Face the Music

Face the Music

Greg Anton

Plus One Press
San Francisco

Plus One Press
www.plusonepress.com

ISBN: 0-9860085-5-9
ISBN: 978-0-9860085-5-9

2014955299

First Edition: December, 2014

10 9 8 7 6 5 4 3 2 1

For my son Jake

The nights are still there, and the winds that move through the trees...
they're filled with being, of which you are a part.

– R. Rilke

Acknowledgements

A heartfelt thank you to my editor Deb Grabien for generously sharing her passion for the craft of writing.

Kudos to the publishing/editing team; Nic Grabien, layout; Jacqueline Smay, copy editing; Jaimee Garbacik, line editing; and Nancy Aronie, Ken Chasser, Ken Greene, Marty Levine, Dennis McNally, Geoffrey Menin, Sophie Menin, Alan Trist, and Craig Wright for reading and re-reading.

Special thanks to Robert Hunter for his inspiration and suggestions on how to actually write, and for his beautiful lyrics to the song "Stephanie", and to Stanley Mouse for his exquisite cover art.

I am forever grateful to my wife Holly, who helped me with this book on our first date twenty years ago, and every day since.

And to my children Chevy, Curry, Georgia, Heidi, and Jake, for their love and support, to my sister Lillian and brother-in-law Gregory and my parents, Paul and Shirley for always believing in me.

And to all the people who gave me encouragement and who's lives inspired me to write: Chris Andrian, Banana, Rob Bloom, Red Cawley, John Cipollina, Dave and Howie Cort, Kenny Feld, Martin Fierro, Jackie Fraser, Wavy Gravy, Liam Hannrahan, Jeff Jacobs, Steve Kimock, Allan Lang, Donna Godchaux Mackay, Algis Makunas, Marian May, Nancy May, Sean McCloskey, Abriana Menin, Brian Risner, Irv Rosenberg, Ed Rosenthal, Robin Sylvester, Isabel Tercero, Steve Turer, and Mary Wilson.

...and to all the wonderful musicians I've had the good fortune to play with, who've provided me with an endless stream of material to write about.

This is a Story About a Love Song

"Stephanie"

Robert Hunter – Lyrics
Greg Anton – Music

Original track credits:

Steve Kimock – Guitar
Melvin Seals – Organ
Tim Hockenberry – Vocals
Robin Sylvester – Bass
Greg Anton – Drums, Piano

Available on iTunes

Face the Music

There are five different intoxications: the intoxication of beauty, youth, and strength; then the intoxication of wealth; the third is of power, the power of ruling; and there is the fourth intoxication which is the intoxication of learning, of knowledge. But all these four intoxications fade away like the stars before the sun in the presence of the intoxication of music.

In music the seer can see the picture of the whole universe. What we call music in everyday life is the exact miniature of the law working through the whole universe.

There are some who on hearing rhythms instantly fall into ecstasy. They can jump into the fire and come out without being burned. They need not be very educated to go into that trance, nor very evolved. Sometimes they are very ordinary people, but sound can have such effect upon them that they are moved to a higher ecstasy. And how much more must it intoxicate those who have touched the perfection of music and meditated on it for years and years!

Often and often the experiment has been made, and one has always seen that snakes of any kind are attracted on hearing the sound of the *pungi* (flute). There is a certain effect on their nervous

1

system which draws them closer and closer to the sound. They forget that instinct of protecting themselves from the attack of man or other creatures. At that time they absolutely forget, they do not see anyone or anything.

Some people are like instruments; when good music is presented before them they respond, they become attuned to it, they are all music.

Music seems to be the bridge over the gulf between form and the formless. If there is anything intelligent, effective and at the same time formless, it is music. It creates also that resonance which vibrates through the whole being, lifting thought above the denseness of matter. It almost turns matter into spirit, into the original condition, through the harmony of vibrations touching every atom of one's whole being.

No other art can inspire and sweeten the personality like music; the lover of music attains sooner or later to the most sublime field of thought.

Music touches our innermost being and produces a life that gives exaltation to the whole being, raising it to that perfection in which lies the fulfillment of man's life.

– Sufi Inayat Khan
The Mysticism of Sound (1916)

Chapter 1

"I'm not saying he can't sing." Woody paced around his little one-room apartment, stopping to sort through the guitar parts that covered almost every surface. "I just can't work with him. Nobody can. And he's worked with everybody."

"Then get another singer."

"I've tried, man. I've totally tried. Singers are nuts. Their job description is to be the center of attention."

Murray shrugged. "All artists want attention, that's why they're artists."

"You see that package of strings I just had?"

Murray glanced at a shoebox overflowing with guitar strings. "I told you what I think. I think your songs sound better when you sing 'em because they're yours."

Woody picked up his Fender Stratocaster and fell back into a dilapidated vinyl chair. He put the electric guitar face-up on his lap and ran his calloused, nicotine-stained fingers up and down the neck, feeling for imperfections. "My songs have a life of their own. I don't want to impose my miserable life on them."

"What are you talking about?" Murray took an empty bag of

3

corn chips off Woody's kitchen counter and reached in for the crumbs.

"I'm talking about getting some fancy-ass rock star to sing my new song to get enough money to get Stephanie out of that job." Woody lit his last cigarette and crumpled the empty pack. "I'd rather not sing anyway. I don't like hanging out with people I don't know, singing to 'em is even worse." A cigarette and wire-cutter in the same hand, he eased the tension on the heavy-gauge strings and snipped them off a quarter-inch from the bridge. An errant string splayed apart, just missed his face and knocked the head off his cigarette. He rotated in his seat, slapping at the hot ashes. "It's like one tree grows in a ditch and gets half the sunlight another tree gets. That's all it ever gets, that's its fate. I've been thinking maybe my music's not destined to be in the light. But now I came up with this song that does everything I've ever wanted a song to do, it just needs a little light. But the only way to really get it out there is to work with some insensitive poser that –"

"You have anything to eat around here?" Murray opened Woody's refrigerator. "Want to go out and get something?"

"No man, I've got work to do." Woody took a guitar string from a square paper envelope, unraveled it full length at eye level and peered over it. "Maybe I don't have the stomach for Ray in my life, but this song has a future of its own." He brought the string down across his knees, released one end and let it coil back together. "There's something about the chord progression, it's got built-in momentum, like an expanding circle. They're simple chords, simple words, but the emotions get complicated. When I play the chorus I can't stop playing."

Murray pulled his head out of the refrigerator, pushed his black plastic-rimmed glasses back on his nose and looked over at Woody.

"I don't know what it is." Woody was staring down at the guitar in his lap, long curly blonde hair covering his face. "I've written a million songs, but I'm ready to bet my life on this one." He flung his hair back, unwinding a tuning peg with much more force than was

4

necessary. "This is the song that ate the New Jersey Turnpike!" He yanked out the high E string. "Ray's got the voice, he'll hit it out of the park. And with Ray Bell singing, the guy on that door can put it all together."

Murray closed the refrigerator door and looked at the magazine page stuck to the door with a hot dog magnet the size of an actual hot dog.

"The guy on the left is Jeff Pearlman," Woody said. "That's him at last year's Grammys with Olivia Newton-John. He's one of the most powerful entertainment lawyers in California. And he's a record producer and he used to manage Ray. I've checked out everything he's done. He'll dig my music. All I have to do is connect the dots." He rubbed down the bare neck of his guitar with furniture polish and a soft chamois cloth. The guitar was immaculate.

Murray reopened the refrigerator. "You must be really into olives."

"I don't like them that much. My refrigerator always has stuff in it I don't like, that's why it's still there."

"Want to go down to Haank's?"

"No man, I've got work to do. Things change fast in the music business. Besides, you know I'm allergic to meat, especially the meat they cook at Haank's. You're the one always talking about your cholesterol and everything."

"You could get a veggie burger or salad or something."

Woody put his guitar down on a pile of laundry, poured the contents of a worn leather pouch onto his already cluttered kitchen table and began sorting through guitar parts, picks and polished stones. "Listen man, I've said it a thousand times; everything at Haank's is cooked in animal fat. Animal fat is cooked flesh from some animal's leg or face or... get it? It's like eating a piece of something's leg that's walking around on it like, would you eat your own foot if you were starving?"

"What about that stuff you were saying about cows being vegetarians and natural food compactors? You said beef's like a dense salad because it's made out of a hundred percent grass."

"I was just goofing around man, I was stoned."

"Were you stoned then or are you stoned now?" Murray's glasses fogged up from the refrigerator and he cleaned them off with the tail of his flannel shirt

"I'm just saying, Haank's vibes are all over the food at that place."

"I'm not going to marry the guy, I'm going to get him to make me a sandwich."

Woody kept sorting through the items on the table, a system of little piles revealing itself. "Food is one of the most absorbent things there are. It's like a sponge, soaking up the vibes anywhere near it. Especially stuff like bread, or corn bread, or scrambled eggs; the fire attracts the energy and the heat seals it in. Haank's energy is in that permanent scowl he has when he's cooking. It *is* like marrying him." Woody pointed a pair of needle-nose pliers at Murray's stomach. "That negativity gets in your food and you take it in, digest it. It's like if a cow knows it's about to be killed and the adrenaline gets in its body and then the meat's all tough. That's why the kosher guys sneak up with a razor or hammer or whatever and the cows don't know what hit 'em and they keep the lines crooked with swinging doors so they can't see what's happening up ahead. If I have to see that moron singer while I'm trying to play, making those contortions with his face like he's constipated or something –"

"I'm going out to get something to eat." Murray's eyes fluttered closed. It was a constant mannerism of Murray's, closing his eyes for the duration of a sentence when he spoke directly to someone. He shuffled around, hands in the pockets of his baggy pants, moving in a roundabout way toward the front door.

Woody glanced at the big school clock on his apartment wall. "Wanna go with me to meet Stephanie when she gets off work? Sometimes they put out free food for the customers. Or there's that pizza-by-the-slice place next door."

"I thought you didn't want anybody, you know, checking her out when she's working."

"At the end of her shift she's just talking to customers. She's connecting with lonely people, man, deeply lonely. She's practically a psychiatrist for guys that are like… she's getting paid to be somebody's friend for a minute. We can walk to Masonic, take the bus to North Beach so we don't have to drive. Save the planet."

"Whatever. I'm walking out the door in five minutes."

"Relax man. Everybody gets to Christmas at the same time." Woody knelt down in front of his backpack, skinny legs bent under him, two bony knees protruding from frayed holes in his jeans. He started stuffing things into his already full backpack; pen, pocketknife, flashlight…

"Can't you ever just walk out the door?"

"I'm twenty seconds from lift-off." The backpack wouldn't close. He removed a large prescription pill bottle from a zippered compartment and held it in his lap. He'd just recently taken to carrying it around, his never to be touched exit-strategy pill bottle, filled with sleeping pills, pain pills, tranquilizers; a healthy stash of fifty or sixty pills and pieces of pills he'd saved over the years that he could swallow in three gulps and never have to deal with anything again. He always knew it was there.

"You can't possibly use all that stuff for going out for an hour."

"Hey man," Woody said defensively, "carrying this shit around actually increases my freedom. If it ends up I can't change my environment," he held up the pill bottle, "I can take a couple of these and change my view of it." He set the bottle back in his lap. "Or I can take a lot of these and *really* change my perspective." He shoved the bottle into his backpack and stood up. "You don't see things the way *they* are man, you see things the way *you* are."

Murray took a step toward the door.

"I'm right behind you," Woody said. "Beginning countdown. Ten… Nine… Eight…"

"Sure you're not forgetting anything?" Murray asked sarcastically.

Woody looked down at his larger-than-life Bob Marley-smoking-a-spliff "Freedom" T-shirt. "Freedom man. We're outta here."

Woody expertly worked the multiple deadbolts, flipped over a dangling cardboard sign that said "Gone To Meet Loaf," lurched down the narrow stairs and burst out onto Ashbury Street. Three blocks from Haight, the sidewalk was full of activity and ripe with patchouli oil. Summer seemed to be a good enough reason for a celebration. People were sharing joints and hanging out up to their waists from second floor windows of decoratively painted Victorians.

They headed down the street. Woody's short sinewy body was an undernourished, sleep-deprived coiled spring of nervous energy. Murray, overweight and out of shape, had trouble keeping up. After two blocks Woody stopped and waited.

"What's the big rush?" Murray hiked up his pants, breathing hard. "I wait around and wait around, you take forever to get your shit together, then you're in this gigantic hurry –" He stopped mid-sentence, looking over Woody's shoulder.

"What's up?" Woody glanced behind him.

"Nothing, let's go." Murray started walking.

Woody caught up. "What's up?"

"Nothing." Murray kept going. "I haven't really had anything to eat all day and I figured I'd just stop by your place and see if you wanted to go out and get something and then this whole ritual starts unraveling." He suddenly stopped in front of a young bearded man sitting on the sidewalk with a blanket covered with handmade jewelry, Grateful Dead stickers and a sleeping dog.

Woody looked down at the blanket and up at Murray. "What's going on, Murray? Feel like doing a little shopping?"

Murray squarely faced him and closed his eyes. "Where's your backpack?"

In slow motion, Woody brought his right hand up to his left shoulder where there was no backpack. Looking back at the three long city blocks they'd come from, he clenched his teeth and mumbled something.

"What?" Murray said.

"Freedom. Let's go."

Chapter 2

When Woody and Murray walked through the velvet curtains at the Chi Chi Club on Broadway, Stephanie was standing near a small table covered with ashtrays, cocktail glasses and beer bottles. Four men in suits with their ties undone were lounging around the table, one with his chair pushed back at an angle facing her, a cigarette dangling from his lips. Stephanie stood in front of him, smiling, wearing only a bra, panties and high heels.

Woody froze in his tracks. Murray, a half step behind, stumbled into Woody's back. They stopped and watched.

Stephanie extended one leg, raised it up in front of her until her knee almost touched her forehead and slowly swung it out perpendicular to her body. She gracefully wrapped her hand around her elevated high heel, held the difficult position for a long ten seconds, turned like a figure skater away from the table and bent over almost in half, eighteen inches from the man's face. He looked at her without expression and sipped his drink.

Woody stepped in front of Murray, blocking his view. "We're outta here. Let's go next door and get some pizza."

Murray peered over Woody's shoulder.

"Hey man! What're you looking at?"

"Your girlfriend's ass, like every other guy in the place."

"Yeah, well you're not every fucking guy. You're you and I'm me and Stephanie's…"

Stephanie slipped on her robe, walked over and gave Woody a kiss on the cheek. "Hi honey. Hi Murray. You guys missed happy hour. I can get you some drink tickets if you want. I've got one more dance, then I'm off."

"A cold beer would be great," Murray said.

"No!" Woody said. "We're going next door for pizza. We'll wait for you over there."

"Suit yourself. I have to get back to work, my boss is watching." She gave him a peck on the cheek, shook out her curly red hair and headed toward the back of the room.

"I've got to get my new song recorded at all costs and make some money so Steph can quit that fucking job."

Woody and Murray were sitting at a tall little table in a brightly-lit pizza shop on Broadway. Just four miles across the city from the smiles and bellbottoms of the Haight, the tight black jeans and sneers of the street punks wandering in and out were like from another world. Woody sprinkled a thick layer of red pepper on his slice.

"Are you going to eat that like that?"

"Like what?"

"Like that, with all that pepper on it."

Woody took a bite. "This is nothing. I'm about to choke down my insecurity and swallow it. An army of one. I'm gonna accost that music lawyer I was telling you about and play him my song on the street if that what it takes. All I can think about is Stephanie with those perverts gawking at her." He picked up the red-pepper shaker and shook it on his pizza using his entire arm. "It's just not natural when a woman says give me twenty bucks and I'll show you my crotch. It ignores the whole gestalt of getting to know somebody, progressing through the layers, the natural unfolding of things. It's like having the crescendo in the first four bars of a song!" He slammed the peppershaker down on the table.

Murray bit into his slice. "Women are different than men. They see things from a whole different perspective."

"No kidding. Stephanie says unzip a man's fly and his brains fall out. The thing she doesn't get is that there's a kind of instinctive modesty. You have to honor that."

"Honor *what?*"

"Monogamy, man. It works so the mother knows who the father is and the father knows who the father is, and there's always a guy around to hunt and protect the kids. The family trip man, the kids are more likely to survive. It's a species protection plan, like a natural HMO. Jealousy is natural."

"I think she actually feels okay about working there," Murray said with his eyes closed. "In fact, I think she kind of likes the attention."

"That's total one hundred percent bullshit! She's doing it for the money!"

"Hey, take it easy." Murray swallowed faster than he'd meant to and wondered if he was feeling chest pains or indigestion. His doctor had said he was too young to be having chest pains, he should lose some weight. Woody said real men have chest pains. "I'm just saying Stephanie knows what she's doing. She's one of the most together women around. Women in some cultures have children by the time they're eighteen and stay home and take care of the kids. In California, they take kickboxing and go to law school. Don't mess with them, they're getting smarter than the men. They probably always have been." Murray took a gulp of soda. "Doesn't it kind of turn you on, all those guys being attracted to her like that?"

"It does just the opposite. Thinking about those cretins gawking at her, I get turned on and pissed off at the same time. It's like we're never alone, there's always three of us...Stephanie, me and my thoughts." Woody looked down at his pizza. "We haven't really gotten it on much lately. She keeps wanting to, but I keep thinking about those jerks where she works. Every time we get started we get in a fight."

"No wonder you're so uptight," Murray said. "Is your mouth burning or what? I can't believe you can eat that with that much pepper on it."

"This is nothing man. I've got a cast iron stomach."

"You ever try this?" Murray took a small bottle of hot sauce off the counter next to them. The pizza shop was famous for its selection of exotic hot sauces. "This is the hottest thing known to man."

Woody shook a dollop on the corner of his slice and took the bite. "Hot pepper's good for you. It's a natural antibiotic and cleanser and full of vitamin C. I can eat it all day."

"Five bucks you can't put the rest of that bottle on there and eat it." There was a half-inch of hot sauce at the bottom of the little bottle.

"Show me the five. " Woody emptied the bottle, his half-piece of pizza now covered with a red-pepper soup. After two bites he was sweating profusely. He chewed fast, wiping his forehead with the flimsy paper napkins and reached for Murray's Coke.

"Hey, you didn't say anything about drinking Coke."

"You didn't say anything about no Coke." Woody took a swallow and kept chewing. He finished the piece and picked up the five-dollar bill.

"You all right? Your face is all purple."

Woody turned towards the door and kept draining Murray's Coke that was now nothing but ice cubes. "Where is she? She was supposed to be off work a half-hour ago."

"I heard drinking can make it worse," Murray said. "Maybe you should eat some bread or something."

"I should drink some gasoline. I'm going to see what happened to her." He went next door, took two steps inside the dark club and froze. He could barely make out Stephanie in the back of the room, sitting at a booth with a balding businessman just reaching over to cup her breast.

"Hey!" Woody yelled.

12

All heads turned. Stephanie stood up and Woody started toward them. The bouncer at the bar caught what was happening and headed diagonally across the room. He was a giant, taking huge strides, passing a table with each step. They arrived at the booth at the same time.

"You said they never touch you!" Woody shouted at Stephanie. "You told me –"

"He didn't touch me. Wait for me out front."

The bouncer put his oversized hand on Woody's bony shoulder. "Let's go."

Woody jerked away. "Get your hands off me, freak! I'm talking to my girlfriend!"

"Just turn around and walk out." The bouncer towered over him, the timbre of his voice so low it sounded like a slowed-down tape.

"Fuck you, moron!" Woody's face was red, his fists clenched at his sides. "I'm talking to my girlfriend!"

"She's working right now." He took a step in front of her and put his hand back on Woody's shoulder. "Move out."

"Stephanie! Tell this goon to back off!"

Stephanie tried to see past the bouncer in the narrow aisle. "Woody! Wait outside. I'll meet you out front in five minutes."

Woody pulled the bouncer's hand off him. The bouncer held onto his shirt and tore it halfway off his shoulder. "You fucking asshole!" Woody sprayed spit. "Stephanie!"

Stephanie managed to step around the bouncer and she and Woody stared at each other's bare breasts, his exposed by a surreal-looking hole in one of Bob Marley's eyes, hers flopping out of her flimsy robe. Woody looked like he was about to cry. "What are you doing here?"

Stephanie cinched up her robe, the bouncer spun Woody around, twisted his arm halfway up his back and shoved him toward the door. "You're out of here pal."

"You're breaking my arm you fucking asshole! I'm gonna sue your drooling moronic ass outta business!"

13

The bouncer shoved harder, weaving between tables, trying not to knock over drinks. Woody dug in his heels and suddenly felt a cramping surge in his bowels.

"Shit!" He put his free hand across his stomach. He was dead weight, hanging by the bouncer's grip on his arm, one knee up to his chest. "I gotta use your bathroom."

The bouncer let go of him. "I want you to leave, now."

"Hey man, I'm begging you." Woody was doubled over. "I ate all this hot sauce and I'm gonna fucking explode. Let me use your bathroom for two minutes and I'm outta here, no more hassles, I swear."

Woody farted and the air turned putrid. The bouncer took a step back. "Five minutes. Five minutes and I never want to see you in here again."

Woody quickly made his way to the men's room that wasn't much bigger than a closet, with a urinal, a stall and a sink. He took two steps to the stall and flung the door open. The businessman in the suit who'd been sitting with Stephanie was on the toilet with his pants at his ankles, his erection in his hand.

"Shit!" Woody turned and took in his remaining options; the urinal, the sink, a plastic trashcan. "You're jerking off thinking about my girlfriend you old fuck! She'd never get near a decrepit pervert like you if you didn't pay for it!"

He bolted out the door and into the ladies' room five feet away, made it to one of the two stalls and held on through a burning explosion of his bowels. In between waves of dizziness and nausea, he imagined the bouncer coming in and dragging him out, his pants not pulled up properly, Stephanie seeing him like that.

But maybe the bouncer hadn't seen him switch bathrooms, maybe he was okay. He definitely didn't have to worry about any women coming in; this was for customers and there were rarely any women customers. Maybe the bouncer would look for him in the men's room and think he'd left. Maybe the bouncer would find that guy jerking off, it probably happened all the time.

14

Doubled over on the toilet, Woody thought of his backpack and how everybody always gave him flak about lugging all that stuff around. This was the exact kind of thing he was usually prepared for with Rolaids, bottled water, maybe a clean T-shirt. People were so damn shortsighted.

The next wave of diarrhea was so nauseating, it blurred his vision. He felt like he was about to throw up but didn't have the strength to stand and face the toilet. He put his hands on the metal walls to brace himself, heard the bathroom door open and watched a pair of silver glittered high heels walk into the stall next to him and turn around. White panties fell onto the shoes and the spiked heels rose up on their toes. Woody lifted his feet off the floor and held his breath.

Stephanie walked out in front of the club, looking for Woody. A doorman in a cheap suit, white shirt and skinny tie was standing under an enormous pair of flashing neon breasts, hawking to the tourists; "Come in and take a look. First one's free." The doorman saw Stephanie, winked at her, and turned his attention to a group of Asian businessmen approaching on the sidewalk.

Stephanie found Murray next door at the pizza shop. "Where's Woody?"

"He went to the club twenty minutes ago looking for you. Didn't you see him?" Murray was at the same table with his third slice of pizza and a Styrofoam cup of coffee.

"I saw him. He made a big scene and got in a fight with Rick the bouncer. Rick said Woody was sick, he let him use the bathroom and he thought Woody left. He's not around anywhere."

"He ate a slice of pizza with way too much hot sauce," Murray shrugged. "It probably made him sick."

"What did he do that for?"

"Five bucks."

"At least he's doing something to supplement his music career." Stephanie smiled and sat down.

Murray noticed her perfume and dramatic green eyes outlined with thick black liner. She was wearing a loose sweatshirt, jeans, and sneakers; a stark contrast to her work makeup. He held out his piece of pizza. "Want a bite?"

She shook her head no, thinking about the helpless expression on Woody's face when the bouncer dragged him away.

"Wouldn't it be great if Woody could get a break with his music?" Murray said. "He works so hard at it."

She looked thoughtfully toward the front door. "Sometimes he tries *too* hard. It's like he trips himself up, putting a stick in his own spokes. But somehow, out of complete chaos, he makes such beautiful music. When he plays, all the clutter falls away and he seems so clear and clean. He should be considered a national treasure. His music's so beautiful, it could stop wars."

"How about a cup of coffee?" Murray asked. "I'll buy you one."

"No thanks." She ran her hands through her hair. She had the same wild curly hair as Woody, only hers was shiny auburn-red and about half as long as his.

Murray looked at her sheepishly, wondering if she only wore her ultra-sexy underwear for work. He kept seeing the image of her bending over.

"I can understand Woody being jealous about my job," she said, looking down at her long fingernails that were painted the same color as her hair. "Sometimes the customers try to touch me. Unfortunately, once was tonight when Woody walked in. I don't think he saw me slap the man's hand away. I never let them touch me, ever." She sighed. "I thought I could maintain my integrity and still keep that job. The money's great, but I guess it doesn't work for Woody." She folded her arms across her chest. "I just like to dance. I have an audition with a modern dance company coming up and God knows I'd rather do that."

She watched Murray trying to open a package of powdered coffee creamer and wondered, as she often did, if she was kidding herself that her job had anything to do with dancing. "You'd think Woody might like it that other men think I'm attractive. You need help with that? I've got a couple of good nails."

He handed her the package and she opened it for him. "Seems like people are always struggling with packaging," she said. "One thing about Woody, he usually has a knife or something with him."

She walked to the door and looked down the street. When she came back, Murray was smiling.

"What's so funny?"

"Woody was just here doing the same thing, getting up every few minutes looking for you. You're a perfect couple."

"I just wish he'd relax about my job. It's not like either of us have much money coming from anywhere else. The thing is, I really believe he'll get a break with his music. I respect the way he focuses on it and won't compromise. And I don't mind paying for some things right now, but if he keeps freaking out on me…"

"You have to admit," Murray said with his eyes closed, "it must feel strange having a room full of guys looking at your girlfriend in her underwear."

Just then Woody walked into the pizza shop and stood directly behind Stephanie. She didn't see him come in. Murray couldn't believe how he looked, ashen gray, shirt torn open, curls of hair stuck to his face.

"His jealousy is driving me crazy," she said. "I was hoping maybe you'd talk to him."

"Why don't you talk to him yourself?" Murray motioned toward Woody, but she was on a roll and didn't notice.

"We've talked and talked and talked. If he wasn't so –"

"He's right –"

"Stuck. The guy's stuck in a muck and just keeps mucking around, making this big mess everywhere he goes." She gestured with her hands.

Murray glanced up at Woody, his eyes glazed over, swaying back and forth without bending at the waist. It looked like he was about to fall straight back or collapse onto Stephanie.

"His jealousy is poisoning our whole trip."

Murray closed his eyes. "But you're still in love with him, aren't you?"

"He's the only guy I've ever fallen in love with! I might've stepped in it a couple of times, but I've never actually *fallen* in love before. He's the most loveable, creative, completely insane guy I've ever met. And he almost cost me my job tonight. Then we'd both be broke! Where the hell is he?"

She stood up just as Woody bent down, met her motion and kissed her on the mouth.

"What happened to you? You look awful." She brushed the hair from his face and put her hand on his forehead. "Are you okay? You taste like you threw up."

"I love you too."

Chapter 3

The next night, at The North Beach Saloon on Grant Street, there were three bands on the bill, one playing on stage, the other two with their gear stashed in a cramped hallway. On a triangle shaped stage barely big enough for a drum kit, four musicians, their amps, and a blues singer were squeezed together and spilling onto the floor. The musicians that weren't playing paced the hallway like caged animals, unable to exchange more than a few words over the blaring music, pressing past each other to get to their equipment cases.

The sailor saloon turned blues club was the oldest drinking establishment in San Francisco, and it smelled like it. In 1860, the ten-stool bar had a copper trough underneath that patrons could pee into without having to risk standing up.

Damp heat and live blues poured out of the always-open front door, and the tourists poured in. The odd-shaped room had scuffed wooden floors, dust-covered sailor nostalgia on the walls and realistic local drunks that made the experience authentic for the tourists. Two blocks from Chinatown, around the corner from Broadway, and lined with Italian restaurants, the narrowness of

Grant Street seemed to funnel the crowds on the sidewalk right into the saloon.

Woody sat on a beer keg in the hallway, playing scales on his unplugged electric guitar while his drummer did paradiddles on a phone book. A young woman with long straight hair, a beaded headband and a blouse tied in a knot exposing her bare stomach, walked up to Woody. "What time do you guys go on?"

Woody ignored her and kept playing. His unplugged guitar was virtually silent but he intuitively knew what every fret sounded like, his left hand traveling up and down the neck like a giant spider in configurations that looked physically impossible.

The woman stared blankly at Woody's hands and yelled in his ear. "Wanna smoke a joint?"

Just then the keyboard player walked up and yelled in Woody's other ear. "We don't have time for 'Squish.' Our set got cut short and Dave the owner wants his girlfriend to sit in. We can lose the solo in 'Bury This' and have time for 'Squish,' or just jam on 'Bury.'"

The girl with the headband leaned in. "This is a killer joint of Thai stick my ex-boyfriend smuggled back from Vietnam in his –"

"Whatever!" Woody yelled at both of them. "It's so loud in here I can't think!" He walked out the rusted metal door to the back alley and lit a cigarette. Sick from eating all the hot sauce the night before, he'd barely gotten any sleep. He had a pounding headache.

The keyboard player came out to the alley followed by a blast of loud distorted guitar. "We go on in twenty minutes. What should we open with?"

"Whatever you want, man." Woody kicked the door closed. "Just pick some songs."

"Feel like playing that new ballad you showed me? The guys'll pick it up if you show them the changes to the bridge."

"I don't feel like singing tonight."

"We should do it sometime. What's it called again?"

"'Stephanie.'"

The bass player joined them, his bass hanging low across his waist. "Short set tonight," the keyboard player said, "and Dave wants Tami to sit in. She sings okay when she's not too drunk and we need to keep Dave happy." While the keyboard player was talking, the band inside finished their song. It became dramatically quieter but the keyboard player, oblivious, kept on in the same loud voice. "When we get on stage we should tune up real quick and go right into the first song."

The bass player slapped a funky groove with his thumb and Woody responded with a fast chord progression. The drummer came out and tapped his sticks on the door in a metallic cadence. The bass player put the headstock of his electric bass against the metal door, Woody did the same with his guitar, and the door amplified the trio like a big acoustic resonator. They played like that until the band on stage started their next song and drowned them out.

A half-hour later, the first band left the stage and Woody, making numerous trips, carried up his eighty-five-pound amplifier, pedal board, effects and guitars. When the band had finally set up, stashed their instrument cases in the hallway and were walking back up the two stairs to the small stage, the girl with the joint gave them each a hit.

Facing his amp, Woody glanced over his shoulder at the audience and quickly looked away. Everyone in the room was staring at him. Whenever *he* went to see a band, from the moment the musicians took the stage, he checked out their every move. Plugging cables into his guitar effects, he remembered the words of his fifth grade choir teacher: *Just listen. Your body knows how to make music, just listen to it.*

He finished setting up, dug a pick out of the coin pocket of his jeans and ran it down his strings. As if acting of their own volition, his hands went into a repeating pattern of harmonics, echoing like clanging church bells, and the sound took him out of his head. The drummer turned on his swivel-throne, quietly exchanging his sticks for a pair of mallets, and drew a gentle swell out of his ride cymbal. The sax came in with a long, low foghorn, the organ laid down a chordal bed and the bass player added marshmallow whole notes that filled the corners of the room like expanding foam earplugs.

With consummate control, the band sustained the vibrating cacophony, increasing the volume and intensity until it seemed like they had no place to go when the sax player suddenly spat out a flood of notes that sounded like the screech of an animal being torn apart. The drummer grabbed his sticks, whacked his snare drum four times and Woody took off with a chunky chord progression that congealed the chaotic energy into a driving rhythm.

The band ducked and weaved, notes flying back and forth across the stage. When Woody introduced one of his signature soaring guitar lines, the sax player put down his tenor, picked up his soprano and like a magician performing alchemy, blew long angelic phrases that bonded to the notes of the guitar, lifting them even higher.

Woody recognized the rare synchronicity that was happening, as did everyone in the room. It was nights like this that kept him going. Playing his instrument felt effortless, selfless; five musicians collaborating in service of some sixth entity. The energy surged, palpable waves of sound flowing off the stage until, on some invisible intuitive signal, they simultaneously descended on one big chord and dissolved into silence. The small audience of locals and tourists, a blend of nationalities melded together by the music, all held the silence for a moment then burst into applause.

"You guys know 'I Ain't Talkin' About What I Gotta Say' in A?" It was the owner's girlfriend Tami, staggering onto the stage with a beer in her hand. "How's everybody doin' tonight?" she yelled into the microphone. She was a big girl with a booming voice. "Aren't these guys great? Anybody out there ever had the blues? I said has anybody out there…"

His back to the audience, Woody hit a dissonant minor chord.

Tami took a gulp of beer. "Ok everybody, we're gonna play the blues to cure your blues. One… two… three…"

The band came in on the downbeat. Tami came in on the third beat, throwing everyone off balance. The drummer quickly straightened out the groove and Tami sang two more verses, coming in wrong each time. Woody played a blistering solo, just reaching the climax into the chorus when the singer started a verse. Frustrated, he slowed the song down and ended it while she was still singing. She waved her arm like a windmill, trying to keep the band going, but the drummer followed Woody who retarded the song to a close.

"Thank you Tami," the keyboard player said into his microphone. "Let's hear it for Tami!" There was a smattering of applause.

"How about one more?" Tami said to the keyboard player. "I didn't get to finish that one."

"We don't really have time, we only have a short set and..."

"How about it, folks?" Tami yelled into the mic. "Wanna hear one more?" One person clapped. Tami turned toward the band. "'Stormy Monday' in A. One... two..."

"We just played a slow blues in A," Woody said across the stage to the keyboard player.

Tami took a swig of beer. "'Stormy Monday' in B...one... two... three..." She took so much time between each count, the song came in as an excruciatingly slow dirge. With time to spare between backbeats, the drummer got the barmaid's attention, pointed to his empty glass and pantomimed another shot of tequila. She brought it over and he slugged it down with his right hand without missing a beat on the snare with his left. Tami made her way through the song, mostly singing in the old key.

Woody strummed the weirdest blues chords he could think of and scanned the room looking for Stephanie. The Chi Chi Club was two blocks away. Was she working tonight? They were both whores, baring their souls for the tourists. He hit another jarring chord. If things weren't okay with Stephanie, nothing else mattered; if things *were* okay with Stephanie, nothing else mattered.

After a half-dozen trips lugging equipment out to his car double-parked in the alley, Woody finished packing, went back inside and found the keyboard player at the bar. "We get paid yet?"

"Hey man, you played great. Want a beer? Sorry about Tami. Dave really appreciates us letting her sit in. He gave me extra drink tickets and offered us a Saturday night next month. Think you'll be available?"

"You get the money for tonight?"

The keyboard player took a twenty, a ten and a five out of his wallet. "Dave says we ran up a big drink tab but he still gave us two hundred. I took out money for the posters. We made thirty-five each."

"I didn't have any drinks."

"I think it was Mickey that ran up the tab. I gave him twenty-five, I still lost money on the posters."

Woody stuffed the money in his pocket. "With the rehearsal, driving, load-in, load-out, setting up and playing, I'm making about three dollars an hour, not counting guitar strings."

"I know what you mean," the keyboard player said. "It's Thursday night. We'll definitely do better on a Saturday."

"Maybe we can get it up to four dollars an hour. Maybe I can pay my parking ticket with my drink ticket."

Woody walked out and got in his old four-door Buick Electra that was packed to the roof with equipment. He'd just slid into the driver's seat, his hand on the door, when a voice startled him.

"Hi. Didn't mean to sneak up on you. I just wanted to say I've been watching you play the last couple of years. You play as good as anyone I've heard. You've got the magic touch." The man was well dressed, with an air of confidence about him; not a typical patron at The Saloon.

"Thanks." Woody gave a little salute and closed the big car door. He remembered a time when he was just learning to play. He'd gone to a concert to see one of his guitar heroes perform and had waited by the stage door after the show, hoping to catch a glimpse of the band and their entourage. To his surprise, the guitar player came out alone, carrying his equipment. When Woody said something to him about how inspired he was by the music, the guy's only response had been to ask for help loading his amplifier into his car.

The last ten times Woody had played at The North Beach Saloon, he swore it would be the last. The pay was bad, the sound sucked, no place to park, but he always needed the money. He started his car, lit a cigarette and noticed that the well-dressed man was still standing there. He rolled down his window. "Hey, thanks for the kind words. Stuff like that keeps me going."

"I know it's hard," the man said. "Don't give up. Your playing is important. It's truth."

Woody gave another little salute and headed to Daly City to see Stephanie.

Chapter 4

Just ten miles south of the Haight, going to Daly City was like going to a different country, as if the counter-culture revolution in the city had bypassed certain suburbs. The polar opposite of the creativity and communal brother and sisterhood permeating San Francisco, the land developers' dream of low-cost construction was devoid of soul, style or sense of community. Rows and rows of identical houses, all made out of ticky-tacky, were so much alike they resembled a Hollywood movie set. Each weekday morning, as if it were choreographed, virtually every electric garage door in Daly City swung up to let the commuters out to work.

Stephanie didn't care for the modern surroundings, but the rent in her small apartment complex was cheap and when she'd first moved in, she'd been attending San Francisco State a few miles away. Now, two years out of school, barely getting by with local dance and theater performances, she'd taken the job at the Chi Chi Club on Broadway, at the opposite end of San Francisco. Working there part-time for two months, she was constantly looking for another job.

The next morning, Stephanie walked into her living room in her bathrobe with her hair wrapped in a towel turban. She found Woody sitting in her beanbag chair, the centerfold of a Penthouse magazine draped over his leg.

"I see you found something to entertain yourself," she said. "I heard you get up early after you got here so late. Did you get any sleep? Sorry I didn't make it over to your gig."

"I can't even tell what this is." Woody nodded at the centerfold. "It's such a close-up, it looks like a piece of dried fruit. I'd rather look at underwear ads in the newspaper."

"It's what happens in a world run by men." Stephanie patted down her hair with the towel. "Guys prefer the linear approach. They just keep using up things like trees, air, water and women. Penthouse Magazine's been showing a little more each issue until it's all used up. Men have turned women inside out and crashed into a blank pink wall."

"People." Woody closed the magazine. "Living proof that women have sex. What are you doing with a Penthouse magazine anyway?"

"I use it for work, to get an idea of what different angles look like."

"So you can open your legs for the best exposure?"

"Actually, for the least exposure. People's imaginations are always better than the real thing."

She went to the kitchen and poured a cup of coffee from the pot Woody had made. "There's no harm in letting people have fantasies, although I think most men would like to realize their fantasies. For women, they're just fantasies. They'd never want them to actually happen." She bent forward at the waist, shaking out her hair.

Woody thought how incredibly beautiful she looked, in spite of, or maybe because she'd just woken up and had no makeup on. "Fantasies? Like guys have about you when you take your clothes off?"

"Woody, please." She felt herself tense up. "Let's not go there first thing in the morning."

He saw the anxious expression on her face but kept on. "Isn't it your job to be somebody's fantasy?" he said as evenly as he could. "So guys can go home to their wives and fantasize about you."

She shrugged. "I just dance. The customers do what they do. People constantly fantasize about what they think they want. We even fantasize about things we don't want; about our worst fears."

Don't push it, he told himself. When she bent over at the waist again and shook out her hair, he could see her breasts. She looked incredibly beautiful, and any guy off the street could share this intimacy with her. His throat tightened. "My girlfriend's available to any guy with ten bucks."

"Woody, please..."

"No need to fantasize. Step right up and feel my girlfriend's tits, ten bucks each. Two for twenty. Step right up. Step right –"

"Damnit Woody! I told you, no one in that place has ever touched me! Got twenty bucks?" She flung open her bathrobe, stood facing him with her legs apart for a long moment, then turned on her heel and disappeared down the hallway. He didn't see the tears in her eyes.

Five minutes later, she came out of the bedroom fully dressed, walked out the front door and slammed it so hard, her coffee cup fell off the edge of the counter and broke on the tile floor.

Woody sat staring at the closed door. *One of these times she's going to just walk out and not come back.*

He cleaned up the shards of glass, replaying their conversation in his head. *Whatever her reasons are for working that job, it doesn't help to insult her.*

As he'd done many times before, he decided to not bring up her job again. He'd focus on his music and figure out a way to make enough money for both of them.

When Stephanie got to her car she realized she didn't have her purse: no driver's license, no money, just the keys clutched in her hand. She didn't feel like going back.

She got into her royal blue,1967 Mustang, her pride and joy. No work today, a full tank of gas; she decided to head to the beach.

She rolled down her window, drove to the garage exit she rarely used because of traffic on Eastmoor Avenue, and pulled out over the severe-tire-damage grate. There was a solid row of cars parked on the street, with a narrow space just wide enough to drive through. Beyond the parked cars, she could see the boulevard, a fast moving stream of traffic where no one slowed down long enough to let anyone else in. She gripped the steering wheel with both hands and pulled forward.

Suddenly, out of nowhere, there was a large man in a sleeveless T-shirt standing in front of her car. He had a broad stomach, shaved head and over-sized tattooed arms folded across his chest. She couldn't figure out where he'd come from or why he was standing there, his knees almost touching her front bumper.

"We need money." It was another man standing at her open window. Startled, she whipped around in her seat. He was small and emaciated, with pasty blue-white skin. "We ain't gonna hurt you if you give us yer money."

"I don't have any money." She quickly reached over and locked the door.

"Just be cool lady, and we be cool. You ain't goin' nowhere."

When she started rolling up the window, the man jammed a piece of 2x4 in the curved part of the opening that instantly stopped it from going up. She noticed the multiple marks from other windows on the piece of wood.

"Don't fuck wif us bitch! Just gimme your purse so you don't get messed up."

She thought of the severe-tire-damage spikes behind her and wondered if it would stop her car or how far she could get on four flat tires. They must have picked this spot because they knew she couldn't back up. She definitely didn't want to get stuck alone with these men inside the parking garage. What would they do when they found out she really didn't have any money?

She made the quick judgment that she'd be safer near the street, where someone might see her and call the police. She took her foot off the brake, pulled forward a few inches and nudged into the big man's shins. The man did an exaggerated body-slam down on her hood and his face came almost up to the windshield, his thick forearms splayed on the glass.

"Hey bitch!" the man next to her window yelled. "You just run over my buddy. Now we gotta get a lawyer and sue yer pretty ass."

Reaching into the car, he grabbed the back of her hair, shoved her head forward and smashed her mouth into the steering wheel. Her vision blurred for a moment, she felt blood drooling from her mouth and she wondered if her front teeth were knocked out. Her vision cleared as the man on the hood grabbed a windshield wiper in each hand, ripped them off and gave her a toothless, demonic grin.

"All we wanted is your fucking money. Now we gonna take s'more." The man at the window leaned into the car and grabbed her breast with his free hand while he held on to the back of her hair.

Stephanie sat there in shock, unable to process what was happening. Paralyzed with fear, she felt like she was watching it happen to someone else. Time froze, she stayed motionless for what seemed an eternity, then the pain and reality of being manhandled suddenly broke through to her consciousness. Survival mode kicked in, fear became anger, the air turned red… she swung her head over her left shoulder and bit down into the muscle of the man's skinny forearm, clenching her jaw as hard as she could until she felt her front teeth come together. She had a momentary flash of relief that she still had her teeth as the man released his grip on her hair and jerked his arm away.

"Fucking bitch!" He thrust his right arm back into the car and dug his fingers into the side of her neck while he groped her chest more violently with his other hand.

She turned her upper body toward the passenger seat, pulling away from him. He held on to her, leaning inside the window up to his waist, tugging back, his right hand on her neck, his left arm across her chest. She resisted, straining in the opposite direction as far as the seat belt would stretch, held the position for a long moment, then gave in slightly, intentionally letting him pull her back a few inches until she felt him tugging with all his strength. Using the power he was using to pull on her, she suddenly swung around toward him, torqued her hips and drove the heel of her right hand into the tip of his nose. His head was straining back against the inside of the doorjamb above the window. There was no give.

His nose disappeared into his face and a stream of warm blood spurted over her and the white interior of the car. He yelled out and let go of her. Blinded, trying to extricate himself from the car, he had one hand up to his face and one hand gripping the steering wheel.

Stephanie hit her seat belt release, peeled his hand off the wheel and held it flat against her chest with both hands. Turning so she faced the back of her seat, she brought the full weight of her body down and counter-clockwise against his little finger. She heard a snap and saw an inch-long splinter of bone protrude through his skin.

The man jerked himself out of the window and stumbled backwards onto the ground, screaming and spurting blood. She felt the car moving and saw she was rolling out toward the traffic with the big man half off the hood, trying to get a purchase with one foot on the pavement. Spinning back into the drivers seat, she grabbed the wheel, aimed the car right at him and put the accelerator to the floor. The front bumper rammed into his shins and he collapsed on the hood again, this time for real, smashing his face at the base of the windshield.

She put the automatic gearshift in reverse and floored it. The man on the hood fell to the sidewalk and she felt a soft impact behind her. The wheels started spinning and she knew she'd hit the small man in back of her car, maybe pushing him into the severe-tire-damage spikes. A sickening wave of nausea rose up in her throat and she realized she was holding her breath. Letting off the gas, she started gasping for air when the big man in front of the car got up, came around to her open window and wrapped his huge hands around her throat.

Seething mad, a bloody gash on his forehead, he got a stranglehold and bore down, choking off her circulation. She swung the her wheel to the right, put her car in low, felt herself about to black out and stomped on the throttle.

The man's feet went out from under him. Losing his grip on her neck, he grabbed her blouse and the strap of her bra and tore them apart as his forehead smashed into the side of the door and he body-slammed face-first onto the concrete. She headed down the sidewalk at high speed and never looked back.

When she got to the corner she jumped the curb, going the wrong way down a one-way street, oncoming cars veering out of her way. Hoping a policeman would see her, she made it to the next intersection and swerved around the corner, this time going with traffic.

She drove for two blocks in shock, rolled down her window and watched in her side-view mirror as the jammed piece of 2x4 bounced off the side of her car and careened down the street. Her hand shaking, she adjusted the mirror and saw her face and hair covered with blood, her upper lip cracked and bleeding.

Involuntarily licking her lips, she put the back of her hand to her mouth. When she took it away she saw the fresh blood, remembered biting into the man's arm, then saw the image of his pale bluish skin. She stuck her head out the window and spat violently until there was nothing left in her mouth to spit.

She pulled into the next gas station. "Please be open. Please be open."

"RESTROOM OUT OF ORDER."

She put her head down on the steering wheel and began sobbing uncontrollably.

A man in a gas station uniform walked up to her open window. "Excuse me miss, your car is blocking –"

Startled, she screamed and slammed her gear shifter into reverse. A car coming up hit its horn, brakes screeching.

She eased out into traffic, made her way to the Cabrillo Highway and headed toward the beach. The dried blood on her skin felt tacky and terrible. She glanced around the car for something to drink, there was nothing but an empty paper coffee cup. She thought of finding a phone booth and calling the police. But what would the police do? The men would be gone by now. She didn't even have her driver's license and they'd ask her where she lived and worked and then she'd be on the defensive. She remembered the one experience she'd had when one of the girls at work had gotten roughed up by a customer. When two young policemen showed up, they were condescending, flirted with her and did nothing to find the assailant.

She drove down the coast, through Half Moon Bay, past beaches and tide pools, driving in a trance for almost an hour. Her view was the splattered windshield, the two stubs of the wipers and her bloodstained dashboard. It was like the screen of some gory arcade game, as if her car was stationary and the sky, the road and the scenery were streaming by, obscured by the blotches of blood on her windshield.

Eventually, she came to a small beach with no one around, parked her car, stripped off her clothes and jumped in the ocean. It was a warm summer day, but the water was cold. Trying to escape the replaying images in her mind, she pushed the limits of her endurance. It felt comforting looking at the horizon, feeling small in the vastness.

When she came out of the water and walked back toward her car, there was another car in the small parking lot with two people in it. About to put the bloody clothes she was carrying back on, she felt a shudder of revulsion. Throwing the clothes in a trashcan, she walked stoically past the car, making no effort to hide her nakedness.

She found some dance leotards and a sweatshirt in her trunk, put them on, and sat down in her car. It was hot and stuffy, bloodstained white seats with a rancid smell. She quickly got out again and went back to the beach, looking for something to clean her car with. Noticing how fast she was walking, she made herself slow down, going slower and slower until she was taking a step with each breath.

She found her spot in the sand and sat in a lotus position facing the ocean, palms up, head tilted back. When her mind involuntarily leaped out at some thought, she visualized the thought being enclosed in a bubble and popped into thin air. The technique usually worked, but today her thoughts were relentless.

Her attractive body, that she was so proud of, was becoming her nemesis. Her thoughts spun out to the horrific possibilities of what could have happened; she opened her eyes... she was at the beach and safe. She was actually lucky. The moves she'd made, the palm strike, the reverse finger lock, she'd practiced them a thousand times in karate class. Another woman might not have those skills.

Inhaling calmness, exhaling anxiety, she imagined the ocean breeze being channeled through pockets of tension in her muscles. She put a smile on her face, though she didn't feel like smiling; mouth yoga, sending a message to her body that, in this moment, she was okay. Like turning a big ship, she slowly pushed her perspective back until she was a passive observer, thoughts flowing out with the waves, worries diluted by the vastness of the sea.

Walking back to her car, she wondered what to do with the rest of her day, or the rest of her life. Where was Woody right now? She'd feel better if he was with her, but his jealousy was becoming unbearable for both of them. She knew she couldn't keep her job and keep their relationship. She already knew she wasn't going to tell him what had happened to her, at least not right away. He might turn it around and blame her for it.

Things had been so light and easy between them before she'd taken the job. Their lives flowed together effortlessly. He'd play his guitar for hours while she worked out dance routines. And when they weren't inspiring each other, they were laughing. She'd never laughed so much in her life.

He was doing his gigs, she was doing whatever fill-in dance performances she could find, but they were barely scraping by financially. When another dancer told her about the money she was making, working just a few nights a week at the Chi Chi Club, she'd decided to give it a try. Then everything had changed.

She thought back to the time they first met: going with a girlfriend to see him play at a coffee shop. He was sitting on a little stage, looking down at his guitar, singing like he was singing to himself. She'd had the experience before, feeling as if she personally knew a singer-songwriter when she heard them reveal themselves through their music. But Woody's lyrics were so poignant and insightful, it made her feel like *he* knew *her*. And in between his emotion-filled vocals, he weaved in guitar lines that were even more compelling than his poetic lines. Like everyone in the room, she was both elated and exhausted when he finished his set.

She'd wanted to meet this guy who was performing on stage and trying to hide at the same time. Her girlfriend, who had met him once at a gig, introduced her and she and Woody sat together, drank coffee, and had a long, intense discussion about the relationship of music and dance. They talked until they were the last two people in the place.

Standing out front, saying goodbye, there was an awkward silence. "I want to ask you something I've never asked anyone," Woody said, looking down at the sidewalk.

Stephanie waited.

"You know what I like most about you?" Woody asked.

Another silence.

"You don't talk during the pauses."

She smiled. "Do I know what you like about me? That's the question you've never asked anyone?"

"No. I mean, maybe, but that's not the question."

"So what's the big question?"

35

"Will you marry me?"

Another long silence. "Shouldn't we get to know each other a little better?"

He gave her a look she couldn't decipher. "If we get to know each other better," he said, "it could go either way." They shared a brief hug and he walked away.

Now, pulling out of the little beach parking lot, she smelled the dried blood again and thought of what Woody often said about how listening to music diminished your other senses. She tuned her radio to KSAN, turned it up and drove back to Daly City.

Chapter 5

Looking straight up to where the point of the Transamerica Pyramid Building met the sky, passing clouds made it seem like he was moving and Woody felt dizzy. He looked down to get his bearings and strummed his acoustic guitar. He was sitting on a stone ledge in a small park at the base of the tallest building in San Francisco. Thirty thousand tons of granite, concrete and steel pressing down on the San Andreas Fault, it was the power center of the financial district and housed Northern California's most prominent entertainment law firm.

Woody's open guitar case had about twelve dollars in it, including the five he'd started with. Tuning his guitar, he shook the hair out of his face and contemplated the never-ending flow of people. The ones there on business, with suits and briefcases, seemed to lean forward at the greatest angle. The better dressed they were, the faster they walked. The people in more casual attire walked more slowly, and only one bearded man with a shopping cart wandered from a set path.

Woody watched the man slowly pushing his cart in expanding circles until he was almost back to where he'd started. When the man stopped right in front of him, Woody nodded and played him a song. *The perfect size audience,* he thought, *one person.* Anything more than that and the stage fright kicked in. No worries here in the financial district, even the people who tossed coins into his guitar case didn't stop to listen.

It occurred to him that it was a city of distinct micro-cultures; downtown bankers, Chinatown two blocks away, hippies in the Haight, fishermen at the wharf, punks on Broadway, and the occasional crossover at all-night diners when the suits on their way to work mixed it up with nocturnal weirdoes that hadn't gone to bed.

Surrounded by the bustling whirlpool of activity, fragments of lyric lines began popping into Woody's head. Putting down his guitar, he grabbed his notebook and jotted down phrases that described the expressions on people's face; everyone already at the meetings they were trying to get to or still at the one they'd just left, oblivious to where they were in the moment. He stopped writing as quickly as he'd started, remembering he had a purpose of his own.

After Stephanie had stormed out of her apartment that morning, he knew he needed to get in touch with Jeff Pearlman, and soon. Getting no response on the phone, he'd made the decision to just go to Pearlman's office and wait until he was available, but he hadn't even made it past security in the lobby. He'd been waiting in front of the building, hoping to catch Pearlman on his way out. The more time that went by, the more agitated he felt. He had no way of knowing if Pearlman was even there. The guy could be in Hong Kong.

Wrapping his hair into a ponytail, Woody inadvertently knocked his backpack over and watched his emergency bottle of pain pills roll across the polished surface of the stone wall. Stretching out prone, he retrieved it before it hit the ground, sat up, and for a moment pictured himself swallowing the contents. Whenever he contemplated his own inevitable death, the impossible challenges facing him seemed unimportant, even manageable. If he kicked back, put on his sunglasses, hands folded on his chest, he could lay there indefinitely, peacefully unconscious in the cyclone of activity.

It could be a day, or even more, before someone took the time to check him out. It would take a security guard or someone in the middle of the night, probably after somebody else stole his guitar.

He stowed the bottle safely away and focused on the front of the building, trying to visualize Pearlman walking out. He imagined tiny Jeff Pearlman, scurrying with all the ant-like people out of the miniature revolving doors at the bottom of the enormous wall of steel and glass. Big important Jeff Pearlman suddenly seemed small and insignificant and the idea of sitting in front of an office building waiting for a chance to approach some guy he didn't even know felt ridiculous, humiliating to his music.

Putting his guitar away, he wondered what Stephanie was doing right now; probably getting dressed for work. He shook off the thought and headed out of the plaza. Stepping off the curb in the middle of the block, weaving between stopped cars, he looked up and there, a few steps ahead of him, was Jeff Pearlman.

Woody quickened his pace, a car horn blared and Pearlman glanced back.

"Hey Jeff."

Pearlman looked at him quizzically.

"You don't know me." Woody caught up and switched his guitar case to his other hand. "My name's Woody. I was hoping to talk to you for just a minute about a song I wrote, if that's okay."

Pearlman raised his eyebrows and kept going. They crossed the street, headed down the sidewalk and Woody saw what he took to be a spooked, staring-straight-ahead look on Pearlman's face. "I didn't mean to scare you," Woody said. "I'm not saying you have to keep walking or any kind of a directive or anything. I'm just like, I'm a harmless musician, you can ignore me or say you don't feel like talking to me and I'll never bother you again."

Pearlman kept walking, Woody kept pace, careful not to crowd him. He reviewed their conversation, trying to recall if Pearlman had said anything yet. He hadn't. Maybe this ridiculous idea was over.

Pearlman wasn't anything like he'd imagined. He was short, probably in his late-forties, with longish hair, jeans, white sneakers and a navy-blue sweatshirt. He looked more like a tennis player than a lawyer. "Sorry to bug you like this," Woody said.

Pearlman gave him a thoughtful look. "You just want to walk next to me? That's it?"

Woody smiled. "No. I've got a proposal for you about a song I wrote."

Pearlman wasn't smiling. "You can contact me at my office."

"I tried calling you a few times. I didn't get anywhere."

"I don't really have time to talk right now, I'm late for a meeting. And I don't appreciate being approached like this."

Woody immediately slowed his pace, letting Pearlman walk ahead. When he came to the red light at the next intersection and Pearlman was standing there, Woody kept his distance. Pearlman glanced over at him, they locked eyes for a moment, then Woody looked away.

Pearlman saw the resignation in Woody's expression. He also recognized the determination and confidence in the way he held himself; obviously accustomed to carrying the worn guitar case.

The light turned green, Pearlman hesitated and this time let Woody walk ahead. When Pearlman approached the red light at the next corner, he went up to Woody. "What's your song proposal?"

Woody took a moment to gather his thoughts, the light turned green and they walked. "I know it's pretty pushy, approaching a stranger on the street like this. I've listened to every song you ever produced and I've written one I think could be a hit like your other ones, but it's different. I'll play it for you any time, but I figured a guy like you wouldn't have time for all the calls it would take to arrange the event. I could play it right here, or anywhere. It'd be virtually no imposition on your time." About to mention Ray Bell, Woody decided to hold off. Once he mentioned Ray Bell's name, the bell couldn't be un-rung.

As they walked, it seemed to Woody as if Pearlman was about to say something then decided against it. "I know this is nuts," Woody said. "Check out my song for one minute and if you don't like it, I'll never bother you again."

Pearlman stopped, Woody beside him. Was this his chance? Should he take out his guitar? When Pearlman looked past him, Woody turned and saw they were standing in front of a crowded restaurant, a sidewalk-patio full of well-dressed patrons. A short, rotund man in a tan suit pushed his way through the crowd waiting for tables and scurried up to Pearlman.

"Jeff, you're almost an hour late for a half-hour meeting. I told you Barry had to leave by four. I tried calling –"

Pearlman turned to Woody. "Do you have a recording of your song?"

"No, but if I could just play it for you sometime… it's the best song I've ever written. I'm pretty sure you'll like it."

"Live music is always better," Pearlman said. "Unfortunately, cassette tapes are what works for my schedule these days."

"Jeff," the man in the tan suit gestured with his hands, "if we don't take care of this right now, Barry's…"

"You caught me at a bad time," Pearlman said to Woody. "Maybe you could get me a tape and I'll…"

"Ray Bell's gonna do the vocals." Woody saw an expression of interest he hadn't seen during their ten-minute encounter.

The short man in the suit patted his forehead with his handkerchief, rocking back and forth in his loafers. "Jeff, this is absolutely the only chance we'll have before Barry leaves on a…"

Pearlman handed Woody his business card. "Call me when you have a recording with Bell on it." He walked into the restaurant, the man in the tan suit a half step behind him.

Without Woody making any move to follow them inside, a uniformed doorman stepped out and blocked his path to the front door.

Chapter 6

"Hello?"

"Ray, it's Woody."

"Woody? I was expecting another call. What's up?"

"I left you a couple of messages and didn't know if you tried calling back. My answering machine's been messed up." Woody held the phone to his ear with one hand while he opened a pack of cigarettes with his free hand and his teeth. Expecting to leave a message, he was thrown off balance when Ray picked up on the first ring. "I've got a new song. It's perfect for your voice. And I have a recording session scheduled this Wednesday, maybe we could see how you sound on it."

"You caught me at a really bad…

"I talked to Jeff Pearlman about the song."

"Pearlman? You talked to him yourself?"

"Yeah. I had a meeting with him."

"How'd you get a meeting with Jeff Pearlman?"

"It took some scheduling. I got it together."

"That guy can definitely make things happen," Ray said, "if he feels like it. But me and him had a falling out over a deal he screwed up. If this is real and you get Pearlman behind the project, I'm interested. But I get these kinds of raps all the time."

"Pearlman's ready, we just need to get him a demo. I've got some players coming over on Wednesday, and a guy to record. Just come by and put down a scratch vocal. It'll take an hour. The song's perfect for your voice, it really is."

Woody waited. There were background noises, as if Ray was on a speakerphone. Woody thought about the one time he'd been to Ray's apartment. He'd gone to drop off a tape and some Barbie Doll looking woman who was high on something answered the door, stared at him vacantly, then left the door open and walked back inside. Ray was lounging in his all-white living room, people hanging around everywhere. He'd barely acknowledged Woody's presence.

"What about Wednesday?" Woody said into the phone.

"Where's the session?"

"My place; a demo with a few guys and a two-track recording."

"You have the song arranged, ready to record?"

"The song's together, its all the phone calls that are the rub. I wonder what the ratio is of phone calls to playing time. It's like what Hunter Thompson says; Hells Angels look ridiculous walking down the street. They're not supposed to be walking, and musicians aren't supposed to be talking, they're supposed to be playing music, you know what I mean?"

Ray didn't answer. It sounded like he was doing something across the room. Woody decided not to say anything until Ray did. He'd waited almost five minutes and was about to hang up when he heard a loud crashing noise.

"Ray?"

"Yeah."

"What the hell was that?"

"It's the bathroom speaker phone. It's all the tile and glass. I'm shaving. Listen, I need to get going."

"What about the session?"

"What's the pay?"

"I don't have a budget," Woody said. "It's just a demo, but if Pearlman gets some air play, it could be great exposure."

"I don't need exposure. I need to make my car payment."

"I can probably get together a hundred bucks."

"I'll tell you right now, there's no way I'm putting my voice on a song for a hundred bucks."

"If it ends up doing anything, you'll get your fair share for singing it. Maybe I can make us both some money."

"I thought there's some trip with your landlord about playing music there."

Woody was surprised Ray would remember him talking about that. "I've got it under control. It'd be just swimmingly if you'd come by and grace us with your presence."

"You think that woman Stephanie will be there?"

Woody realized how hard he was pressing the phone against his ear. "I don't know," he said as evenly as he could.

"She still working at that place on Broadway?"

"No! You gonna make it over or not or what?"

"Don't get your panties in a bunch, I'll see how things shake down. Somebody's at my door."

Woody slammed down the phone and looked over at Murray watching TV with one hand in his pants and one in a bag of corn chips.

"Looks like Jimmy Carter could be president," Murray said without looking up. "He seems like a pretty nice guy."

"Does that mean he gets his own TV show?" Woody reached into the back of his guitar amplifier with a thin piece of cloth and, one by one, gently rocked the delicate glass tubes, making sure they were properly seated in their connectors. "Getting Jimmy Carter to do something for you is like me trying to get Ray Bell to sing my song."

"You go through the same trip every time you deal with Ray," Murray said. "It's like what they say about insanity; you expect different results by doing the same thing over and over." Murray turned his attention back to the TV. "How'd you get hooked up

44

with Ray anyway? He seems like he's in a whole different musical world than you."

"He walked into this little bar where I was doing a solo acoustic gig. He was on his way home from his concert, stopped in for a nightcap, told me he liked my songs, and said he might be interested in singing a couple of them. He had two beautiful women, a limo waiting out front, and I figured my songs could get a ride in a limo instead of trying to hitchhike across the country with me. God knows I've tried everything else."

Murray muted the remote and prepared for the impending tirade about Ray.

"Whenever I mention he might be singing my songs, people start paying attention. But Ray just keeps jerking me around. I call him, he says he's into doing stuff, then I don't hear from him. I went over to his place once and gave him a tape. He came over here once, I played him a couple of songs, and he says something about taking too long to get to the chorus. He wasn't even listening. All he did was look at Stephanie the whole time. This session guy I met told me Ray glued a little piece of mirror on his shoe so he could look up the back-up singers' dresses. What kinda guy would do something like that?"

"You had any sleep?" Murray asked. "You seemed like you got pretty sick from all that hot sauce."

"That whole sleeping thing's a hoax."

"You're saying you don't need to sleep?"

"You don't have to let it run your life. You think it's just a coincidence they have us sleeping and working eight hours a day? It's big of them to leave a little time in between for procreation." Woody removed the pot from his Mr. Coffee, stuck in a cup midstream, and replaced the pot without losing a drop. "Just when you're getting momentum, you're supposed to go to some designated sleeping area, put on an official sleeping outfit and terminate all progress. Then you wake up discombobulated, you stink, your face is messed up and you have to put everything back together. Thirty years of your life, sleeping. I'll sleep when I'm dead."

Woody sat down, picked up a basketball-sized wad of tangled guitar cables on the floor in front of him, and began pulling it apart. "This whole discussion is moot anyway. I couldn't sleep through the night if my life depended on it. I lie in bed, my mind's going a million miles an hour…" Strands of his hair got caught in the cables. "Shit!" He hurled the wires to the ground. "Oh, by the way," he said in a high whiney voice, "is Stephanie working at that place on Broadway? If he ever gets near her…" He fished the remains of a joint out of an ashtray. "I've got Pearlman, a great song, great musicians, it's all in motion, just like the music. People don't get that *when* is more important than *what*. Everybody's focused on space when the secret is time. We're lost in space, man."

He gave Murray a hit, then expertly smoked the joint down to a quarter of an inch without burning his fingers. "Math doesn't explain music, music explains math. There's nothing's like music, except maybe sex, but sex is only a poor imitation on some kind of base physical plane. Music is the plane, man, a rocket ship."

Woody picked up the ball of wires again; extension cords and guitar strings tangled up with instrument cables. The wad grew bigger as he worked on it. He threw it back on the floor. "If you spent your life trying to design an extension cord or garden hose that always gets tangled up in itself, you couldn't. But they always do, every fucking time!"

Murray shrugged. "Maybe things are meant to intertwine, like roots of trees, or relationships, or practically everything. If strands of cotton or wool didn't naturally get tangled, we wouldn't have clothes."

Woody looked at him blankly. "Things aren't coming together, they're coming apart." He nudged the ball of wires with his foot. "Entropy, the only thing that doesn't need maintenance… except art. Giving an artist energy is like feeding a fire. It can come from a Rolling Stones' audience or an appreciative cat, an artist will give it back a thousand times." He stared up at the ceiling and began speaking slowly and softly. Murray had never heard Woody speak slowly *or* softly.

"There's this natural symmetry in the universe," Woody said. "It's everywhere, like the symmetry of people's faces. It drives people crazy to even look at somebody with a piece of food on their cheek. Anyone can hear the wrong note in a scale. We just don't see that we can see it, like fish don't see the water."

The cadence of Woody's voice sounded unnaturally even, as if he was in a trance. When Murray looked over at him, Woody's head was half-submerged in a six-inch-wide tear in the vinyl upholstery of his reclining chair. Murray did a double take. Puffy strands of yellow stuffing were coming out of the chair and intermingling with Woody's blonde curly hair, giving it a surreal look.

"Bring a radio into this room," Woody went on in his trance-like tone, "it'll play the music that's in the air. The radio waves are always here, and some day we'll be able to perceive them. Musicians can actually take those invisible vibrations and transform them into something visceral."

Woody was now barely audible. "Mozart was a heavy sleeper as a kid. They'd wake him up by playing seven notes of an eight-note scale on the piano… do, ray, me, fa, so, la, ti—he'd wake up, drag himself outta bed, go over to the piano and hit that last note. That last note. He had no choice."

Murray waited for Woody to go on. Woody was asleep.

Three hours later, Woody opened his eyes and quickly closed them. Then the thoughts came crashing in and he knew he wouldn't get back to sleep.

He looked to see if Murray was still there. His apartment was empty, light from the muted TV bouncing off the walls. Reaching for the chain of his reading lamp, he glanced at the clock. Where was Stephanie right now? 2:10 am, she'd been off work for two hours.

What was he doing up? The whole band and a recording engineer were coming over tomorrow. Would Ray even make an appearance? He lit a cigarette and started pacing. He knew the routine: wake up raw, vulnerable, his pathetic life over-exposed, thoughts cutting like knives. Maybe he should smoke a joint or take a pill or make some coffee, anything to change how he felt, kill time until his emotional armor assembled itself; his morning jacket.

The phone rang, startling him. It had to be Stephanie, at two in the morning! Something must've happened to her. His hand shaking, he picked up the phone. "Hello?"

"Jack?""

"Hello?"

"Jack there?"

"Jack?"

"Sorry, wrong number."

Woody hung up. His next thought made him sick to his stomach. He'd actually felt relieved by the idea that Stephanie might be in trouble, maybe in a hospital, rather than with some guy from work. What kind of selfish asshole was he?

He crushed out his cigarette, went to his backpack and dug out his pill bottle. How many pills would he take? A couple of sleeping pills, he didn't have the balls to take more. Was this even a real emergency that justified going into his emergency pill stash? He jerked his head to the left. "Fuck off!"

Dropping his hands to his sides, he stood listening to his voice echoing off the walls. *I'm actually talking out loud to myself.* He quickly sifted out two sleeping pills and chewed them up; they tasted terrible but they worked faster when he chewed them.

A half-hour later, the pills started coming on and he felt less desperate. Things might work out if Ray actually showed up and he managed to record his song.

Chapter 7

The next night, Woody took a headcount of the people crammed into his little apartment: a bass player, conga player, keyboard player, the keyboard player's girlfriend, saxophone player, his girlfriend, and a recording engineer. People had drifted in over the course of the evening and everyone was lounging around, drinking beer and smoking pot. The two girls were chattering.

"Is this a recording session or just like a rehearsal or something?"

"Is Ray really coming?"

"I thought Ray was the reason people were even going to like check out the music."

"I don't think Ray's that big of a deal anymore? I mean he had like one hit song and everything he's done since then is all about what he *did*, not what he's *doing*? I actually like know Ray, personally, from being backstage at a concert where we totally hung out. But I don't think Ray's still that big of a draw."

"I don't know about his drawers, but he's totally got the cutest butt. Anybody see what happened to that last joint?"

"Let's play something to warm up," Woody said.

"Do 'Squish' first," the keyboard player's girlfriend suggested. "I love that song. It's like totally contagious. Every time I hear it, I hear it in my head for days."

"Didn't somebody order a pizza?" the sax player's girlfriend asked no one in particular.

"I thought we were doing a recording at six." The engineer had a two-track reel-to-reel recording system set up on the floor in front of him, with a pair of bullet-shaped microphones on a tripod. "It's after eight. If I don't return these mics tonight, I pay for another day. If we're going to do it, let's do it."

"I thought the whole idea was to make a recording with Ray," the keyboard player's girlfriend said. "I heard there's some big-shot music lawyer that's –"

"Let's jam on something to warm up," Woody interrupted her. He connected cables to his guitar amp and the percussionist started a soft percolating conga beat.

The sax player adjusted his reed and began a rhythmic counterpoint to the congas. It took the bass player about thirty seconds to plug his bass into a practice amp at his feet and lay down a groove. The keyboard player had a portable electric keyboard with built-in speakers. He played swelling church-organ chords with his left hand, adding a right-hand melody that floated on top of everything like frosting on a cake. The keyboard player's girlfriend stood in the middle of the room, twirling to the music.

Woody plugged in his electric guitar and played a catchy single-note riff, creating a focal point for all the parts. For the next twenty minutes, they played a relaxed repeating pattern with soft bubbling rhythms, then slowly faded into silence.

The recording engineer hit the stop button on his recorder. "That was great! Way better than some sappy Ray Bell vocals. Looks like he's a no-show anyway, and these microphones are past their bedtime."

"The sound of shit happening," Woody said.

Downstairs, in the dirty alcove of Woody's apartment building, Stephanie stood sorting through her key ring. A bare light bulb exposed rows of metal mailboxes and dusty walls covered with graffiti. She'd just found the right key and stuck it in the lock when Ray Bell walked up.

"Hi."

She jumped back, startled. "Ray. What are you doing here?"

"I wouldn't miss a recording session. I was hoping you might be here. What happened to your mouth?"

She put the back of her hand to her lip. "Is tonight Woody's recording session?"

"Tonight's the big night." Ray put his arm across the doorway. "So how're things going down at the club? Any big tips?" He was wearing his usual rock-star Hawaiian shirt halfway unbuttoned under a casual sport coat, faded jeans and expensive shoes with no socks. His medium-length black hair was slightly messy and he hadn't shaved for two days.

Stephanie slipped under his arm and opened the door. "You coming in?" Without giving him a chance to respond, she started closing the door behind her.

"Hey, slow down." Walking up the narrow stairway to Woody's apartment, they heard the music and smelled the pot. The apartment door was locked. She took out her keys.

"Why don't you just knock?" Ray suggested.

"I don't want to disturb Woody when he's playing."

"Sounds to me like they're just tuning up."

When her key wouldn't turn, he reached to help her and pressed against her back. She leaned away, the door popped opened and they fell in holding onto each other.

Woody held his hand in mid-stroke over his guitar. Stephanie went quickly across the room. "Hi honey. Sorry I'm late."

"You came with Ray? From work?" he glared at Ray.

"I ran into him downstairs as I was coming in."

"Hey Steph," Ray called, "don't forget these." He tossed her keys, a high gentle toss, but she ducked and the keys hit her elbow and fell to the floor.

"What happened to your mouth, did somebody hit you?" The muscles twitched in Woody's jaw.

"There must be some pretty rough customers at The Chi Chi Club," Ray said.

Stephanie put her hand on Woody's shoulder. "It didn't happen at work. We'll talk later."

Just then the sax player's girlfriend brushed past Stephanie and Woody and sidled up to Ray. "Hi Ray. Remember me? Crystal? We met backstage at your concert? Remember? I had to keep switching with my girlfriend 'cause we only had one backstage pass and you were all like, you were tripping out that you couldn't tell us apart. Remember? I was the one that we were like totally talking about your music and everything and I was saying how when the first time I heard you sing I was all like totally like –"

Woody had an array of sound effects connected to his amp that could alter his guitar sound anywhere from Jimi Hendrix to Simon and Garfunkel. He cranked the knob on the master volume and raked his hand across his strings. The room imploded into a wall of sound. When he stomped on his distortion pedal, activated his flanger and ran his hand up the neck, it sounded like a freight train derailing sideways across steel rails.

He let it feed back for ten agonizing seconds, held the strings, stepped on another pedal and began finger picking harmonic arpeggios with a tone as pure as Zen finger bells. The contrast was dramatic, as if a bomb had exploded in the room and now the floating harmonic notes were binding to suspended particles of shrapnel, purifying the air.

The tone effects on Woody's guitar made it sound more acoustic than electric. With an efficient circular motion, he created a repeating pattern that sounded the way his hand moved, folding in on itself. The conga drummer, a delicate young Cuban man, slipped in a fingertip counter-point, the keyboard crept underneath, the bass came in under that and the sax blew a long high melody.

When Ray looked around the room, everyone had the same

enraptured expression. He began humming softly, adeptly blending notes with the saxophone in harmony, unison, then back to harmony, weaving in a melody he remembered from one of Woody's songs. Woody glanced up, impressed with Ray's perfect pitch, surprised he would remember the little melody. Then he looked over at Stephanie in her small space in the opposite corner, moving her hips and upper body in a fluid, understated motion that looked like bottled music. *This is what music can do, bring people together, vaporize all the personality, ego bullshit.*

Suddenly there was a loud forceful knocking, much louder than was necessary; the door was wide open. It was Woody's landlord, Mr. Huo.

Woody slipped out into the hallway, closing the door behind him. *I've got a band of great musicians, Ray Bell singing, and now this!* "What the hell's going on?" he demanded.

"Too loud music, rent not paid.

"What're you talking about, man? I paid the rent two weeks ago."

"Fifty dollars short."

"You don't come pounding' on my door for fifty bucks. I told you I'd pay you!"

"Every month short. Now you owe three hundred dollars. Too many loud people, too many –"

Woody looked down at his landlord, three inches shorter than him. "We need some peaceful conflict-resolution," he said quietly.

Mr. Huo was thrown off by the sudden change in volume. "Conflict revolution?"

Woody smiled. "Yeah, that's it." He held up his index finger. "One sec." He went in, got the hundred dollars he had for Ray, and gave it to his landlord. "Sorry for the trouble." He started to close the door.

"Still must move." Mr. Huo shook the twenty-dollar bills at him. "Too loud noise. Too many –"

"We'll try being more quiet." He kept slowly closing the door.

"Must move, must –"

53

"Thanks for your understanding. Let's both try to think positive thoughts." Woody gently closed the door.

By this time, the bass player and keyboard player were packing up their gear while their girlfriends smoked a joint with Ray. Woody lured Ray away from the girls and sat him down on his unmade bed to show him "Stephanie". He'd just started playing when the keyboard player got in a loud argument with his girlfriend about how many beers he'd had. She said he was too drunk to drive. The bass player's girlfriend agreed. The guys left without their girlfriends and the conga and sax players grabbed a ride.

Woody kept trying to show Ray his song, but Ray was distracted by the girls across the room. Woody and Stephanie glanced at each other and shared a knowing look.

"Hey," she reached for the coffee, "can I get you girls a cup?"

With the girls' attention elsewhere, Woody managed to get Ray to sing a couple of verses into his portable tape recorder.

"That's pretty good. The line into the bridge goes up an octave." He let the recorder run and played the melody on his guitar. "Let's try the bridge." Ray was looking over Woody's shoulder, smiling at the girls.

Woody stood up with his guitar, walked around Ray, sat down on the other side of him, and played the bridge. Ray had to turn his back to the women.

"Dude," Ray opened his hands, "when we get into a real studio, I'll know exactly what to do. Play the last chorus." Woody played and Ray belted out the chorus with such resounding authority, Stephanie and the two women stopped talking and the room became quiet.

"That's it!" Woody said. "Let's get a complete version."

"I'll try one take," Ray said, "I don't have all night."

Woody was adamant about getting the phrasing and melody exactly the way he wanted, and Ray continually complained that Woody was being too picky. But they kept at it, both of them recognizing the quality of what was happening. The key was just right for Ray's voice and the power of the music and words was coming through.

After numerous tries, they finally got one complete version recorded. When Woody pointed out where the melody in the verses could be improved, Ray asked for a lyric sheet. It turned out that the napkin Woody had written the lyrics on had been inadvertently used by one of the girls eating her pizza. There was nervous laughter, Woody offered to rewrite the lyrics, but Ray just stood up, made a comment about wanting to get paid to work on somebody else's song, and offered the women a ride home.

As the three of them walked out, Ray winked at Stephanie and she heard him whistling "Whistle While You Work."

Woody rewound the cassette tape and hit the playback button. While his song played, he watched Stephanie standing at the sink cleaning coffee cups, moving her hips to the music.

He walked up behind her and began rubbing her shoulders. "Thanks for cleaning up. You know, I first got the groove for that song watching you dance in the kitchen."

She shut off the water and turned to face him. He gently touched her cheek near where her lip was swollen.

"I hit my mouth on the steering wheel. I was driving out of my garage and had to slam on the brakes." She saw the uncertain look in his eyes. "I'm fine, really, I'm just exhausted right now. Can we please talk tomorrow?"

"You weren't wearing your seat belt?"

"I hadn't put it on yet."

She knew he knew she always put her seatbelt on when she got in her car. They looked in each other's eyes for a long moment. "Does it hurt?" he asked.

"Only when I laugh." She smiled and it made her wince. "We'll talk tomorrow. I'm fine." She kissed him on the cheek with the side of her mouth. "Good night. I love you."

"Just a sec." He went to the little freezer compartment of his refrigerator, took out a package of frozen peas and handed it to her.

This time she broke into a serious smile that hurt even more. She put the frozen peas on her swollen lip and, still smiling, left to go home.

Chapter 8

"American Management."

"Janet, it's Ray."

"Hi Ray. Jason's in a meeting."

"Tell him it's me. Tell him it's important."

Jason picked up a minute later. "Ray, what's up? I'm in a meeting."

"What's happening with the tour?"

"Nothing's changed. We've got a couple of tentative weekend dates with low guarantees, we're having trouble filling the weekdays. Even when I suggest smaller rooms, they're not interested. Promoters we've worked with aren't even returning my calls."

The young woman sitting next to Ray was running her fingers through his hair. He shrugged her off and stood up, looking for some privacy. People were hanging around everywhere. His extra-long phone cord dragging behind him, he went out into the hallway and closed the door on the cord.

"Jason, I'm running on empty. My credit cards are maxed out, I need to make something happen. What about your idea of doing an opening set on somebody else's tour, using the headlining band to back me up to save expenses? If I don't get some cash flowing soon I'm —" The elevator door next to him opened and three people stepped out, a woman Ray knew and two men he didn't recognize.

"Hi Ray," the woman said. "I tried calling you. These are the two friends I wanted you to meet, they do lighting design."

"I'm on the phone."

She gave a nervous laugh. "You moved your office into the hallway?"

Ray felt like telling her to just get back in the elevator. "Ray, are you there?" Jason said. "I have to get back to my meeting."

Ray waved the woman and her friends inside. "Jason, we need to make something happen. What about finishing the album?"

"Ray, there's not one hit on there. I've said it before; you should work with a co-writer. 'I Wanna Be On You Again' is just a rehash of 'I Wanna Be On You'. I don't sell tickets, Ray; hit songs sell tickets. You need a song that's at least on the charts. As time passes you're becoming more of a novelty act. If something doesn't change soon, we'll be booking casinos. I've got to get back to my meeting. Get me something new I can work with."

Woody woke up from a vivid dream to the sound of knocking, stumbled around and opened his apartment door. When he saw Ray standing there, he thought he was still dreaming.

In recent months, since he'd met Ray, he'd had recurring nightmares about his music career. He was trying to play without a guitar, or sing but nothing came out, or unable to get on stage. The dreams were different scenarios with the same panic-stricken frustration. And Ray was in many of them, standing in his way, blocking his path.

Trying to make sense of Ray standing in his doorway, Woody stretched his jaw in jerky contortions, swung the door open and walked back in. "You're just in time for breakfast, caffeine and nicotine. If we're gonna jam, I guess it'll have to be a morning raga." Woody was wearing a tattered bathrobe over a Charles Manson T-shirt and plaid boxer shorts. Taking a step inside, Ray was confronted by the smell of stale cigarettes and body odor.

"What's happenin', Ray?" Woody asked through a hacking cough. "You here for what I owe you? I had some money last night, but my landlord kind of cut ahead in line." He stopped in front of his Mr. Coffee machine, transfixed by the little orange light. The machine had been on all night and there was nothing but a burnt black film at the bottom of the pot. "Want a cup of coffee?"

"I don't really have time to hang out," Ray said. "I just came by to see if I could borrow that tape we made last night. That song 'Stephanie' is pretty good."

Woody turned and looked at him. Even this early in the day, he thought, Ray looks like he stepped out of a Gentlemen's Quarterly magazine. "You like my song?"

"There's some good ideas there," Ray said. "Let me do some work on it, maybe I can make it a little more radio friendly."

"Radio friendly? That song's radio fellatio. It's ready to go."

"It's up to you," Ray shrugged. "I can try working on it, or if you'd rather just pay me for what I've already done. I'm double-parked out front."

"It would be cool if you got familiar with it so we can record it properly. I listened to it last night, there's talking in the background that's as loud as the music. I can't give this version to Pearlman."

"Let me check it out."

"I have a friend that makes copies," Woody said, "I'll get you one."

Ray shrugged. "Why don't you just give me the one we made? You know how the song goes. I'll make a copy and get it back to you if you want."

Woody reached up under his long hair and scratched the back of his head. "I guess so," he mumbled, "it's a messed-up recording, I can't really use it for anything."

Ray watched Woody shuffling around in a daze. "The tape recorder's right there on the table."

"Oh yeah." Woody ejected the cassette. "So when can we get together and make a decent recording?"

"Give me a buzz, we'll find a time. I gotta split."

Woody contemplated the cassette in his hand.

"Lookit man," Ray said, "if you're not into this."

Woody gave him the tape. Ray nodded and turned to walk out.

"Wait a minute, let me label it." Woody took it, applied a strip of masking tape, wrote "Stephanie" and his name on it, and handed it back to Ray.

Ray turned to walk out again.

"One sec," Woody held out his hand. "I need to put one more thing on it."

"My car's about to get towed."

Woody extended his hand further. Ray gave him an obsequious little smile and handed it back.

Woody added the date and a copyright symbol; a small letter c with a circle around it. He held the tape out flat on his hand.

When Ray reached for it, Woody unexpectedly leaned forward a few inches and shook Ray's hand, the cassette pressed between them. For a clumsy moment, Ray continued shaking hands; if they disengaged, they'd drop the tape. Woody waited until Ray made direct eye contact, then pulled away and left the tape in Ray's upturned palm.

Looking like an embarrassed victim of some sleight-of-hand, Ray walked out.

A few hours later, Murray knocked on Woody's door and woke him up. "Looks like you figured out how to sleep." Murray sat down in the warm reclining chair Woody had just been just sleeping in. "You still want to make that trip to the Laundromat?"

"I had a dream that Ray came by this morning and told me he liked my song. Looks like me and Ray Bell might be working together. Hey, what time is it? I gotta check in with Steph."

"If you're not into doing laundry today."

"How about we do it over at Stephanie's? Today's her day off." Woody started gathering clothes off the backs of chairs.

"I don't know if I feel like driving all the way over there."

"We can do it over there for free."

"Maybe just go yourself."

"Whatever man, laundry's about my least favorite thing to do." Woody stuffed clothes into a laundry bag. "I think Stephanie's friend Cherrie might be around. They've been taking a karate class together. She told Steph she thinks you're enigmatic."

"I'm what?"

"Enigmatic. She got it from a fortune cookie."

They filled the big back seat of Woody's faded, gold-colored Buick with dirty clothes and headed out 19th Avenue past miles of neat little stucco houses joined at the hip like one long monopoly-board house, each with a manicured lawn the size of a bedspread.

Woody had a pen and a dog-eared notebook next to him on the seat, jotting down notes while he drove. At one red light he wrote for an extra few seconds, horns started blowing, he hit the gas and Murray spilled his soda on the seat.

"What the hell are you doing?" Murray said.

"I write songs about driving when I'm driving, being blind in the dark, hangovers on a hangover. I'm writing a song about this biker chick taking a piss off the back of a Harley on the freeway. I actually saw it happen, but if I get too descriptive it'll weird people out. The truth is what weirds people out the most. I'm going to make it about generic freedom but keep the hard athletic prose." He went to write down "hard athletic prose."

"Look out!" Murray yelled.

Woody snapped his head up, saw the stopped car in front of them and stood on the brakes. They screeched to a halt two inches from the car's bumper and Murray caught himself with a straight-arm against the dashboard. "Damnit! Can't you wait until we get there?"

61

"The ideas don't come when I'm trying to think of them. They come when it's happening."

"I suppose you write about sex when you're having sex." Murray tightened his seat belt.

"No, man. And I don't write about music when I'm playing music. Some things are sacred. It's like, did you see that guy sleeping back there on that bus-stop bench? His collar all scrunched against his puffy face with that piece of sleeping-bag hanging down to the sidewalk?"

"I've been watching the road. Somebody has to."

"Well that's the stuff, that image, like Van Gogh's work boots, you get one chance to capture it, like taking a picture with words." Woody glanced down at his notebook on the seat, covered with soda. "You can always tell a book by its cover."

It was early evening when they drove up to Stephanie's security gate and pressed the intercom buzzer. When her voice came out of the little metal speaker-box and she buzzed them in, Woody breathed a sigh of relief.

"You think her friend Cherrie will be around?" Murray asked.

"Maybe," Woody said. "She's kinda sweet, but she doesn't have much going on upstairs. I bet she couldn't put shampoo, rinse, repeat in the right order. I'm surprised Steph even hangs out with her. When she starts a sentence you never know where she's gonna end up, and she always ends up laughing. It's weird how she laughs at everything she says."

"There's something about her that turns me on," Murray said.

"I think you've got testosterone poisoning. Try sitting on your hand until it falls asleep, then jerk off with it. It'll feel like somebody else's hand."

Stephanie's apartment complex was a modern two-story structure with a heated pool. Woody and Murray, with their pale complexions, jeans and T-shirts, looked out of place among the young professionals coming and going. A young man in a polo shirt and pleated slacks walked past Woody, brushed his shoulder, and kept going without a word.

When they walked into Stephanie's apartment, she and Cherrie were in the kitchenette in sweat pants, tank tops and running shoes, drinking margaritas. Stephanie's condo was spotless, the polar opposite of Woody's place. Woody hugged Stephanie and noticed that her mouth didn't look as bad as he remembered. He decided not to bring it up. He and Murray flopped down on Stephanie's beanbag chairs and they both almost slid off.

Cherrie laughed. "We just came from the karate class, we're having margaritas. You guys want one?"

"Sure," Woody said. "I need a drink to handle all the preppies smashing into people around here. Everybody in this place thinks they're movie stars. It's the movies that are messing things up."

"Not every movie," Cherrie said with a nervous laugh. "There are some excellent choices out there and some very worthwhile –"

"*Every* movie." Woody stood up. "Movies, TV, air-brushed magazine people all looking perfect. It's like Plato's perfect table, as if there's an ideal pose or macho line for every situation. It affects you unconsciously, like you're supposed to be Paul Newman having some profound existential experience whenever you talk to a woman or look at the ocean. People actually think phony movie relationships are how real relationships are supposed to be."

Cherrie picked up the pitcher of Margaritas. "You guys want salt or no salt?"

"I'll take salt." Murray hoisted himself off the beanbag and went over and leaned awkwardly against the kitchen counter.

"You live in the same building as Woody, don't you?" Cherrie said. A dollop of wet salt fell on the strap of her tank top.

"I live on the floor right above Woody's apartment," Murray said, trying not to look at her chest. "I hear him playing all the time. I think music rises."

Woody took two margaritas off the counter and brought one

across the room to Stephanie. He gestured over at Murray and Cherrie, he and Stephanie clicked glasses in a conspiratorial toast, and she went to take a shower.

Cherrie pressed the button on the refrigerator ice machine. Two cubes fell out and a red light came on. "I've only got ice for you," she laughed. Missing the pun, Murray looked at her quizzically. "I've got some ice over at my place," she said. "Want to take a walk?"

"We were supposed to be doing our laundry." Murray looked across the room at Woody. He was reading the paper. Murray shrugged. "Our laundry's still in the car. Might as well leave it there."

Walking to her apartment on a gravel path lit by yellow sodium bulbs that gave their skin a greenish mosquito-light hue, Cherrie and Murray came to the swimming pool lit up with underwater lights. Cherrie saw that no one was around and looked at him with a mischievous flash in her eyes.

"How about a swim?"

Murray shrugged and looked down at his jeans.

"If God had meant us to swim naked, we would've been born that way," Cherrie giggled. "Wednesday is the official, unofficial clothing optional day."

She ran down the steps to the pool, stripped off her clothes and dove in. Gliding underwater, she put the little gold cross on her necklace up to her lips and prayed she wasn't still having her period.

Murray stood at the edge, watching her. When she passed the underwater lights, her silhouette surrounded by swirling bubbles looked like a Disney movie. He watched for as long as he could without gawking, waited until she was at the deep end, took off his own clothes and waded into the shallow end. Self-conscious about being overweight and naked in front of her, he stayed in the water up to his neck when she swam by.

"The water's yummy, isn't it?" When she swam back toward the deep end, Murray followed, keenly aware of the water flowing past him.

Cherrie glided around the perimeter with a gentle breaststroke. Tracking closely behind her, Murray watched her frog kick spread wide and snap together, sending a wake rippling down the length of his body. He felt himself growing excited. As his excitement increased, so did his water resistance. He swam harder, closing in until his hands were just out of reach of her feet. The pool was like a hydraulic connection, hydro-sex. It occurred to him that no matter how close they came, there would always be a thin liquid layer between them.

Murray put his head down and pulled himself through the water. Coming up for air, he got another good look at her. He hadn't had sex in almost a year. On fluid drive, his hard-on furrowing a path through the water, Murray felt as if he were touching her. Slipstreaming, his frog kick matched hers and he focused in with concentration that pulled him along like a tandem trailer.

They passed an underwater light, voyaged through the hot water jet, navigated the Gulf Stream and once again Murray became privy to a centerfold view. At that moment he noticed the slightest film of red drifting out of her like a wisp of underwater smoke.

It was too much. He came in the water.

Relative to their slow speed, Murray gained momentum and gently collided with the soft pink palms of her feet. She stopped and turned. They stood inches apart in shoulder-deep water, her blue-white breasts buoyed on the surface like water balloons. Their eyes met for a moment when a slight ripple in the water caught their attention and a milky jellyfish delicately laced with blood floated by. It was the most fragile of moments. Murray closed his eyes and shrugged his shoulders, she gave a small nervous laugh and they simultaneously reached out of the water and embraced.

When Murray and Cherrie left Stephanie's apartment, Woody had walked back to Stephanie's bedroom. She was just getting out of the shower.

"What happened to your chest?"

She turned away and slipped on her bathrobe.

"What happened to you?" He held out his hands as if he was reaching for her. "What are those bruises?"

She sat on the end of the bed and took a deep breath. "Two men tried to rob me on the sidewalk in front of my apartment. I was just driving out of the parking garage and they came up and wanted some money. I didn't have any and they got mad."

"What did they do to you?" He sat down next to her.

"Nothing really. They reached in the car and tried to grab me. That was it." She looked down, tears welling up in her eyes.

"Did you call the police?"

"No, I should have. I guess I wasn't thinking clearly."

"That's all that happened? They didn't... do anything to you? How did you get those bruises?"

She sat up straighter. "The whole thing only lasted a few minutes. They reached in my car window, tried to grab me and I drove away. I never even got out of my car."

He took her hands in his. "It must've scared you."

"It was pretty intense, but the fear didn't really sink in until it was over. Now I'm here, and I'm okay."

"It didn't have anything to do with any guys from work?"

"I've never seen those men before in my life! My job had nothing to do with it!" She withdrew her hands from his and gave him a hard look. "I appreciate your concern, I don't feel like talking about it anymore."

Woody stood up, walked in a little circle, then went to the door. He had his door on the doorknob. "Sorry."

She stood and folded her arms across her chest. "I'm ok, I'm just trying to process all this. I need to figure out some things on my own."

Without a word, he kissed her on the forehead and left. Figuring Murray would be okay either spending the night with Cherrie or catching a bus, Woody headed home.

It was almost midnight when Murray caught the last bus home to the Haight and saw Woody's apartment lights still on. He found him sitting with an acoustic guitar at his kitchen table, wearing headphones, eating a bowl of cornflakes with one hand and writing in his notebook with the other. Getting a whiff of fresh coffee, Murray felt better. He knew Woody knew he had a difficult time with women, and hoped he wouldn't ask about Cherrie.

Woody pulled his headphones off one ear. "Whaddya get?"

"Cops and hardons. They're always around except when you need one."

Woody let the headphones snap back on his head and wrote down what Murray had said.

"There's coffee."

Murray poured himself a cup. "This is some of the strongest coffee I've ever tasted. What are you..."

"What?" Woody took off the headphones.

"What are you doing with all this stuff?"

"I'm writing a song with AM-radio-mind." Woody pointed to the headphones on the table with a tiny talk-radio voice coming out. "AM radio, mindless moronic chatter. It's the manifestation of the American thought process. The other day I watched people at a bus stop eating, reading and listening to transistor radios; all in the middle of a million cars and sirens. That's my audience. I'm trying to write a song in the environment it's gonna be heard in. These distractions hone my focus." Woody was talking so fast, pieces of cornflakes were flying out of his mouth. Murray took a piece of shrapnel on the cheek.

"Hey! How about honing your focus on your cornflakes?"

"I'd have to be a lot more enlightened to do something like that. With a zillion facts bouncing around in my head, I'm a hero being mindful of anything. I've got information stored in my brain about everything I've ever known about math, music, nature, hungry people in Africa, Stephanie's past sex life..." He went blank for a moment and took another gulp of coffee, barely taking time to swallow. "For me to ignore all that knowledge and perceive just one thing, like how my heartburn feels from this coffee… it's impossible."

"Whoa there Cowboy, I was just talking about some cornflakes. This whole thing reminds me of that story about the Zen monks doing a silent meditation."

"It's like listening to music." Woody kept on as if Murray hadn't spoken. "You can't hear anything else when you really listen to music. Music's the exact opposite of silence, so they're practically the same. In fact…"

"So these four monks…" Murray decided to press on regardless. Unlike Woody, he was used to going to bed early and getting nine hours of sleep and right now, up late and buzzed on coffee, he was sick of Woody interrupting him. "…so these four monks sit down to do a silent meditation…"

"Like try listening to a song while you listen to me talk," Woody kept on. There was no stopping Woody. There was no stopping either of them.

"So these monks start this silent meditation," Murray continued, "and the first monk says…"

"… you couldn't repeat the lyrics or you couldn't repeat what I said. One or the other. You can't hear both."

"… 'we should close the door'…"

"… in fact, you can't really see and…"

"… and the second monk says, 'you just talked' …"

"… hear music."

"… and the third monk says …"

"… you can't even think and hear music …"

"… hey, you just talked telling him he talked'…"

"… music is accurate communication. Talking isn't."

"… and the last monk says, 'I'm the only one who hasn't talked.'"

Woody lit a joint and passed it to Murray. There was a minute of unusual quiet between them. "I read somewhere that there are seven kinds of silence."

Chapter 9

Ray sat at his piano with his cassette player and headphones, listening to the song he'd recorded with Woody. After a frustrating hour, he still couldn't figure out the chords to the bridge. He could usually rely on his intuitive sense of pitch and melody and could sing just about anything. And once he could sing something, he could find the notes and chords on the piano. But Woody's chords were as weird as he was.

Ray picked up his phone to make a call and put it down. *I have to at least figure out how to play the song myself.* He went at it for another twenty minutes, then pounded his fist on the keys in frustration. *So what if there's a couple of chords missing. Woody's a goddamn street musician! He doesn't have a clue about the real world of radio and record companies. My voice and delivery make "Stephanie" into a real song. It isn't even the same song when I sing it.*

Ray picked up his phone and pressed the auto-dial button.

"American Music."

"It's Ray for Jason."

Jason came on. "Hi Ray. I've got no news. I've tried everything to get this tour booked but it's just not –"

"I've got a new song," Ray cut in, "a guaranteed hit. The last time I said that to you, I was right. This song will do it for us Jason, everything we need."

"A new song? Whose is it?"

"It's mine."

"I didn't know you were writing. Get me a tape."

"I haven't recorded it yet."

"Even just vocal and piano is fine. Let me hear what you've got. What's it called?"

"'Stephanie.'"

Ray hung up and went back at it. After numerous tries, he finally got a version recorded by featuring his singing and playing one note on the piano over places he was unsure of. It wasn't great, but with the lyric sheet he'd written out, it was adequate to use for a federal copyright application.

It had been almost two weeks since Woody gave the cassette to Ray, and he'd called Ray and left more messages than he'd wanted to. He decided to try going directly to Pearlman. After several calls in several days, Pearlman's receptionist curtly informed him that leaving more messages would have the opposite effect of what he was trying to accomplish.

Woody figured Pearlman was probably inundated with phone calls and tapes and had a feeling that if he could just play him his song in person, that would do it; the song would speak for itself. Woody packed up his guitar and took a bus downtown to The Transamerica Building.

Woody had read everything he could find about Jeff Pearlman; an entertainment-lawyer-turned-music-producer with an uncanny knack for recognizing hit songs. There were stories about him early-on in his career, discovering unknown artists, even street musicians, and doing things like taking a mortgage out on his house in order to get them into a studio and record their music. Pearlman had discovered Ray

Bell when he was singing top forty songs in hotel lounges. He'd paired him up with a songwriter and produced his only hit song.

Woody scanned the lobby of the Transamerica Pyramid; there was a security desk in front of the elevators, the entry to the stairs beyond that. Going back outside, he walked down the ramp to the underground parking garage, found the elevator and waited ten feet away until a group of businessmen accessed it with a key. Woody casually joined them and rode up forty-four floors. The elevator opened into a private lobby with panoramic views of the city, the Golden Gate Bride and the Pacific Ocean.

"Can I help you?"

"I'd like to see Jeff Pearlman."

"Your name please."

Woody hesitated, wondering if the receptionist would remember him from the messages he'd left. "My name's Woody."

It didn't faze her. "Do you have an appointment?"

"No. I met with Mr. Pearlman last week. He asked me to contact him."

She sized him up, standing there with his guitar case. "If Mr. Pearlman isn't expecting you, you can't just see him. You need an appointment."

The phone rang. "Just a moment please. Pierce and Pearlman, how may I direct your call?" She turned her attention back to Woody. "I'm sorry sir, everyone in the office is extremely busy today. We don't do walk-up business here."

"Can I make an appointment? Mr. Pearlman asked me to contact him."

"You'll have to talk to Mr. Pearlman's assistant. You won't be able to see him today, his schedule is completely full."

"What's his name?"

"Whose name?"

"His assistant."

"*Her* name is Holly Wilson. Holly's currently on the phone." The phone rang. "Pierce and Pearlman, how may I direct your call?"

The calls kept coming, one after another. "Is there a phone I can use to make a local call?" Woody asked between calls.

Without looking up she said, "There's a phone by the couch, any line that's not in use, press 9. Pierce and Pearlman, how may I direct your call?"

Woody walked across an expansive oriental rug, sat down on a chrome and leather couch and recognized John Coltrane coming out of hidden speakers in the ceiling. He picked up the phone on a glass side-table, tried calling Stephanie and got her answering machine.

He wandered around the waiting room, checking out the gold records and concert posters, then went back to the receptionist. Her desk was behind a counter almost as high as the top of her head. She spoke into her headpiece while she worked the phone and typed notes.

The calls finally stopped and she looked up. "Who was it you were waiting to see?"

"Holly."

"Holly is still on the phone. We're extremely busy here today. I'm afraid you'll have to come back when you've scheduled an appointment."

"I'm working on a project with Ray Bell." Woody saw the same interested expression he'd seen on Pearlman's face when he'd first mentioned Ray's name.

"You work with Ray Bell?"

"We're working on a recording project."

"Really? How's Ray doing these days?"

"You know Ray?"

"He used to be one of Mr. Pearlman's clients. Actually, Ray and I became close friends."

"I'm not surprised," Woody said. "Ray's pretty friendly with women."

Her face changed dramatically, going cold and formal. She slapped a notebook and pen on the counter. "Leave your contact information."

She answered two more calls and looked up. Woody was still standing there. "I'm extremely busy. Leave your contact information." "Can I please wait for Holly and make an appointment?" The phone rang. "Suit yourself." She answered the call.

Amazed at the receptionist's attitude, he went back to the couch, took out his acoustic guitar and played along quietly with 'Trane. He wondered what Stephanie was doing right now. He could feel her pulling away. If he lost her he'd probably be losing the only woman who could see through all the confusion in his life and still care about him.

"Sir! Please!" the receptionist yelled across the room. "I can't hear the person on the phone." She must've been twenty feet away. Woody thought he'd been playing softly. He put his guitar down and watched the top of her head bobbing up and down like a machine playing 'Pierce and Pearlman' with no connection to a brain. When another fifteen minutes passed, he knew she was ignoring him. On impulse he picked up the phone next to the couch and called the office number. The receptionist answered across the room. "Pierce and Pearlman, can you please hold?"

"Sure." Now he was on double hold, in person and on the phone. She came back on the line. "How may I direct your call?"

"I'm calling for Jeff Pearlman."

"Mr. Pearlman's assistant Holly receives his calls. She's currently on the phone, may I take a message?"

"I'll hold."

"Whom may I say is calling?"

"Billy Button, Columbia Records. "

"Will she know what this is regarding?"

"Yes." The phone rang.

Woody was impressed with the receptionist's composure while she juggled all the action. It was just the kind of equanimity he needed to have to work with a bunch of crazy musicians. She put two more calls on hold and went back to Woody's line. "Mr. Button?"

"Yes."

"Holly is still on the phone. Can I take a message?"

Just then Jeff Pearlman walked into the reception area. "Brenda, what's going on with the phones? I can't get an outside line."

"I'm sorry, Mr. Pearlman, it's unusually busy, I have three calls on hold and –"

Woody popped off the couch. "Hey Jeff, it's Woody. I talked to you on the sidewalk about my song. If you could just give me three minutes of your time."

"Mr. Pearlman, you have two calls waiting and there's –"

"I've been here longer than any of those calls and I'm a live person."

"Hold on," Jeff Pearlman put his hands up. "Let me take these calls, then I've got one call to make, and then I'll see you, but it has to be very brief, okay?"

"Okay!" Woody spun around and headed toward the couch.

Pearlman disappeared down the hall and Brenda went to the calls on hold. "Mr. Button? Hello?" The caller ID display on Brenda's console showed the call coming from the office number. It made no sense.

The call was suddenly disconnected. She looked across the waiting room, saw Woody pressing the button on the phone, and called security.

Woody leaned back on the couch and thought about what he'd do when he got into Jeff Pearlman's office. This was a chance of a lifetime. He'd tell him he wanted to play him one song… no talking, just music. Then it would be up to Pearlman.

"Sir, you'll have to leave. Please come with me."

Woody looked up. "What?"

The guard looked to be about sixty years old with chocolate brown skin and silver hair. "There's been a problem, you'll have to leave."

"What're you talking about man? I've got an appointment."

"I'm asking you to leave," the guard said more forcefully. "Please come with me."

"Hey, I don't know what your trip is, but I've got an appointment with the main man here. Brenda?" Woody called across the room. "Tell this guy I'm waiting for Pearlman."

"That man barged in here without an appointment and has been harassing me," Brenda snapped.

"Let's go," the guard said.

Woody gathered up his things and walked out with the guard close behind. Passing the reception desk, he said to Brenda; "Using your little job with your little brain to pull a power trip on people... feel important?"

The guard had an elevator key that ensured an express ride with no stops. They rode down forty-four floors in silence, walked through the lobby, out a revolving door and the guard took his position.

"Sorry about the hassle," Woody said.

The guard nodded.

"You think it'd be ok if I waited out here for Pearlman?" Woody asked. "I actually had an appointment with him. That receptionist has a real attitude."

"If you don't bother anyone, you can do whatever you want out here."

"I didn't mean to cause a scene, I'm just trying to get my music career going. I know you're just doing your job."

"What kind of music do you make?"

Woody considered the question. "I don't really make music. I'm more like a midwife."

The guard nodded.

"My stuff is kinda like rock and jazz and blues all rolled into one."

"I like the blues."

"Everyone gets the blues," Woody said. "John D. Rockefeller can get the blues."

The guard smiled.

It occurred to Woody that with all the people around, it might be a good place to try to make some money. "Want to hear a song?"

The guard nodded. "I don't have much else going on."

Woody knelt down and unlatched his case. "I've got a song I was going to play for Pearlman. There's this singer, Ray Bell, who might sing it."

"Ray Bell?"

"You know who he is?"

"He used to come around here quite a bit. There were always a bunch of kids trying to get his autograph. I asked him once for his autograph for my nephew, but he didn't have time. Doesn't take much time to sign your name."

"Time," Woody strummed a minor chord. "The most valuable thing there is. And people in America have everything but time." Four businessmen walking abreast transitioned to single-file formation and streamed through the revolving door next to them with marching-band-precision. Woody strummed the chord again. "There's two ways to get rich; have more or need less. Before washing machines, people washed their clothes once a month and had time to hang out. Now they do laundry every day because they can, they're spic 'n span."

The security guard looked amused.

Woody added a simple guitar melody. "The first people, hunter-gatherers, had time to travel and enjoy life. They owned nothing, so they had everything. Then they got insecure about running out of food, people stayed put, grew food in one spot, the spot got depleted, they all over-eated." He went to the four chord. "When men said God was a man, people got mean, fighting on principle, spend their time fixing broken tools 'cause Mother Nature's invincible." He strummed harder, bending over his guitar. "Ain't no coincidence, after years of huntin' and fishin'; agriculture and religion show up and people start bitchin'." Woody hit the big five chord. "And then… tah dah… here comes people with the least time in history; with cars and clocks and life without mystery." He went back to the top of the chord progression. "Time is Mother Nature's way of putting space between events. Now we use up all the time, so everything's happening at once."

The security guard watched as Woody started a pulsating beat on his low E string. "It's gonna be Mother Earth one, white people nothing. And it's gonna come fast, hit critical mass, some oil-spill-ozone-nuclear freak-out, not enough rain, too much rain, earthquakes and hurricanes. We'll drive 'till the last drop of gas, freeways of dead cars, no lane to pass."

He dug into his strings. "Grass'll grow through shopping mall walls, bust open the tarmac and take it all back, jack. Mother Nature, with her infinite wisdom, can increase the cancer rate from breathing smog a thousand percent by snapping her fingers." Woody stopped for four beats and snapped his fingers. "Mushrooms. Per square foot, they're the smartest, most muscular creatures on earth. And they're gonna get together and pick up the sidewalks. Don't pave over the hand that feeds you. Don't pave over your... own... Mother... Earth!" Woody hit his final chord.

A man walked by and dropped some coins in Woody's open guitar case. "That's an interesting song," the guard said.

"Thanks, I was just goofing around." Woody took a few minutes to tune his guitar. "Want to hear a real song?"

"Go ahead and play. I'm just standing here."

Woody sang the first verses of "Stephanie," started feeling sad in the chorus, and transitioned to another song in the same key; a poignant ballad about how alone everyone is no matter how many people they're surrounded by. While he sang, a constant flow of people streamed by.

"Sounds real good," the security guard said.

"I've been working on my songs forever," Woody said. "It's like, everybody's trying to write a hit song, be a movie star, get people to tell them they're cool. I don't need to be rich and famous to know I'm cool. I just want to be able to pay my rent and be with my girlfriend."

"You have a group together?"

"I'm trying man, but getting a band together is like, you ever know any artists who've tried making a living painting pictures?"

"There was one fellow I knew from high school, he was a little odd."

"Well imagine getting a bunch of crazy artists together to paint one picture, on one big canvas, and they all have to decide how it should look and, and this is the killer, they all have to paint at the same time, standing right next to each other, even if one of 'em just broke up with their girlfriend or has the flu or –" Woody noticed the guard glancing around and realized how loud he was talking. He lowered his voice. "So when does Pearlman leave at the end of the day? Maybe we could ambush him."

The guard stiffened.

"Hey man, I was just kidding. I'm not stalking the guy. I had an actual appointment until his receptionist decided she didn't like me. You think if I hang out here I might eventually get to see his royal highness?"

"From what I can tell, Jeff Pearlman's a pretty nice guy. He's one of the only people in the building that takes time to say hi or remembers when it's Christmas. As far as waiting out here, it's a free country. But I should tell you, Mr. Pearlman doesn't always leave out of this door. It's a big building."

"Thanks for the tip. My name's Woody."

"Ernie."

"Here's my card." Woody gave him a card with a picture of a turtle playing a guitar and his phone number.

"Your music's real nice. Don't give up. I need to go check in for my second shift." The guard shook his hand and walked inside.

Playing music was the last thing Woody felt like doing. He noticed that the flow of foot traffic had shifted, like a changing tide, from people coming in to people going out. He packed up his things, went in through the revolving door, and scanned the lobby. Businessmen and women were rushing in every direction like a movie on fast-forward. The blur of motion had a disorienting effect and he suddenly felt like he was drowning in a roiling sea of suits.

Watch the elevators? Wait outside? Try another entrance? What the fuck am I doing here? He swung back around into the revolving door and stayed there, going round and round until he was the only one in the door; a growing line of confused commuters quickly backing up. He kept his head down, following the end of his guitar case. *In or out? Where's Pearlman? Spin the bottle. In or out?* He lurched out, unsteady on his feet, and kept walking to the closest bus stop.

An hour later, Jeff Pearlman walked out of the revolving doors.

"Good night Mr. Pearlman."

Pearlman stopped. "Hey Ernie, what happened with that guy in my waiting room? Was there a problem?"

"No sir. He turned out to be a pretty nice guy. He played some of his music for me. Says he plays with Ray Bell."

"That's what I heard. Did you happen to get his name?"

Ernie took out Woody's card.

"Let me write down the number."

"You can keep the card," Ernie told him. "I don't have any use for it."

Pearlman merged his black Jaguar into the thick traffic on Montgomery Street and picked up the car-phone mounted on the center console.

Holly answered. "Hi Jeff, what'd you forget?"

"Nothing for once. When you get a chance, give this guy a call and see if he'll come in for an appointment." Pearlman held up the card. "W-O-O-D-Y, phone number 415 M-E-W S-I-C-K. And you better notify security when he's coming, or they might not let him in."

"Is that the guy Ernie escorted out today?" Holly asked. "Brenda says he's a real creep."

"I met him once on the street. He actually seems like an interesting guy, very genuine. I'm curious to hear what his music's like. And he says he works with Ray Bell. I'd like to find out what Ray's up to. He's got an outstanding debt with the office that I've let go too long."

Chapter 10

Three in the afternoon, Murray got off work early and stopped by Woody's apartment. The door was wide open, Woody in his reclining chair, a cigarette in one hand, a cup of coffee in the other. Several times in recent days, Murray had found Woody sitting in his apartment, staring into space. It was especially noticeable with Woody because he rarely sat in one place, and when he did, he almost always had a guitar in his hands. The first thing Murray noticed was how much smaller Woody looked without his guitar.

"I thought you had your big appointment today with that music lawyer," Murray said.

"Yeah."

"What time's your appointment?"

"Four-thirty."

"You better get it together," Murray said. "Seems like traffic downtown is getting worse all the time."

"The future's not what it used to be."

"Haven't heard from Steph?"

"Haven't heard from her in like five days. The last time we were together, I saw these bruises on her chest. I told you about what happened with those guys on the sidewalk. I think she's going through some heavy changes."

"Maybe she's just not answering the phone," Murray said. "Why don't you go over there?"

"I went over, she wasn't around." Woody picked up a banana and peeled it. "Can you believe how much packaging they put on these things? It's like fifty percent packaging. What a waste." He threw the peel at a bag of trash and missed by a foot.

Woody was acting strange, even for Woody. Murray couldn't tell if he was serious or joking about the banana peel.

"You know the evolution rap?" Woody said. "Amoebas evolve into fish, crawl out of the sea and evolve into apes and people?"

"Yeah." Murray moved a pile of laundry off a chair and sat down. He knew Woody would go to his meeting when he felt like it, and there wasn't much he could do about it.

"It's upside down." Woody got up, took a box of guitar strings and dumped it upside down it in the middle of the floor. "We're de-evolving. Human beings are the lowest form of life yet. We're the only animal that needs clothes, condoms, vitamins, refrigerators, forks, toilet paper, religion, weddings, art… we think we need everything, that's why we're always fighting." Woody dropped to his knees in front of the pile of strings. "I bought a new set of guitar strings that vanished into thin air."

Murray picked up an unopened package next to him "These?"

"No man. I bought a set of extra heavies for the audition. I just had 'em."

"It'd probably be better to play with old strings than miss the appointment."

Woody picked up his pace, circling the apartment. "Animals are divine the way they live. They don't make mistakes. Man is the only animal that makes mistakes. Man, man, builds a square room in a round world, throwing trash everywhere, hassling with everybody." Woody glanced at the clock and quickly looked away. "And we're all de-evolving together."

81

"You really think this is the time to get into all this?"

"If we were e-volving, you'd think there'd be a bigger difference between all people that ever lived." Woody went back to the pile of strings. "The difference between cultures and language is just superficial. Like say a guy's here from Iran. He sees a sign that says BOB'S FOOT LONG, tries to translate it with a little pocket dictionary and the rule in the front of the dictionary talks about antecedent adjectives or some shit. So he's thinking, 'foot-long', that's copasetic for 'long foot'. But the rule says adjectives come first in English and the guy suffers typical human confusion. All I'm saying is, the difference between cultures, like the difference between spaghetti and chow mein, is no difference at all."

"I think I lost you at the last turn," Murray said. "You going to that meeting or what?"

"Turn? You can't get lost if you're not going anywhere."

"I guess that explains why you're not going anywhere."

Woody unearthed another box of strings. "Like, take the two most opposite people on earth. Take a ninety-year-old lady in Africa and a twelve-year-old kid in Brooklyn. They're the same; insecurities, humor, everything. The relative difference in height, weight, body temperature of all people that ever lived is infinitesimal. Mother Nature's so conservative, she probably votes Republican." Woody let himself fall back into his reclining chair.

"What're you doing? You're gonna miss your big appointment."

"I can't find my strings, I can't find Stephanie, I can't find shit! I'm like, like... every other fucking word out of my mouth is *like*! If I ever say like again, shoot me!"

Murray stood up. "I can't watch."

"Can't watch what? Where you going?"

"I can't watch you miss the biggest opportunity of your music career. And I'll have to listen to you complain about being broke for another ten years." Murray pushed his glasses back and held Woody's gaze, which Murray rarely did. "Sometimes I think you don't really want what you say you want."

"What're you talking about? My music is all I have. I'm doing everything known to man to get it happening."

"That's exactly what I'm saying. How about just going from point A to point B?" Murray lowered his voice. "Look, I know you've got a lot on your mind about Stephanie, and I know you've always got a lot on your mind. I guess all I'm saying is, if you have an appointment, maybe just go to it. The life you ordered has arrived."

Woody looked at Murray for a moment, stood up, gave him a little salute, picked up his guitar and walked out the door, leaving it open behind him.

Murray considered Woody's empty chair and knew Woody would still be sitting there if he hadn't come by. He wondered if he really understood the creative process. He'd seen movies about artists like Beethoven and Janis Joplin and Leonardo da Vinci. Maybe being broke or bummed out was what got an artist's creative juices flowing. Murray realized he liked comedy films okay, but drama and tragedy seemed more appealing, as if unhappiness was more interesting than happiness.

He picked up a small stack of Woody's drawings: intricate pencil sketches of Stephanie, designs for guitars, self-portraits, even an exaggerated caricature of Murray watching TV. Seeing the unique perspectives of images he was so familiar with felt eerie, like he'd stumbled into a place in Woody's psyche where he didn't belong.

The phone rang. He was sure Woody had forgotten something. "Hello?"

"Hi Murray, it's Stephanie. Is Woody around?"

"He just left for a meeting to play his song 'Stephanie' for some music lawyer downtown at the Transam building." Murray sat down in the reclining chair Woody had just been sitting in. It was warm and smelled like him. He'd seen him sitting there a million times, talking to Stephanie. "Woody's been acting kind of strange since he hasn't heard from you."

"I just needed some space," she said.

"Too bad you didn't call before he left for the meeting, it might have brought him out of his funk." She didn't respond. "Steph?"

"I'm still here. Did Woody drive or take the bus?"

"I think he took the bus."

"With a little luck with traffic, I could get downtown and meet up with him, maybe give him a little emotional support. We need to talk anyway."

The end of the day, the sky just starting to turn the buildings pink, Woody approached the front of The Transamerica Building. He thought of the Great Pyramids in Egypt, squat and majestic; the world's tallest buildings for four thousand years. San Francisco's gangly Transamerica Pyramid was twice as tall, but he noticed the specially designed, minimal urban shadow it cast over the city. "Hey Ernie, what's happening?"

"Hello. They told me you were coming. There was a woman named Stephanie just here looking for you."

Woody felt an adrenalin rush up the back of his neck. "Stephanie was here? What'd she say?"

"She just asked for you and went inside."

Woody spotted her across the crowded lobby, sitting on a marble bench. He went and stood behind her. It took her about ten seconds to sense his presence.

They hugged while people tripped over Woody's bulky guitar case. "It's great to see you," he said. "Where've you been?"

"I just needed to take some space for myself." She paused. "When I heard about your meeting, I came over here to see you."

"I saw those bruises and didn't hear from you and didn't know what to think."

"I just needed to be alone, but here I am." He went to hug her again; she took a step back. "I came to tell you something." She glanced around, leaned back in and lowered her voice. "The changes I've been going through lately made me realize something. I realized I want to share *all* my feelings with you, good *and* bad. God knows, whatever else we do, something between us brings out our deepest feelings. I know it's taking a risk, opening my heart to someone like you. But I've decided it's more risky to *not* open my heart. That's why I came here, to tell you that." She gestured to the elevator. "You better get to your meeting."

"What're *you* going to do?"

"I'll have a cup of coffee and wait for you."

She looked so sweet, his whole being ached for her.

"Go to your meeting," she said. "It's for both of us."

"Sorry I'm late," Woody said to the receptionist.

"Have a seat," she said curtly, without looking up.

Heading for the couch, he immediately regretted not bringing Stephanie with him. She could be there while he played his song for Pearlman. He always played better for her. He put his guitar down and walked back past the receptionist. "I'll be back in five minutes."

Jeff Pearlman came out into the reception area. "Woody?"

Woody spun around.

"Are you leaving?"

"I was just going down to the lobby to get my girlfriend. I thought it might be a few minutes until you were ready."

"You're late, and my schedule's very tight today."

Woody started across the waiting room to get his guitar.

"You can leave your things. They'll be safe. I only have a few minutes."

"I was going to play you my song," Woody said. "I haven't recorded it yet with Ray, but if I could just play it for you."

"I don't really have time now. Come into my office and we can talk."

Pearlman's corner office had windows from floor to ceiling. Looking down, Woody got vertigo, involuntarily took a step back, then sat in front of the biggest desk he'd ever seen.

"So you're a songwriter. Have you made any recordings?"

"I've got a bunch of original songs. There's one song in particular, a new one I wrote. I think it's your kind of music. If I could play it for you, it'll take three minutes."

"I'll be glad to review your material, but my schedule's very tight today. I need to be available for some calls and I'm not in a space to focus on music right now. You're working with Ray Bell?" Pearlman asked.

"Ray and I plan on recording my new song."

Pearlman looked interested. "Where will you be recording with Ray?"

"I'm not really sure yet."

"You actually have a commitment from Ray Bell to do the vocals?"

"Ray's definitely interested. But the song stands on it's own. If this is just about Ray..."

"I have some unfinished business with him. I'll contact him directly. You've also piqued my interest about your music. I'd like to hear your song, this is just an extremely busy day."

"Excuse me Mr. Pearlman," Brenda's voice came over the intercom. "The call from London you've been expecting is on line two."

"Thanks Brenda. Sorry," he said to Woody, "I've been waiting for this call all day." He picked up the phone and swung around in his high-back chair that was so big, it was as if he'd created another private office. Woody felt like he was back in the waiting room. He half-listened to the officious-sounding conversation and looked at the rows of framed photos on the wall of Pearlman with his arm around Barbara Streisand, George Harrison, Mohammed Ali, Jane Fonda, Bill Cosby... "Mr. Pearlman," Brenda came on the intercom, "you asked me to interrupt you when your call from Tokyo came in."

Pearlman swung his chair around like it was jet propelled and hit a button on the phone. "Brenda, tell him to hold on." He hit another button. "Mark, listen, I know we have to wrap this up today but something came up I absolutely have to deal with. Call Clapton, tell him to look at the royalty statement before the last one, it's more accurate. If he's okay with it, call Dylan's lawyer, reconfirm and call me back. I know, I know, we're going around in circles, I gotta grab this call. You're the man Mark, put it together." Pearlman hit the phone button, hard. "Brenda, put Tokyo on but give me the heads up when Mark calls back." He looked up at Woody. "Hang in there buddy." Pearlman spun his chair around fast enough to set a land speed record.

After waiting ten more minutes, Woody got up quietly and walked to the waiting room. Brenda had her head down, talking a mile a minute into her headpiece. He picked up his guitar and walked back toward Pearlman's office.

Shuffling down the hallway, head down, he wondered why it was so easy for him to write a love song about Stephanie, but so hard to just be with her. Maybe his song was a personal message, not meant for public consumption. Deep in thought, he inadvertently opened the door to the wrong office, took a half step in and froze.

A dark-haired woman was sitting on the desk with her blouse completely unbuttoned over a black lace bra. Her skirt was hiked up to her waist exposing a garter belt, black stockings, and a ten-inch tattoo of a black panther clawing up the inside of her thigh. A buff young man with a shaved head was sitting on a leather couch in a tank-top T-shirt with his belt undone and the top of his trousers open.

Woody stood there, his hand on the doorknob, feeling like he'd walked into a Fellini movie. Everyone stayed motionless for an interminable moment, the woman jumped to her feet, grabbed together the two sides of her blouse and Woody stepped back out. The moment he closed the door he heard the woman inside yelling; "Brenda! Pickup! Brenda! Where the hell are you?"

Woody headed down the hall to Pearlman's office, opened the door more slowly this time, and sat down. He could hear Pearlman using a fair amount of fluent Japanese and knew he was still on the same call. Woody couldn't get the scene from the other office out of his mind. He picked up his guitar and quietly strummed, the telephone conversation faded into the background, his mind cleared and he sang softly to the back of Pearlman's big chair.

Five minutes later Pearlman finished his call and spun around. He started to say something then stopped, struck by the expression on Woody's face, singing and playing with his eyes closed. Pearlman leaned back and listened, fascinated by the amount of emotion coming from such quiet music. The song was simple and beautiful, with powerful lyrical metaphors and a repeating melodic chorus.

Completely taken with the musical moment, Pearlman felt the tension from the phone calls draining from his body and sat up straight. When Woody went into the last chorus and the intensity began to build, Pearlman gripped the arms of his chair, anticipating the crescendo. Amazingly, the crescendo stayed just out of reach as the song continued to build and he found himself hoping it wouldn't end. The intercom suddenly crackled on. "Excuse me Mr. Pearlman, your call from –" He hit the privacy button and cut her off.

Woody stopped playing and opened his eyes. The two men sat looking at each other.

"That song is beautiful," Pearlman said.

"Thanks."

"Is it one of your originals?"

"Yeah. It's the song I was telling you about.""

"It's really amazing. What's it called?"

"Stephanie." Woody put his guitar in its case. "You interested in my song?

"I think your song is exceptional. I'm definitely interested in doing something with it. Unfortunately today I'm very distracted."

Just then, Brenda knocked on the door and stuck her head in. "Mr. Pearlman, Mark's on the phone. He's called back twice. He says the entire deal is about to fall through."

Getting up to leave, Woody accidentally swung his guitar case into Brenda's knee. It was a glancing blow and he brushed past her.

"Mr. Pearlman," Brenda was bent over, holding her knee, "I think you better speak to Mark. It sounds important."

Pearlman ignored her and walked out to the waiting room. Woody was gone. "He couldn't get an elevator that fast," he said to no one, "he must have taken the stairs."

Brenda came hobbling out. "Mr. Pearlman. Are you going to take this call? Mark says –"

"I heard you the first time Brenda!" He walked into his office, slammed the door and picked up the phone.

Chapter 11

Walking hand in hand, Woody and Stephanie headed out of the crowded lobby of the Transamerica Building. "Let's go to your place," she said.

Woody was pleasantly surprised. She usually insisted that they stay at her place when they spent the night together; Woody's apartment was too cluttered, there wasn't a clean dish or coffee cup, and he never changed the sheets. "The maid's been out sick. You sure?"

She smiled. "I'm sure." It occurred to him that she might actually be afraid to go home. Her experience being assaulted seemed to have affected her more than she was letting on.

When they walked into Woody's apartment, he felt self-conscious and started cleaning up. "My mom has a little plaque in her kitchen," he said. "Nature abhors a vacuum, and so do I."

They enjoyed the bottle of wine, cheese, and fruit they'd gotten, then Stephanie lit a candle, got undressed and got in bed.

Sitting on the bed next to her, Woody noticed she still had her blouse on.

She saw his furrowed brow. "I didn't want to upset you again, seeing those bruises. Nothing happened I haven't told you about. *Nothing.* Two guys reached in my car window and I drove away. The worst part was when one of them tried to choke me." She pulled back her hair and showed him a black and blue mark.

They stayed up late, drinking wine, smoking pot and enjoying an incredible night of lovemaking. At one point, thinking he was asleep, she came back from the bathroom and found him staring at the ceiling. "Of all the times we've ever slept together," she murmured as she got under the covers, "you're awake when I go to sleep and awake when I get up."

"Pearlman liked my song," Woody said, still staring up.

She rolled over, facing him. "I'll look harder for another job, and I'll find one soon. I'm ready for a change. You work on your music and we'll make things happen the way we want them to."

He kissed her and they made slow, passionate love. He kept it slow and sensuous the entire time. He'd heard her refer to it fondly as mid-week lovemaking. They fell asleep in each other's arms.

When Woody woke up and looked at the big clock on the wall, it was 10 am. Careful not to wake Stephanie, he went to the table and lit a candle. From across the room, all he could see was a mound of shiny red curls and the back of one leg sticking out from under the tangled sheets as if it wasn't connected to anything. It occurred to him that if he could accurately render the image in a painting, it would look like one of those Renaissance masterpieces where the angles of body parts looked unreal.

Listening to the steady somnolent cadence of her breathing, he reached for the metronome on the table, matched her tempo and hummed the melody of his new song. It was the tempo he'd been looking for, the perfect ballad. He picked up his guitar and quietly played along with the rhythm section; her gentle snoring and the click of the metronome.

Like looking at a sunset, when he looked away for a few minutes her appearance seemed to change. He recalled a stop-action video he'd seen, a ceiling-mounted camera taking a snapshot every ten seconds of a married couple sleeping in a double bed. Played back at high speed, it looked like a wrestling match with limbs flopping everywhere.

Looking at her, asleep in his bed, he felt exceedingly grateful. "Pray for what you have," he told himself. He was doing a pencil sketch of her when the phone rang. It was Jeff Pearlman.

"Am I disturbing you?" Pearlman asked.

Surprised to hear from Pearlman, only a croak came out when Woody went to speak.

"Woody?"

He cleared his throat. "Sorry, I'm here."

"I apologize for the confusion when you were at my office. I liked the song you played for me quite a bit. It's very well crafted. I'd like to record it."

This time Woody couldn't even muster a croak.

"Woody, are you there?"

"Yeah, sorry… you want to record my song?"

"Yes. I generally work at The Palace Studios. Do you know The Palace?"

"I know the place. I've never worked there."

"It's very musician-friendly. If you're settled on an arrangement, we should be able to get it done in one evening. Let's book a session, say ten days from now, if that works for you. We can record it solo acoustic or, if you have some players you like working with, I can't help but wonder how the song would sound with a full band."

"I know some great players who'd love to do it," Woody said. As they talked, the nagging question in his mind was whether Pearlman still wanted Ray to sing. All Pearlman's comments had been about his song, not his singing. He looked across the room at Stephanie, still asleep. Doing his best to hide the trepidation in his voice, he asked; "Are you still interested in getting Ray Bell to do the vocals?"

Pearlman took a few seconds to respond. "I like the way you sing it. And you're right, Ray's voice might also work well. We could record your vocal on the basic, that would give the band the right feel. And Ray could come down and take a pass at it. Then we'll decide together which vocal sounds better."

When Stephanie woke up, Woody was asleep in his chair. She got dressed, wrote him a note, and was about to leave when his drawing caught her eye. She picked up the sketch he'd made of her sleeping in his bed. The minimalistic pencil lines perfectly captured the entwined relationship of pillows, blankets and her hair. Looking across the room, she half-expected to see herself in the unmade bed. Then she glanced at Woody, asleep in his chair, the curvy contours of his own tangled hair draping over his face like the lines in the drawing. Smiling, she spread a blanket over him and headed home to get ready for work.

Chapter 12

Woody sat at his table looking at Stephanie's one-line note: "ONE THING AT A TIME." He put down his coffee and picked up his guitar. *"One thing at a time,"* he sang, *"one thing… one thing…one thing at a time."*

His first volley of calls about the recording session had yielded nothing but answering machines. Now the return calls were coming in. He'd called Ray, a keyboard player, bass player, sax player and drummer. When word got out about a session at The Palace, things started buzzing.

The keyboard player called back with questions about the grand piano: Steinway or Yamaha? Seven foot or nine? Could it be tuned the day before so the strings could settle? Also, his girlfriend's sister was in town and they'd had plans that night, so he'd be bringing them to the session, which was cool anyway because they both sang backups. He also mentioned that he thought the sax player overplayed.

The sax player called, he was into doing it, but he'd committed to a gig that night. He could get a sub, but the sub wouldn't play for less than fifty bucks. He was into doing it, it was just a matter of economics. Also, the choice of players was totally up to Woody, but the keyboard player was acting like a jerk lately and tried to make up for his lack of talent by criticizing others. Also, in case Woody didn't know it, the drummer was drinking more than usual.

The bass player called back. He was available, and did Woody know the sax player's girlfriend had a thing going on with the keyboard player, so those guys weren't getting along? Also, the drummer was totally obnoxious after a few drinks.

Woody's recording engineer called, said he heard about the session and volunteered his services. He knew Woody's sound and could capture it in the most transparent way. A photographer friend called and insisted this was the kind of event that should be documented.

The drummer didn't call back.

With all the action, Woody figured Ray was the key. He wished he'd never resorted to name-dropping, but Pearlman probably wouldn't have talked to him in the first place if he hadn't mentioned Ray's name. Besides, it might be good to have Ray at the session in case his own vocals didn't cut it.

And, of course, Ray hadn't returned his calls. He picked up the phone to try him once more.

Teisha and Melissa were sitting on white leather bar stools at a white marble bar under a rack of upside-down wine glasses in Ray's living room. "I've known Ray like forever," Melissa said, and passed a joint to Teisha. "I mean we've been through it all. We were like together and un-together and together before he was even like, you know, before anybody even knew who he was."

"Well Ray's made it clear he's pretty serious about us, I mean about our relationship and everything." Teisha took the joint. "Just last night he was all like, he definitely let me know how he felt. Whatever his past is, is whatever. Ray's guru Baba Nanda says the present is a gift, that's why they call it the present."

"Hey sister," Melissa expelled a cloud of smoke. "I'm not saying anything about anything. I mean we don't even consider our trip a trip. My thing with Ray is so not a thing that it can flow with whatever's happening, or even be a part of it. I mean who says two's the magic number? It's all multiples of one anyway, you know what I mean?"

There was a moment of silence that neither of the women were comfortable with.

"Are you into the Stones?" Teisha asked.

"I like their real early stuff."

"Their new record is totally awesome," Teisha said. "Wanna see something far out?"

Melissa raised her eyebrows. "Lay it on me, sister."

"I've got a girlfriend whose boyfriend's brother goes out with a girl that knows a guy on the Stones' equipment crew. She got backstage at their Denver show and got this off an actual Stones' guitar." Teisha reached into her purse and produced a plastic sandwich bag containing a wadded piece of soiled cloth with dangling strips of black electrical tape. "Keith Richards had it on his guitar to keep it from getting scratched by his belt buckle," she said proudly.

Melissa hadn't followed the story and was trying to make sense of what Teisha was holding up when the white phone on the counter rang. It being closer to Teisha, she reached to answer it.

Melissa put her hand on Teisha's hand on the phone. "I'll get it. I answer the phone here so nobody gets the wrong message. I'm neutral, like Switzerland. Hello? Who's calling?" Melissa put the phone down in a cradle that played a tape loop of Ray's hit song while the caller waited. "Ray," she called across the room. "You here?"

Ray was sitting with another guy on a white crescent-shaped couch, playing an Atari video game. They each had a joystick in one hand and a drink in the other. "Who is it?" Ray said, without taking his eyes off the black box.

"Someone named Woody."

"Shit!" Ray yelled. "I lost an aircraft carrier!"

"Incoming! Incoming!" the other guy yelled. The two of them frantically worked their controllers.

"Fuck!" Ray yelled. "You wiped out half my country. This calls for mutually assured obliteration!"

"Ray," Melissa said, "are you going to talk to this guy or what?"

"Hold on, I'm under attack."

On hold, Woody listened to the recording of Ray's hit song being played. He'd heard it before but had never checked it out so closely. It had sappy lyrics, but there was a catchy melody line. The production was the "wall of sound" approach with orchestral strings, a full horn section and a choir of background singers. Ray's voice, doubled and expanded with reverb and sound effects, sounded huge. That kind of production could make anyone sound good.

Holding the phone on his shoulder, Woody picked up his guitar and played along. On his third time through, realizing how long he'd been on hold, he put down his guitar and started pacing. Remembering the one time he'd been to Ray's place, he could picture the scene: a bunch of Hollywood bimbos, each one thinking Ray was their guy, and a bunch of musicians that all thought Ray was in their band. And everything was white, everything; the furniture, the carpet, a white grand piano that Ray could barely play.

"Ray," Melissa called across the room, "this guy's been on hold like forever."

"Damn! I blew up the Southern Hemisphere. Put him on the speakerphone. Check this guy out, he's a classic." Ray flopped back into the couch. "What's happening, Woody?"

"Being on hold."

"Sorry, I was dealing with something global." The girls giggled. "What's up, you got a gig for us at the Coliseum?"

"I've got a session scheduled to lay down a track of that demo we did. That heavy music manager heard my song and he digs it."

"How heavy is he? Will we need a forklift at the session?" The girls put their hands over their mouths, muffling their laughter.

"Hey man," Woody said, "I've got a session at The Palace, Studio D, with Jeff Pearlman producing. You interested?"

The vibe in the room changed dramatically and everyone went

97

quiet, staring at the speakerphone. They all knew who Jeff Pearlman was. And they knew The Palace was one of the best recording facilities in the country. Everyone in the room also knew it was where Ray had recorded his first and only hit song, and that he'd been wanting to get back there ever since.

"You got a session at the Palace?" Ray said, trying to sound nonchalant. "I'll have to call you back." He ran his finger across his neck, signaling Melissa to hang up the phone.

"I need to know if you're gonna do it," Woody said. "We're going to record that ballad that me and you…"

Ray jumped up, picked up the phone and cut off the speaker. "I'm right in the middle of something. I'll call you back tonight."

Eleven-thirty that night, Woody's phone rang.

"Woody, it's Ray. I can make the session. I'll put a vocal down, but I need to know about the publishing. If I put my voice on that song I want a share of the writer's royalties, an equal share."

Woody was exhausted. He'd been on the phone all day and had just smoked a joint, figuring he could take the rest of the night off. Ray had never called him before and he felt way too stoned and spaced-out to deal with him. "Hold on a second."

Woody put the phone down, lit a cigarette, reached for the phone then stopped himself. He took a couple of drags, watched the thin red sweep-second hand circling the big school clock on his wall, and thought of his fourth grade school desk: blonde Formica with the initials JFK carved in it. He remembered sitting at that desk forever, watching the motion of the same red second hand, always waiting for the bell to ring. The big school clock seemed to control time, not just report it. He picked up the phone.

"It's my song. I wrote it."

"Look man," Ray insisted, "when I sing a song, I make it into something that's recognizable, that's associated with me. When Frank Sinatra sings a song, it doesn't matter who's playing guitar. You can change the chords, play a hundred guitar solos, or get girls in mini skirts in the band. None of that matters. It's the vocal. You want to sing the song in the shower for the rest of your life and get a hundred percent of nothing, or you want fifty percent of a million bucks?"

Woody watched the second hand. It stopped for a beat at each mark, holding the inertia, compressing the energy before surging forward to the next moment. Does time actually flow that way, hesitate then surge ahead? Maybe it doesn't move like a clock at all. Maybe it moves like a lava lamp, swelling, separating into globs, then congealing and heaving forward. Time; a ravenous black hole, sucking in a sea of school clocks like a grey whale sucking down plankton.

"Woody, you there?"

"Yeah."

"What're you gonna do?'

"If you sing it and the song does well, I'll make sure you're treated fairly. It's *my* song, I wrote it about *my* girlfriend. You can work out the details with Pearlman."

"I'll put down a vocal, but I'm not signing a release until we agree on a deal that works for me."

When Woody hung up, he noticed a half-bottle of cheap tequila on his kitchen counter, left over from a jam session. He didn't care much for tequila; he rarely drank hard liquor. He took a big gulp and relit the joint. Fifteen minutes, later the phone rang again.

It was Ray's manager, Jason, calling to say that with things getting serious, with a session at The Palace, Woody should deal with him and not call Ray directly. Ray was an artist, he needed to be insulated from business issues. Jason sounded like he'd just woken up and had three cups of coffee.

Woody set the phone down on the table, swigged tequila and listened to the manager's annoying little voice. It reminded him of AM radio chatter with a whiney quality, like an off-key Arabic melody. He'd finished most of what was left of the bottle, glanced around for his guitar, and heard a soft knock on the door and the sound of the lock opening. It had to be his landlord, he was the only one besides Stephanie who had a key. He grabbed the baggie of pot off the table and picked up a can of air freshener.

It was Stephanie. Woody was so surprised, he stood there spraying air freshener on his foot. Stephanie backed out into the hallway. Woody threw the can down and followed her.

"Is that insecticide?" She held her hand over her nose.

"It's strawberry air freshener. What're you doing here? I thought you were my landlord."

"I just got off work, I didn't feel like going home. Are you drunk?"

He gave her a goofy grin. "It's happy hour. You felt like coming here two nights in a row?"

They went back in, Woody opened a window and they burst out laughing. Then they heard the little voice of Ray's manager, still coming out of the phone. "... only reason I'm bringing this up is to facilitate the creative process; get the business out of the way so the music can flow." They kissed while the voice kept jabbering away. "I'm a musician myself so I understand what it takes to —"

"Call me tomorrow." Woody hung up and walked Stephanie over to the bed. They were fondling each other, when the phone rang again.

The answering machine clicked on. "Hi Woody, this is Angel, Ron's girlfriend? Ron told me about the recording session and he was all like why don't you and Glen, that's my girlfriend, short for Glenda... why don't you ask Woody about catering the session because people get hungry and you need to concentrate on your music and everything and we —"

Stephanie threw a pillow across the room. It was an excellent shot and knocked the phone off the table. She rolled over on top of Woody, sat up, and began unbuttoning her blouse while she slowly rotated her hips. He put his hands on her waist and stopped her.

"What's the matter?"

"Strip for me."

"What?"

"Do your dance for me. Turn me on."

"Having trouble getting turned on?" She reached behind her.

"Feels like you're doing fine."

"I want to see you dance."

"We're dancing together, right now." She reached back again.

He stopped her. "I mean it. I want to see you do your thing, just for me."

"How much have you had to drink?"

"I know you know how to turn a guy on without touching him. Do it for me."

"You're really set on it, aren't you?"

Woody saw an immediate change in her expression, like she suddenly came under a sultry, sexual spell with the snap of a hypnotist's fingers. He felt himself getting turned on and angry at the same time.

She stood up next to the bed, cupped her breasts, and gazed at him, her eyes half closed, her mouth half open. In slow motion, she lifted her skirt and ran her hand up the inside of her thighs. She was wearing thong panties and black fishnet stockings, her standard work clothes. When she slid her hand between her legs, Woody felt as if he was going to explode with a confusion of sexual energy and rage.

"I could use a little music." Stephanie slipped off her blouse and stepped out of her skirt. In her bra, stockings and panties, she got Woody's acoustic guitar from across the room and set it down next to him on the bed. Stepping back, she began to gyrate.

Woody picked up his guitar but didn't play. Thinking about other men seeing her like this twisted his stomach into a knot. *Stop*, he thought, *just stop*.

Reaching behind her, she snapped off the bra, leaving just her panties and stockings, her eyes now three-quarters closed. He felt like a stranger; anyone could be watching her. He hit a dissonant chord on his guitar. As if in a trance, she kept moving, slowly spinning with her hands over her head. Woody recognized the move, the same move she did when he played music for her, the same move she did for her customers.

The two times he'd been to the Chi Chi Club, he'd obsessively checked out the customers. Pasty-white businessmen with their ties undone, giving the girls perverted sneers, Hispanic punks jabbing elbows in each others ribs, cocky black drug dealers with gold chains, noxious cologne and huge meaty faces. Woody hit another jarring chord. Stephanie kept dancing and turning, slowly coming to a stop with her back toward him. She gradually bent forward from the waist until her forehead was almost at her knees, her legs slightly apart. Then, for what felt to him like an eternity, she slowly ran her hands up the inside of her legs, pulled her panties aside and delicately slipped a finger inside herself.

Woody jumped to his feet, his whole body shaking. Grabbing his guitar by the neck, he swung it over his head and brought it down full force, smashing it on the floor next to her.

Stephanie grabbed her clothes off the floor and clutched them in front of her. Her face blanched white, she pulled her clothes back on while he stood by the bed, staring at her.

"Be careful what you ask for!" She kicked the shattered guitar and sent it skittering across the floor. A moment later she was gone, the slammed door echoing behind her.

Chapter 13

The day of the recording session, Woody was an emotional wreck. He packed his equipment into his car, ran back upstairs and opened the crumpled piece of paper on his table.

Dear Woody,

I love you, but your jealousy is tearing us apart. I'll find another job as soon as I can. In the meantime, I don't think we should be together. It's destroying the possibility of any future we have.

I love who you are and honor your music. Please honor my desire to have my own space right now,

Stephanie

P.S. Good luck with your recording session. I'll be thinking of you.

It was hard to read because he'd crumpled it into a ball the first time he'd read it. He knew what it said. He crumpled it up again and threw it in a corner, into a morass of newspapers, guitar parts and cassettes. *What woman in her right mind would want to share this life?*

He was running late for the session, but had the urge to take three minutes and play his song one more time in a familiar environment. His electric guitar was in his car, his faithful old Harmony acoustic was still lying in pieces on the floor; an homage to his failed relationship.

He sat down and, without accompaniment, closed his eyes and quietly sang his song, his voice quivering. Halfway through the first chorus he felt a presence in the room, opened his eyes, and saw the girl that lived down the hall standing in his doorway holding a bag of groceries.

"Your car's getting towed, brother."

By the time Woody dealt with the tow truck driver, he was almost an hour late getting to the session. The entrance to The Palace was a plain metal door in the warehouse district of San Francisco, with no sign or markings. Woody knew it well. He'd driven past it for years, checking out the exotic cars and limos parked out front.

He spoke into an intercom and was let into a palatial entrance adorned with gold records and rock stars' guitars. The girl at the front desk was a Marilyn Monroe look-alike with a small studded diamond in her cheek where Marilyn's beauty mark was.

"You must be Woody," she said in a breathy Marilyn voice.

"He nodded."

"Welcome to The Palace. Have you worked here before?"

"No." He gazed up at the guitars on the walls.

"You'll be working in studio D. Most of your musicians are already here. Actually, there are quite a few people waiting for you. Mr. Pearlman left word he'll be here by the time you're ready to record. Ray Bell also called—he's running late." She maintained her smile and breathiness while she conveyed the information with consummate efficiency. "If you have equipment, we have loading assistants and complimentary valet parking. Studio D is down this hallway, then right, left, left, right. You'll see the neon 'D'. Kitchen and dining room will be to your right, restrooms left, lounge and game room across the hall with complimentary drinks and snacks. The hot tub and sauna are off the lounge. Two runners are assigned to your session to go out for food, equipment, or whatever you need. A guitar tech, drum tech and maintenance engineer are on staff twenty-four hours, masseuse on staff until midnight. My name is Marilyn." She breathed her name. "Let me know if there's anything you need."

Studio D was a zoo, people drinking, smoking pot, wandering back and forth between the rooms. The musicians were set up in an expansive studio of polished hardwood floors and mirrored walls. An array of rotating tie-dye covered sound panels hung from the twenty-foot ceiling. The position of the panels could be adjusted with motorized levers that the saxophone player's girlfriend was operating. Walking in, Woody immediately felt disoriented.

"Woody!" The keyboard player's girlfriend was the first to notice him and sashayed across the room in a dramatic purple bathrobe with a gold 'D' embossed on the front. "This place is totally awesome! Is Ray coming? This is my friend Amanda?" Amanda was in a matching purple bathrobe. "Amanda works with a publicist that used to work with Ray and she totally knows everybody. Wanna take a hot tub? The water's perfect."

"Hi Woody. I'm Brian, the house engineer. We're getting sounds, going to a two-inch Studer with isolation for everyone. The drums will be in what we call the fish tank, total iso with lots of reflection. Drums sound huge. We'll print four tracks of acoustic grand piano with close micing and also capture the ambiance of the big room. The sax will be in the booth, the bass will go direct. Will you be going direct or using a mic for your guitar amp?"

"What's with all these spinning panels on the ceiling?" Woody said. "I feel dizzy."

"The woman that came with the sax player says she helps with sound design. Actually, I think she's just stoned and having fun with the control levers."

"Woody?" It was the photographer.

Woody jerked his head around.

"Sorry man, didn't mean to scare you. I just need to know if you want stills of guys wearing headphones or you want video footage. I brought a hand-held Super 8 that we can sync-."

"Woody!" He jumped again. The girls in bathrobes were back from the kitchen. "Angel said you said she could do the catering but we're making this nice organic salad we know you're into and she's talking about some scuzzy take-out pizza. We said let's figure it out together and she's all like, yeah, but then she just does what she wants."

Woody looked at her like she was speaking a foreign language. "Snare drum please," a voice came booming over the talkback speakers, and the drummer whacked the snare drum.

"Turn the drums off in the monitors!" the house engineer yelled into the control room. He wasn't heard. He turned to Woody. "Lookit man, it's cool you brought your own engineer, but it might be faster if I did the set-up. He's not familiar with the Neve board. It's definitely got some quirks."

When Jeff Pearlman walked in, the panels were still spinning, drums were crashing, people were eating pizza and drinking beer and the room was thick with pot smoke. "What's happening here, Woody?"

"Hi Mr. Pearlman, how're you doing?" Woody wiped the sweat off his forehead with his sleeve.

"Call me Jeff. Have you recorded anything?"

"Not yet, we're still setting up."

"The session was booked for five o'clock to record one song. It's almost eight. Who are all these people?"

"They're the band, and some friends to help out."

A woman in a metallic-gold halter top, heart-shaped sunglasses and hoop earrings so big they rested on her shoulders, stepped between him and Pearlman. "Are you Woody? I'm a friend of Ray's? He told me about the session and, is Ray here? Somebody said you'd know?"

Woody stared at her like a deer in the headlights. Pearlman took him by the arm. "Come with me." They walked into the hallway. Pearlman checked his watch. "Is Ray here yet?"

"I haven't seen him."

"Do you have an acoustic guitar with you?"

"No. I had one. I don't have it any more."

"Follow me." They wound through a catacomb of tunnel-like hallways lit with tubes of colored neon and into a small studio. Pearlman closed the door, picked up the phone and called the front desk. "Marilyn, this is Jeff. I'm in studio B. Is anything scheduled in here tonight?"

"No sir."

"Then I'll be working here. Send someone over to align the heads on the two-inch machine. I need two mics, one for vocal, one for acoustic guitar. And I need an acoustic guitar. You have one?"

"We have several."

"Bring me your best one, I think it's the Martin. Have the tech put on new strings, tune it and bring me a fresh roll of tape, Ampex 456. I need it all right away. This will be a closed session, no disturbances, no exceptions."

Woody watched Pearlman setting up. "Before I was a lawyer," Pearlman said, "before I was a producer, I was a recording engineer."

A young man showed up with the tape, microphones and guitar, and aligned the recording heads on the reel-to-reel machine. Pearlman handed the guitar case to Woody. "Go in that vocal booth and play your song like you played it for me in my office."

"What about the band?"

"They'll be fine in the hot tub."

"What about Ray?"

"He just missed his chance to sing the best song of his life."

The isolation booth was the size of a walk-in closet, covered floor to ceiling with thick gray foam padding. It was like a vault. With every move he made, adjusting the microphone stand, putting on his guitar strap, clearing his throat, the sound stopped a millisecond after it started, controlled by the insulation. Strumming the guitar, it sounded deep and rich with a beautiful bell-like tone perfectly contained by the minimal ambience of the room; pure guitar.

"Woody!" he heard a tiny voice. "Headphones!" He found them hanging on the mic stand and put them on.

"Can you hear me now?" Pearlman said through the talkback system from the control room. "Step up to the mic and play. I need to get some levels."

Woody started the song, got halfway through the first chorus and stopped.

"Okay, let's try one," Pearlman said.

"I've been trying."

"I've just been getting levels. Now the tape's rolling. Go for it."

Woody sang two verses but stopped when he got to the chorus.

"Is something wrong?"

"I think I started it too slow."

"Let's try it again. Are the levels in your headphones okay?"

"Yeah."

"Is the balance between your voice and guitar working? Want more reverb on your voice?"

"I'm okay."

"Tape's rolling."

Woody got through the first verses, halfway through the chorus and stopped again.

"It was sounding good," Pearlman said. "What happened?"

"I don't know, I guess I'm feeling a little emotional."

"That's a good thing. Emotional is good. Use it to your advantage and put it in the song. Here, let me try something... okay, we're rolling."

When Woody started singing again his voice sounded huge in the headphones, like he was singing in a concert hall. It reminded him of Ray's voice on his hit song. Woody got through most of the song, including a beautiful solo, but when the chorus repeated at the end he felt as if he was trying to sing with a weight on his chest. Every time he sang the word "Stephanie" he had to fight back tears.

Pearlman stopped the tape. "Woody, take a break. Come in here for a minute."

Woody took off his headphones, set the guitar carefully in its stand, and pushed open the thick soundproof door into the control room.

"Sit down and relax until you feel like playing."

"I'm okay." Woody remained standing.

"You want a glass of water or coffee or a beer?"

"No thanks."

"Feel like smoking a joint?"

"Not right now."

Pearlman rolled his chair back a few inches and folded his hands. "You sound pretty good, just a little tentative. Is something bothering you? You worried about the band?"

"They probably haven't even noticed I'm gone."

"How's that guitar?"

"It's incredible. Way nicer than mine was."

"It's a '59 Martin. I love the sound, I use it whenever I can. What happened to your guitar?"

Woody looked down at the floor.

"Woody," Pearlman said gently, "if you're not up to doing this tonight..."

"Let's just do it." Woody walked out to the booth, got his headphones, guitar and microphone in position and started playing. He sang in a monotone but made it through the song.

"That's better, but it lacks the oomph you had when you sang it in my office. Sing one like your life depends on it."

Woody played stronger but his voice sounded forced. He was going into the last verse when the phone rang in the control room. Pearlman let it ring. It stopped, then rang again. Pearlman picked it up. "What?"

"Sorry to disturb you, Mr. Pearlman." It was Marilyn. "I have a message for Woody."

"I told you no interruptions."

109

"The woman said it's important. She says she knows Woody's working but she insisted she get a message to him."

"So what's the message?"

"She said I have to give the message to Woody, no one else."

"Who's it from?"

"A women named Stephanie."

Pearlman had turned the monitor speakers down in the control room, but he could hear the last repeating refrain into the chorus with Woody singing "Stephanie". "Hold on, Marilyn."

When Woody finished the take, Pearlman spoke into the talkback mic. "Woody, there's a call for you. Pick up the phone on the back wall and press 7."

Woody glared at the phone. Who could be calling? Pearlman had told Marilyn no interruptions, and he was having enough trouble getting the song recorded without dealing with anything else. He grabbed the phone off the wall. "What?"

"This is Marilyn at the front desk. I'm sorry to disturb you. A woman named Stephanie called and said to tell you she loves you and to sing one for her."

Pearlman waited. There was only silence in the booth. He pressed the talkback button. "Woody, are you there?"

"Roll the tape."

"Stephanie!" Woody sang with so much more power than he had been, the recording levels instantly maxed out, the thin needles on the VU meters pegged to the right, red lights flashing everywhere.

My heart's busted open
My sky cerulean blue
I fell in love with you
As I was born to do

Pearlman reached for the controls, trying to prevent it from distorting, thankful for the limiter he'd put on the input channels in case of a radical change in levels. He'd no sooner got things under

110

control when Woody transitioned to a soft, delicate voice, almost whispering.

Your eyes
Your lips
Your hair
I see your face
I see you everywhere

Pearlman adjusted the faders again, checked the meters, then sat back and listened. When Woody came to the last chorus, he cried out "Stephaniee!" in the most emotive, plaintive voice Pearlman had ever heard.

Reluctant to have the song end, Pearlman just let the tape roll, as if he could somehow capture the sound waves still moving through the air. When he finally turned to the big tape machine behind him, there were three people standing in the back of the room: Ray and two women. "Hey Jeff," Ray said. "How've you been? That last take sounded pretty good."

"You're late," Pearlman said dryly. He walked past Ray out to the vocal booth, pulling the thick door closed behind him.

Woody had set the guitar in its case and was kneeling on the floor in front of it. It had a beautifully aged spruce patina, with white mother-of-pearl dots on a rosewood fingerboard.

Pearlman had always appreciated the special, almost devotional relationship musicians had with their instruments. "You really know how to pull the sound out of that guitar."

"It's the nicest guitar I've ever played."

He watched Woody running his fingers back and forth across the neck. "It's yours."

Woody looked up to see if he was serious.

"It's a gift, from me. I'll work it out with the studio."

When they walked back into the control room, Ray and the women were gone. "You did really well," Pearlman said. "Ready to hear it?"

Woody contemplated the expansive rows of knobs and faders on the recording console. "I feel like I've been through the wringer. I think I'll let it meld on the tape before I listen to it."

"It was a great performance," Pearlman said. "Maybe we should listen back one time before you leave and make sure we've got everything the way we want it."

Woody was by the door, holding his new guitar . "You mean that was perfect, let's try to do it better?

Pearlman smiled.

"I've given all I've got for tonight. Thanks for hanging in there with me."

Back in studio D, the party was in full swing. As Woody reached for his electric guitar still in its case, he locked eyes with Ray who was across the room standing with a group of people. He gave Ray a slow-motion beauty-queen wave and walked out, a guitar in each hand.

When Pearlman went to the kitchen for some coffee before listening back, Marilyn walked in. "How's your session going?"

"It's over. It went great."

"Can I get you anything?"

"I'm just having a cup of coffee."

"We have an espresso machine. Can I make you one?"

"This is fine."

"How about a shot of some very special Cognac to go with your coffee?" She raised her eyebrows.

He raised his own eyebrows. "Normally I wouldn't, but for a smooth talker like you... This *is* a special occasion. I just recorded a hit song."

Marilyn reached to a high cupboard, brought down a dirty, half-filled bottle of French brandy, and poured some into a crystal brandy snifter.

"What *is* this stuff?" Pearlman eyes widened. "It tastes amazing, like liquid velvet."

"Paul McCartney left it here. A 1760 vintage, from an old pirate ship pulled out of the English Channel." She poured him a little more. "Can I get you anything else?"

"I'm fine. I'll be working in studio B a little longer. Did you give those papers to Ray Bell yet?"

"Not yet."

"Might as well wait until he's leaving," Pearlman smiled. "Why spoil the party?"

Pearlman sipped his brandy and settled back into the big producer's chair for a listen. Woody played a beautiful intro on the guitar, a taste of things to come. The first verses told a soulful, poignant love story, imagery of one man's battle against loneliness. Then the understated first chorus, creating tension to draw the listener in. The bridge gathered momentum followed by a solo and quiet last verse with a tender emotional release into the final chorus; a slow, compelling build that once again had Pearlman gripping the arms of his chair. At the peak of the chorus, with Woody wailing out his climatic "Stephanie!", a crackling audio distortion hit Pearlman like a slap in the face.

He snapped up from his chair, rewound the tape, and played the section back. The defect was blatant, both sonically and visually on the meters. Frustrated, wondering how he'd missed it when he was recording, he replayed the section over and over, trying every trick he knew to camouflage the spike on the over-saturated magnetic tape.

For the next few hours, Pearlman and the best engineer the Palace had on staff worked together, trying to repair the glitch on the tape. Using all the high-tech gear available, they tried taking parts from a previous chorus, flying them in to use on the last chorus, then combining and layering them. At each step, Pearlman wondered whether he should just get Woody back in to perform it again, but he had a feeling that this was a one-of-a-kind performance. He felt as if he'd witnessed Woody having an emotional catharsis that he'd been lucky enough to capture on tape.

113

If that was the case, his chances of getting another version like this one were nil.

When Pearlman had done everything possible to salvage the recording, he decided it sounded good enough to use as a demo but probably wasn't good enough for radio. The compelling nature of the song had distracted him from hearing the distortion; all he could do was hope other listeners would have the same experience. He left the tape in the mastering room for any final EQ that might help and, on his way out, stopped by the kitchen for another shot of Paul McCartney's brandy.

Two hours later, Ray and two women, two different women than the ones he'd come with, stumbled into the reception area. They were laughing, all talking at once, the women hanging onto Ray's neck in a way that looked to Marilyn like they were choking him.

"Pardon me ma'am," Ray leaned halfway over the reception desk, pulling the women off their feet. "I'm a professional musician trying to keep up with the specs on the latest studio equipment. Would you happen to know the legal capacity of the hot tub in Studio D?" The girls laughed.

Marilyn gave Ray a patronizing smile and waited for the laughter to die down. "Are you Ray Bell?"

"The one and only." Ray pointed a wavering finger at a gold record on the wall. "That's me right up there."

"I have something for you." Marilyn served him with a file-endorsed summons and complaint with a notice to appear in San Francisco Superior Court for breach of contract with the Law Offices of Jeff Pearlman.

Chapter 14

Woody took the long way home over one of the highest points in San Francisco. Twin Peaks, once called "Breasts of the Indian Maiden," was where he often went to contemplate the big picture, and to think.

He parked, got out of his car and watched the pulsating glitter of millions of lights under a crescent moon. He felt elated, depleted, the night's events almost too much to assimilate. It was as if the endless obstacles of his life had happened for a reason; years of swirling circumstances on the verge of synchronicity, but not until he was in the perfect studio with the perfect song. Now it was recorded, and he'd sung it himself.

He sat on the hood of his car until sunrise, smoking cigarettes, contemplating the infinity of fading lights, each one representing someone's life of struggles, successes, failures and ultimately, the extinguishing light of mortality.

Driving down the figure-eight road back to sea level and the crowded morning city streets, it felt like a reentry back to real life. Unbelievably, it was only a few days ago that he'd smashed his guitar at Stephanie's feet. He'd seen the look on her face and thought he might never see her again. But she'd called the studio, left that wonderful message. Things might be okay.

Back at his apartment, he cleaned up the splintered remains of his old guitar and got out his new one. The Martin was the finest instrument he'd ever owned. It felt like it somehow justified his existence. Only the best musicians had instruments like this. He meticulously cleaned and polished it and put on another new set of strings, but when he tried playing, everything felt stale. He got out file folders of old songs, looking through the hundreds of unused lyric lines he'd written, hoping for some inspiration. Nothing clicked. Finally getting his song recorded was like giving birth, a long laborious childbirth. Now came the post-partum depression.

It was almost three in the afternoon when Woody's cumulative exhaustion finally caught up with him, and he decided to make a commitment he rarely made when he wasn't with Stephanie. He took off all his clothes and got in bed, under the covers, not on top. He was asleep in five minutes.

When Woody woke up, he stumbled around his apartment, groggy, wondering what to do with himself. All the energy he'd put into finally getting his song recorded, and now what? Pearlman had cautioned him against expecting any overnight miracles. There'd be plenty for Woody to do, but right now Pearlman needed time to spin his magic with the record companies.

Woody made himself a cup of coffee and sat on the inside ledge of his window. He could see just a sliver of the dim gray sky above the narrow alleyway two stories up. He glanced at the clock: 5:10. He must have slept for a couple of hours—that was plenty for now. Stephanie was probably getting ready for work, her regular shift was seven to midnight. He hadn't tried calling her since the recording session, since she'd called him. He picked up the phone.

"Hello?"

"Hi, Steph."

116

"Woody?"

"Yeah. How're you doing?"

"How am I doing?" There was an edge to her voice. "Is something wrong?"

"No. Actually, things went great." Woody stood up. "I got your message when I was recording and I thought maybe we could go out for coffee or something."

"Coffee?"

"Or whatever. I was just calling to say I got your message."

"You're crazy." She hung up.

Woody stood there holding the phone at his side until he heard the disconnected-busy signal. Her voice sounded so strange, like she was high or maybe drunk. Maybe she was with someone. He called Murray.

"Hello."

"Hey Murray, what's up?"

"Woody?"

"Yeah. You feel like going out to get something to eat?"

"When?"

"In a little while or whenever. Have you talked to Stephanie lately? I can't tell what's going on with her."

"Huh?"

"What're you doing? You sound really out of it."

"I'm sleeping. What did you think I'd be doing at five in the morning?"

"Five in the *morning?*"

"Don't you know the difference between night and day? You're crazy." Murray hung up.

Woody went to the window, looked at the sky and did the math. He'd slept for fourteen hours, not two! He'd never slept that long in his life. It was the first time he'd spoken to Stephanie since he'd smashed his guitar, and now he'd called her at five in the morning. "She and Murray are right," he thought, "I *am* crazy.'

His refrigerator was empty. He looked in his wallet; six bucks.

117

Going to his closet, he lugged out his global-disaster change-jar: a gallon jug of coins, to be used when there was no electricity or banks, just cash and barter.

He tilted the jar on its side, wondering whether the circumstances justified using it. He was always short on cash and always thinking about using it, but this was different. He'd finally gotten his song recorded and, for the first time in his career, maybe a jar of coins wouldn't matter. And he was hungry.

He turned it upside-down, a few coins came out and a quarter got jammed in the spout. He got a butter knife, dislodged it, a few more coins came out and another quarter got stuck. Frustrated, he lugged the entire jar to his car and went back for his guitar, thinking he'd get something to eat and then try playing in a different environment.

Sitting with his motor idling in front of a 24-hour diner, he noticed a man with scraggly long hair sitting alone in a booth, staring into a cup of coffee. The troubled expression on the man's face reminded him of himself. It made him uncomfortable. *It's time for a change, a real change. Stephanie needs a break, Pearlman needs a break and I need a break.*

At a gas station, he smashed the neck off the change jar, filled up with gas, corn chips, bananas and bottled water, and headed east. Except for more gas, he didn't stop driving until he got to the Grand Canyon, a day later.

Chapter 15

One o'clock in the morning, Stephanie was just getting home from work when she saw someone that looked like the man that had been splayed across the hood of her car.

She rolled up her windows, locked her doors and circled the block, taking notice of the phone booth at the corner. When she came back the second time, she got a better look. It wasn't him.

That night, in the middle of a fitful nightmare about a rainstorm of blood splattering on her windshield, Woody woke her up with his five a.m. phone call. Unable to get back to sleep, she walked around her dark apartment, too raw to even face the glare from a light bulb. Using the kitchen nightlight, she filled her glass teapot, put it on the stove and patiently kept watch until the water came to a boil. Standing in the dim light, both hands wrapped around a cup of herb tea, she let the vapors warm her face and tried to let go of the nightmarish images that were still vividly present.

Her life wasn't working. Since being assaulted by those men, she was actually afraid to come home. Woody was completely unpredictable, her job felt more and more creepy; the universe was telling her the city wasn't where she was supposed to be right now. It was time to go.

Spending the day packing boxes, when it came time to get ready for work she picked up the phone to call in sick. When the manager answered, she told him she was quitting for good, surprising herself at how instantly liberating and right the decision felt.

She called and had her phone disconnected and decided she'd go to Marin County and stay with her Aunt Auddie and Uncle Max, two of her favorite people on the planet. She'd figure the rest out from there.

As the day wore on, the piles of clothes, boxes and suitcases became overwhelming. Trying to decide what to do with Woody's poetry, artwork and tapes felt more painful than dealing with her own things. Wacky and wonderful, his artwork was everywhere. Throughout their three-year relationship she'd found poems on phone bills, in the margins of books, even on the inside of a roll of toilet paper he must've spent forever rolling back together.

Just when she was about to take a break and get something to eat, she took a small picture off the wall and found a poem on the back that began "I hope we're still groovin' when you're movin'." Tears came to her eyes. It was a reminder of how dramatically their relationship had changed when she took the dancing job. The playfulness in his poems and songs had been replaced with existential inquiries into the meaning of their most innocuous interactions.

In a hallway closet, Stephanie found a large, dust-covered piece of art. She remembered Woody disappearing after her second day at work; a few days later, she'd found it leaning against her door: a Bosch-like oil painting, four feet tall, of a nude dancer standing in front of an audience of men with veined eyes popping out of their heads. The men were sitting at little desks much too small for their bodies, gawking at the dancer. On each desk Woody had glued a little paper poem about the secretiveness the men felt when they went home to their wives.

She almost ran down the hall to her bedroom. Reaching into the closet for her suitcase, she was showered with a shoebox of Woody's cassette tapes. She'd put the box there herself, collecting the tapes that Woody left everywhere. He was constantly accumulating recordings of everything: gigs, songs, African drummers, Tibetan monks. She accidentally stepped on a cassette and heard the crunch of the plastic case.

Collecting the tapes off the floor, she put them in an overflowing garbage bag and carried it outside to the dumpster. She felt guilty walking out, but relieved walking back. Woody liked chaos and clutter; she liked simplicity and she was entitled to it.

She finished packing one suitcase with just the basics and left everything else for another time; the need to get out was overwhelming. As soon as she'd locked the door, she realized she'd forgotten her birth control pills, an issue she didn't feel like dealing with. The simplest thing would be to just bring them with her. She put her key in the lock, felt herself tearing up again and walked away.

Driving through the parking garage, she kept her eyes straight ahead, went out over the severe tire damage spikes and headed toward the Golden Gate Bridge.

Chapter 16

In the middle of Arizona, in the middle of the night, Woody took the Grand Canyon exit off Highway US 89. Following signs to the North Rim, he drove past miles of "FULL" campgrounds. A talkative attendant at the last gas station had told him that people traveled thousands of miles, phoning and writing in advance, just to reserve a campsite. Right now he'd settle for a place to pull over and sleep in his car. He was so tired, he could barely keep his eyes open.

Woody had visited the area once before as a child, when his parents were still together. He remembered the enormity of the canyon, how it magically made the stress in his family feel minor and inconsequential. The canyon seemed to swallow everything. He'd always wanted to go back.

Spotting a gated utility road with a National Park Service lock left hanging open, he drove in and pulled the gate shut behind him. The pitch-black gravel road wasn't much more than a trail, branches scraping loudly against the sides of his car, his windshield almost opaque with dead bugs.

The darkness in front of the car seemed to suddenly thicken, his headlights disappearing into nothingness. Getting out, he peered into the abyss and could sense the depth but couldn't see more than a few feet in front of him. He saw what looked like a flickering star, but it didn't make any sense; he was looking down. Overwhelmed with fatigue, he took a pile of laundry out of his back seat, made a lumpy bed on the ground, gazed up at the stars, down at the little out-of-place star, and fell asleep trying to figure it out.

Opening his eyes with the first light of day, he found himself looking into the rusty right front wheel of his car, a sharp rock poking him in the ribs. It was the wheel with no hubcap. He blinked, trying to bring the mud-packed lug nuts into focus, then rolled over onto his other side to within inches of a sheer three-thousand-foot drop-off.

For a horrified moment, staring straight down, he thought he was still dreaming. Gripping the loose dirt with his outstretched hand, he tried to force himself awake.

A wave of dizziness swept over him and everything started spinning. He was sure that if he tried getting up, he'd lose his balance and fall over the edge.

Holding on for dear life, the realization of where he was, leaving San Francisco, leaving Stephanie, all flooded into his consciousness at once and he had a sudden urge to just roll forward and parachute with his laundry into the open arms of the void. *Do it! Let go and just roll over, she won't even miss you!*

Woody's focus landed straight down on a boulder on the canyon floor. At first it seemed miles away, like looking through the wrong end of a telescope. Then the boulder appeared to be getting closer, sparkling granite hurtling up at him. A vivid image of his body impaled on the jagged edge of the rock made him involuntarily jerk back and stand up. He realized he could get his bearings by not looking down.

Leaning back against his car, he kept seeing flashes of the big rock, like a transparent meteor whooshing through him. He'd parked his front wheels within inches of the edge, his front bumper actually hanging over.

123

He picked up his guitar, sat on the ground and tried playing. His fingers felt jerky. Gently prodding the strings, he eventually regained his coordination and was able to play something soothing. When he finally felt grounded, he got in his car and very carefully backed it away from the edge.

Woody stayed on the rim of the canyon for the next five days, sleeping in his back seat and playing his guitar. At night he made a small campfire of pinecones and twigs, the firelight penetrating only a few feet into the canyon, making a shallow dent in the darkness as if the darkness was heavier, flickering yellow light floating on the surface.

From sunrise to sundown, Woody played his guitar. He played until his fingers were raw, then propped his guitar against a rock and positioned it so it was surrounded by the vista of the canyon. He could write a song, hearing notes and chords in his mind, just by looking at the neck of his guitar.

One afternoon, strumming a new song, he realized how much his music had changed since Stephanie said she wanted to be alone. The same major chords that had always seemed uplifting now sounded sickly sweet. Combinations of notes with a natural angst felt pleasing. *Some notes could go to counseling together for the rest of their lives*, he thought, *and nothing would ever get resolved.* He sang the first verse.

I can't even get myself
To act the way I want
How can I get you
To act that way too

On the third day, having run out of bananas on the first day and corn chips on the second, Woody began to feel the spaced-out intoxication from not eating. He was down to water and pot. When he smoked, it distracted him and allayed his hunger. When the pot wore off, the edge of the hunger returned. On the fourth day, he ran out of pot.

He knew he'd needed to get away, reevaluate his life, confront the possibility that he and Stephanie might be breaking up for good. Permanently losing her would be like losing a limb, something you think you can never get used to and then, eventually, you do.

Sitting on the edge, playing to the vast emptiness, it felt like trying to fill the canyon with music. The only signs of life, besides the birds and lizards darting in and out of the brush, were two people all the way down on the canyon floor, camping next to the Colorado River. It was their campfire that he'd first seen in the darkness, thinking it was a flickering star. Miles away, as big as ants, he couldn't stop checking them out. He worried about them leaving, leaving him really alone. The first thing he did every morning was look to see if they were still there. At night, he watched their tiny campfire almost as much as his own.

Late afternoon on his fifth day, lightheaded from lack of nourishment, he took a break from playing the guitar and tracked the giant cumulous clouds casting fast-moving black shadows across the rock walls; clouds so big they dwarfed even the enormous canyon. *Stephanie looks at the same sky, breathes the same air…* the separate self he'd been clinging to suddenly felt like an illusion. Filling his pockets with coins, he walked a quarter-mile and stood staring at an outdoor public phone lit by a fluorescent bulb and covered with moths. He had no idea what time it was, there or in California.

It seemed like a futile gesture, trying to get justification for his existence from a little voice on a telephone line a thousand miles away. But he wanted to feel that connection. He put in the coins and called Stephanie; her phone was disconnected. He called his own phone to check for messages; it was disconnected.

He called Jeff Pearlman's office.

"Pierce and Pearlman, how may I direct your call?" It was Brenda, the receptionist. He pictured himself standing there on hold, depositing all his coins.

"This is Woody for Jeff Pearlman. It's important."

"Mr. Pearlman is unavailable. I'll put you through to his assistant."

Woody was surprised when Holly immediately came on the line.

"This is Woody. I'm calling for Jeff to see what's happening with my song."

"Hello Woody, I'm glad you called."

"Really? What's up?"

"I'm very sorry to tell you this, but Mr. Pearlman has had a heart attack."

"What?"

"He's in the hospital scheduled for bypass surgery."

Woody turned half-circles back and forth, tethered by the short, metal-wound phone cord. "Is he going to be all right?"

"Mr. Pearlman's condition is stable. That's all the information I have. We're all as concerned as you are."

He hesitated. "Will anyone else there be working on my song?"

"This has all been very sudden. We're not sure who will be handling Mr. Pearlman's affairs. Can I put you on hold for a moment? As you might imagine, things are quite hectic around here."

He was on hold for twenty seconds when he heard the coins drop. He felt like his stomach dropped with the coins and heard the buzzing tone of the disconnected call.

Woody walked slowly back to his little campsite and stood at the precipice. When he looked straight down, the toes of his sneakers hanging over the three-thousand-foot cliff, he realized how comfortable he'd become, being on the edge. Then he saw that it was getting dark and there was no little flickering fire on the canyon floor; the campers keeping him company were gone. Time for him to go.

He packed up his stuff and drove back to San Francisco, using the rest of his change for gas, coffee, and a gas-station sandwich. He was greeted by a padlock and eviction notice on his apartment door.

Chapter 17

Dressed in a sharp navy-blue skirt, suit jacket, stockings and high heels, Maria Angelista sat with a yellow legal pad on her lap at Jeff Pearlman's bedside in his private hospital room. She wore red lipstick, her jet-black hair was in a tight bun and she had a figure that defied the confines of her formal business suit.

"I'm sick of dealing with egocentric assholes who spend twenty thousand dollars on legal fees just to get their name an inch bigger on a movie screen," Pearlman said. "What's next on the list?"

Maria made some notes and flipped the page. "It just says 'Woody'."

"Woody," Pearlman smiled, "He sings and plays guitar. He's a total space case, but he's got a hit song. The song is amazing. The guy somehow finagled his way into my office and in a period of about two minutes took me on an emotional journey just singing and playing acoustic guitar. The melody stays in your head for days. A slow song with a catchy beat… that's not easy to do. Do you see that control to raise up the bed?" Pearlman pulled his covers down to his waist. "Brenda was supposed to send over some real pajamas instead of this hospital garb. And maybe a couple of cigars."

"I'll check with her." She pressed a button and slowly raised the head of his bed. "Say when. Do we have a demo of Woody's song?"

"That's fine. I have a track with vocal and guitar. It has some technical glitches, but it presents the song. There's something about the starkness of the recording that's appealing. It's a very passionate performance."

"What do you want me to do with it?"

"Get it to some labels right away."

"Clive Davis called yesterday about the Santana project," Maria suggested. "He owes us a favor."

Pearlman shook his head. "You don't get it. Clive wouldn't be doing us any favors with this one. Four or five times in my career, out of a million songs, I've heard a song that's a certain hit. I've been right every time. Send a copy to Arista, CBS, Polygram and Warner Brothers. They'll hear what I'm talking about by the first chorus, and they'll all want to hear any other material he has. So do I. And get a copy to Robert Redford, he's working at Paramount on a new feature, a love story. This would make a perfect theme opener. Who knows; the song's so strong, they might consider re-naming a character 'Stephanie'."

"Where's the master tape?" Maria asked.

"It's at The Palace. Unfortunately, I messed it up a little when I recorded it."

She uncrossed and crossed her legs and just kept writing. Stanford Law School, top of her class with a specialty in entertainment law, Maria was extremely bright, gorgeous and unflappable. That's why he'd hired her. Pearlman knew that every rock star and music executive he referred to her would hit on her, and they'd hit a stone wall. She was all business.

"Let's send a sample to radio programmers across the board," Pearlman said. "Maybe the first minute of the song, just to give them a taste. Rock, Pop, Adult Contemporary, even Country; they'll want to play the whole thing, but it won't be available. They'll contact the labels and that'll start a bidding war. And get in touch with

Woody. Make sure it's a hundred percent registered and copyrighted."

"Holly can't reach him. His phone is disconnected and he hasn't responded to any of our correspondence. He called once from a public phone in Arizona and didn't leave a number. Holly even sent out a private investigator; it appears he's moved with no forwarding address. His landlord wasn't helpful, and his neighbors on the floor of his apartment building were understandably reluctant to share any information about him."

Pearlman sighed. "Woody's the key to all this and, unfortunately, he might be the weakest link. It'll take a substantial investment of time and money on our part, and he'll be under a lot of pressure. We've got to find him before we commit."

Maria stopped writing and straightened her skirt. "If you don't mind me saying so, your doctor says it's not a good time to take on more stress at work. This guy sounds very high-maintenance. The first time he came to the office, Brenda had to call security. The second time he was seen snooping around where he wasn't supposed to be." She looked for his reaction. Pearlman was gazing out the window.

"He's definitely a character," Pearlman said thoughtfully. "We'll just have to figure out how to deal with him. Do you know Ray Bell?"

"I know who he is."

"He might know how to reach Woody. He was set to sing the song, but Woody sang it himself. Woody originally got my attention by dropping Ray's name, and I went along with it. I figured I could use Ray to sell the song and collect the money he owes me at the same time. I did the same thing Woody did, trying to use a name instead of letting the song stand on its own. He had his reasons, he's in survival mode. There's no excuse for me." He shook his head. "One of the files I gave you is a delinquent breach of contract matter I have with Bell. It's probably approaching fifty grand with penalties and interest. When you talk to him, ask him if he's in contact with Woody. But don't trust him. The guy's a snake. He'll be after that song himself. I'm sure he knows how good it is." Pearlman went back to staring out the window. From his upper floor room at San Francisco General, he could see his office at the top of the Transamerica Pyramid.

"Do you feel all right, Mr. Pearlman?"

"Please call me Jeff." He gestured at the heart monitor. "How many guys on their death bed say 'I wish I'd spent more time at the office'. That's why I'm making changes. I've got enough money to not work another day of my life."

"You're a long way from your death bed... Jeff."

A large blue jay landed on the windowsill outside. Pearlman kept his head motionless against his pillow and met its sideways stare until it flew off. "It's been a long time since music affected me the way Woody's song did. That's why I got in this business in the first place, for music like that. Woody loves someone so deeply you can actually feel it when you hear the song. And you can feel his pain." Pearlman paused. "I felt pain like that once in my life, when my wife took my kids away from me."

Maria, like everyone else at the firm, knew that Pearlman had recently been through a difficult divorce. She'd heard his ex-wife had done everything she could to hurt him during the breakup, including making it hard for him to see their two young children.

Maria was also aware that he was now an eligible bachelor, but she'd discovered that working for Jeff Pearlman, with his reputation for dealing with the world's biggest stars, didn't automatically translate to a glamorous social life. Since her first day on the job, she'd been buried in paperwork and hadn't even met the famous people whose files she was working on. She was having serious doubts about this law firm being the right place for her to climb the entertainment industry ladder.

Looking up, Maria realized that Pearlman had shifted his gaze from the window back to her. She flipped the page on her legal pad. "Does Woody have more songs?"

"He says he's got a lot more. He was giving me a private performance in my office when Brenda scared him off. She's becoming the office negatron. It's like an abuse of power, the way she gives some people special treatment while she keeps others on hold." He stopped himself and put his head back on the pillow. "I'll deal with Brenda. Right now, we've got to find Woody. We need to know how deep of a bench he has. Is he a one hit wonder, does he have an album of songs, or ten albums?"

"What's the name of the song you recorded?"

"'Stephanie'."

"Hello?"

"Ray Bell, please."

"Who's calling?"

"Attorney Maria Angelista from Jeff Pearlman's office."

"This is Ray." His palms were suddenly sweating. "What can I do for you?"

"I have some legal issues I'd like to discuss with you."

"I'm glad you called. I have some business to discuss with Pearlman, but I heard he had a heart attack."

"Mr. Pearlman is taking a leave of absence. I'm handling some of his matters. Have you retained an attorney to respond to Mr. Pearlman's lawsuit?"

He shifted the phone from one ear to the other. "Not yet."

"Good, we can talk directly. Are you available to come to my office? Say Thursday at two o'clock?"

"See you Thursday."

Chapter 18

Standing in his hallway, guitar case in hand, Woody stared at the over-sized padlock on his apartment door. No phone, no bed, no bathroom, locked out of his life; he should've stayed on the edge of the Grand Canyon. He gave the door a resounding kick and walked up one flight to Murray's.

"Where've you been?" Murray held his door open. "You look like you lost some weight. You been sick or something?"

Woody walked past him, set his guitar down and fell back on Murray's couch. "I went to the Grand Canyon to do a little work on my suicide note and ended up going on a water and corn chip fast, except I ran out of corn chips. You got anything to eat around here?"

"Corn chips."

"Perfect."

Murray headed into his kitchen. "You just left everything and went to the Grand Canyon?"

"Life's not for everyone." Woody sat up and gestured with his hands. "I finally got my song recorded, which by the way, it turns out was recorded by a guy that just had a heart attack. I was getting hit with all these bills, not sure what was going on with Stephanie, I needed a break. You think by any chance I could borrow fifty bucks?"

Murray's face went slack. "You want to borrow fifty bucks?"

"Maybe if I give Huo fifty bucks he'll let me in my apartment to get my stuff."

"You can't get into your apartment?" Murray took a handful of corn chips from a bag on the counter and offered the bag to Woody.

"I've had enough corn chips for this lifetime." Woody leaned forward on the edge of the couch. "There's a padlock on my door. I pretty much used the last of my money on gas, driving back from the edge."

"I don't get paid until the fifteenth," Murray said. "And I was out a few days with the flu so my check will be light. Besides, you told me you'd pay me that hundred you owe me right after your recording session."

"Give up all hope of a better past."

"What're you going to do with all your stuff?"

"I thought maybe I could leave some things here for a minute. You might be able to use some of it. It's all temporary. Like I said, I finally got my song recorded so something should be happening pretty quick." He knew Murray had heard his raps a million times. He got up and helped himself to a handful of chips. They tasted unusually salty. "Murray, you know how when someone you don't care for invites you to some great event, you probably don't feel like going? But when your best buddy asks you to take a ride to the dump, you're always ready to go?"

"Yeah."

"Well, I did a lot of thinking at the Grand Canyon, and a lot of guitar playing. I figured out that music is the only way to actually experience time." Woody saw the expression on Murray's face and stopped himself. It was obvious Murray wasn't in the mood for music theory.

Woody looked down the length of the couch, resisted the urge to lie down, and forced himself to sit up straighter. "Anyways, I've realized that I dig hanging out with friends like you more than trying to hang out with rock stars."

"I know what you mean." Murray pushed his glasses back on his nose. "You want to put all your amplifiers and stuff in here?" Murray's apartment was the same size as Woody's, a one-room studio with a kitchenette, but it somehow seemed larger. The bed was made, the sink was empty and there were clean uncluttered surfaces. "I don't really have room for any more stuff than I already have."

Woody shrugged. "I can deal with the stuff part. I just need to make a couple phone calls from somewhere for a minute. I know I've been saying this for a long time, but I finally did get one of my songs recorded and I'm on the verge of getting some cash flowing." Woody glanced down the length of the funky brown couch. They felt the strong territorial vibe; it was an uncomfortable moment for both of them.

"Lookit, man." Woody suddenly stood up. "I don't want you feeling like you gotta perform or whatever."

"Where you going?"

"To find a bolt cutter."

Murray nodded toward Woody's guitar. "What about your guitar?"

Woody knelt down on the floor, opened the case and ran his fingers across the strings. "I thought I'd leave it here, just for today if that's okay."

Murray looked at the canopy of curly blonde hair draped over Woody's bony shoulders. The way he was kneeling in front of his guitar, it looked like he was praying. "Wow," Murray knelt down next to him. "This guitar is beautiful. Where'd you get it?"

"Pearlman gave it to me."

"You mean it's yours?"

"Yeah. And it's definitely worth some money. I'll tell you what, lend me fifty bucks and you can own part of it, a secured loan."

"What good's that going do me, unless you sell it? What do you think it's worth?"

"A lot more than fifty bucks."

Murray noticed that Woody was badly in need of a shower. He stood up. "If you want, you can use my shower or have something to eat before you go."

Woody closed his guitar case and leaned it against the wall. "Thanks man, but if you just lend me a few bucks for a fishing pole instead of like giving me a fish, maybe I could get in and use my own shower."

"I can give you twenty bucks. That's all I can spare right now."

"You're a real prince, Murray." Woody took the twenty and turned toward the door.

"Hey Woody."

Woody stopped in the doorway. Murray stuck his hands in his pockets and for a moment, Woody thought he was going to give him more money. "I know what you mean about friends being important and everything," Murray said with his eyes closed. "I just think we can be better friends if we don't live together."

Leaving the building, Woody peered through the little square inch of glass on the door of his mailbox. It was filled with letters, probably junk mail and bills. The key to his mailbox, with everything else, was locked in his apartment.

He walked down the dusty steps onto the sidewalk and felt the oppressive afternoon heat. The summer sun seemed to have more of an edge than usual, searing his pale skin.

The only place he could think of to borrow a bolt cutter was the mechanic's shop where he had his car worked on, fifteen blocks away. Fifteen meant thirty round-trip, if the mechanic even had a bolt cutter and would lend it out. Was it too far to walk? His car, if it wasn't towed or ticketed, was almost out of gas. He had to preserve the twenty at all costs. And, bottom line, even if he could get his stuff out of his apartment, where was he going to go?

135

He thought about getting something to eat; that tank felt pretty low too. Looking down at his sneakers, he remembered something he'd read about people in Africa eating boiled shoe leather to ward off starvation. He walked faster.

In three blocks he came to Oak Street, a wide, one-way boulevard, and beyond that, the Panhandle of Golden Gate Park. In the middle of a field, he could see a row of aproned, bearded men standing behind a long table under a colorful sign made from a bed sheet: "FREE SOUP." In front of the table was a meandering, hundred-foot line of barefoot young people in glitter and face paint, kicking hacky-sacks and tossing Frisbees. Mixed in with the daydreamers were genuinely hungry street people, ready for a warm meal. It looked like at least an hour wait, standing in the circus, for a bowl of soup. Woody headed down the street toward the mechanic's shop.

After a few long blocks, he realized how thirsty he was. Those salty chips at Murray's were the last thing in the world he'd wanted. He'd meant to get a drink of water, and now he'd end up paying for bottled water. The hot summer sun was high in the sky. He needed a break.

Passing by a two-family house with a small wooden porch, it looked like no one was home. He walked up the steps, sat down and felt instant relief from the heat.

He was reevaluating his plan when it occurred to him that he didn't have to actually possess his stuff, he just needed access to it. If he got a lock like the one on his apartment door, cut the real one off and replaced it with his own, Mr. Huo would never be the wiser. If he was quiet, he could get in and just live there, rent-free. There were plenty of vacant apartments in the building, Mr. Huo would probably leave his stuff, hoping to get some back-rent.

Woody suddenly felt a sense of regret over his failed relationship with his landlord. How did *he* feel dealing with Woody's crazy friends, coming and going all hours of the night? *Everyone's pain, to them, is as painful as it gets,* he thought. Mr. Huo, with his little wife who didn't speak English, shuttling white plastic bags up and down the stairs; she always seemed scared. He decided to do something nice for her, maybe get her some flowers, commit a random act of kindness.

Woody leaned back against the porch railing. Across the street was a gigantic billboard of a hamburger on a sesame bun with melted cheese, oozing mayonnaise sauce. He hadn't eaten red meat in two years. The hamburger looked moist and succulent. He could feel what it would be like to have a wet sensuous bite in his dry mouth and pictured himself with arms spread wide, clinging to the slippery slope of the six-foot-slab of greasy meat, his head buried up to his ears, chewing furiously while he tried to get a purchase with his foot on the bottom rung of the sesame bun. He smiled at the thought of a slow-motion Niagara Falls of pink mayonnaise sauce cascading over him, followed by a fifty-pound slice of Bermuda onion bouncing off his shoulder, crushing the roof of a car in traffic below. He shifted his position on the porch step and realized how spaced out he was from not eating and sleeping. He at least needed a drink of water.

A nicely dressed black woman with two young children came around the corner at the end of the block and stopped at the bottom of the stairs. The woman saw Woody, hesitated, then quickly led the children up the stairs toward the door. They looked to Woody like they were coming from church, or a wedding. He awkwardly moved aside while the woman stepped past him and unlocked the door.

"Sorry to be on your porch," Woody said. "I was just getting out of the sun for a minute. Do you think I could possibly get a glass of water, if it's not too much trouble?"

The woman ignored him, shuttled her kids through the door and locked it behind her. Woody let his back slide down the railing, sat on the step, and kept talking to the closed door. "I mean, I'm so thirsty I could drink a horse, and I'd hate to collapse here on your porch and every time you wanted to go out you'd have to shove my body back and forth with the back of the door and you'd have to explain it when company came over for lemonade and sandwiches and…"

The door opened six inches and the small hand of a little girl set a glass of water down. "You can leave the glass on the porch when you're done." She closed the door before Woody could thank her.

Woody drank the water, San Francisco tap water, cool and delicious. He was always generous with street people and now his good karma was coming back. He'd be even more generous when he got his first big royalty check. The thought yanked him back to reality, back to his predicament with Pearlman. What the hell was he doing, starving on the street? A week ago he was in a top recording studio. Maybe Pearlman was permanently gone from work and his recording deal was permanently gone. He'd better get used to it. The thought felt like a weight pressing down on him. *Now what? Back to the crummy gigs? Playing on the street? Back to square one, without a place to live.*

Looking around the tidy little porch, bright red hanging geranium plants and fresh green paint on the floorboards, he felt like a filthy intruder and stood up to leave.

"Here, mister." It was the little girl again. She looked about six years old, this time offering a candy bar through the slightly open door.

Woody took the candy. The girl's sparkling brown eyes, filled with eagerness and anticipation, gave him instant relief from the heaviness he was feeling. *Second-hand hope,* he thought. When she started to close the door he blurted out, "Wait, what's your name?"

"My mom says I have to come right back." She closed the door most of the way. "Samantha."

Woody quickly reached into his pockets for something to give to her. The little girl kept the door open a crack, watching him. Woody always had extra stuff with him, and now he had nothing. Reaching down to the bottom of his pocket, he pulled out a guitar pick, a piece of electrical wire, a matchbook and Murray's twenty-dollar bill. Through the slightly open door, wide little eyes watched his every move.

He raised his eyebrows and motioned with his head to the items in his hand. Samantha opened the door another inch to get a better look.

"Go ahead. Pick one."

She reached out tentatively, her hand hovering over his. She held it there for a few seconds, then took the twenty, quickly looking up to see what would happen next. All he could do was smile.

"Thanks mister." She disappeared behind the door.

Woody sat down, ate the candy bar and read the ingredients on the wrapper. It occurred to him that what trickled down to people on the street wasn't the romantic version of stale bread and bruised apples, but usually some preservative-packed junk food. He never should've given away his last twenty. That was crazy. But that little girl's face; it felt like she'd practically saved his life. That was worth twenty bucks.

A bus went by and he remembered that some buses on that line had back doors that opened. He could sneak in the back door and get most of the way to Stephanie's. A bolt cutter wasn't in the cards today. He'd explain to her what happened when he'd woken her up with his 5 am phone call. Maybe she'd even be glad to see him.

Behind him, the front door to the house opened again. It was the little girl, with the twenty-dollar bill in her hand and a look of determination. "My mom says I can't keep it." She put the twenty down, placed a shiny red apple on top of it, and quickly closed the door behind her.

Woody stared at the apple, savoring the miracle he'd just witnessed. He half expected the door to reopen with the little girl balancing a silver tray of fresh fruit on her head. Smiling, he walked across the street, bought a bottle of cold water and a banana, and got on the next bus. It felt way better getting on through the front door than slinking in the back.

It was early evening by the time Woody got to Stephanie's in Daly

City. The security code he had wouldn't open the front gate. He was standing there wondering what to do when a neighbor of Stephanie's came walking out. "Hi Woody, looking for Stephanie?"

"Yeah."

"She moved out."

Numb with disbelief, Woody spent most of what was left of Murray's twenty on beer and pretzels at a bar near his apartment. With the bartender on the phone and a young couple at a table in the corner, he sat alone and drank beer, staring at a yellowed paper sign on the wall that said "FREE DRINKS TOMORROW."

He'd recorded his song for Stephanie, and now it all felt useless. In a half-hearted effort to ease his pain, he tried to muster a feeling of anger toward her. He couldn't. She had the qualities of a goddess, not a speck of negativity toward anyone. And she had the good sense to just leave him instead of trying to change him. He looked over at the couple in the corner, shoulders touching, laughing. He wasn't part of a couple anymore.

The only place he had to go right now was Murray's and Murray would have to be okay with it. Woody had run out of options.

It was past midnight when he climbed the steps and knocked on Murray's door. No answer. He knew Murray was a sound sleeper and had to get up early for work, but this was an emergency. He knocked harder.

"Who's there?" Murray said through the closed door.

"It's me."

Murray opened it with the safety chain still on and closed his eyes against the hallway light.

"Sorry to wake you up," Woody said.

Through his torpor and the crack in the door, Murray could smell the alcohol on Woody's breath and his foul body odor. He undid the chain, swung open the door and headed back to bed. "You can stay on the couch tonight, that's it. And be quiet, I gotta get up for work."

"Thanks man, I really appreciate it." Woody quietly closed the door and made his way to the couch. "Murray, you awake?"

"No."

"Sorry man, I wouldn't have come in the middle of the night but you wouldn't believe the shit that happened. I was feeling about as low as you can go, then I went over to Stephanie's and –"

"I gotta sleep back to work inna' morning," Murray mumbled incoherently.

"Sorry man. I hope this noise in my head doesn't keep you up."

Murray threw a pillow at Woody. "Will you for once just shut up! You buttered your bread, now lie in it."

Three minutes later, Murray was snoring. Woody was amazed at how some people could fall asleep so easily. The slightest unfamiliar sound, other people in the room, anything unusual, made it impossible for him to sleep. He wondered how long he should wait to get in the refrigerator, he was starving. He'd never looked inside Murray's refrigerator, he'd rarely been in his apartment. Murray was always coming over to his place for short visits. Woody had realized long ago that Murray was attracted to energy, never initiated it, and could only take so much.

When Woody's eyes adjusted to the dim light, he quietly walked across the room and opened the refrigerator. It was clean and organized, with little plastic containers labeled with masking tape that said "Murray." Woody opened one, a square of lasagna cut to the shape of the small container. Using light from the refrigerator, he spent a few seconds looking for a fork, then scarfed down the lasagna with his hands while he investigated the other shelves. He considered only eating part of the lasagna but couldn't stop himself. His body craved food; he'd replace it tomorrow.

Checking further, he found carrot cake and potato salad. Opening a drawer with his greasy fingers, he picked up a fork and dropped it.

"What the hell? Can't you ever be quiet!" Murray rolled over and put a pillow over his head. "And don't eat my lunch in those containers."

Woody tiptoed back to the couch. He had to pee. There was no way he could wait until morning. He'd have to walk within six inches of Murray's head, but it had to be okay to go the bathroom.

He slipped past Murray, turned on the light, and there was Murray's everything: deodorant, dirty razor, cold sore cream, hemorrhoid cream, a stack of soiled Hustler magazines. Woody hated it in there. He finished peeing, walked out into the dark and knocked over a lamp.

This time it took a while for Murray to get back to sleep. Woody lay on the couch listening to Murray's restlessness, thankful for the blanket he'd found and the pillow Murray threw at him. He noticed, with a kind of scary amusement, that the more Murray's breathing settled into a steady rhythm, the more lonely he felt. The last place he wanted to be was in this apartment. "Macbeth murdered sleep," he whispered, and was amazed that he'd spoken out loud.

He pulled the blanket up to his neck, staring at the ceiling. As the minutes passed he became uncertain of whether he'd actually said something out loud or had imagined saying it. He tried screaming "Macbeth murdered sleep" as loud as he could in his head without making any noise. *I'm losing it,* he thought. He could just get up and walk out, but he had nowhere to go. The idea of being out on the street seemed scarier than where he was: sentenced to freedom.

He was feeling queasy. He'd eaten way too fast, practically inhaling the food. The air in the apartment felt hot and stuffy, oppressive, beads of sweat forming on his forehead… he stood, facing the couch, heart pounding, and couldn't remember standing up. *Now I'm really losing it.* He lay back down and tried watching his breath, like Stephanie said; when in doubt, breathe in, breathe out.

He suddenly became aware of the imposing hum of the refrigerator. *Did it just come on, or has it been there the whole time?* It sounded like B flat or A. He hummed softly in unison, then departed up a third and a fifth, harmonizing. In some indefinable way, that little bit of music seemed to take the edge off his anxiety.

What were his real bottom-line options? His mother still worked in Eastern California as a part-time waitress. It was a constant feeling of consternation, waiting for some good news as a reason to call her and the good news never coming and him always needing money. She never had any extra, but would come through with a hundred bucks in a pinch, especially around Christmas. Her place was about the same size as his. He'd rather die than show up in the shape he was in and impose on her delicate little-old-lady living space. He'd always fantasized that, someday, he'd get a big royalty check and buy her a house.

His thoughts became progressively more disjointed, unraveling in a vortex of guitar cables swirling around the bum on the bus stop bench, the torn piece of hanging-down sleeping bag a ground-wire connecting the man to the earth and all of humanity; billions of people like miniature planets, each one orbiting in their own gravitational field, a gigantic river of bodies pouring onto the rocks of the Grand Canyon with a shrill scream, howling sirens of universal pain reverberating off canyon walls…

Woody's eyes burst open to the electric buzzer of Murray's alarm clock.

"What the hell!" Murray hit the off button. "You've been making a racket all fucking night!" He stumbled into the bathroom.

Woody listened to the sound of the shower and thought about leaving before Murray came out, but he was deeply tired. Besides, where would he go? He rolled over toward the back of the couch hoping Murray would just go to work and leave him there.

When Murray came out, Woody was sure he was making more noise than necessary, trying to wake him up. Murray made himself some toast and instant coffee and saw the empty plastic containers in the sink that had his name on them for the refrigerator at work. He glared at Woody on the couch. "Now you sleep!" He stormed out.

Wednesday night was bowling night for employees at the movie theater where Murray worked as a ticket-taker. He rarely went

143

bowling, and when he did, he left early. This time he stayed until the last game, not wanting to go home and deal with Woody. When he finally did go home, Woody wasn't there. And to his surprise, the place was cleaned up, blanket folded, dishes washed. The only sign of Woody was his guitar in its case against the wall.

Chapter 19

"Brenda?"

Brenda looked up from her reception desk. Maria Angelista was standing there holding a stack of files.

"I tried calling you twice from my car and got the answering service. I thought we had a live receptionist here."

"It's been very busy today."

"Ray Bell will be coming in." Maria turned and walked away.

"Ray Bell?"

"Yes," Maria said without looking back. "Let me know as soon as he arrives."

"Hi Ray. I heard you were coming in today. How've you been?"

"Still kickin'. How about you Brenda? Still living out by the coast?"

"The commute gets worse every day, but I couldn't live without a view of the ocean. And Georgia loves the beach."

"Georgia?"

"You remember Georgia, my Saint Bernard."

"Does she still get in bed with you in the morning?"

145

Brenda blushed and pushed her hair back from her face. Ray was reminded of how much perfume she wore.

"It's been a long time Ray. I expected to hear from you."

"I've been meaning to call you. I've been totally jammed."

"After what happened between us? Too busy to call for almost a year?"

"C'mon Brenda, don't get all gooey on me. It was a Christmas party."

"I didn't know holidays were so important to you." The phone rang. "Every musician in the world calls here but you... Pierce and Pearlman."

Brenda dealt with the call. "You're working with Maria?"

"I'm here about a song I wrote."

"Glad to hear you're making music.

"Do you know a guy named Woody?"

"Isn't that another word for dick?" she sneered. "That guy's repulsive."

Ray raised his eyebrows, surprised at her attitude. "Is he one of Pearlman's clients?"

"I guess they're talking about it. I sure hope not. I wouldn't want that creep coming around here."

Ray stepped closer. "That fucker's trying to steal one of my songs."

The comment clearly piqued her interest. "Does Jeff know about it?"

"I heard Jeff might be permanently out of commission."

She raised her own eyebrows; Pearlman's health condition was supposed to be confidential. "He's taking a medical leave. We're not sure when he'll be back.

When Brenda answered another call, Ray glanced down at her low-cut dress, sauntered behind the reception desk and began massaging her shoulders. "I know you know how special that night was," he said when she hung up. "I've been thinking about you, Brenda, I really have. I just wanted to clear some space in my life and not try to jam you in with a bunch of other things. You know what I mean?"

Rubbing her shoulders, he moved his hands down toward her chest. She leaned forward so his hands ended up in the middle of her back. "Let's go out for a drink sometime," Ray said, "maybe we could start up where we left off."

"I'd enjoy that, Ray." She called Maria's secretary. "Maria will see you now."

"I'll call you soon." He walked toward the back offices, looking at his watch.

"Ray," Brenda said quietly.

He stopped and looked back at her.

She held his stare as long as she could without smiling. "That's the wrong way. I'll show you where Maria's office is."

"You look great, Brenda," Ray said, following her down the hall.

"The only other time you've said that to me, we were walking down this same hallway at the Christmas party. Both times, all you could see was my ass." She held open a door.

He stepped in and turned around. "I'll call you soon Brenda, I really will."

She nodded and closed the door.

Ray realized he was standing in a bathroom. Combing his hair in the mirror, he thought about Brenda's spunkiness; that was what he liked about her. He walked down the hallway to an alcove where a buff young man with a shaved head was sitting at a desk.

"I'm looking for Maria Angelista," Ray said.

"I'm Bruce, Maria's secretary. You must be Mr. Bell. One moment please." He buzzed the inner office. "Ray Bell is here to see you."

"Send him in."

Maria shook Ray's hand, waved him toward a chair and sat down on a leather couch by the window. The office was stark and immaculate with black enamel art-deco furniture and a Jackson Pollack painting of dramatic red and yellow brush strokes. Ray walked past the chair and sat next to her on the couch.

Without expression, she slid a few inches away. "Thank you for coming, Mr. Bell."

"I'm glad I did. You're a lot easier on the eyes than Jeff Pearlman."

Ignoring his comment, she picked up her yellow legal pad. "We have some matters to discuss regarding your pending litigation with Mr. Pearlman."

"Before we get into that, do you represent a guy named Woody?"

"Yes. I understand you're working with him."

"Did he tell you he wrote that song 'Stephanie'?"

"I've been informed it's his song."

"It's my song. I showed the song to Woody before he recorded it."

Maria gave him a curious look. "You composed the melody and the lyrics?"

"*Everything*. The song's copyrighted in my name."

She jotted down a note. "This is the first I've heard about another composer."

"There's this topless dancer me and Woody both know," Ray smirked. "Her name's Stephanie. I guess Woody's got a thing for her. When I showed him the song I wrote about her, he went ballistic. Now he's saying Stephanie is *his* girlfriend so 'Stephanie' must be *his* song. He thinks it's a package deal. The guy's crazy with jealousy and can't handle that someone would write a song about a woman he's gaga over."

"I'd like to discuss this with Woody directly," Maria said.

"The guy's psycho. It's my song." Ray laid his arm across the back of the couch, his hand a half-inch from Maria's shoulder. "How long have you been working here? You're about the best looking attorney I've met. Most women lawyers I know ride brooms to work."

She stiffened. "So, let me get this straight, Mr. Bell. You wrote a love song about a stripper that Woody cares about but you don't?"

The desk phone intercom crackled on. "Ms. Angelista, I have Mr. Grantham on the phone."

"Brenda, I'm in a meeting."

"Sorry to disturb you. You asked me to let you know as soon as I was able to reach Mr. Grantham."

"That was two days ago, Brenda. You know I'm in a meeting."

"Sorry to disturb you. Shall I tell Mr. Grantham you'll call him back?"

Maria went to her desk and glared at the intercom speaker. "Tell him you made a mistake calling him. I'm in a meeting!" She turned off the intercom, and headed back to the couch. "I'm surprised Brenda would do something like that. She's usually so efficient."

"There's more to Brenda than meets the eye," Ray said. "Some people think she's the most important person to know in the music business."

Maria sat down abruptly and slapped her legal pad back on her lap. "You haven't replied to Mr. Pearlman's complaint regarding the contract dispute you have with him."

"I've been a little busy trying to survive," Ray said. "But here I am, and I could sing my own song and Pearlman could get the money he thinks I owe him and everybody'd be happy."

Maria pointed to a thick document on the glass-top coffee table in front of them. "This complaint was filed in San Francisco Superior Court. You've been served. What are your intentions?"

"My intentions?"

"Do you plan on hiring an attorney, filing an answer In Pro Per, or is your defense strategy to hope for a woman judge and flirt your way out of the case?"

Ray took his arm off the back of the couch and sat up straight. "You can tell Pearlman he's trying to get blood out of a stone. And Woody's trying to steal my song. Pearlman invited me down to the Palace to sing "Stephanie," then it turns out the whole thing was a setup to serve me with those legal papers. If that's the way he's gonna handle things, fuck him. You're going to end up with your own lawsuit and it's going to be my word against Woody's. And who do you think people are going to believe, an international recording artist or some drugged-out hippy that's never recorded anything? You're going to have one of us as a client, your choice."

Maria stood up. "I don't think we have anything else to discuss. We intend to file a request for a default judgment regarding the contract dispute. If you'll excuse me now."

Ray was on his feet. "Woody is scamming you guys. It's my song and I'm going to make it a hit. My voice is instantly recognizable on a thousand radio stations." He gestured at the wall. "Wouldn't it be nice to have a gold record on *your* wall?" Framed gold records in every other part of the office complex were conspicuously absent from Maria's office.

"Thank you for coming in, Mr. Bell."

As soon as Ray was gone, Maria went to the office library, read Ray's entire file and pored over back-issues of Billboard, Rolling Stone and Variety. There were dozens of articles about Ray's concert tours and his tabloid relationships with models and movie stars.

Back in her office, she called a former law school classmate, Chris Andrian, who worked at the Copyright Office in Washington DC. He checked the ledger and told her they had received a copyright application from Raymond Bell for the song "Stephanie" two weeks ago.

"Thanks Chris, that's helpful information. So how do you like Washington?"

"The work's interesting, but my office doesn't have any windows. How about you Maria? What's it like working for Jeff Pearlman?"

"Actually, Jeff has had health issues and I'm taking over responsibility for some pretty interesting cases."

"I'll bet your office has a window."

She laughed, looking out her 44th story view of the city. "You'd win the bet. I was hoping we'd get a chance to get together again before you left for Washington."

"Yeah, sorry about that. You know how crazy things are when you're getting ready to move across the country. Definitely let me know if you need any more help with the copyright stuff. Nice to hear from you, Maria."

The next day, at the plush listening room she'd reserved at the Palace Studio, Maria waited in a high-back producer's chair while an intern engineer worked quietly in the back of the room, winding two-inch-wide magnetic tape around the spoked aluminum wheels of the recording machine. "Ready?" The young man asked.

"Any time," Maria said.

Standing next to the machine, the engineer played Woody's solo recording of "Stephanie." The moment it ended, he spoke up. "Wow. That song's amazing. It almost makes you feel like crying. Who is that guy? I've never heard of him." He rewound the tape. "Too bad about that recording glitch in the last chorus. I heard they tried to fix it. Ready to listen again?"

Maria was sitting with her back to him, facing the speakers. "No," she said without turning around.

"You don't want to listen to it one more time? It's less than five minutes. I wouldn't mind hearing it again, if that's okay."

Maria stood and walked toward the tape machine with such a stern expression on her face, the young man involuntarily took a step back. "Show me how to run this machine," she said. "I'd like to listen to it alone."

The engineer programmed the machine for continuous replay. Sitting by herself, Maria listened to the song from beginning to end a dozen times.

Chapter 20

When Murray opened his apartment door to leave for work, he found Woody standing there with his hand in the air, about to knock.

"Hey Murray, what's up?"

"I'm late for work."

"I'm going to talk to Mr. Huo today. The stuff in my apartment is worth more than what I owe him. I was hoping maybe I could –"

"I'm pretty late for work." Murray started to sidestep him and close the door behind him.

"You think I could use your bathroom? You don't have to wait around. Just let me use your bathroom and you won't even know I was here."

"Where'd you stay last night?"

"I just hung out, took a walk around the Haight."

Murray hesitated. "There's a couple slices of pizza in the fridge. Just make sure the door's locked when you leave. And the toaster oven's kinda weird. The oven part's okay but the toaster switch sticks. Use the temperature knob if you use it, don't use the toaster part."

"Thanks a lot, Murray."

Woody took a shower and had a slice of burnt pizza. He'd been up all night, walking the streets, drinking coffee, killing time until he knew Murray would be leaving for work. Now he had nine hours until Murray got home. Things had reached a new low and his standards for what he could accomplish in a day were getting lower all the time.

Expecting to be disappointed, Woody called Stephanie. Her number was still disconnected. Before the disappointment could sink in, he called Pearlman's office. Brenda curtly informed him that Mr. Pearlman's condition hadn't changed. Woody asked to speak with Holly.

"Holly is on the phone. Someone will contact you when we have anything new."

Woody insisted that he hold on until he got to speak to somebody. "Suit yourself," Brenda said, and left him on hold.

Making a face at the phone, he hung up and tried directing his attention toward something constructive. He made a list of musicians, possible solo gigs, and bands that might need a guitar player. Hooking up with a local band going on the road could net him enough money to get into his apartment. And while he was on the road, he wouldn't have to worry about a place to stay. But getting a gig without a callback number in the frantic phone-tag world of musicians presented quite a challenge. And he knew the chances of a band needing a guitar player on such short notice were slim. He'd played plenty of local gigs, in bars and cafes, but he'd only been on tour a few times. They were low-budget runs with four guys squeezed into a vanload of equipment, sharing cheap motel rooms, no one getting any sleep. The situation was ripe for conflict, and usually ended that way.

It didn't help that Woody was constantly dealing with his fear of being onstage. It wasn't an uncommon issue with some of the musicians he played with, but for him it could be paralyzing. When

153

it was time to play, he didn't get much sympathy if he did anything else.

But he was more confident about his guitar playing now and he knew that if you played well enough, it didn't matter if people thought you were a jerk. Accomplished musicians would put up with almost any kind of personality disorder, drug habit, or obnoxious behavior, just to play with other great players. The better the music, the more it blinded musicians to the personality making the music.

Woody spent his nights roaming the streets, playing for spare change, waiting for morning to come. Occasionally, he'd stay on other people's couches. More often than not, he'd show up at Murray's when he was leaving for work, spend the day, and leave before Murray got home. It seemed like the situation couldn't go on but, impossibly, the days slipped into weeks.

The prickly vibe between Woody and Murray became progressively more uncomfortable. Then, when Murray was about to just not answer his door, Woody would get a gig, buy some groceries, a six-pack of beer and a bag of pot. They'd get stoned, Woody would play him some songs and things would be okay for a few days.

Woody was hitting rock bottom, pushing Murray's limits and depleting his possibilities of places to stay. He'd been gravitating toward the open-all-night section of Market Street, the nocturnal underbelly of San Francisco, where the city's homeless and insomniacs congregated and did their business. Late one night, wandering down a wide sidewalk of brightly lit store-fronts, adult theaters and pizza and burrito shops, Woody spotted what he needed in a pile of tools in a 24-hour pawnshop window: a made-in-Japan bolt cutter for thirty dollars.

He had fifteen bucks. The pawnbroker wouldn't go for it. Woody went back the next night with his guitar and struck a deal to leave the guitar, borrow the bolt cutter for a day, get his guitar back, and give up his fifteen dollars.

The cheap bolt cutter dented the tempered steel lock on Woody's apartment door but wouldn't cut through. He kept trying, putting the bolt cutter at different angles until he bent one of the handles and the tool became unusable. Angry and frustrated, wondering how he was going to get his guitar back, he was on his way out of the apartment building when he noticed the little metal bar on his locked mailbox. He wedged the bent handle of the bolt cutter against the wall and managed to cut the thin metal but damaged the handle more in the process. He panicked. What if the pawnshop wouldn't take back the bolt-cutter and sold his guitar? He headed down the street, then remembered his mail and went back.

With some difficulty, he pulled out the overstuffed wad of letters. There were telephone bills, car insurance bills, utility bills, shut-off notices, an offer for a pre-approved credit card and two letters from the Law Offices of Jeff Pearlman.

Sitting on the dusty steps, one letter in each hand, he looked at the professional envelopes with his name typed on them. Was this his rejection letter? *Stop bugging our receptionist, see you later pal.* Why were there two letters? One felt thicker. He turned them over twice, examined the postmarks, and held them up to the light. When he reread the address, he saw his hand was shaking.

The first one he opened was a form letter informing Pearlman's clients of his absence from the office due to health reasons. The second letter, with an earlier postmark, was a two-page contract, giving Pearlman's office the rights to represent him and to place his song with record labels, in soundtracks or with other artists. An advance on publishing royalties was included as part of the agreement; a check made out to Woody for five thousand dollars. Woody could accept the terms of the contract by endorsing and cashing the check.

Chapter 21

After a month at her Aunt and Uncle's place in Marin County, Stephanie felt more peaceful than she had in years.

Her Aunt Auddie and Uncle Max were a sibling-looking couple in their late sixties. Max was a retired physician, Auddie was his social director. Stephanie had spent most of her teenage years living with them. Stephanie's mother, a struggling single mom, had left her to her own devices with a string of baby-sitters until, at age twelve, she went on her summer visit to California. Max and Auddie made some mysterious arrangements and she found herself permanently living with them. After high school she'd attended college in San Francisco and moved to Daly City, but they remained her closest friends.

When Stephanie showed up and told them she was moving back to Marin, they were thrilled, and enthusiastically offered their guest room for as long as she wanted.

Through a friend of Auddie's, Stephanie auditioned for and was accepted into The Mill Valley Dance Company. The rehearsals kept her busy, gave her a great workout and for the first time in her life, she was actually making money as a professional dancer.

She found herself thinking about Woody less and less. When she'd first left the city, thoughts of him called up images of being strangled by his jealously. He'd left her messages everywhere, but she'd decided to wait a while before contacting him. Now, the tincture of time had smoothed over the rough edges and her memories were gradually becoming less negative. It occurred to her how ironic it was that leaving her old job—the thing that had soured their relationship—had happened when they were no longer together.

In retrospect, it was hard for Stephanie to believe she'd actually done the job at all. It was the smell of the place she disliked the most, the stale beer and cigarettes. And the constant, revolting battle to keep the customers' filthy hands off her.

One thing about Woody, his hands were always manicured and immaculate, with titillating guitar calluses on each finger. With all the mess around him, he kept his hands and guitars obsessively clean. There were so many things about him she liked; his humor, sense of adventure, intentionally breaking social rules most people weren't even aware of, unintentionally breaking rules most people lived by. His unique way of conceptualizing things was amazing. She'd learned more from him than anyone she'd ever known

With Pearlman's check cashed, Woody was back in his apartment, his guitar was out of hock and his phone was back on. Listening to the messages that were left on his answering machine before his phone had been disconnected, he found a message from Stephanie.

"Hi Woody. Hope things are okay. Just wanted to let you know I quit my job and moved out of my place. I'm at Max and Auddie's in Marin."

When she paused, Woody felt an incredible sense of elation.

"It'd be nice to hear from you."

He let out a joyous yelp, picked up the phone to call her, put it back down, and with a surge of energy, ran up and down the stairs, packing his car with everything he might need for a weekend out of town. He knew he always did better with her in person, and for once he had some money.

He put the money he owed Murray in an envelope, added a little extra, slipped it under Murray's door, then drove around and paid back everyone else he owed money to. His last stop was at the house where the little girl had given him the water and candy bar on her front porch. He put a box of candy in a paper bag with an apple and a twenty-dollar bill, wrote *Samantha* on it and left it on the doorstep. He headed for the Golden Gate Bridge.

Cruising north out of the city, Woody felt great. Stephanie had quit her job, he was going to see her and he had over four thousand dollars in his pocket.

He thought of the times he'd been to Stephanie's aunt and uncle's place and the weird vibe he always got from her aunt Auddie. He and Max kind of hit it off, especially after a couple of drinks, but he knew Auddie thought Stephanie could do better. *For some reason,* he thought, *Auddie thinks I'm a crazy unemployed musician.* He smiled to himself and stepped on the gas.

"Oh, hello Woody, we weren't expecting you." Auddie's voice squawked out of a metal box at the security gate that looked like a fast-food drive-up speaker.

"How've you been, Auddie?"

"Fine."

"How's Max?"

"Fine."

Woody looked at the little speaker box and felt like saying "Gimme a cheeseburger and fries." Instead, he went with, "Is Stephanie around?"

"She should be back soon, would you like to come in?"

It was a good sign. Then he saw himself in the rear-view mirror, looking scraggly in his sweat-soaked shirt. "Thanks Auddie, I've got something I need to do, I'll check back in a little while."

"I'll let Stephanie know you're in town."

He couldn't believe how thoughtless he'd been, so intent on

getting there, he hadn't even gotten himself halfway presentable. He remembered a public restroom at a park in Tiburon, a few miles away, where he could clean up and change his clothes. He was about to drive away when the parking space next to him caught his attention. It was marked CAR/SMALL, with the word CAR above the word SMALL. A similarly marked parking space was in front of Stephanie's apartment complex in Daly City. He understood the concept: people supposedly read SMALL CAR as they pulled in. But he knew everyone actually read it backwards.

Shortly after he and Stephanie had met, he'd taken a can of white spray paint and painted an L after the word CAR... CARL SMALL. Stephanie thought it was cute when he did it at her place. He considered doing it here, at Max and Auddie's, decided Max and Auddie might not think it was so cute, and headed toward Tiburon.

Creeping along the single lane road in rush hour through a tony neighborhood of adobe-style homes, Woody's engine began to overheat. The traffic thickened until it stopped, his temperature gauge began climbing and he turned off his motor. As soon as he did, the traffic started moving and horns blared behind him. He knew he had a leaky radiator. Every time he filled up with gas he had to put water in, he'd been meaning to fix it for months. He drove twenty feet, traffic stopped again and he turned on the heater and fan to help cool the engine. The heat in the car was quickly becoming unbearable.

The only way the electric windows would work in Woody's old Buick was by the individual controls on each door. Pulling his hair off his neck, he wrapped it in a ponytail and reached over the seats to get to the windows. Traffic crawled forward the width of one front lawn and stopped again.

Woody looked over his guitar and the pile of clothes in the front seat and out the passenger window. Thirty feet away a balding, sunburned man in sagging Bermuda shorts and a sleeveless T-shirt, a can of beer in one hand and a garden hose in the other, was squirting piles of dog shit across his manicured lawn toward the gutter. The incongruous presence of the slovenly-looking man on the neat-as-a-pin landscaping was somehow offset by the adeptness and skill he displayed. Woody watched with interest at the way he maneuvered the piles by slightly varying the water pressure. The man obviously had experience, moving with the confidence and focus of a master at his craft.

Woody had always been fascinated by the efficiency of motion displayed by master athletes, artists and tradesmen of every kind. He knew musicians who could create prodigious, complex sounds while barely moving their bodies. They all shared a kind of confident relaxation. The man squirting the hose was as focused as a professional golfer, probably drunk, playing on his home course.

As the man got closer, Woody realized that if the traffic didn't move soon, it was inevitable that spraying specks of dog shit would get on the side of his car, maybe come in his windows. He looked at the stopped cars in front and behind him, the street had turned into a parking lot. "Hey," he yelled out the passenger window. The man didn't look up. Maybe he couldn't hear him. "Hey!" No response.

The man advanced toward the street, squirting additional mounds toward the center of the procession, the size of the pile growing exponentially, the threat becoming more ominous. A few feet from the street the lawn sloped down steeply, the tsunami of turds approaching the crest.

"Hey man! Hey!" Woody yelled. The man was now definitely in hearing range. When he took a step forward without looking up, Woody saw the expression on his face and realized what was going on. The guy knew exactly what he was doing. It was intentional. Knowing the cars were trapped, he was getting revenge against the incessant traffic in front of his house. Or maybe he'd been watching Woody's oil-burning junk-heap creeping towards his house and he'd planned the trajectory, a personal vendetta.

Five cars ahead, the traffic started moving. Woody gripped the steering wheel, one foot on the gas, one on the brake, unconsciously revving his hot motor against the locked brakes. He hit his horn that hadn't worked in years. "Hey! Mr. Dog Shit!" He was sure he saw a smirk on the man's face. "Keep away from my car!"

Just then the traffic broke, cars in front started moving and horns behind him sounded. His car lurched forward, almost running into the car in front of him. He looked in his mirror; a truck blocked his view of the man on the lawn.

The traffic crept forward another fifty feet and stopped again. Steam coming from under his hood, Woody looked to his left and saw The Bayside Mission Inn, an exclusive-looking resort hotel perched on a hill. He touched the wad of cash in his pocket, wheeled down the long driveway through a tunnel of palm trees and pulled up to the front entrance.

Valet parking attendants were scurrying between large potted plants on marble steps, shuttling luggage to and from Mercedes, Ferraris and BMWs. An attendant walked up to Woody's car and opened the door. "Checking in sir?"

"Yeah." Woody stepped out.

"Do you have luggage I can help you with?" The young man observed the contents of the car and smelled something burning.

Woody checked out the sharply dressed, clean-cut young man. "I'll probably need everything."

The man looked at Woody like he had his pants on backwards. "Everything, sir?"

"I haven't decided what I'm wearing for dinner. Leave the stuff in the trunk, bring the rest in. I'll take the guitar." When Woody pulled his guitar out, a small pile of clothes fell on the ground. He saw the expression on the attendant's face and gave him a ten-dollar bill.

The lobby was an expansive glass arboretum filled with ferns, high-backed wicker furniture and beautiful, tanned men and women lounging around with tennis racquets propped against their chairs. "Can I help you sir?" The man behind the reservation desk was dressed like an Egyptian military officer in a white jacket with gold buttons.

161

"I'd like a room."

"Do have a reservation?"

"No."

"How many people are in your party?"

"Two, I hope."

The man sized up Woody. "And how many nights will you be staying with us?"

"How much are the rooms?"

"Let's have a look." He scanned an open reservation book. "We have a standard room available for two-fifty-five per night, a standard with bay view for three hundred, a standard suite with kitchenette and Jacuzzi for three-fifty and our four-room Bjorn Borg suite with private tennis court and personal tennis pro for seven-fifty per night."

"How much for just a shower and a tennis pro?"

"I beg your pardon?"

"Just kidding. How much is your cheapest room?"

"Two-fifty-five for our standard room with king-size bed and garden view. All of our rooms include complimentary breakfast, mini-bar, use of our swimming pool, golf course, spa, gym and tennis courts."

"Do you have a recording studio?"

"I'm sorry. You're inquiring about –"

"How much for the room with a hot tub?"

"That would be our standard suite for three-fifty per night, including bay view and private verandah. "

"That's the cheapest room you have with a hot tub?"

"Yes sir."

Woody pictured himself with Stephanie in a private hot tub, sipping champagne. But $350 a night? "The room with the hot tub has a kitchen?"

"Yes sir."

He could save money if he had a room with a kitchen. What else was he going to do, show up like a bum and stay in the spare bedroom with one thin wall separating them from Max and

Auddie's bedroom? And then, in the morning, having to hang around drinking coffee, wondering if they'd heard anything. "I'll take the room with the hot tub."

"How many nights will you be staying with us?"

"One."

When the man pressed him for a credit card, Woody flashed his wad of cash and put a thousand dollars on the counter. A bellhop appeared, a lanky young olive-skinned man who looked like he'd out-grown his uniform, long arms hanging past the sleeves of his white jacket. He picked up Woody's guitar. "Your suite is on the second floor of the west wing. This way, please."

They walked outside on a stone path lined with tropical plants. "Are you here on business or pleasure sir?" the bellhop asked.

"Pleasure," Woody said. "Strictly pleasure." He held out his hand, the bellhop slapped it and his formal stride shifted to a soul-brother slide. "Name's Henry. Haven't seen you here before."

"I just kind of landed here, trying to impress my girlfriend."

"Some of the staff at this place is a little stiff. Let me know if you need help cutting through the attitude. Call the concierge any time and ask for Helpful Henry."

They arrived at Woody's suite and Henry started moving around the rooms, using his long arms like a Harlem Globe Trotter, adjusting lights, curtains, air conditioner, hot tub jets. "Cold beer?"

"Sure."

Henry opened a bottle of Heineken from the mini-bar, poured a glass, grabbed a bag of peanuts, pretzels and a banana and juggled the three items, keeping them all in the air at once. He spun a 360, caught them, put them by the beer and took a perfectly rolled joint out of his pocket. "*Accoutrement, Monsieur?*"

"Merci beaucoup," Woody said.

Henry took a small ashtray out of his pocket, set it on the table, held the joint in the palm of his hand and slapped his forearm. The joint spun in the air and landed in a propped-up position in the ashtray. He pulled out a pack of matches and set it next to the ashtray. Woody gave him ten dollars, slapped him five and Henry slipped out the door.

Woody wandered around checking out the bathroom full of lotions, mini-bar, two TV's, three telephones and a complimentary bottle of champagne. When he saw the king-size bed with frilly pillows and a pair of chocolate truffles, he immediately wanted to call Stephanie. It'd only been an hour since he'd talked to Auddie. He'd show a little patience, present himself as a new man, with some money in his pocket, money from his music.

He took a shower and brought his guitar out on the verandah. Strumming a chord progression, he looked for a melody to put over it and surprised himself with how easily the musical ideas flowed. It could be like this from now on, he thought, sitting in luxury, writing songs. Between him and the water was a virtual sea of tennis courts. Playing his guitar, listening to the soft boinging of tennis balls, Woody thought of using the sound as a percussion track on his next recording.

"You're staying at The Bayside Inn?" Stephanie said in disbelief. "That place in Tiburon?"

"I'll explain everything when I see you. C'mon over."

"I've got a dance rehearsal this evening. Maybe we could meet for breakfast."

"I've got this nice place for one night and… I was really hoping to see you."

She took the extra time to answer, as she often did. Woody knew to wait. "I wasn't expecting you and I'm always tired after rehearsal. I'd prefer to see you tomorrow."

This is the time to be cool, he thought. *$350… the price of love.* "I'll keep my room another day, come over in the morning."

"But it must be so expensive."

"Just come over in the morning, I'll be here. I can't wait to see you."

"You sound good Woody. You sound calm."

"I love the way you say the L in calm."

"Woody." She sounded serious. "The last times we were together, you really scared me. You smashed your guitar and I felt like I didn't know you, like you could've hurt me. I'd had that encounter with those men on the sidewalk and then to have you act so violently…"

"I just flipped out for a minute. I was really uptight about your job and I'd had a bunch of tequila… I never drink tequila. I just lost it for a second."

"Woody?" she said softly.

"Yeah?"

"It's not okay to act like that, ever. You really scared me."

"It'll never happen again."

Woody took his guitar back out on the balcony, played to the moonlit bay and the musical ideas flowed. He'd often considered the mystery of the creative process and how, for many great artists, living in emotional pain seemed to spark their creativity. The theory was that you've got to live the blues to play the blues. Woody didn't buy it. Sitting on the balcony of a luxury hotel; that's what sparked his creativity, not trying to write a song with his landlord pounding on his door.

He leaned back in the padded lounge chair and watched an ultra-slow procession of moonlit ripples in the bay appear out of the black void. When their white edge first came into view, the small waves seemed stationary. Then, almost imperceptibly, they made their deliberate progress towards shore.

When Woody walked into the living room the next morning, his heart sank. All his things from his car were piled by the door, as if the squalor followed him wherever he went. He picked up the phone. "I need a maid."

"Our maid service occurs in the West Wing at eleven a.m."

"Tell the maid I've got a big tip waiting for her."

"I'll send someone right up."

Fifteen minutes later, a pretty young Latina girl knocked softly on the door. Woody let her in.

"*Hola.*" The girl stopped just inside the doorway

"What's your name?"

She smiled.

Woody searched his memory for the words. "*Como te llamas?*"

"Sunita."

"*Como estas?*" Woody said.

"*Yo estoy muy bien. Hay algo que puedo ayudar a limpiar Senor?*"

He stared at her. He'd used up all his Spanish. "Here's the deal." He waved at the pile. "My girlfriend's going to show up soon and I want to get these clothes folded and put away and everything cleaned up and... want to sit down for a minute?" Woody gestured to an armchair. She sat down and looked at the floor.

"Like I was saying, I haven't seen my girlfriend for a while. I think she's tired of me being scatterbrained and I've got all this stuff like it follows me wherever I go."

Sunita sat stiffly, hands folded in her lap.

"You don't understand a word I'm saying, do you?"

She looked back at the floor.

"I guess it's like music, the emotion comes through."

"*Yo no entiendo nada de lo que estas diciendo.*"

Woody shrugged. "I don't understand you, you don't understand me and I'm blathering on because I'm so nervous that if I blow it this time I... I've realized how important the important stuff is and I want her to see that, not all this *stuff*. I'm trying to simplify my life, maybe even demonstrate a little progress in that direction. I could say anything and you'd just smile."

She smiled.

Woody took out his wallet and produced a photograph of Stephanie. "This is who all this blabbing is about." He rocked the little photo back and forth and mimicked a high-pitched woman's voice. "Hi. My name's Stephanie. I stopped by your hotel room, but there was so much junk everywhere, I thought I'd accidentally gone to the dump and I left."

She looked up, looked past him, and her smile disappeared. Stephanie was standing in the doorway.

Woody waited, not sure how Stephanie would react. With a stern look, she held the tension for as long as she could, then burst out laughing. It took him a moment to get it, then he started laughing himself. When Sunita, totally confused, eventually burst out laughing, Woody and Stephanie became hysterical.

Sunita stood up, picked up the photo of Stephanie that Woody had dropped on the carpet, rocked it back and forth, said something in Spanish, and the three of them stood in a circle, bent over at the waist, laughing until they were crying.

Chapter 22

Sunlight streaming through the panoramic windows, Jeff Pearlman looked around his office at the staff he'd called in. "Let's get this meeting started. Holly? Where are we on this?"

"We've received responses from CBS, Arista, Polygram and Warner Brothers." Holly read from her notes. "They're all interested. They all want to hear more."

"And we can't find Woody." Pearlman ran his hands through his hair in frustration. "I can't believe the guy would push his way in here the way he did, then we don't hear from him. Maria? You have something?"

"Before we go any further; I recently had a meeting with Ray Bell." Maria's face was void of expression. "Ray claims he wrote the song "Stephanie.""

"What?"

"Ray Bell is adamant that he wrote the music and lyrics and that the song is copyrighted in his name. He claims he and Woody both knew a topless dancer named Stephanie. Apparently Woody struck up a relationship with her and couldn't accept the fact that someone else had written a song about her. I'm told that Woody has some serious psychological problems and that he –"

"Bell didn't write that song!" Pearlman put his hands on his hips. "He's not capable of writing a song like that. When you hear Woody sing it, he owns it, there's no question." He hit the intercom button. "Brenda. Come in here please."

Brenda didn't acknowledge anyone except Pearlman when she walked in. She knew who was there; she'd made the arrangements for the meeting herself.

Pearlman motioned her to a seat. Brenda remained standing.

"You remember that fellow Woody." It was more an accusation than a question.

"The guy that was so crazy I called security?"

"Do you know how to get in touch with him?"

"I think Holly talked to him." She didn't look at Holly, sitting a few feet away.

"I spoke with him once," Holly said. "He was calling from an out-of-state public telephone. We were disconnected and he didn't call back. I tried calling his home phone, but it was disconnected. Our investigator reports that he's moved with no forwarding address."

"Has he cashed the check we sent him?" Pearlman asked.

Holly shook her head. "We sent him the check over a month ago. According to our bank statement from a week ago, the check hasn't been cashed."

Pearlman paced back and forth with his arms folded across his chest. "I can't believe I can meet with a guy in my office, do a recording session with him at The Palace, and we can't figure out how to get in touch with him. You didn't do an intake sheet, Brenda?"

"The first time he came to the office, he just barged in." Brenda insisted. "He's called here a couple of times, but when I ask him to hold on to transfer him or take a message, he just hangs up. He's never once left a callback number. When he first came in he was acting very strange, stalking around the waiting room. He used the waiting-room phone to harass me. I thought he could be dangerous.

I don't know what you expect me to do when someone acts like that."

Pearlman stopped pacing and dropped his hands to his sides. "I worked with him in the studio, the guy's harmless. Artists aren't normal people, Brenda. They're our natural resource and they require special handling. No one's going to walk in here all proper and punctual like it's a dentist's office."

"But he was acting so crazy."

"Brenda! If we didn't deal with crazy artists we wouldn't have *one* client. Vincent Van Gogh could come in with his ear cut off and you'd probably put him on hold! Receptionists are easy to replace, great artists aren't. Now why don't you get back to work and figure out how to get in touch with Woody!"

There was a tense silence after Brenda left. "Mr. Pearlman, if I may," Maria ventured, "it doesn't matter how great a musician Woody is if we can't find him. We could resolve this matter by recording the song with Ray Bell. He claims to have composed the song and after interviewing him, I believe he did. His voice is perfectly suited for it and he'll do a professional job. Program directors all over the country will be interested to hear something new from Bell. He's a known, proven commodity. And we'll be in a perfect position to put a lien on his royalties and get his past debt paid."

"Ray does have a compelling voice," Bruce offered, spinning a thick silver earring. "I can understand why the young girls buy his records."

Ignoring the comment, Pearlman suddenly slapped his desk with his open hand. "You'd expect a guy like Woody to be calling here ten times a day!"

"Excuse me, Mr. Pearlman," Holly said. "You asked me to remind you not to get worked up over office matters. Your doctor says you shouldn't even be working. And if I can add my two cents, that fellow Woody does seem quite unreliable. He's certainly caused a lot of disruption around here in the short time we've tried working with him. Right now you have over twenty calls waiting to be returned from some very talented songwriters who, by the way, all have addresses and phone numbers. I would also like to say that, from experiences too numerous to mention, all of us here are painfully aware that the idiosyncrasies of a potentially great artist can often overshadow the artistic process and make it impossible to actually get anything done."

Pearlman leaned back in his big chair and sighed.

Maria sensed the energy shifting. "When you balance all the considerations, and the fact that the song is legally copyrighted in Bell's name, the option with the least risk and highest economic potential would be to record the song with a professional like Bell and use our resources most effectively to achieve the greatest return on our –"

"When the paramedics arrived I was lying right here on the floor." Pearlman began talking while Maria was still talking. She let her sentence trail off. He spoke softly, looking into the middle distance. "I was under my desk, on my back, with four calls on hold, every one of them urgent. Calls about the world's greatest new band or some prima-donna rock star keeping twenty thousand fans waiting in the hot sun because there weren't enough blue M&M's in the dressing room… and I couldn't breathe. Right then I would've traded all the ticket sales and record royalties in the world for one deep breath."

He took a long, slow breath while everyone remained quiet.

"I imagined that I was under water, an inch from the surface, reaching for air. Then everything went black and when I woke up I was looking down at myself, my heart stopped, the paramedics going crazy, the phone on the floor with the reflection of the blinking lights bouncing off my face… I actually watched myself die."

Pearlman looked at Maria. "I don't give a shit about the highest return with the least risk."

Maria kept her eyes on the legal pad in her lap.

"Maria, I'm talking to all of you!"

171

She snapped her head up and her face turned red, incredulous that he'd talk to her like that in front of the others.

Pearlman looked at everyone in the room individually. "You all know Ray Bell. You all know he's not capable of writing a song like 'Stephanie'. He didn't write his last hit song. I hired someone to write it for him. Of the twelve songs on his album, he only wrote one, the worst one, 'I Wanna Be On You.'" Pearlman shook his head. "What an idiotic song. If we can't find Woody, I won't work on the project. Meeting adjourned."

Chapter 23

"Pierce and Pearlman, how may I direct your call?"

"Hi Brenda, it's Ray. Been getting any phone calls?"

"I got this one, but I know you're not calling for *me*. "

"I've actually been thinking about you, Brenda. Want to go out for dinner sometime?"

"Sometime?"

"This week?"

"You mean for the whole week?"

"You know what I mean, Brenda. How about Thursday? You know Alfredo's, that Italian place down the street from your office?"

"Alfredo's? Really?"

"Seven o'clock?"

"Hold on a sec." Brenda answered another call and put it on hold. "I have to be at work early the next morning, but I've always wanted to go to Alfredo's. I walk by it every day."

"Is Pearlman still out sick?" Ray asked.

"He comes in once in a while. Sorry Ray, but it's crazy here today. You calling for Maria?"

"You mean there's a lawyer that's not in a meeting or on the phone?"

"Thursday at seven?"

"Thursday?"

"Alfredo's?"

"See you Thursday."

"Hello Ray, thank you for returning my call."

"Hi, Maria. Did you decide you'd rather go out dancing than go to court?"

"Actually, I've got a business proposition I'd like to discuss with you."

"I'm all ears."

"I'd prefer to discuss it with you in person."

"I'll come over, when's good?"

"I'd prefer to meet with you out of the office," she said. "Would you like to talk over lunch?"

"Sure."

"Does two o'clock this Thursday work for you?"

"Sure."

"Do you know Alfredo's, two blocks east of my office?"

"I know the place. Do I need to bring anything?"

"Just your charming self."

At two o'clock on Thursday, Alfredo's, an exclusive reservations-only Italian restaurant, was filled to capacity. Crowded with power-lunchers, it was open to the public, but was actually more like a private club. Tourists were lucky to get a reservation a month in advance, regular customers could usually just show up.

Ray arrived late and was shown to a private booth in the back that was made even more private by a maze of straw-wrapped Chianti bottles hanging from the low ceiling. Maria was sitting at a table of brightly colored ceramic tile with a spread of antipasto and a bottle of Pinot Bianco in an ice bucket.

174

When he went to kiss her on the cheek, she leaned away and stuck out her hand. He sat across from her, topped off her glass of wine and poured himself one. They ate antipasto, talked about the music business and Ray felt himself being mesmerized by her dramatic dark eyes and the sharp dimples in her cheeks when she spoke. He knew she was Italian, but with her olive skin, jet-black hair and international flair, she could be Indian or even African.

Continually dropping names, Ray talked about his work with this or that musician and the well-known producers he was considering for his next project. They were halfway through the bottle of wine and had ordered salads and pasta when she took a thick document out of a soft leather briefcase next to her on the seat and slid it across the table: PERSONAL MANAGEMENT AND LEGAL REPRESENTATION AGREEMENT.

"Here's my business proposal." She put her hand on top of the document and left it there. "I'm leaving Jeff Pearlman's office and going out on my own. I heard a recording of the song 'Stephanie' with Woody singing. It's an exceptional song. He sings it well, but it would be perfect for your voice. You composed the song, is that correct?"

Ray looked her straight in the eyes. "I wrote it. It's my song."

"Do you have any recordings of you singing it?"

"Not yet, but I can sing it for you right now." He leaned toward her and broke into a soft chorus of "Stephanie," singing the melody with expert restraint. She looked around, obviously uncomfortable. He sang one chorus and held up his glass. "To Stephanie."

In the ten seconds of quiet singing, she could hear what a strong hook the song had, and how resonant Ray's voice sounded on it. It took her a minute to regain her composure. "I'm quite serious about exploiting the potential of that song with your voice, but only if the authorship is clear. If we come to an agreement, I expect to participate in the publishing and the last thing I'd want for either of us is to have some itinerant musician claiming authorship."

"Woody's never gotten it together to publish one song. The guy

175

plays on the street. He knows I wrote the song. We'll never hear from that space cadet."

"My hunch is that we *will* hear from him and I want to be prepared for that eventuality."

The food arrived. Interspersing Italian with broken English, the flashy waiter seasoned their dishes with black pepper and grated Parmesan and brought them another bottle of white wine, *Bianchello del Metauro,* compliments of the chef, who was a Ray Bell fan.

They ate and drank while Maria not so subtly suggested that Ray's stature in the music business was wavering and that effective management was the key to his future. They agreed that the timing of using this song to rejuvenate his career would be perfect. She told him Jeff Pearlman had lost his drive since his heart attack and she was going out on her own with clients that had the potential to break through conventional entertainment barriers. Her concept was to create multimedia crossovers that included film, TV, advertising and corporate branding. Ray would be performing at Ray Bell Stadium, schmoozing at Ray Bell Steak Houses, there'd be Ray Bell casual wear, Ray Bell surfboards... all this going on while he cranked out one mega-hit after another.

As they made their way through the second bottle of wine, Ray was surprised at how cool and clear she remained. He noticed that she'd ordered the most pricey things on the menu, but had barely touched her food.

She talked about how his camera-friendly good looks could potentially take him beyond pop singing into acting and film, but the first critical step was to score another hit song. Through contacts at Pearlman's office she'd developed a relationship with the president of A&M Records. A&M was instituting a fast-track album release program for their top recording artists. They'd bring an artist into their in-house studio, record an album, focus on one song, and prepare it for national airplay and distribution in twelve weeks, strategically coordinated with People/Rolling Stone/Time Magazine stories, merchandising and tour support. Everything was in place.

"A&M also has a top notch staff of songwriters." Maria kept her eyes on him. "We can work with them for future songs."

Ray let the comment go, his mind spinning from all the alcohol and heady conversation, He reached for the French Press of coffee the waiter had brought and accidentally spilled coffee on the corner of the management contract. "Let's get this out of the way." He wiped it off with his red cloth napkin and flipped to the back page. Under the signature line it said Ray Bellini aka Ray Bell. "I haven't used Bellini in years. You must've done your homework."

"I probably know more about you than you do."

Ray shrugged. "So who should sign the contract, Bell or Bellini?"

"Ray Bell is fine."

He signed it with a dramatic gesture and tossed it onto the seat next to her.

"You might want to consult another attorney before signing it," she told him. "At the very least, you should read it."

"If the partnership works, we'll both want to keep doing it. If it doesn't, neither of us will. It definitely won't work if we don't trust each other." He picked up his wine glass and noticed that she'd switched from wine to Perrier. "Here's to trust."

She clicked his wine glass with her water glass, took the contract off the seat and opened it to a publishing sharing clause. "Please read this paragraph and put your initials next to it. There's also a place for your initials at the bottom of every page." She watched him quickly go through it. "I'd like you to keep this to yourself until I've properly severed my business ties with Pearlman's office. In fact, it's imperative."

"Let's talk about something besides business." He initialed the last page, slapped the document closed and tossed it again, Frisbee-style, onto the bench. "When's your birthday? I'll bet you're a Scorpio."

She picked up the contract. "Gemini. One last thing, I promise." She turned to an addendum page entitled AUTHORSHIP RIGHTS AND LIABILITES. It stated that Ray was representing that he composed the words and music and controlled all rights to the song

"Stephanie." It relieved Maria of any potential liability in case of an authorship dispute and held Ray personally responsible for costs and attorney's fees in the event of litigation on the issue. "Please read this carefully and put your signature and the date under it." While Ray scanned the page, Maria said, "You copyrighted 'Stephanie' just less than month ago, is that correct?"

Ray whipped his head up. "You don't miss a thing, do you?" He took a slug of wine. "I showed Woody the song, saw his jealously trip start to come out, and figured I better get it covered. Then Pearlman offered to record it with Woody playing and me singing and I decided to give it a try. I even offered Woody a chance to get in on the publishing. I was scheduled to sing my song at the Palace in studio D, but they went off and recorded it in another studio. I think the whole thing was a setup to serve me with those papers. Pearlman's being conned by that punk. If you don't trust me, this partnership isn't going to work." Ray refilled his wine glass. "Well?"

She sipped her Perrier, watching him over the rim of the glass. "My personal opinion is that Mr. Pearlman would not intentionally suborn perjury or copyright infringement. However, that recording session occurred just days before he had a major heart attack. He was under enormous pressure at the time, with some very high-profile cases and a superhuman workload. The heart surgeon reports that the flow of blood and oxygen through one of his arteries was almost completely constricted; his judgment may have been impaired. It would have been an ideal time for someone like Woody to mislead him. And now; Mr. Pearlman's ability, or even desire to work at full capacity is questionable."

The meal never regained its congenial mood. She paid for lunch and, standing in front of the restaurant in a light rain, Ray had just put his hand on her arm and suggested they go back to his apartment for a celebration drink when she turned and spoke briefly to the doorman. Before Ray realized what was happening, she was whisked away in a cab.

Full of pasta and wine, feeling euphoric, Ray chatted with the doorman for a while then walked to the back parking lot, sat down in his black Porsche, reclined his seat, and fell asleep.

When Brenda arrived at Alfredo's at seven, Ray wasn't there. Getting herself a drink, she settled on a couch in the dimly lit bar that was set up like a living room, with Tiffany lamps and Victorian-style furniture. Halfway through her daiquiri, Ray walked in.

"Sorry I'm late." Kissing her on the cheek, he got a much too strong whiff of perfume and noticed that the slit in the side of her dress went almost to her waist. *Brenda's attractive*, he thought, *but in a different way than Maria.* Everything about Maria seemed to have just the right amount of understatement. Brenda had on a little too much makeup, a little too much perfume and her dress was just tight enough to make her look uncomfortable. When she made a comment about him looking like he'd just woken up, he ordered a drink and went back to the restroom he'd just come from and splashed cold water on his face for the second time.

He had two Crown Royals, she had another daiquiri, and they went to the dining room and were seated at the same booth where he and Maria had been a few hours earlier. The same waiter that had served Ray and Maria lunch, all smiles and ultimately discreet, served Ray and Brenda a beautifully prepared dinner of authentic Northern Italian cuisine. He brought them a bottle of *Brunello di Montalcino Reserva* red wine, again compliments of the chef.

From her reception station at one of the most powerful entertainment law firms in the country, Brenda interacted with virtually everyone that mattered in the music industry. She gave Ray all the latest gossip and he told her about the new song he'd written that he was sure would be a huge success. Maria Angelista's name didn't come up once.

As they made their way through the food and wine, Ray summoned his most sincere expression. "You know Brenda, I've been thinking—how would you feel about playing a more active role in my music career?"

Brenda held her forkful of pasta.

"I'm going to need a personal assistant on the road. Someone to keep my schedule together and keep the groupies and music press at bay. I know right now you've got a full-time job with Pearlman, but –"

"I'm already practically a road manager for some of Jeff's clients." Brenda went back to eating her pasta, gushing with excitement. "I've actually been toying with the idea of going into artist management myself." She put a thick layer of butter on her bread and dipped it in her pasta sauce. "Jeff doesn't really appreciate what I do for him. We've had some serious disagreements recently about how the office should be run. Since his heart attack, it's like the office is flying on radar with no pilot."

The third course with entrees arrived and they ate quietly for a minute. "I don't know how well Pearlman knows this guy Woody," Ray said.

Brenda slathered butter on another piece of bread. "People like Woody try to get to Jeff in every way imaginable. My job is to protect him so he can get his work done. And now, with Jeff acting so strange and the office in chaos, the last thing we need is some dysfunctional energy like Woody's. I'm not surprised to hear he'd try to steal your song—he seems pretty desperate. He's nothing but bad news."

When Brenda began extrapolating on ways Ray could modernize his singing in the style of popular country artists, Ray held up his hand. "Enough talk about music business." He got up and moved to her side of the booth.

After dessert and a generous taste of the chef's best Porto, they almost knocked over the table getting up and walked unsteadily to the bar for a nightcap. Standing in front of the couch they'd been sitting in earlier, they kissed lightly and, like the first time they'd sat down, the seat was deeper than they anticipated. Falling back, Ray's hand accidentally on-purpose went through the slit on the side of Brenda's dress and up her thigh. Glancing around the crowded room, he had a moment of pause about being so risqué, but when he felt the moisture on his hand and realized Brenda was wet through her panty hose, his thoughts evaporated.

As if materializing out of thin air, a waitress was suddenly standing directly in front of them. With a goofy grin on his face, Ray moved his hand and Brenda awkwardly straightened out her dress. When they ordered drinks, the waitress asked, "Would either of you care for some coffee?" Ray couldn't bring her face into focus.

With no response forthcoming about the coffee, the waitress left and Ray saw what looked like a blur of other customers looking at him. He abruptly started to stand up, fell back and, with another effort, got to his feet. "Sitting in that seat is like driving into a goddamn ditch. Let's go."

"But didn't we just order drinks?" Brenda protested.

"It's time to go." He extended his hand, hoisted her up, and they made their way to the door.

After working late at the office, Maria and her assistant Bruce left the Transamerica Building and headed toward North Beach, the sidewalk cafes buzzing with activity. They'd gone two blocks when they literally ran into Ray and Brenda stumbling out of Alfredo's, leaning into each other at such an angle that they couldn't have walked that way individually.

All four of them stopped and straightened up, Ray and Brenda rumpled and unsteady, exuding garlic and alcohol fumes, Maria and Bruce's clothes as neat as when they'd arrived at work that morning. Ray moved imperceptibly to the side, away from Brenda. Maria did the same with Bruce.

"Working late?" Maria asked Brenda.

When Brenda started to reply, Ray blurted out a jumbled sentence about Northern Italy and Northern California. He finished the sentence with a mangled pronunciation of "*Brunel di Montalcino Reserva*" and a feeble bit of Italian-opera-style melody.

The icy stare Maria gave Ray was so penetrating, it almost sobered him up. "Glad to see you're doing something creative with your million-dollar voice. Do you eat all your meals at Alfredo's? Goodnight!"

"Pierce and Pearlman, how may I direct your call?"

"Morning, Brenda."

"Ray, is that you? You sound terrible."

"You must've got up pretty early this morning." Ray sounded like he had a throat full of gravel.

"I've been here since eight. You probably don't remember, but I set your alarm so I could get up for work. Last night was really fun, but my head feels like it's going to explode. I haven't had that much to drink in years."

"You should've woken me up. We could've said goodbye properly."

"I did try waking you up. I even figured out how to work your cappuccino machine and brought you one. You were dead to the world and I was late for work. I'm really glad you called, Ray. You said some pretty nice things last night. So, when will I see you again?"

"Real soon. Is Maria around?"

"Maria?"

"She called me this morning."

Without another word, Brenda jammed her index finger into the transfer button on the phone so hard she broke the tip of her fake fingernail.

"Thanks for calling, Ray," Maria said. "I just wanted to give you an update. I spoke with Marty Levine at A&M today. He's interested in our project, but he wants to hear the song before he'll commit to anything. We need to get him a demo of 'Stephanie' ASAP. It doesn't have to be anything fancy, just something that presents the song with your vocal."

"I'm on it."

Chapter 24

Listening to Woody playing his acoustic guitar on the balcony at the Bayside Mission Inn, Stephanie gazed out at the sailboats and sipped her tea. They'd spent the day making love, taking hot tubs, and ordering room service. When they began talking about ways to integrate his music with her dancing, she saw him looking at the phone.

"You're thinking about calling Jeff Pearlman's office, aren't you?"

"What gave you that idea?"

"When was the last time you called?"

"About a week ago. I don't think Pearlman's back at work yet, his heart attack sounds pretty serious and I doubt anyone else in that office cares about me. Feels like my song stopped when Pearlman's heart stopped. Every time I call there, I'm put on hold, redirected, disconnected, it's impossible. My relationship with Brenda the receptionist started out bad and just gets worse. I wonder if she'd consider going to counseling with me."

Stephanie chuckled. "It sounds like you've left plenty of messages. Be patient. I don't think there's anything else to do but wait to hear from him. We've got this incredible room for one day. Maybe try just being here."

"Be here now? What a concept. I was actually planning on being here later, like maybe in a month from now, when I'm living in my car and thinking about how nice this place was. Has there ever been a receptionist that wasn't a woman?"

"Are you talking about her being a woman, or being a difficult person?" Stephanie stepped over to the balcony, put her leg up on the high railing and began stretching. "There are greater differences between people within a gender than between the genders. They take the crying baby boys the minute they're born, wrap them in blue blankets and the nurse says, 'Listen to the set of lungs on that guy, he knows how to get what he wants.' They take the girls, wrap them in pink and say, 'Listen to the poor thing, there must be something wrong.' Babies all come out crying, the color of their blankets and everything else they experience sets their self-image from birth."

"You're saying there aren't genetic differences between males and females?"

"They're two sides of the same thing, Yin Yang." Stephanie went into a deep stretch until her upper body was flat on her extended leg, long red hair draping over her knee in a cascade of curls. "We're all part of a grand design that's in beautiful balance. We just need to stop trying to be in control and let things happen naturally."

Woody was struck by the natural grace of her lithe body.

"Let's enjoy our time here in this beautiful place." She slowly came out of the stretch.

Woody looked past her, out at the bay. "All I really want is to be with you and write music. I don't care about all the glitz and gigs. I don't even care about the money, just you and music."

"Why not find a simpler way to make money, just play for the enjoyment of playing? Why do you need an audience?"

Woody thought for a moment. "I think it has something to do with why you can't tickle yourself."

Stephanie raised her eyebrows and suddenly reached over and

started tickling him. They wrestled and laughed, then sat back in their chairs. Woody poured himself some tea. "Here's to Stephanie."

"To Stephanie," Stephanie said, "the world's sweetest love song."

They sat in silence, watching the dramatic sunset, bold slashes of crimson, like mercurochrome poured on a powder-blue sky. "When you're content with your life," she said, "even for a day, or an hour, you're a model of equanimity. You're in the moment. You watch the sunset with the same focus as when you're playing music. And when you're making love to me, I can tell when you're distracted and when you're not. Today's been wonderful."

"I keep thinking the reason we're here is because of that song," Woody said. "If I find a way to get it out there, and write more, we could live like this forever."

She gestured at the sunset. "It's happening right now. Your music's too good to not be heard. A man with a lot of experience in the music business heard your song and gave you five thousand dollars. Try being more kind to yourself."

Woody picked up his teacup. "My cup's half empty."

She picked up hers. "Mine's half full."

He furrowed his brow. "How come you always have more than me?"

The bedroom was tastefully decorated with rattan furniture and Gauguin-style oil paintings of Polynesian women carrying baskets of fruit. They went in, flopped down on the bed, made love for the third time that day and lay on their backs watching the shadows of the ceiling fan.

"I left my birth control pills in Daly City," Stephanie said.

"Will you marry me?"

Stephanie watched the fan and said nothing.

"We could have one of those silent Buddhist weddings."

More silence.

"We could have a silent marriage."

"Let's get our own lives together so we're both doing what we want," Stephanie said. "The happier we are individually, the stronger our relationship will be."

185

"I didn't exactly understand the answer. Should I repeat the question?"

"The answer is, for now, let's be patient and stay open to what the universe brings." She rolled over and faced him. "I don't ever want to be in a place where I have to choose between you and happiness, because I'm afraid I might choose you." She pushed the hair back from his face. "I keep thinking that if we do this right, I might not have to choose."

"Let's go down to the dining room and have dinner," Woody suggested. "We'll celebrate the mystery of life."

"You're already spending a fortune staying here. We've got our own little kitchen. We could go to the store and bring something back."

"Let me take you downstairs for dinner."

"Well, I do have a nice dress in my car that Auddie insisted on buying me. But we'll probably need a reservation. All the beautiful people in Marin County come here for dinner."

"I've got connections." Woody called the dining room. There was a two-hour wait. He called the concierge. "Henry? I need a table for two at the restaurant. They're booked up."

"Not for my main man. Hold on a sec… table for two in twenty minutes. I don't suppose you have a sport coat? You need one to get in."

"I left mine home."

"Gotcha covered. See me in the lobby."

Stephanie took a shower and came out of the bathroom with her hair piled in a cluster of auburn swirls, a mid-length black silk dress that clung to every curve on her body and the dangling turquoise earrings Woody had given her early in their relationship. Woody was still in bed, sitting up playing his guitar.

"I think I'll take a walk and look at some of the beautiful artwork they have in the lobby," she said. "See you down there."

"When I see you in the lobby, act like you don't know me."

"What?"

"Just act like you never met me before, but whatever I do, be real friendly. I want to play a little trick on somebody."

"Sir, are you talking to me?" She curtsied and walked out.

Woody always felt frumpy next to Stephanie's natural elegance. He dug through his crumpled clothes trying to find something presentable, settled for his cleanest T-shirt and jeans and headed to the lobby.

"Check it out, brother." Henry held up a black cashmere sport jacket. It fit Woody perfectly, transforming him from hippy to hip entrepreneur, his unruly blonde curls a dramatic contrast to the finely tailored, jet-black dinner jacket. "Cash-meer. The ladies love it." Henry ran the back of his hand down Woody's lapel. "I got you a nice table by the fountain."

"My date stood me up," Woody said.

"Bummer. Especially now that you're looking so sharp."

"I'll just have to find a replacement," Woody said. "I can't let these cool threads go to waste. Hey, Henry, check *her* out." Stephanie was standing close by with her back to them, admiring a naturally pink, life-size alabaster stone sculpture of a woman in a flowing evening gown.

"Ooowweee." Henry turned the word into a soft, high-pitched whistle. Woody looked to see if Henry actually had a whistle in his mouth. "Now there's something that would go nice with dinner."

"Let's see what this cashmere can do." Woody took a step toward Stephanie.

Henry grabbed his sleeve. "Where you going brother?"

"To get a date for dinner."

Henry tightened his grip on Woody's sleeve. "Dig it man, let me fill you in on the scene here. These ladies come here in Ferraris and helicopters with the richest guys in San Francisco. They spend two hundred dollars on a haircut for their poodle. They think they own the world..." he paused for effect, "... and they do. Trust me, you don't want to mess with them."

"I know what these women want." Woody gently removed Henry's hand from his sleeve. "Those rich guys are always negotiating. That's how they got rich. Their women are starved for a direct approach."

"I mean it," Henry said in a low urgent voice. "You gotta watch your step around here. You don't get the power trip these people are on."

"Bet me another joint she has dinner with me." Woody winked at him and went over to Stephanie, now a few feet away, admiring an original Andrew Wyeth painting.

Standing beside her, his eyes on the painting, he said, "Andrew Wyeth said he did most of his work just *dreaming* about painting."

She looked over at him "Oh, hi. You startled me."

"Sorry. You look like a work of art yourself. My name's Woody."

"I'm Stephanie."

"I don't really know what I like," Woody said, "but I know about art."

She did her best to not burst out laughing and looked at him like he'd said something profound. "I've heard that Andrew Wyeth paintings were made out of egg yolks."

He furrowed his eyebrows. "I was wondering why this painting was making me so hungry. Want to get some dinner in the restaurant?"

She ran her fingertips up and down his lapel. "Cashmere? From goats?"

"I'm a vegetarian. I don't eat sport coats." He wrapped her hand around his bicep and they walked toward the dining room.

Henry stood with his arms hanging at his sides, his mouth dropped open.

"Henry," Woody said as they walked by him, "be a sport and run up to my room and make sure the hot tub's hot."

Chapter 25

Ray sat at his piano, trying again to learn "Stephanie" from the cassette he and Woody had recorded. He'd finally figured out the verses, but after working for two hours, he still couldn't figure out the chords to the bridge. *How can I record a demo of the song if I can't play it?*

After calling a half-dozen music services advertised in the back of The San Francisco Bay Guardian, he found what he was looking for. The man was an elderly, classically trained piano teacher, working out of his apartment. He offered music transcription services for five dollars a page. It was a place Ray definitely wouldn't be recognized.

The small stuffy apartment smelled like Vicks VapoRub and felt like it was about eighty degrees. There was a grand piano completely covered with stacks of sheet music and there were piles of books everywhere. The frail looking man had on three sweaters, thick bifocals, and a yarmulke. Ray handed him his portable cassette player with fresh batteries and Woody's tape in it.

The man sat on his piano bench and pointed to a wooden chair. Ray watched as he replayed the tape several times, periodically plunking a note on the piano, transcribing the song with a thick black fountain pen. When he was finished, he went back to the top of the first page. "Name?"

Ray hesitated. "My name?"

The man looked at him curiously, holding his pen in place. "The name of the song?"

"'Stephanie.'"

The man handed him the three pages. "It has an interesting bridge. That will be fifteen dollars."

Ray took the sheet music home, copied it over in his own handwriting and wrote at the top of the first page: "*Stephanie*". *Medium Ballad. Music and Lyrics, R. Bell.* He tore up the transcriber's copy and threw it in the trash.

Stephanie left the Bayside Mission Inn early and went to her morning yoga class. Woody slept in, played his guitar on the balcony until checkout time, and stood at the front desk, staring at the hotel bill in disbelief. The party was officially over, back to reality: $700 room charge, state tax, county tax, parking charges, restaurant charges, phone charges, mini-bar, room-service, total: $1,285.

His car had been brought around and was parked at the elegant front entrance. It was filled with all his belongings and idling blue smoke, the bellhop and parking attendant both waiting for their tips.

He drove to the end of the long driveway and considered his options. Things felt great with Stephanie, but being with her right now meant being with Max and Auddie. He could drive back to the city and try to somehow get the recording of his song. If he couldn't get it from Pearlman's office, maybe he could get a copy from the Palace Studio. He wasn't even clear on who actually owned the recording. Then he heard a hissing sound coming from his engine and saw his temperature gauge moving up. He took the note out of his pocket that Stephanie left that morning.

Thanks for the wonderful time. I have my own room at Max and Auddie's.

Come visit if you like. Love, S.

"I'll have the turtle soup, and make it snappy," Woody said into the gray metal speaker-box at the gate to Max and Auddie's apartment complex.

"Who's there?" Auddie said.

"It's Woody. This speaker looks like one of those fast-food drive-up thingies. Is Stephanie around?"

"She should be back soon. Would you like to come in and wait?"

Auddie served Woody ice tea and they sat at the kitchen table making small talk, both of them uncomfortable. It'd been six months since the last time he and Stephanie had come up for a visit. It looked to her as if Woody hadn't cut his hair, and maybe hadn't even washed it, since then.

While they talked in generalities about the difference between living in Marin and living in the city, Woody fidgeted with the little paper umbrella she'd put in his drink. "I've always wondered what the significance was of these little umbrellas."

"They don't really make much sense, do they?" Auddie shrugged. There was an awkward silence. "So why do you use 'em?"

"You sum?"

"Use *them*."

"Use what?"

"The umbrellas. I never put one in a drink myself, but I thought if anybody knew anything about the subject, it might be someone that used them at home, on their own volition or whatever."

Auddie shrugged again. "To tell you the truth, I've never really thought about it. I guess they're just for decoration, or maybe they shade the ice when you drink outdoors."

Woody suddenly got up and stood behind his chair. "Excuse me a minute." He walked down the hallway to the bathroom.

When he closed the door, his attention landed on a rectangular, aluminum-framed window above the shower stall. It reminded him of a similar rectangle he'd seen on the page of a magazine with the caption: "USING BUTTER SMUGGLED FROM THE KITCHEN,

191

INMATE ESCAPES THROUGH A WINDOW EXACTLY THIS SIZE." There was a bottle of liquid soap on the sink, and Woody pictured himself naked and lubed, stuck halfway through the window, Auddie coming in to see what happened and checking out the dangling view from below. He smiled to himself, closed the lid on the toilet, sat down and began looking through Max's New Yorker magazines.

After ten minutes, he knew it was weird. After fifteen, he knew Auddie was wondering if he was doing drugs in the bathroom. After twenty minutes he heard a faint knock on the door. "Woody? Are you all right?"

"I'm fine, Auddie. I'll be right out."

When Woody came out of the bathroom, Auddie was chopping vegetables, listening to Flamenco music and talking on the phone. He went to the living room and sat at Max's state-of-the-art computerized chess set. Black and silver stainless steel pieces stood on a custom metal tabletop, half the pieces off to one side. He moved a silver pawn to see how the position would look, a beep sounded, and the machine magnetically slid a black bishop across the board, captured the pawn and shuttled it off.

Max walked in the front door. "Woody, how're you doing boy? Don't mess up my game." He kissed Auddie on the cheek and went over to the chess table. Woody had replaced the pawn and was trying to activate the move-back function.

"Don't worry about it. I've got this computer figured out."

"You can beat the computer?" Woody raised his eyebrows.

"I just move my knight back and forth between the same two squares for the first few moves. It doesn't make sense, nobody would ever do it. The computer searches a billion games and gets totally confused. Let's play one."

Woody played white, a queenside bishop's pawn opening which he knew very little about, but figured Max wouldn't know about it either. He was right. Max countered with tricks he used against a traditional king's pawn opening, none of them worked and they slogged their way into the middle game.

"Max, Stephanie will be back soon," Auddie said. "Why don't you open some wine to have with dinner?" She saw the gleam in Max's eye and knew he was already mentally tasting options, always looking for an excuse to open a good bottle.

He went deep into his collection and uncorked a vertical selection, 1961 through 1963, of his Chateau Haut Brion first growth Bordeaux. He poured a glass for Auddie and brought four glasses to the chess table. In between moves, he went on about the polished veneer of the '61, the nervousness of the '62, and the chewy ratatouille of the '63. Max was so enamored with the legs on the 1961, he got out his stop watch and he and Woody measured the length of time the taste from one sip lingered on their tongues, a record breaking finish of forty-four seconds.

Stephanie arrived, dressed in a dance leotard and gave hugs all around. "I was hoping you'd come over," she told Woody. "Have these guys been treating you okay?"

"Beatings will continue until morale improves. Max isn't being very nice to my queen."

When Stephanie came back from taking a shower, Max and Woody were still hunched over the board.

"Dinner's ready," Auddie called across the room. They didn't respond.

"Max?"

No answer.

"Max, I went to the doctor today. I'm pregnant."

"Five minutes," Max said.

Fifteen minutes later, Stephanie brought the guys two plates of food and she and Auddie ate dinner in the kitchen. Stephanie talked about Woody's ambition as a songwriter and her own aspirations for a dancing career and someday, a family.

Auddie was an excellent listener. "That reminds me," she said. "I recently came across that letter you wrote after your first semester at college." She put on her reading glasses and took a piece of notebook paper from her purse.

Reading the letter shoulder to shoulder, Auddie and Stephanie looked like mother and daughter, the color of their hair almost identical auburn red, with a touch of gray in Auddie's.

Dear Aunt Auddie and Uncle Max

Greetings from college. Oh well, I guess college wasn't exactly what it was cracked up to be.

Sorry I haven't written sooner. I didn't want to tell you this stuff on the phone.

I'm not exactly in college any more. I'm definitely going back, but I dropped out for right now. I met a nice guy and, well, here goes, I'm having a baby. I know it's sooner than we all expected, but I know it'll be fine.

My boyfriend's name is Joe. He's really nice. He's got a room we live in that's right behind a gas station and they told him he can have a job at the station as soon as they have an opening. I just know he'll get it. He's had so many jobs he can do practically anything. In the meantime, I've been using my tuition money for our rent. But that's just for now.

I guess I should tell you, the real reason I haven't written sooner is not because I don't love you. It's because I have a broken arm. Joe accidentally broke my arm. He really didn't mean to, he just had too much to drink. And he absolutely promised to never ever hurt me again. I believe him. Wait until you meet him — he's really nice. And I know he'll be a great father. He's got three other kids, but I haven't met them. He says he really likes them. Anyway, I'm getting my cast off on Thursday and in the meantime, the good news; I've learned to type with my left hand.

Well, Uncle Max and Aunt Auddie, you can relax. None of the above is true. Not one bit of it. But, I did get a D in English and I just wanted to put things in their proper perspective.

I'll see you in two weeks during Spring break.

Love, Stephanie

They burst out laughing, even though they both knew how the

letter ended. Then they shared a heart-felt hug, said goodnight to their guys and went off to their respective bedrooms.

Ray reached across the woman asleep next to him in his king-size bed and answered the phone.

"Ray? It's Maria. I know you worked late in the studio last night. I hope I didn't wake you up."

Ray squinted from the light coming through the curtains. "I had to wake up anyway, to answer the phone."

"Sorry, I'm just excited to get things going. This morning I went to the studio and listened to what you did and personally took a copy to Marty at A&M and played it for him. He loved it. I know it's only a vocal demo with piano, but the song comes through. It accomplished just what we hoped it would. The A&R people are pumped. They want to get you into their studio this week. They've got a band of top session players lined up, everything's falling into place."

Ray reached down and rubbed his bedmate's bare leg. "I'm ready."

"There is one other matter I should apprise you of."

"Maybe I should get a cup of coffee and call you back."

"I'll be brief. Pearlman filed a motion requesting a default judgment in the lawsuit he has against you for breach of contract. I'm not concerned about it. It'll just be a money settlement, and a relatively small one compared to what this song will generate. In the pleadings there's also something about a conflict of interest on my part because I used to work for Pearlman. If necessary, I'll get a friend from law school to sign the papers I prepare. Lawyers do it all the time. We'll delay the litigation with simple stalling tactics, then agree on some compromised settlement. The worst that can happen is that they get a lien on song royalties... an amount that will probably be less than a couple month's income."

"Thanks for the update." Ray looked to be sure the woman lying next to him was still asleep. "Maybe you should come over to my place sometime and we can have a glass of wine and discuss all this."

"Let's get the song recorded." She hung up the phone. *Admit it, girl,* she thought. *Singers have sexy voices.*

Looking around her small apartment, she realized that since taking the job with Pearlman and moving to San Francisco, she hadn't had one visitor. Now, since leaving Pearlman's office, she'd been working from home, spending days *and* nights in her empty apartment.

Her relationship with Bruce was weird. The only place they'd ever had sex was in the office; that was the entirety of their relationship. Now that she'd quit her job, she probably wouldn't see him again, unless one or both of them got really horny.

Thinking about Ray's offer, she knew that socializing with a client on an active case was taboo. And Ray was so shallow and egotistical, it was a waste of time even thinking about it. She reached for the thick book on her desk, *Federal Copyright Protection and Derivative Works.*

Max and Woody's chess game ended in a draw at midnight, a pawn and a rook each. They sat back and considered the final positions. "Want a hit of pot, for medical purposes?" Max asked.

"For medical purposes." Woody knew that, as a physician, Max had been one of the first to espouse the medical benefits of marijuana. He also knew that whenever Max smoked, he got on his soapbox about it.

Max took his custom glass pipe and stirred the resin in the bowl with a pipe-cleaning tool. He liked doing things in a big way; he had a loud voice, ate a lot, drank a lot and took big hits on the pipe. "Pot's good for so many ailments, one plant can heal a village." He lit up. "I think of it like any nutrient. No vitamin C, you get scurvy and your teeth fall out; no vitamin D, you get rickets, no THC, people's cognition systems arc and they wage wars." He refilled the pipe. "Psychoactive drugs are nature's way of protecting herself. Nobody's going to sit on a beach, take some pot or mushrooms, and say, 'There's a good place for an oil well.'" Max expelled a cloud of

196

smoke. "What do *you* think pot does to you?"

"It makes me more honest."

Max's eyes glazed over. "That's it?"

Woody shrugged. "It's more fun falling asleep when you're stoned."

Leaning too far back in his chair, Max almost tipped over backwards and caught himself. "So, what do you and Stephanie have planned for the future?"

The question caught Woody off-guard. "Marlon Brando says plans are for squares."

"You calling me a square?"

"You ever hear of Sitting Bull?"

"I heard of him," Max said. "You know him?"

"He's my mentor for decision making."

Max raised his bushy eyebrows. "What does that mean?"

"There was this hard-charging Sioux warrior who rode all day and night and skidded up to the front of Sitting Bull's teepee with an urgent question about a thousand Indians facing off against an army of white guys. Bull listens to the guy, says he'll be right back and goes inside his teepee. The Hunkpapa Sioux Nation is put on hold, everyone expecting Bull to come out at any moment, and he doesn't come out until the next morning." Woody paused.

"So?" Max said.

"So Bull finally emerges from his teepee and says, 'I've eaten on it, I've smoked on it, I've fornicated on it and I've slept on it. Now I have my answer." Woody stood up, gave Max a little bow, and went to Stephanie's bedroom.

Late the next morning, within minutes of each other, Woody and Max emerged from their bedrooms, hung-over, in bathrobes, and nearly collided by the coffee pot Auddie had left warming.

They grunted acknowledgments, Max farted, they both reached for a cup in the dish-rack, bumped shoulders and looked at each other for the first time that morning. Woody's bathrobe had "MAX"

197

embroidered on the front and was way too big. Max's bathrobe said "AUDDIE" and was way too small. Neither of them noticed.

"You go ahead." Woody turned to walk out of the kitchen.

Max grabbed his sleeve. "Rock scissors paper for the first cup."

"Huh?"

"Choose you for the first cup." Max raised his fist and Woody flinched, thinking Max was about to hit him. "Rocks paper scissors," Max said, "rho sham bow."

Holding Woody's sleeve, he demonstrated rock, paper, scissors, with his free hand, then began pumping his fist up and down. "Get ready... here we go... Rho, Sham, Bow!" Max stuck out his flat hand: paper.

Woody stared at Max in bleary-eyed confusion, his right arm in Max's clutch, the other arm dangling at his side. Then, without warning, at the last millisecond, Woody threw scissors with his left hand, two fingers barely protruding from his over-sized bathrobe sleeve. It took Max a few seconds for it to sink in, then he moved his paper-hand forward and stuck it in Woody's scissor-fingers.

"You win, Billy the Kid. Go for it." Max walked over to the chessboard.

Woody poured two cups. "Whaddya take in your coffee?" he called.

"Cream and sugar. I had a move."

"What?"

"It wasn't a stalemate. I had a move. I could've traded rooks."

"You do that, I'll push my pawn, you'll be in check and it's mate in two moves."

Max looked up to see if Woody could see the board from where he was standing. Woody was putting cream in the coffee, his back to the game.

"Hello?"

"It's Maria. Ray, I heard the recording you did with the band. 'Stephanie' is going to be a hit. It's rough, of course, but with post-production and a good mix, it's going to shine. Marty's publicist is setting up advance telephone interviews with Billboard, Melody Maker, and Creem. They'll have artwork for us to review in two weeks. We're hoping for a release date in four to five weeks."

"We still need to remix the rest of the album."

"We'll get it done, Ray. As I've said, the rest of the album is filler. All our energy is going into "Stephanie.""

Woody walked around the little town of Mill Valley, waiting for Stephanie to get out of her dance rehearsal. There was something comfortable and relaxing about the rural enclave of boutique shops and bookstores, where entrepreneurs and hippies who could afford to, went to get away from the city. At the base of serene Mount Tamalpais, the tall redwoods and quiet streets were a welcome relief from the intense urban energy Woody felt just walking out of his apartment on Ashbury Street.

Settling himself on a bench in front of a coffee shop, he opened his guitar case and had just started playing when an old Volkswagen bus loaded with lumber parked across the street. Plywood was tied on the roof and 2x4's stuck out the rear door. A rotund middle-aged man in a colorful Hawaiian shirt climbed out and started carrying boards behind a hardware store. The man had such a broad smile on his face, Woody assumed he'd just shared a joke with someone around back and was still smiling from a good laugh. But the man continued to smile while he dealt with the cumbersome pieces of wood. The bus was half unloaded when Woody packed up his guitar and walked over to help.

Without a word, he took some boards out of the back of the van and was walking in when the man was walking out. The man kept smiling and kept working. They worked for twenty minutes without speaking, evenly paced, passing each other in the same place on the sidewalk. Woody realized he was keeping a smile on his own face. When they finished, the man stuck out his hand.

"My name's Orbit. Thanks for the help." Taking out a little

broom, he swept out the bus and Woody noticed how neat and clean it was inside.

"What are you doing with all that lumber?" Woody asked.

"I found it in a dumpster and traded it for some plumbing parts." He nodded at Woody's guitar case. "You play guitar?"

"Yeah."

"If you're looking for a gig, there's a place down the street called The Sweetwater with live music. Thanks again for your help." Orbit got in his bus and drove off.

Woody walked two blocks to The Sweetwater. Touching the money in his pocket, he went in and sat down. Used to being broke, he had to constantly remind himself that he could go into a bar or restaurant and order what he wanted. The place was small but classy, with attractive lighting, a polished wood and brass bar and a stage at the far end of the room. "You have live music here?" he asked the waitress.

"Wednesdays, Thursdays and weekends." She was about twenty-five, with dreadlocks, a ring on every finger and a half-dozen bracelets on each wrist. When she blinked, Woody did a double take and realized he was seeing a minutely detailed face painting of two open eyes on her eyelids.

"How do you get a gig here?" Woody asked.

"As a waitress?"

"As a belly dancer."

The waitress went blank and glanced down at Woody's stomach.

Woody smiled. "As a musician." He nodded toward the stage. "To play here."

She laughed a nervous laugh and snorted on the inhale. The snort embarrassed her and she laughed and snorted again. Woody looked at her with a straight face and did a snort back. They both laughed

"So how do I get a gig?"

"Leave a tape and promo package for Seven. He books the bands.

My boyfriend plays here with Perpetual Vegetable. It's totally cool. They started on Wednesdays and Seven moved them to Thursdays. They'll probably get a weekend pretty soon. That's how it works here, unless you're Bob Dylan."

Woody ordered a beer and realized he was letting his career be held hostage by one version of a song that he could record again anytime. It was time to let go of any expectations he had of Jeff Pearlman.

He quickly finished his beer and drove down the street to Plum Music. Making some quick shopping decisions, he purchased a cassette recorder, two microphones and a pair of headphones; top-quality, professional equipment. It was definitely time to replace the junky tape machine and mics he had at home.

He sat in the parking lot with the recorder and mics on his dashboard, and played and sang. Listening back after each performance, the song got progressively better. The clear, crisp sibilance of his voice and the trebly twang of his guitar strings sounded as good as a commercial recording. Doing multiple takes, he was modifying subtle vocal phrasing when two teenage boys in a four-wheel-drive truck parked next to him. The truck was two feet higher than Woody's car. The teenagers smoked cigarettes and kept their motor idling, the reverberating bass of the truck's exhaust subsuming everything.

Woody was about to leave when, without thinking, he plucked a note and realized that the rumble of the tuned exhaust was in G, the same key as "Stephanie." The concept fascinated him. Repositioning the recorder, he sang right up on it and recorded a complete version of his song. When the truck drove off and he played it back, the rumble of the motor in the background sounded like he'd recorded the song with a rhythm section.

When Woody drove back to the Sweetwater, there was a different waitress. "Is Seven around?"

"No."

"When does he come in?"

"Seven."

Woody looked to see if she was joking. She was wiping off the bar.

"Seven comes in at seven?"

"Yeah."

"I have a tape for him to check out."

"You can leave it with me. There's a ten dollar listening fee and it takes thirty days."

"Ten dollars and thirty days?"

"We get like fifty cassettes a week here. Leave your tape, or go join the Beatles and come back."

Woody waited around until 7:30 and left. He was just getting into his car when he saw a large man with a big white 7 on his black T-shirt coming down the sidewalk at a fast pace.

"Are you the guy that books the Sweetwater?"

"Yeah." Seven had a full blonde beard, a ponytail and was six inches taller than Woody."

"I'm trying to get a gig."

"Leave a tape at the club, I'm late for work." He turned to walk away.

"Listen man, I could really use a gig. In thirty days I could be –"

"Like the sign over my desk says, your lack of planning is not my emergency."

"I have a pair of headphones and an original song right here." Woody reached in his open window and grabbed the recorder off the front seat. "I'll pay you your ten dollar listening fee to listen to one minute of my song. Ten dollars a minute, that's like six hundred dollars an hour."

"Buddy, you should've been a lawyer instead of a musician. I told you what you need to do to get a gig."

Woody held out the recorder. "This recorder cost me over two hundred bucks, brand new today. Press play and listen for one minute. If you don't like the song, you can keep the recorder."

"You are one tenacious motherfucker." There was a half-smile on

202

his face. "I don't want your tape machine. Play me the damn song so I can get to work."

Woody reached up, put the headphones on Seven's big head and pressed play. Seven leaned back against Woody's car. After a few seconds he was tapping his foot. He listened to the whole song.

"That's your song?"

"Yeah."

"You have any more like that?"

"About a hundred."

"You have a band?"

"Almost."

"Can you play solo acoustic?"

"Sure."

"I have a slot on Saturday, nine o'clock, opening for Oblong. Fifty minutes, fifty bucks. You available?"

"Oblong?"

"Oblong Oolong, it's a local rock band. They sell out Saturday nights. Call me if you want to do it." He started to leave.

"I'll do it."

"You have a photo?"

"No."

"A bio?"

"No."

"How about a name?"

"Name?"

"Yeah, you know, like, my name's Seven." He stuck out his hand.

"Woody."

"If you want a sound check, show up by seven." Seven resumed his long strides down the sidewalk.

Calling Stephanie from a phone booth, Woody got Max and Auddie's answering machine, left a message, and went back to The Sweetwater to check out the music.

The opening act was a young man playing solo acoustic guitar with no one paying attention. The roadies from the headlining rock band walked all around him, even in front of him, setting up their equipment on the stage. The thought of being up there himself, playing his songs, terrified him. He watched as the guy played his heart out to people drinking and talking and ignoring him. Woody didn't want to add to the disrespect by leaving in the middle of his set. Then he stayed to see what the headliner sounded like. They were loud and abrasive; a singer with a nasal voice singing songs devoid of melody. He left after two songs.

When he drove back to Max and Auddie's, it was eleven-thirty and seemed too late to buzz the intercom. He parked on the street and hopped a fence. Wandering among the look-alike apartments, he finally found the right one and tapped softly on the door; no answer. He walked between the buildings, saw a light on in the back bedroom and gently tapped a little beat on the window.

In bed reading, Stephanie recognized the pattern and went up to the window, cupping her face with her hands to see out in the darkness. Woody was right there, his face pressed against the glass a half-inch from hers. She jumped back, startled, then laughed. Sliding open the window, she popped off the screen and Woody climbed in.

Stephanie stood there, naked, smiling. Without a word, he took off his clothes and dropped them in a pile on the floor. When she lay back down on the bed, he knelt down, put his face between her legs, and began kissing her thighs. When she began to moan, he backed off. She laughed.

"What's so funny?" Woody whispered.

"Max and Auddie are out on their friend's boat. They won't be back until tomorrow."

When Stephanie got up the next morning and walked into to the living room, Woody was on the couch playing his guitar and singing, surrounded by lyric sheets and chord charts. She stopped in the doorway and listened. This was what she loved most about him, his music. Hunched over his guitar in Max's oversized bathrobe, bony knuckles and knees under a trellis of hair… it was as if the alchemy of his playing transformed everything into a visceral sensation. She adjusted her position against the door and Woody looked up.

"Good morning." She walked over and sat down next to him. "Have you been up long?"

"I woke up in the middle of the night from this weird dream. I was doing a gig and everybody in the audience had guitars and they were all playing and when I tried to play, the neck of my guitar coiled up like a snake and bit the side of my neck. Now I've got this gig and…"

"You have a gig?"

"Yeah, at the Sweetwater."

"I heard that's a nice place. Congratulations."

"I'm opening for a rock band. I've never played solo acoustic at a rock gig."

"You'll do fine." She sat down next to him and began rubbing his chest.

"I told the guy I've got all these songs, but they're not really together. I need like twelve songs to do a set. And if I don't say anything between songs I need more. It's embarrassing being up there with all those people staring at you."

"Your music is beautiful. What are you embarrassed about?"

"I'm embarrassed about everything I do, things I say, my body. I'm embarrassed sitting here telling you what I'm embarrassed about."

"It's you that feels that way, not your music. Your music is unashamed and proud."

"My songs are as nervous about this gig as I am."

"Maybe I can help you both relax." She took his guitar from his lap, gently placed it on the carpeted floor, put her hands inside his robe and massaged his chest until he eased her down on top of him and they made love on the couch.

They were lying next to each other, naked, when they heard

someone coming in the front door. They panicked, sure it was Max and Auddie. In a slapstick moment, Stephanie covered her chest with Woody's robe, Woody draped a sleeve over his crotch and a clean-cut young man stepped inside the door.

"Hi, I'm Harold the house cleaner." He looked at the floor, embarrassed. "I clean on Tuesdays and Thursdays but I have instructions to…" he took a card from his back pocket, "if anyone's home, leave and come back the following day until no one is home, then resume the Tuesday-Thursday schedule." Avoiding their eyes, he backed out the door.

Chapter 26

From a half-block away, Woody could see the crowd standing outside the front door of the Sweetwater. He walked slower and considered turning around. The thought of being on stage made him start to sweat. These people didn't want to see a guy with an acoustic guitar, they'd be waiting for the rock band to come on. If Stephanie, Max and Auddie weren't already coming to the gig, he'd turn around right now.

Using his guitar case as a lance, Woody pushed his way through the crowd and found Seven.

"You missed sound check," Seven said, "your dressing room's back by the bathroom. I'll announce you in forty-five minutes. Come right up and start playing."

The dressing room was more crowded than anywhere else in the venue. The room was like a bunker with cinder-block walls painted flat black, covered with graffiti and dog-eared rock posters. A torn couch and mismatched armchairs were overflowing with people sitting on the arms, drinking, smoking pot and talking loudly. He looked for a place to tune his guitar and play some scales to warm up. The guitar player from Oblong, the headlining rock band, was changing his guitar strings on the floor in a corner.

Woody staked out another spot on the floor next to a folding table covered with empty beer bottlers, a half bottle of Jack Daniel's and some slices of processed cheese on a metal deli-tray. He was tuning up when a young man, unsteady on his feet, walked up to the table. Eye-level with the back of the man's knees, Woody looked up and watched him fold a piece of cheese into his mouth, take a gulp of Jack and put a second slice of cheese in the back-pocket of his jeans.

Just then another young man with a pleasant smile knelt down in front of Woody. Extending a glass pipe packed with a lime-green crystalline bud, he held a lighter cocked and ready in his other hand. "P.G."

"P.G.?"

"Purple God."

Woody took the pipe in his mouth and the young man lit it. He got a much bigger hit than he expected, exhaled a dense cloud of smoke and started coughing. The young man waited for his cough to subside and offered the pipe again. Woody declined, stood up and spotted a slice of pizza on a paper plate being used as an ashtray. Realizing he'd barely eaten anything all day, he picked up the slice, blew off the ashes and took a bite. A short stocky man in a tight, black Oblong T-shirt came up to him. "You with the band?" He had a military crew cut and a neck so thick it looked like he didn't have one.

"I'm the opening act," Woody said chewing the pizza.

"Woody?"

"Yeah."

"I'm Guff, Oblong's manager. Your dressing room's down the hall. This ain't your food."

"Down the hall?" Woody stopped chewing.

"Next to the bathroom." Guff gave him a deadpan look, raised his fist and slowly extended his index finger toward the door.

Woody laid the half-eaten slice of pizza across the top of Guff's fist. "Should I finish the bite in my mouth or you want that too?"

Holding his guitar in front of him, Woody made his way through the crowded hallway to a broom closet with two chairs and two bottles of water. When he tried playing, his hands were shaking so badly he could barely play a chord without making a mistake.

Stephanie, Max and Auddie got in what they thought was a line to the front door. After being jostled for ten minutes they were further away than when they'd started. Stephanie got the doorman's attention, verified they were on Woody's guest list and they made their way to a little table Woody had reserved for them by the stage.

At nine o'clock the house lights dimmed and the stage lights came up. Seven walked up to the mic, made some announcements about upcoming shows and introduced Woody: "A wonderful, soulful, singer-songwriter, his first time at the Sweetwater, please give it up for... Woody!"

Woody didn't appear. Seven shaded his eyes and looked off stage. "It'll be just a minute, folks." The stage lights dimmed and the house music came back on, the room buzzing with restless energy.

Stephanie left Max and Auddie at their table. Making her way toward the back hallway, she squeezed through the lines in front of the restrooms to the main dressing room. Woody was nowhere to be found. She walked back through the crowd, found Seven standing at the bar and asked him where Woody's dressing room was.

The little room was empty. Standing in the hallway, wondering where he could be, she noticed the line in front of the men's room was longer than the line to the ladies room; very unusual. Cutting to the front, she knocked on the men's room door.

"Woody? Are you in there?"

The door opened just enough to let her in and Woody locked it behind her.

He looked terrible. His long-sleeved shirt was unbuttoned, his face and bare chest blanched white, a wad of paper towels in one hand, his guitar in the other. The room smelled like vomit. "I can't do it," he pleaded.

"Can't do what?"

"Go out there in front of those people."

"What do you mean?"

"I mean I can't do it! They're a bunch of head bangers. They don't want to see me. They're here to see a loud rock band, not a guy with an acoustic guitar." He looked at the floor. "Some guy gave me a hit of pot. It's like the strongest pot I've ever smoked. I tried playing, my hands won't even listen to me."

"Just try to relax. They'll love your songs. Everyone does."

"People like sausages too, but they don't wanna see how they're made."

"You're a musician. Get yourself together." She took the paper towels from his hand and brushed away the hair stuck to his face. "What's the worst thing that can happen?"

"My voice, when I sing, it's so personal. I don't even know those people and they just sit there and stare at you."

"It's not about you, it's about your music." There was a loud knocking on the door.

"Maybe I'm not meant to be a performer." The sound of rapping knuckles turned to a pounding fist.

"Then don't perform. You're not an actor, you're a musician. Just go out there and play."

Someone started kicking the bottom of the door.

"I'm going out in the audience," she said calmly. "I'll be sitting in front of the stage. Forget about everyone else and just play for me." She tried pushing his hair back from his face again. It was useless. She buttoned up his shirt and put her hand on the doorknob. "You okay?"

"Thanks."

"You look great, you play great." She kissed him on the mouth. "And you taste like you just threw up."

When Stephanie got back to the table, Auddie looked at her and raised her eyebrows.

"He's just putting the finishing touches on his makeup, he'll be right out."

Ten minutes later Woody walked onto the stage, sat down on the brown metal folding chair and looked at his feet, long hair covering his face and draped over his guitar. The lights in the room dimmed and the stage lights came up. The house music being turned off got some people's attention, but most people barely took notice and kept on talking.

Oblong had all their gear set up on the stage behind Woody; guitar amps, four guitars on stands, a bass amp, a multi-keyboard set-up and a full drum set with a half-dozen shiny cymbals cocked at different angles.

Woody sat on the stage, motionless. Within a minute the audience was back to full volume, loud and boisterous, many of the patrons with their backs to the stage, girls squealing with laughter, young men ordering beer. Some people were checking out Woody, asking each other what he was doing up there staring at the floor.

There were about five times as many people in the room as there were seats, everyone in a constant jockey for position. Most people were preoccupied with their own conversations, but the longer Woody sat there, the more distracting his presence became. After several minutes, he was difficult to ignore. The sheer strangeness of him sitting there, a faceless mop of tangled hair and a guitar, began to permeate the room. People became unsettled, conjecturing loudly to each other about what might be happening on the stage. The noise swelled, gradually increasing to a fever pitch, individual voices merging into one cacophonous bleating that sounded about to require crowd control.

Woody suddenly leaned his acoustic guitar into the microphone and struck a power chord with an exaggerated Pete Townsend windmill stroke across the strings. He kept his arm extended, letting the chord ring out and fade. People were startled, stopped talking and looked toward the stage. Woody kept his face down, his arm straight out, parallel to the ground.

Talking erupted and sputtered around the room, people speculating again on what was happening, who the guy on the stage was, how long he could keep his arm extended like that. Woody's right hand was positioned like a claw in mid-air, shiny metal finger picks gleaming with reflections from the multi-colored stage lights. He stayed frozen in position. It got weird fast. A few people got up and left, everyone else remained focused on the stage. Bartenders and waitresses stopped in their tracks. The sound engineer walked out of the sound booth and stood next to Seven who was stationed at the bar, checking out the scene in disbelief. A muted intense buzz of whispers, like a swarm of bees, hovered in the room. There was speculation about some kind of hidden stage prop holding up Woody's arm, maybe hidden in his hair, his hair didn't look real. When it seemed humanly impossible to keep his arm like that, Woody pushed it further, beyond any reasonable limits of the laws of nature.

The crowd slowly dissolved into silence and stayed silent until the silence became unbearable and sporadic bursts of nervous chatter flared up. A young man sitting near the stage stood and took a step forward to get a closer look. His movement silenced the crowd again. When another young man moved toward the stage, the crowd noise came back, this time in a low rumble, building, the audience feeling the need to act, like bystanders to an emergency, or a public lynching.

"Stephanie," Woody said under his breath, his arm still extended. The room plummeted to silence and stayed silent for a full minute until people started asking each other in hushed voices if they'd heard what he'd said. Woody leaned an inch closer to the microphone and said it again, a decibel louder, adding a touch of melody, "Stephanie." He brought his arm down and lightly played his second chord of the night. There was an audible, communal sigh as Woody moved up on the mic and delicately started the opening chorus to his song.

He built it up moderately and transitioned into the verses, the audience straining to hear every nuance of every word. He played through multiple verses, each lyrical line revealing hints of an unfolding story of profound love and crippling insecurity. At a natural break in the story, he seamlessly transitioned into an instrumental section of fluid single-note runs and polyrhythmic harmonics that expanded dynamically until it sounded like four guitar players playing. Minutes later, he brought it all the way back down again for the last vocal verse.

When Woody went into the final chorus the room was so quiet the crowd heard the rubbing of his fingers across the steel-wound strings. His voice was a whisper. He began repeating the chorus, over and over, taking his time, the audience floating along on a gently building wave of energy until, without anyone realizing how he'd gotten there, he was playing full volume, almost screaming, thrashing at his guitar. When the momentum had accelerated to where it seemed it had nowhere to go, he kept going, finally reaching a point of collective agreement, a communal climax and release. Everyone let out the breath they'd been holding, checked their seatbelts, and the slow descent began.

Woody incrementally backed off the microphone, singing softer, segueing into a circular finger picking motion, repeating arpeggios ringing like syncopated chimes. He picked his head up slightly, his hair fell back and Stephanie, in the front row, saw the tears on his cheek. Tears came to her own eyes.

Prodding the ringing harmonics out of his strings, Woody added a double-time bass line on his low E string with his thumb. He alternated the bass line every four beats by smacking the wooden body of the guitar, creating a reverberating sound that lasted the entire measure until the next whack of his thumb. The groove was infectious.

He slipped in a throaty vocal rhythm that worked like another instrument. It gradually became apparent that the sounds were lyrics; a poignant repeating poem about a girl at a dance, dancing by herself. Halfway through the song, people were swaying in their seats, tapping on the tables. A couple of drunk frenetic girls danced on their chairs. Woody stomped his foot and sang and played his guitar like a drum, a one-man band, the congregation clapping along in unison.

Saturday night at The Sweetwater, the fanatical group of music fans were hard to win over. But once they were into something, there was no stopping them. They were there to be part of the performance, to be squeezed into the confined space and become one sweaty pulsating body.

Woody played harder, exuding a vitality that seemed boundless. The audience soaked it up and worked with it like an exponentially expanding force field, the entire room pumping together in orgiastic abandon. Guff, Oblong's manager, pushed his way through the crowd to Seven, who was still standing at the bar.

"He's gone over."

"What?" Seven towered over him, intentionally not bending down to hear him. He was enjoying Woody's set and resented being disturbed.

The stocky manager cupped his mouth, went up on his toes and yelled toward Seven's ear. "Woody's gone over his time! We're supposed to be on in ten minutes. We need time for the set change."

"He started late," Seven said, "he's only been on for twenty minutes."

"That ain't our problem, he's ten minutes over."

Seven looked at the audience, not a single person without a smile on their face. He looked down at the manager. "Let's give him a couple more songs."

"Everybody in this place is an Oblong fan. That guy didn't sell one ticket. We got a contract!"

Seven turned his attention back to the stage. "Let the guy do a couple more songs."

When Woody decelerated the beat and slowly brought the intensity down again, it was as if he gently took each sweaty dancer and personally escorted them back to their seats. One at a time, he eliminated the thump on his guitar, then the bass line, the finger picking and finally snuck back into the soft repeating chorus of "Stephanie." People in the audience sang the chorus with him, the atmosphere like a church, sweet, sensual, everyone feeling connected by the magic they were creating together.

Woody slowly leaned away from the microphone, letting the choral wave in the room swell on its own when he heard an urgent low voice on the side of the stage.

"Hey!" "Hey!" He looked over and saw Guff, frantically running his finger across his throat.

Woody kept playing. Everyone was on their feet chanting "Stephanie" like a drunken hundred-person choir. A minute later, when he felt the physical presence of the manager approaching, he stood up, still playing, and stepped right off the front of the twelve-inch stage into the audience. The audience opened a path like parting the Red Sea, making room for Woody and his guitar to pass through. A young woman reached out and touched his hair.

Making his way down the length of the room, he played and sang himself right out the front door. The moment he left, the audience burst into applause, clapping and whistling, expecting him to reappear. When he didn't, the clapping gradually dissipated and returned to the same talking and confusion that started the show.

Hot and flushed from the biggest adrenalin rush of his life, Woody didn't stop playing. He sang to people on the sidewalk and in front of restaurant windows. He walked into traffic and played for stopped cars. When they honked their horns, he just kept playing. He was floating ten feet off the ground, nothing could bring him down.

In the small town square, Woody sat on a park bench and slowed down the chorus to one repeating muted note, humming the melody. *Stephanie, Max and Auddie are probably waiting for me*, he thought. *I'll take a minute to decompress, then go back and take them out for a late-night dinner with the fifty dollars I get from Seven.*

215

Closing his eyes, he imagined himself still on the stage. He could feel the heat of the audience… "Stephanie…" they were singing his song.

"Hey brother, you play good."

Startled, Woody opened his eyes and stopped playing. Two young women dressed in black jeans, black T-shirts and engineer boots were standing in front of him. One girl was stocky with a butch haircut, one was slim and petite with the sleeves of her T-shirt rolled up exposing buffed-up biceps.

"Don't stop, you sound good," the big girl said.

"I just finished doing a gig," Woody said, "I'm ready for a break."

"Where were you playing?"

"The Sweetwater."

""That's cool. That's a nice guitar. It looks like it's worth some bucks."

"Yeah, it's pretty nice," Woody said.

The heavy girl sat down on the bench next to him. "I play guitar a little. Mind if I try it?"

"Not really. I mean, yeah I mind. Sorry, it's my main axe and I don't feel like lending it out."

"Some folks can't afford fancy things like that." She reached over and put her hand on the guitar.

"Hey, what're you doing?" He pulled it away from her.

"Take it easy brother, I just want to check it out." She reached out again, put her hand next to Woody's on the neck and pulled it towards her.

"Don't mess with my guitar!" Woody laid his arm across the front of it when he felt a sharp pain at the back of his neck. A bright white light, like a flashbulb, went off in his eyes. He felt himself falling and saw that the girl who had been in front of him wasn't there anymore. He slumped forward, looked over his shoulder and saw her standing behind the bench slapping a flexible lead-filled blackjack in the palm of her hand. He noticed how her muscular forearms looked strangely out of place with her small hands. He looked to see where he was falling, a close-up of the worn varnished grain of the wooden park-bench passed through his field of vision and the cement surface of the sidewalk came up at him like it was coming up from the bottom of the Grand Canyon.

The girl sitting next to him held her grip on the neck of the guitar and he collapsed over it onto the ground, smacking his forehead hard on the concrete. His hand stayed twisted upside-down, holding onto the guitar.

"Let's get outta here!" the girl with the blackjack said urgently.

"He won't let go." The other girl was prying at Woody's fingers. "He's got a fucking death grip. You killed him!"

"He's not dead, he's breathing. I can see him breathing."

"His fucking fingers are frozen!" The large girl stood up, picked up the guitar with both hands and pulled at it. Woody's body dragged a few inches along the ground, his grip still intact, his hand wrapped around the thin end of the neck by the tuning pegs.

"C'mon!" The girl with the blackjack jerked her head back and forth, looking up and down the street. "Let's get outta here!"

The large girl repositioned herself, shoved the guitar towards Woody's chest so his arm folded in on itself, then yanked back hard. Woody's arm went limp, he released his grip and the thin wooden body slammed into the iron armrest of the bench. "Fuck!" She held up the broken guitar, pieces of bridgework hanging from dangling strings, and threw it on the sidewalk next to Woody.

"With a guitar like that, maybe he's carrying some cash." The smaller girl checked his pockets; guitar picks, coins, and his driver's license. She tossed them away, then found what she'd been looking for: a wad of bills. "Bingo!" She quickly counted it. "Eighteen hundred bucks!"

The big girl let out a yelp, raised two fists in the air and put her foot through the remains of the splintered guitar. "All that money and he wouldn't even let me play it!" She looked at Woody's hand lying palm-down on the cement. "Fucking rich hippie asshole!" With all her weight, she brought the cleated heel of her engineer boot down into the back of Woody's right hand.

Chapter 27

Stephanie's arms sliced through the icy cold water, barely rippling the surface. Over the last few days, she'd increased her daily jog on the beach to two miles and then a polar bear plunge in the ocean.

Every morning, she'd drive over Mount Tamalpais, park in a desolate area near Muir Beach, and run on a winding trail through smooth-skinned madrone trees. The packed-dirt path followed a creek and gradually changed to sand as the creek flowed across a beach and emptied into the ocean. The ocean waves flowed upstream as far as they could, each wave advancing with determination, the unfazed creek pouring forward, blurring the distinction between salt water and fresh water.

Stephanie would run north on the beach, jump into the surf, then take a short swim in the cold water toward a point of vertical rocks. From her days surfing there, she knew of a tidal inlet that carried her through a small opening in the cliffs onto a ten-foot secluded beach. She'd do yoga, stretch out on the warm sand and sometimes sleep in the morning sun.

She hadn't heard from Woody in five days, since he'd walked out of The Sweetwater. Every day she went through the same thought process; had he just exploded with emotion after the gig? Gone off with some fans? Another woman? He'd done this kind of thing before, disappearing for no apparent reason, sometimes for days. It was usually that he'd either conjured up some jealous scenario about her or sequestered himself away, working on his songs for days with no sleep. Throughout their relationship, the only consistent thing about Woody was his inconsistency. But lately things had felt different. She thought they'd moved beyond their tumultuous, back and forth relationship.

Watching Woody play at The Sweetwater, seeing him in his element, something had clicked for her. His guitar playing and emotion-filled voice had moved her in a way they never had before. Looking at the rapt faces around her, she'd realized that his music was evocative in a universal sense, like it could make a difference in the world. More than anything, she'd felt how much love was coming through his music. The minute he'd walked out the door, playing and singing, she'd made up her mind to give it a try; they'd get a place and live together.

She'd intended to share all this with him when he got off stage, and even made arrangements to have a bottle of champagne sent to his little dressing room. But he never returned.

At first she figured it was part of the show, his artistic statement, leaving everyone with the anti-climax of his departure. But when she'd checked his dressing room and his guitar case and jacket weren't there, she figured he'd come back for his things after the show, intentionally avoiding her.

As the days passed, her uncertainty turned to anger, then back to uncertainty. Maybe he'd had some kind of cathartic experience at his show, a validation of his art. Maybe he didn't need all her doubt and criticism and her aunt and uncle's weird vibes. In some ways Woody was oblivious to the energy around him, in other ways he was sensitive to the point where a questionable glance would send him reeling out the door.

She called Murray; he hadn't seen him. They talked about going

219

to the police, but agreed it wasn't unusual for Woody to be out of touch. The next day, she drove over to Woody's apartment and used her key to get in. It was dark and musty; clearly, he hadn't been there in a while. Could he have gone to his mother's in eastern California? She thought of calling her, but it was highly unlikely that Woody was there, and Stephanie didn't want to worry her.

Eight days after the gig, Stephanie returned from her daily swim, sat at Max and Auddie's kitchen table and looked at the list of people she and Murray had compiled who might have seen Woody. It was mainly a list of musicians she didn't know very well. If Woody needed a break, she could deal with it. It was the uncertainty she couldn't handle.

The phone rang, startling her from her thoughts.

"Hello?"

"Is Woody there?"

"Who's calling?"

"It's Seven from The Sweetwater. Woody gave me this number."

"My name's Stephanie, I'm Woody's girlfriend. I haven't seen him since the show."

"Stephanie. I imagine you have some relation to that song of his. Great song. I've been getting calls asking when he's coming back. I've never had so many calls for a solo acoustic act. That guy can really play."

She was quiet.

"Hello?"

"I'm here. You haven't seen Woody since the show?"

"He didn't even come back to get paid. He left his coat and guitar case in the other band's dressing room."

Stephanie took the receiver away from her ear and it slipped from her fingers into her lap.

A minute later Auddie came in, took one look at her niece's face, and knew something was very wrong.

"They found Woody's things at the club." Stephanie's voice was

220

trembling. "I'm calling the police."

Auddie took the receiver from her lap and set it back in the cradle. "Try the hospitals first."

"Your friend will be glad to see you." The nurse at Marin General Hospital offered Stephanie a kind smile. "He has a badly fractured hand, a serious concussion and is confused and disoriented. We were hoping a familiar face might help."

Stephanie walked slowly down the brightly lit hallway to his hospital room. Holding a bouquet of flowers in front of her, she stopped at the door, closed her eyes and visualized Woody with a healthy white light around him.

Woody's head was bandaged, his right arm in a cast and he was very groggy.

"Woody it's me, Stephanie."

"Hi Steph, how ya' doin'?" His eyes weren't focusing.

She hugged him and broke into tears. "What happened to you?"

"I dunno." He was slurring his words like he was drunk.

"You don't know how this happened?"

"I been lying here trying to figure it out. Everything's kinda fuzzy."

"Do you remember your gig?"

"Kinda. I 'member my low E string was outta tune."

"You played great," she said, almost in a whisper.

"I 'member walking outta the gig then wakin' up here with this gigantic headache. Where's my guitar?" He picked up his right hand to push back the bandage on his forehead, hit himself with the plaster cast and winced in pain.

She adjusted his bandage. "They said you got hit on the back of your head with something and hit your forehead on the sidewalk when you fell. And your hand... the nurse said you might not..." She choked up and didn't finish her sentence.

He looked down at his right hand, a cast up to his elbow with the tips of his fingers sticking out. "I can't feel my fingers."

Fighting back tears, she got up off the bed, turned away and

221

began rearranging the flowers. "This whole time while you were gone... at first I was angry, then I just prayed that you were alive."

"Y'ever notice how it's always somebody else that dies?"

Woody." She was still facing away from him. "I want to say what's been on my mind and... this might not be the best time to bring this up, but maybe it's the perfect time, maybe it'll help you heal. I love you and I've decided I'm ready to give it a try, get a place together, see if we can create the life we both want."

She turned to see Woody's reaction. Woody was asleep.

A week later, Woody was released from the hospital and Stephanie brought him back to Max and Auddie's. She set him up in the guest room with a cassette player, video player and some of his favorite books and magazines. She prepared nutritious meals and administered healing herbs recommended by the supplement specialist at the local health food store. Woody supplemented the herbs with prescription narcotics.

Sitting up in bed, Woody had been reading the same paragraph on a page of Guitar Player Magazine for an hour. His head felt like it was being squeezed in a vise. He hurled the magazine to the floor, reached with his left hand to the side table covered with pill bottles, and knocked them over. When he automatically reached out with his right hand to catch a bottle, it just bounced off his cast.

The motion had twisted his shirt, the top button pressing against his neck. He couldn't undo the button with his left hand. Frustrated, he ripped open his shirt, threw off the blankets and was on the floor, scattering pill bottles, looking for his pain pills. When he found the right bottle, he tried turning the cap and turned it the wrong way. It seemed like every time he turned anything with his left hand; a doorknob, the cap on a toothpaste tube, the dial on a radio; he turned it the wrong way.

Finally getting the plastic bottle open, he took some pills, climbed back into bed and gazed down at his useless right hand. There was nothing but dead numbness. It felt like he'd pressed his fingertips into a hot frying pan. *I can't even dress myself. How will I ever play the guitar again? How will I do anything?"*

The doctor had told Woody to stay in bed for two weeks. After two days he was stalking around the apartment; another two days, around the neighborhood, at times incoherent on pain pills.

While Max, Auddie and Stephanie did their best to make Woody comfortable, he vacillated unpredictably between sullen sadness and outright belligerence. When he tried playing chess with Max, the headaches made it impossible to concentrate. At one point, when Stephanie mentioned that it'd been a while since he'd checked in with Jeff Pearlman, Woody looked down at his cast. "What's Pearlman gonna do with a one-handed guitar player?"

Max went to a local music store, explained the situation to a salesman, and spent $500 on a lap-size synthesizer with a small keyboard that could be programmed to sound like an electric guitar. That evening after dinner, when Woody was sitting in the living room, Max took it out of the box, plugged it in, and carefully set it on Woody's lap. Woody thanked him and clumsily tried to position it so he could play left-handed. Watching him, Max, Auddie and Stephanie heard him mumble, "Hire the handicapped, they're fun to watch."

When Woody turned it on, dialed up the "electric guitar" setting and played a note, the fake synthesized tone sounded to him like fingernails scraping across a blackboard. "Gee," he said sarcastically, "if you close your eyes, you'd think James Taylor was in the room." Making a move to get up, Woody realized, as had been happening with so many things, he was trapped. He couldn't get the keyboard off his lap with one hand without dropping it. He looked over at Stephanie; *Can't she see I can't get up?* Lowering one knee, he did his best to let the keyboard slide onto the floor without breaking it, and headed toward the door.

"Where are you going?" Stephanie asked.

"Out."

"Please don't drive. The doctor said the concussion could still affect your vision. You've taken a lot of pain pills tonight and... the doctor said you should practice with someone in the car to get used to driving with one –"

"I'm fine!"

"You're not fine, you're too high to drive!"

Keeping his eyes down on the keyboard instruction manual in his hands, Max said; "My professional medical opinion is that your ability to operate machinery is impaired. You're legally intoxicated, under the influence of opiates and maladapted to your disability."

"Why don't you just say it in plain English!" Auddie yelled at Max. She was holding a metal folding TV table she'd gotten for Woody to set the keyboard on.

Max's head snapped up from the manual. "Don't get on *my* case, woman!"

Woody reached for the doorknob with his left hand, turned it the wrong way and slapped the door.

"Woody!" Stephanie walked over to him, glanced across the room at Max and Auddie and whispered urgently in his ear. "Please!" Grabbing his arm, she leaned in closer. "I've never heard my aunt and uncle talk to each other like that!"

"Don't get on *my* case, *woman!*" He said it loud enough for everyone to hear and slammed the door behind him. He got to his car, took the two pain pills he had in his pocket, then drove to the Sweetwater.

Woody sat at the bar and drank three drinks in twenty minutes. When he ordered a fourth, the barmaid said; "You better talk to Seven."

"Talk to Seven? About what?"

"About your bar tab." She walked away.

A minute later Seven was standing next to Woody at the bar, towering over him. "How're you doing man?"

"Pretty good." Woody glanced over his shoulder into Seven's

chest, then took a drink from his glass that was nothing but ice cubes. "I could use a drink."

"It's good to see you're getting out. When you're ready, we'd like to have you back, to play here again."

Woody stared into his empty glass. "How about a drink?"

Seven signaled to the bar maid to get him one more.

"Thanks," Woody said when the drink appeared.

Seven patted him on the back. "I know you been dealing with a lot. And we're glad to have you around. But the last few times you came in, you were pretty rude to my employees. I've been personally paying for your drinks and your cab fare home."

"Thanks." Woody grunted. "You're the hostess with the mostess." He looked quizzically at his empty glass. He couldn't remember drinking it. Seven caught the whole thing and gently took Woody by the arm

"Woody, I'm going to do you a big favor. You've got enough problems right now, you don't need to make things worse. I'm cutting you off, bro. This place, with all those shelves of booze in front of you, is not where you should be right now." Seven slid him off the bar stool like he was a rag doll, and escorted him out. Woody didn't fully understand what was happening until the door shut in his face.

Out front on the sidewalk, looking at the closed door in disbelief, Woody was trying to figure out where to go when two young couples came out. "Anybody got an extra smoke?" he mumbled.

They stopped and one of the men gave Woody a cigarette and lit it for him. "Hey, aren't you the guy that played here last month?"

Woody took a slow drag and gazed down the street. "No."

The young man looked to his friends, then back at Woody. "What're you talking about man, we were here. We saw you open for Oblong. You were great."

Woody ignored him and kept smoking.

"When are you playing here again? No kidding, you were really great."

"Must've been a different guy," Woody said without looking at him. "I'm not even allowed in this place."

The other young man took a step forward with his girlfriend on his arm. "We were here too. We were completely blown away by your music. We're huge Oblong fans, but everybody was talking *your* set. That song 'Stephanie' was one of the best –"

Woody suddenly spun around and got right up in the man's face. "Are you fucking deaf! You saw a guy playing guitar! A guy with two hands! I can't even get in the fucking door of this place!" He took the two steps across the sidewalk and violently swung his heavy plaster cast into the small front window of the club.

Seven burst out of the door, took in the scene and slapped his hand flat on Woody's chest. Gathering the front of Woody's shirt into his fist, Seven lifted him six inches off the ground and held him up against the wall. "Listen asshole! You're one of the most talented motherfuckers around. You took a bad fall. You gonna stay down, groveling in your own shit, or you gonna get back up and have a life? Your choice!"

Seven dropped him as fast as he'd picked him up, went back in and called the police. He agreed not to press charges if Woody agreed to stay away. The police impounded Woody's car and it was after midnight when they dropped him off at the front gate of Max and Auddie's.

Using the key they'd given him, he went through the security gate, stumbled around the look-alike buildings, and tried his key in the wrong apartment. He tried it a half-dozen times before he decided that the problem wasn't that he couldn't do it with his left hand; Max and Auddie must have changed their lock. He kicked the door, walked back out to the road and stuck out his cast. He stood there, unsteady on his feet, imagining the conversation that had taken place when Stephanie, Max, and Auddie had decided to lock him out.

Finally getting a ride into town, he walked to the square and sat down on the same bench where he'd been assaulted. Too high on pain pills and alcohol to even notice where he was, he lay down and fell asleep.

He woke up on the hard bench at dawn, cold, hungry, and hung over, with a pounding headache and spasms of pain shooting up his arm. His pain pills were back at Max and Auddie's; he knew he'd never go back there. Reaching in his pocket, he found a few dollars he'd taken out of Auddie's purse and realized how far he'd degenerated into a junkie mentality, stealing money from someone who had shown him nothing but kindness. He shook off the stab of guilt and walked two blocks to a convenience store. Spending what he had on a small bottle of Tylenol, he used his teeth and left hand, but still couldn't get it open. Even when he put it on the edge of the sidewalk and put his shoe on it, he couldn't remove the childproof cap. He picked up a loose piece of concrete from the parking lot, smashed open the plastic bottle, swallowed the contents without water, and hitchhiked to the hospital.

Every chair in the emergency room was taken, everyone trying to avoid eye contact under the bright fluorescent lights. "ID and proof of insurance?" the receptionist said to Woody when he finally got to the front of the line

Woody showed her his cast. "You guys put this cast on a few weeks ago, I lost my wallet, I lost my pain pills. My name's-

"You need some kind of Identification to be seen."

"This is my ID." Woody shoved his cast in closer. "My doctor was a red-headed guy named Dr. Cawley. The nurses called him Dr. Red. Save us both a bunch of time and hassle and just tell Dr. Red Woody the guitar player with the broken hand needs some pain pills. It's an emergency!"

"Sorry, but you need identification, hospital regulations."

"I'm gonna wait right here until I pass out from the pain. Just ask the doctor, he'll remember me." Woody stepped away a few feet and leaned against the wall in view of the receptionist.

Forty-five minutes later Dr. Red, in a white coat, came out of the

227

swinging doors, obviously in a big hurry. He spoke to Woody for two minutes, produced a pad and scribbled a prescription for a small amount of pain medication. He wrote across the top; LOST MEDS / NO CHARGE REPLACEMENT / NO ID / NO CHILDPROOF CAP, and disappeared through the swinging doors.

After another hour at the pharmacy, Woody got his pills, took four and stood in front of the hospital, waving his cast in its sling until a young, long-haired man going to San Francisco stopped and gave him a ride. It was a small, dirty sedan, covered with bumper sticks and a surfboard tied to the top.

"What happened to you?" the driver asked. "You look pretty banged up."

"Yeah." Woody leaned his head back on the seat and closed his eyes.

"Where you going?"

"San Francisco," Woody said with his eyes closed. "The Haight, or anywhere."

"I'm going to the beach, but I'll get you to the city. What happened to your hand?"

Woody didn't answer. He was asleep.

Shaking Woody's shoulder, it took the surfer several tries to wake him up. When he reached over and opened the passenger door, Woody almost fell out. They were at the west end of Golden Gate Park by the beach, five miles from Woody's apartment.

Late morning, a mild sunny day, Woody walked to the beach and sat down in the sand. He carefully slipped his jacket over his cast, rolled it into a pillow, and decided to finish his nap before making his way across the city to his apartment. He took two more pain pills.

Enjoying the warm sun and the waves of narcotic euphoria, it occurred to him that even with no food, no money, no girlfriend, no right hand... he could still enjoy a day at the beach.

An image came to mind of an account he'd read of German

concentration camp survivors being transferred to a location where there were no tall chimneys, which meant there were no ovens. The prisoners got off the train and stood in the snow, half naked, half-starved, and rejoiced. The writer described them as actually giddy with happiness. Everything's relative, Woody thought. The warm sun felt luxurious. Like counting sheep, he mentally counted the pain pills in his pocket and dozed off to sleep.

Woody dreamt that Ray and Stephanie were sitting together holding hands, the only people in an ornate balcony high above the stage at the Sweetwater. Woody was on an operating table on the stage, a team of doctors in white coats cutting off his right hand with a chrome hack saw. There was no blood, his hand lopped off like a half-loaf of bread, falling from his arm in slow motion and landing on his smashed guitar that lay in pieces, smoldering on the stage.

He woke up with a start, sweaty and disoriented, one side of his face burnt from the sun. Relieved to see his hand was still there, he looked over at a group of teenagers that had set up a camp of blankets and coolers twenty feet away. They were gathered like a pile of puppies, drinking beer and laughing over the sound of a blaring battery-powered radio.

Woody felt as if something had woken him up, not just the dream. He sat up and blinked his eyes, trying to shake off the drug haze, connect up the synapse. He felt an urgency to clear his head, discern the source of the strange sensation before it disappeared. He looked all around, up at the sky, out across the beach. It felt like there was some ominous presence, but the harder he tried to focus on it, the more vague it felt. He couldn't think. Exasperated, he lay back down and put his head on his pillow. As soon as he closed his eyes, he heard it, coming out of the teenager's radio... the last chorus of his song "Stephanie."

In ten seconds it was over and a DJ launched into a rapid-fire monologue about ten hits in a row with no interruptions. Trying to get up quickly, Woody leaned on his right hand, winced in pain, raised his cast and felt sand flow into it. He walked awkwardly over to the teenagers. "Whuddya listenin' to?"

They looked at him warily; he was obviously very high.

"Ninety-seven point five, the chit," a girl said.

"The shit?" Woody mumbled.

They laughed. "K.C.H.T," she said. "It's the name of the station. They play the good chit." They all laughed again.

"What was that last song?" Woody asked.

When no one else answered, the girl that had spoken said, "I guess we weren't really listening. We were just hanging out talking and stuff."

"You want a beer, man?" one of the guys offered. "You look like you could use one."

Woody stared out at the ocean, adjusting his stance in the sand.

"You okay?" the girl said.

Without answering, Woody walked away, sat back down by his jacket and took two more pain pills. He knew he was pretty out of it, he must've still been dreaming when he heard the song. That chorus had been playing in his head for years. He lay back, closed his eyes and listened to the radio DJ. The hyper-paced chatter tugged him in the opposite direction of the nodding-out drowsiness he so badly wanted to slip into.

He was considering what it would take to drag himself back to the surface of full consciousness and move out of earshot of the blaring radio, when he felt a shadow come over him, blocking the sun. He opened his eyes. It was the teenage girl he'd spoken to.

"You still want to know about that song?" she asked.

"Yeah."

"Well, my friend's kind of shy and she didn't feel like saying anything, but she totally knows every song on the radio. It was the new Ray Bell song, "Stephanie." They play it all the time. There's a Ray Bell concert at The Greek Theater tomorrow and we're totally going if we can score some tickets."

Chapter 28

Woody headed in the direction of his apartment. Tomorrow he was going to The Greek Theater.

Saturated with codeine, he imagined himself walking onto the stage, a roadie putting a guitar on his neck, joining Ray for the last chorus of "Stephanie," ten thousand fans giving the songwriter a standing ovation. He wondered how big of a production they'd have, female back-up singers—three black divas would be perfect, maybe three or four horns, even a string section. He had a hit song.

As the hot afternoon wore on and the medication wore off, Woody's mood plummeted. Four more miles to his apartment. He went for his pills; they were already almost gone. He took two and trudged on, cars and trucks whizzing by, litter swirling around him. He began to wonder what kind of reception he'd really get from Ray when he showed up at the Greek Theater. Maybe he was getting ripped off, not getting credit for the song. How long had he been out of touch with Ray and Pearlman? It was Saturday, the concert was on Sunday. He'd call Ray as soon as he got home and make sure his name was on the guest list.

He made his way to Lincoln Avenue, a main thoroughfare where he might be able to hitchhike or sneak on a bus. His hand was throbbing. When he tried adjusting his sling to elevate it, it put more pressure on his neck and made his headache worse. Then he realized that in his drug-induced fantasies about playing with Ray, he'd completely forgotten about his hand. It occurred to him with brutal clarity that he might never play the guitar again.

With his shoddy appearance, hitchhiking wasn't working. The headache and pain in his hand were merciless. He took his last two pills, went into a crowded drug store, and stealthily pocketed a bottle of over-the-counter pain medication. On the way out, he found himself in the liquor section. He didn't like hard liquor, *or* shoplifting, but he was getting accustomed to both. He just had to make it through one day and get to the Greek Theater. When he noticed a security guard at the cash register with his back to him, he stuck a pint bottle of scotch in his pants and slipped out the door.

Emboldened by the liquor, he went into the next restaurant he came to and ordered a meal to go: a New York steak, the most expensive thing on the menu. When the food came out, he stood in front of the cashier, flipped open the Styrofoam container, picked up the greasy meat with his left hand and tore off a bite. "I'm usually a vegetarian, that's how hungry I am. I don't have any money, so go ahead and call the cops." The manager threw him out and let him keep the food.

Head down, dragging his feet, Woody was slowly crossing an intersection when an old Volkswagen bus pulled over and the driver offered him a ride.

"What happened to your hand, Woody?"

There was something familiar about the man's voice. "How'd you know my name?"

"You helped me unload some lumber up in Mill Valley. My name's Orbit. Where you going?"

"Ashbury Street."

"I'm going toward Berkeley, but I can swing through the Haight."

"Berkeley? I'm trying to get to The Greek Theater. Mind if I go that way with you?"

"Sure."

Woody looked at him and remembered his smile.

They drove for a half-hour in silence, the old Volkswagen doing its top speed of 55. When they got over the Bay Bridge, Orbit said, "You're going to the Greek Theater?"

"Yeah. I actually don't have to be there until tomorrow. I was thinking I'd just hang out on Telegraph Avenue."

"It must be a little tricky getting around with that cast. You right handed?"

Woody looked down at his hand. "I guess I used to be."

"I live not too far from here. Come over and rest for a little while, I'll make you a meal."

Orbit took the next exit and turned into an alley behind a shopping center. Surrounded by piles of plastic milk crates and wooden pallets, in the middle of a sea of stores and pavement, was a semi-secluded vacant lot with its own streetlight. "This place is a black hole of city planning," Orbit said with a smile.

Orbit's home was a lean-to affair of old boards attached to an abandoned bulldozer; a house of cards supported by skyhooks. It didn't look like it was going to fall down, it looked like it already had.

Woody ducked in a low doorway and followed Orbit inside. There was a surprisingly clean comfortable central living space with nooks and crannies going off in every direction. "Everything here, every possession I have, was discarded by somebody," Orbit said. "A lot of it comes from the shopping center dumpsters. People are constantly throwing stuff away. Where do they think *away* is, another dimension where trash goes?"

Orbit went to the orderly little kitchen area and began assembling an assortment of jars that contained what looked like leaves and twigs. "I found a diesel engine at the dump, put it in that

233

old Volkswagen and I run it on vegetable oil that was used to make French fries. They eat a lot of French fries around here. It's amazing what they discard; a board with a couple of nails in it, perfectly good food with a torn label or a day past the expiration date. I eat as well as anybody in Berkeley and enjoy the occasional luxury of wiping my ass with a tortilla. Have a seat." Orbit nodded to an old dentist's chair in the corner and proceeded to light an array of candles and hanging lanterns. Making his way to the chair, the low ceiling and crooked walls made it difficult for Woody to get his bearings.

Orbit moved around the room with amazing grace, fitting into uneven corners that seemed contoured to his bulbous shape. He mixed the vegetable matter from the jars in a hand-operated blender and served Woody what he called an "hallucinogen and tonic."

"It's mostly fruit juice, with a little foliage from the Amazon. Drink it slowly. It'll relax you, change your perspective."

"You happen to have any pain pills or aspirin or anything?" Woody asked.

"That drink should help. If your hand doesn't stop hurting in a little while, I'll see if I can find you something else."

"If I don't get some pain pills pretty soon..." Woody's looked down at his hand. "I can't even think with this pain in my hand."

"Try to relax." Orbit smiled, a kind gentle smile. "When you're tangled up in your mind, it's hard to get untangled using your mind. That drink has herbs in it that are good at untangling things. It'll lubricate your thoughts so they don't get so much traction. Get a little rest, I've got some last minute shopping to do." Orbit bounded out the door. Woody watched him move down the alley in a kind of hopping-skipping motion then disappear behind a dumpster.

Woody stood up and looked around at Orbit's strange collection of objects in unusual applications. His head hurt and his hand hurt and that foul-tasting drink was making him sick. He looked for the bathroom, hoping to find some pain pills in the medicine cabinet. There was no bathroom. He went to Orbit's tidy little sleeping area that had hand-painted jewelry boxes neatly arranged on shelves around a sheepskin bed. Looking for pills or drugs of any kind, he opened the miniature wooden drawers and pullout compartments. They contained an assortment of crystals, feathers and pouches of intense smelling powders, but no pills. He found a blurry Polaroid photo of Orbit in a graduation gown in front of an Ivy-league looking building; a confident, trim young man, almost unrecognizable but for the signature smile. Woody suddenly felt panicky. What the hell was he doing in this weird place, going through someone's personal stuff?'

He struggled to put the objects back and close the little drawers with his left hand. Something fell out and he automatically reached for it with his right hand, withdrew in pain and knocked over a vase of flowers. He picked up the vase, set it back on the shelf and clumsily tried to replace the flowers. The long stems went everywhere but into the narrow opening. The more he tried, the more frustrated he became. The vase fell over again, spilling water on him. He instinctively went to grab it with his cast and broke it... "Fuck!"

"Here."

Startled, Woody spun around. Orbit was standing behind him holding another vase of flowers. He set it on the shelf where the first vase had been. "Go ahead, smash it."

Woody looked at him wide-eyed.

"Smash it!"

Hyperventilating, Woody looked at the vase, back at Orbit, then back at the vase. He raised his cast up to his opposite shoulder and swung full force. The vase exploded, water, flowers and shards of glass going everywhere. Orbit immediately picked up a twelve-inch porcelain sculpture of a little girl petting a dog and set it on the shelf where the vases had been. "Go for it slugger, knock it out of the park."

Dripping sweat, chest heaving, Woody looked at the sculpture, back at Orbit, then spun around and lurched out the door. He put his hand up against the huge, windowless back wall of the shopping center, bent over at the waist and threw up. He gagged and dry-heaved for ten minutes, tasting the bitterness of Orbit's drink.

When his stomach finally settled down, he leaned his back against the building, slumped down onto the pavement, and surveyed his surroundings. It was getting dark, piles of wooden pallets and scrap lumber looming in the shadows. Orbit's rambling shack, with beams of yellow light shooting out of the cracks, blended into the landscape like a Frank Lloyd Wright design.

Daylight seemed to be disappearing faster than he'd ever seen it, shades of black-and-white rapidly replacing colors. He couldn't tell how much time had passed when he began to feel a mild, stimulating body rush and wondered what was in Orbit's frothy cocktail. He felt a sensation of lightness, like being weightless or even body-less, as if he was in another dimension, observing his huddled body at the bottom of the expansive white wall.

A sharp spasm in his right hand suddenly demanded his attention. He laid his cast in his lap and made a conscious decision to return to his body and address the pain, hold it lovingly like a mother holding a crying child. For the first time in his life he welcomed pain as something familiar, like an old friend. *What an interesting concept,* he thought. He remembered pictures he'd seen of a Buddhist monk doused with gasoline, burning himself to death in protest of the Vietnam War. The series of photographs showed the monk sitting in a lotus position with a calm, peaceful look on his face as he was reduced to a pillar of ash. The incredible distress he must have felt, but didn't feel at all.

Woody was amazed at how comfortable he was at that moment with the pain in his hand, looking at it objectively, as if it were someone else's pain, or even some kind of universal pain. A figure suddenly emerged out of the shadows and startled him. It was Orbit, cradling an arm-full of vegetables. "Hors d'oeuvres in ten minutes," Orbit said with a smile, "main seating in twenty, your promptness is appreciated." He ducked inside.

Ten minutes later, as soon as he stepped through the narrow

doorway, Woody felt the warmth and security of the candle-lit room with its thick aroma of garlic and ginger. It was a stark contrast to the disorienting weirdness he'd experienced there earlier. He sat down in the dentist chair, propped his feet up on the footrest, leaned back into the wrap-around head supports and watched Orbit prepare dinner.

The space in the bulldozer that the engine had once occupied now held a wood cooking stove with the smokestack protruding through the roof. A slab of lumber on the bulldozer's cleats served as a chopping block with overhead dangling copper pots teetering in rhythm with Orbit's motion. "Things can be so simple," Orbit said. "When you're cold, you get warm just making a fire. That's a little more direct than driving to a condo owner's meeting to talk about financing for a new heating system."

Woody noticed the broken glass was cleaned up and a new vase of fresh flowers was on the shelf. "Sorry about breaking that stuff."

"No worries," Orbit smiled. "A nearby florist discards a dumpster full of flowers and chipped vases every day." He wielded a butcher knife into an onion. "I talked to a doctor once about getting a couple of my taste buds transplanted to my little finger."

Woody looked down at the numb fingertips of his right hand. "You think you can taste something and hear music at the same time?"

Orbit stopped what he was doing, cut himself a chunk of parmesan cheese and chewed thoughtfully while he tapped a simple clave rhythm on the chopping block. "Yeah, but when I do them at the same time they're both diminished a little." He went back to the onion. "We get two eyes for depth perception, two ears for stereo, but only one mono mouth. Go figure."

Twenty minutes later, Orbit served up a vegetarian feast. There were no plates. Orbit served each course with a *splat*, on a clean, jagged-edge sheet of plate-glass. The sauces spread like fresh poured pancakes, almost but not quite reaching the other guy's serving. Woody had several helpings and felt his body absorbing the

237

nutrition he so badly needed. Using a spoon, he fashioned an organic mural of string beans and brown rice. It was the first bit of artwork he'd done with his left hand and he surprised himself with his facility of motion. "Plate glass, I get it."

"And that's why they call it fireplace." Orbit was tending the fire in the kitchen.

"And that's why they call it dope." Woody blinked his eyes, half expecting to wake up from a dream. Everything about Orbit and his environment seemed dreamlike.

Orbit cleaned the table with a chrome squeegee and hot soapy water heated on the wood stove, and they retired to two bucket seats from an old Chrysler New Yorker. "There *is* life after dinner," Orbit said and served up cigars, chocolate and Kona coffee.

Woody, sated and relaxed, realized that getting to the Greek Theater, or even thinking about Stephanie, were all things in the past or future. *Don't miss this amazing moment with this crazy guy. Be present. Don't miss this one.*

"The night's a pup," Orbit said and produced a bottle of cognac. "Can you believe somebody actually threw out this bottle because the label was torn?"

Woody felt a wonderful intellectual bond with Orbit. He couldn't remember ever being with someone that made him feel so at ease, so normal. He took off his shoes, handily enjoyed his cigar and the dual ashtrays in the armrests of the old car seat and noticed it was getting easier to do things with his left hand.

"The things I find in dumpsters never cease to amaze me." Orbit set a pair of brass goblets on the plate glass. "Americans feel so entitled, we fill cavernous landfills with disposable lighters just to avoid the effort it takes to light a match." Orbit served the brandy and flicked the ash of his cigar into the fire, his face hidden in a low spot in the ceiling. Woody could only make out the silhouette of his shapeless body and the glow of his cigar going back and forth into the void. He looked headless. They smoked in silence.

Orbit finished his cigar, walked across the room and produced a coverless volume of Shakespeare he'd found in the dumpster when he was collecting food for dinner. He let it fall open in his hands, held it under a hanging oil lamp and read aloud; "When the sea is calm, all ships alike show mastership in floating."

"A coward dies a thousand deaths," Woody said. "The valiant tastes death but once."

Orbit looked at Woody thoughtfully, put down Shakespeare and went back to cleaning up from dinner.

Watching Orbit glide around the kitchen, Woody was transfixed by his efficiency of motion. His stomach was so big, he should have been bumping into things. It was as if the room was moving around Orbit, rather than *vice versa*.

"That your guitar?" Woody nodded at an acoustic guitar in the corner with candle wax dripping on it.

"I found it in a dumpster. Help yourself."

Woody looked down at his hand. "I used to play guitar. I wrote a song, this music lawyer recorded it, and now it's on the radio with another guy singing. It's a long story."

"Decisions that affect the most people in this country are made by lawyers," Orbit said. "Artists, architects, Jaguar mechanics, mothers, people who know how to solve problems; that's who should be making the important decisions."

"Sounds like you're not too thrilled about lawyers," Woody said.

"I used to be one." Orbit shrugged. "I dropped out. Some lawyers do some good, a lot of them just perpetuate the conflicts."

"Everyone's stuck in everyone else's ruts," Woody said. "You can set a precedent by laying a board across a mud puddle. Most people won't consider a better way across, not even caring that maybe the guy that laid that board down might've been a drunk four-year-old."

"It's all relative." Orbit threw aside his dishtowel and let himself fall back into a car seat with a thud. "When that four-year-old drunk laid that board in the mud, anybody could walk across it, dance across it, in their pajamas. Take that same board, ten feet long, twelve inches wide, lay it between two rooftops, then see how it feels to walk across."

"Everything *is* relative," Woody said quietly.

Orbit nodded agreement. "No exceptions. Try to find one thing everyone agrees on. You can't. Put a chair by a dumpster in an alley that smells like piss and put a chair on the most idyllic beach in Hawaii. Then get everyone in the world to sit in both chairs and agree which place is better. You can't. Most of them will like the beach, but there will always be somebody that had a friend drown at the beach or has a nice memory of a dumpster. It's... all... relative."

Picking his feet up one at a time, Orbit plopped them on a leather ottoman, took in a deep breath and started a low reverberating chant. A multi-layered sound emanated out from the recesses of his big chest, gradually expanding into a rumble that filled the room like an earthquake, jangling jars and rattling Woody's bones. Woody held on to his armrests. Orbit's eyes were closed, his cheeks full of air, the sound continuous: circular breathing.

After a few minutes, Woody relaxed into the car seat and let the vibrations massage his body. He couldn't tell how long it had lasted, but after the chanting dissolved into silence and Orbit's cheeks were deflated, he still felt a tiny vibration on the surface of his skin. "Motion," he said softly.

Orbit emitted one more guttural sound, like the last bit of air let out of a tire.

"Motion's the one thing everyone agrees on," Woody said, not sure if Orbit was listening. "Heartbeats, tides, orbiting planets. Music is pure motion, that's all it is."

Orbit's breathing segued into snoring. *Deja Vu*, Woody thought, *I spend half my life watching other people sleep.* The fire's embers faded to a faint orange glow and he fell into the first restful sleep he'd had in a long time.

When Woody awoke the next morning, Orbit was gone. There was an envelope on the plate glass table with a hand-written note in beautifully scripted penmanship:

"A coward dies a thousand deaths, the valiant tastes death but once."
Good luck on your journey.
See you in the future or see you in the pasture.
This is for you, I found it in the dumpster.

Inside the envelope was a ten-dollar bill.

With one hand and consummate patience, Woody folded his blanket and neatened up the room. He took one last look around Orbit's amazing home and walked out across the expansive parking lot. He felt light on his feet, well rested and enjoyed the fragrance of the eucalyptus trees lining the street. The pain in his hand was still there, but it felt tolerable; he'd get to a doctor soon. He tried hitchhiking, didn't get a ride and didn't care.

Walking the mile to the nearest bus station, he found out about a bus to the Greek Theater and bought a ticket. Then he called Ray from a phone booth and left a message that he was coming to the show and to be sure to put him on the guest list. Woody decided that if he didn't see Pearlman at Ray's show, he'd call him tomorrow, Monday morning.

He thought about calling Stephanie. After all the kindness she and Max and Auddie had shown him, he'd just walked away in a drugged-out stupor. He wondered whether they'd really locked him out or if he'd just been too high to open their apartment door. He decided to wait until after the concert before calling her; one more day and everything in his life might be different.

Stephanie was always saying that Buddhists were always saying that of all the virtues; kindness, compassion, honesty, generosity... the greatest virtue of all was patience. He remembered the first time they'd talked about it. While she'd explained the concept, he'd made a little protest sign, an index card thumb-tacked to a Popsicle stick:

241

WHAT DO WE WANT?
PATIENCE.
WHEN DO WE WANT IT?
NOW!

Remembering the laugh they'd shared, Woody ran the fingers of his left hand across the wooden slats of the bus-stop bench he was sitting on. Shortly after he'd gotten out of the hospital, he'd gone back to the town square where the police had found him lying on the ground unconscious. He'd walked around, sat on different benches and couldn't remember ever being there. The experience was like an impenetrable opaque part of his brain, a blurry image he couldn't bring into focus. Thinking about it gave him a headache.

Chapter 29

Two bus transfers got Woody to within four blocks of the Greek Theater. The headaches and throbbing pain in his hand were back, and it was hard for him to even look up in the bright sunlight. Thinking about Orbit and the last meal he'd had, Woody counted his money. With the buses, phone call, and cold drink he'd bought, he had about five bucks left. He went behind a grocery store, found a green dumpster with six-foot-high sides and wondered how Orbit managed to get in and back out carrying all the things he retrieved. With great difficulty, Woody leaned a wooden pallet against the side and climbed up high enough to peer over the edge. He couldn't believe what he saw. It was as if someone had taken an aisle from the store, tipped it on its end and poured the entire contents into the dumpster. It was half-filled with wilted vegetables, bruised fruit, hundreds of packages of lunch meat, cheese, cookies, bread... enough food to feed a village. Pulling himself up further, he realized that if he managed to get in, he could be stuck in there.

He pictured himself eating sliced cheese sandwiches until he was trapped on his back like a distended wood tick with a bloated body

243

and tiny flailing arms. Suddenly losing his one-handed grip on the slippery metal side, he fell off and smacked his cast on the pavement.

The pain was worse than ever, the plaster cast barely intact. He sat on the ground with his back against the dumpster and waited for his body to calm down. Sitting there, he noticed a penny on the ground next to him. He picked it up with his left hand, put it between the numb fingers of his right hand and tried an up and down motion as if the penny was a guitar pick. He was only able to do the motion twice before the penny fell to the pavement.

As Woody got close to the concert, his mind was spinning with possibilities. Was Ray working with Pearlman? Was there a royalty check waiting for him somewhere? Would he be on the guest list and treated like a special guest, or was Ray stealing his song and he wouldn't even get into the concert?

The area was crowded with festive concertgoers. There were hawkers selling T-shirts, food vendors and throngs of giddy young people swinging day-glow fluorescent tubes. He was wondering what kind of food they'd have backstage when he passed a food cart with the fragrant smell of steaming hot dogs. Woody hadn't eaten all day, the hot dogs were two bucks. Was he still a vegetarian? Not today, today he needed protein. He stepped up to the vendor. "Make me one with everything."

The man looked at Woody, dirty and disheveled, his hand in a dilapidated cast. He could smell Woody's body odor even from behind the hot dog steamer. He put a dog on a bun with mustard, relish, and onions.

"You by chance have any sauerkraut?" Woody asked.

The vendor put a much-too-high pile of sauerkraut on top and handed it to Woody. It was warm and delicious, but hard to manage with one hand.

The vendor noticed the difficulty Woody was having, losing half of his condiments while he ate. "So you must be a Ray Bell fan."

"Actually, I know him."

"No kidding?" The vendor took a closer look at Woody, strands of sauerkraut hanging from his two-week-old beard.

"How about you?" Woody asked through a mouthful of mustard. "You like Ray Bell?"

"Oh, I'm here every night." He was concentrating on pouring steaming water from one stainless steel container to another. "All the bands sound pretty much the same to me. Once in a while, I got a buddy that works the back door, I go see a few numbers at the start of a show. I'm too busy afterwards. Hot dogs are a lot more popular *after* the concert." He covered the steaming pan. "I don't really care for the loud stuff, though I have to say, that song 'Stephanie' is pretty nice. It just came out of nowhere and now it's on the radio and they've got pictures of Ray Bell everywhere."

The vendor nodded at the T-shirts for sale hanging up behind him. One had a picture of Ray with a sultry Elvis Presley expression: *"RAY BELL AT THE GREEK."* Another T-shirt said *"STEPHANIE ROCKS!"*

The vendor kept talking. Woody stopped listening. He couldn't believe the T-shirts. Woody had read stories about Ray's last hit song. The guy had been playing in hotel lounges, then two months later he was riding in limos. Now the same thing had happened again. "I wrote that song," Woody said to the hot dog vendor.

"What song?"

""Stephanie.""

"No kidding?" the vendor said, unwrapping a plastic bag of buns. Just then two young men stepped in front of Woody and ordered hot dogs.

Approaching the outdoor amphitheater, Woody thought of its remarkable history; everyone from Theodore Roosevelt to the Dalai Lama to Jerry Garcia had been on its stage. *Whatever else happens,* he thought, *the song I wrote is going to be played here tonight.*

There were long lines at every entrance. Woody found the box office: "SOLD OUT, WILL CALL ONLY." He cut to the front of the line.

"Excuse me!" a young girl yelled, and pushed herself in front of him.

"I'm with the band," Woody said.

"So am I!"

Woody got in the back of the line. It took him fifteen minutes to get to the window. "I'm with the band, I'm on Ray Bell's guest list," he told the man behind the thick glass.

"Can I see a photo ID?"

"I don't have one," Woody said.

"I need to see some kind of picture ID to verify a guest pass."

"I lost my wallet, my name's Woody. I just walked here from San Francisco, I'm with the band."

The man picked up a clipboard and scanned a long list of names. "Nobody named Woody on the list."

"I'm a personal friend of Ray Bell's. I wrote the song "Stephanie." Get a message to him or his manager, Jason Nett, and he'll okay it. This is important, just do it!"

Woody looked wild. The man rolled his chair back slightly from the window. "I'm sorry sir, but you're not on the list. There's nothing I can do."

"Where's somebody from management that I can talk to?"

"At the backstage door, around the side to the right."

Going against the flow of fans, Woody walked a hundred feet around the concrete building and found the backstage door. A man in a suit with a security guard on each side of him was blocking the metal door, a dozen people trying to talk to him at once. Two men pushed their way to the front, the man in the suit nodded and quickly let them in. Woody stepped forward. "My name's Woody. I work with Ray Bell."

"Do you have a wristband? You can't use this entrance without a white wristband."

"Tell Ray Woody's here. Or get word to his manager Jason Nett, he'll let me in."

"You have to go to the box office and get a wristband."

246

"I've already been to the box office. I'm telling you man, just talk to Ray for two seconds and he'll okay it. Just tell him –"

"For this entrance you need a wristband. No wristband, no –"

"Hey man! I wrote 'Stephanie'! The song they're playing tonight! Tell Ray Woody's here and he'll let me in. I'm with the goddamn band!" Just then a young man walked up, flashed his wristband and slipped in the door. A girl started walking in right behind him. The man in the suit grabbed her arm. "Can I see your wristband?"

"I'm Ray Bell's sister, Patricia Bell." She put her driver's license in his face.

"You'll have to go to the box office."

"I'm Ray's sister!" The man positioned his body in front of her, a security guard moved closer. She started to protest when a nicely dressed woman walked up and interrupted her. "Excuse me, I'm Clarisse Johnson. I sing backups with Ray. I'm on his new album. I didn't have time to make advance arrangements, but if you check with Ray's road manager Bill Vitt –"

"Hey honey! I'm Ray's sister," the other girl snapped. "Wait your turn with every other backup singer in town!"

"Don't honey me, sister! I work with Ray and he never said anything about having a sister, honey!"

"Sorry ladies, you both need a wristband to get in this door." Just then, two buff young guys pushed past the women and flashed official-looking laminates on neckbands. The security guards converged on them. "We're with the sound company," one of the guys said with authority.

"You need prior clearance for tonight, no exceptions. If you didn't get advance clearance..."

Woody was now ten feet back from the door. He heard the music starting up inside and knew he wasn't getting in. The band was onstage; there was no way to get word to Ray. He stepped back, leaned against the cement wall and watched the people milling around, some holding their index fingers up and little handmade "I need a miracle" signs.

Totally depressed, he stood listening to the rumble of the music echoing off the concrete structure, trying to recognize what the band was playing. He listened to one song, then another, wanting to leave but waiting to see if they played "Stephanie." He wondered what kind of arrangement they'd use in a concert like this. He'd heard that projecting the energy of a song out into a venue this big could require an entirely different treatment, different than what worked in an intimate setting like, as Ray had pointed out, Woody's shower.

Half the set had gone by before Woody realized that, if they hadn't played "Stephanie" yet, it was probably scheduled as the show closer, or the encore. Too depressed to wait around any longer, he shuffled towards the front of the building, half-heartedly hoping to see someone he knew working at one of the entrances.

Walking back down the hill, he thought about calling Stephanie and apologizing. Wondering where the closest hospital emergency room was, he found himself walking past the hot dog vendor.

"What happened?" the vendor said."

"I couldn't get in."

"You feel like checking out the rest of the show?"

"They're sold out."

"I got a friend that works the door by the north parking lot where they let people out. A small guy with a ponytail named Ron. Tell him Hot Dog Harry says to let you in with extra mustard. That's the password. I trade him once in a while for a couple of hot dogs. You can only get in where the cheap seats are, but maybe you can catch a couple of songs."

When Ron let Woody slip in, he told him he'd only have time to see the encore. The moment the metal door slammed closed, Woody was engulfed in a swirling mass of shrieking fans. The volume was deafening, his senses bombarded from every direction, people crushed together in the aisles, spotlight beams of white light racing erratically over the seething mass. No one was onstage. The entire audience was on its feet chanting: *RAY! RAY! RAY!*

248

Woody tried maneuvering to where he could get a sight line to the stage. The crowd was packed so tightly, it was impossible to move forward even a few inches. But he was moving, involuntarily, being carried sideways by the shifting crowd. He had a moment of panic, feeling that if he resisted, he'd lose his footing and be trampled. He let himself go with the flow, doing his best to protect his hand.

Five minutes later, when the band came out, the sideways motion stopped and the audience burst into an explosive roar. Woody strained to see past the screaming kids in front of him. They were mostly girls, standing on seats where there were seats, waving their hands over their heads.

Two guitarists dressed in black came out on each side of the stage, guitars slung low, feet wide apart. The drummer, bass player, keyboardist, and three women backup singers, all dressed in black, took their positions. Then Ray, all in white, came running out, prancing back and forth across the front of the stage, waving a microphone over his head, egging on the audience. People were in a frenzy, jockeying for position to see the stage. Woody tried covering his ears against the deafening noise, using his left hand against one ear and pressing the top of his right shoulder against the other side of his head, holding his cast in the air.

Ray put his hand in the air, signaling the audience to quiet down. "Thank you! Thank you! You're a great audience! I'm in love with every one of you!" There was another explosion of sound. Ray raised his hands over his head, palms toward the audience, and held the pose until the crowd finally settled down. "For this last song I'd like to thank someone. Someone very special to me. I'd like to thank a beautiful red-haired woman I once knew, but never got to know the way I'd like to. I'm still waiting! This song's for you... STEPHANIEEE!"

The guitars hit the opening power chords and the audience erupted again. The band performed a powerful anthemic rock and roll version of the song with Ray cavorting across the stage, playing air guitar, gyrating his hips, inciting roaring waves of cheers. When the band went into the last chorus, an enormous panel of white lights came down across the back of the stage with STEPHANIE! STEPHANIE! STEPHANIE! flashing on and off in time with the music.

Fireworks exploded above the open amphitheater and the crowd around Woody immediately started moving toward the back door. A throng of teenager boys were somehow wedging themselves like a riptide through the aisle faster than everyone else. Woody hunched over to shield his hand, wondering if there was any hope of getting to the dressing room to talk to Ray. He looked toward the stage. The musicians were gone, replaced by an army of security guards in blue uniforms. Woody put his attention back to just trying to stay upright and let himself be carried toward the exit.

As soon as he got outside, the momentum of the crowd increased dramatically, like stepping into a fast-moving river. When he finally managed to get to the edge and could walk at his own pace, his legs felt wobbly. Emotionally devastated, physically depleted, he walked slowly into a wooded area beyond the parking lot, sat down on the ground littered with bottles and cans and leaned back against a tree. The noise of the audience still raged in his ears, the back of his neck felt like a giant hand was digging its fingers into the base of his skull. And through the agony, "Stephanie" was playing in his head. Trying to wrap his mind around the spectacle he'd just witnessed, he felt like crying but couldn't. He'd never felt this bad.

Sliding sideways down the base of the tree, he put his head on the hard dirt. It smelled like piss. The Bayside Mission Inn? Murray's soft corduroy couch? Everything in his life seemed like a distant dream, but the pain in his head and hand were brutally present. Shifting the position of his hand, a jolt shot up his arm. He clenched his teeth, knowing that if he just waited, the feeling would subside back to what he could tolerate, to what seemed intolerable a few minutes ago. Could things get any worse? *This song's for you, Stephaniee!*

Woody wanted to die. How much energy would it take to stand up and walk to some tall structure or freeway overpass? He visualized his hand under a huge truck wheel, crushing it badly enough to have it amputated, anything to remove the source of the pain. Closing his eyes, he felt consciousness slipping away and imagined being curled-up inside his mind, left alone to die.

Suddenly jerked back to awareness by an eerie, high-pitched sound, Woody saw the dirt a few inches from his face. What was that sound? Where was it coming from? It had a primal quality, like an animal in distress, or an injured child. Should he lift his head to check it out? Could he even get up to do anything about it? The sound seemed so close, echoing in his ears. A shudder of deep sadness suddenly coursed through his body when he realized he was making the sound himself, whimpering like a puppy.

Chink... chink... chink chink. Woody heard the metallic sound before he opened his eyes. Had he died? Was he dreaming? It was daylight, a man with a long gray beard and a clear plastic garbage bag was twenty feet away, collecting aluminum cans off the ground. Woody lifted his head and saw that he was lying in a pile of trash behind the Greek Theater. He automatically pushed down on his right hand and groaned, startling the man with the aluminum cans who hadn't noticed him lying in the litter.

Woody stood up, kicking trash out of his way until he found a bottle with some juice in it. Emptying what was left, he tossed the empty bottle on the ground and started walking. He kept up a slow, relentless pace to a bus stop and spent the last of his money on a bus that took him across the Bay Bridge to First and Mission, a ten-minute walk to the Transamerica Building.

A busy Monday afternoon, Brenda looked up, saw Woody standing in front of her reception desk and gasped so hard she swallowed her gum.

"Where's Pearlman?" Woody jammed his left hand into the jar of candy on Brenda's desk and tore at a piece, trying to open it with his teeth.

At first Brenda didn't recognize him. He looked like a wild animal, his hair a rat's nest of dreadlocks, face covered with dirt. His sling was made of lengths of electrical cord, swollen purple nubs of sausage-like fingers sticking out of his filthy cast, webbed strands of plaster hanging down to his waist.

"I said, where the fuck is Pearlman!" Woody pounded his left fist on the reception desk.

Brenda hit the auto-dial button that called security. She was speaking urgently into her headset when Woody realized what she was doing, reached over and tore the headset off her head. He started around the desk toward the back offices. Brenda stood up and blocked his path. "Mr. Pearlman is in a very private meeting! You can't –"

Woody tried walking around her. She shifted her position and managed to get a shoulder in his path. Staring straight ahead, he shoved her out of the way and just kept going. Off balance, she caught one of her high heels on the corner of the reception desk, and it broke off. Limping after him, she was quickly losing ground. When he reached the end of the hallway and rounded the corner, she kicked off her shoes, ran back to her desk and called security.

Woody burst into Pearlman's office. Two clean-cut men in expensive suits and a younger guy in jeans and a T-shirt were sitting in front his desk. The younger man looked familiar to Woody, but he couldn't place him. He suddenly felt dizzy and put his hand on the door to brace himself.

Pearlman jumped to his feet. "Woody!"

"Hi, Jeff. I know I don't have an appointment or anything, but I've called here a million times and, what's going on with my song? You gave my song to Ray?"

"I didn't give it to Ray, he's stealing it. I've been trying to reach you. Are you okay? You look like you need medical attention.

Pearlman took Woody by the arm and led him into the room. As

252

the men in suits looked on, the man in the T-shirt stood up and offered Woody his seat. "You look a bit rough, mate." He had an English accent. "Can I get you a glass of water or anything?"

Woody sat down and cradled his broken cast. "Do you by any chance have an aspirin or Tylenol?"

Just then Ernie hurried in. "I heard there was some trouble here, Mr. Pearlman." He looked across the room at Woody.

"Hey Ernie." Woody gave a weak smile. Confused, Ernie glanced back at Pearlman.

"Everything's okay here, Ernie. Thanks." Pearlman turned to the Englishman. "Sorry Eric, I think I need to cut this short. If you can talk to Holly about rescheduling?"

Brenda came in barefoot through the open office door. "Mr. Pearlman! That man assaulted me! He charged in here, I tried to stop him and he –"

"You're fired, Brenda."

"What? I haven't done anything wrong! He came in here and hit me! He –"

Pearlman held up his hand. "Get your things together, walk out the door and don't come back."

"But he *attacked* me! I was keeping your meeting private, like you asked me to, and I –"

Leading Woody out of the office, Pearlman glanced over his shoulder at Ernie. Ernie quickly walked up to Brenda and put his big hand on her shoulder.

"What!" Brenda screamed. "You're siccing security on me? That man should be arrested! I didn't do anything but do my job!" She violently jerked her shoulder, Ernie's hand stayed where he'd put it, and Pearlman and Woody walked out.

Chapter 30

Pearlman took Woody to his home in Pacific Heights and set him up with him a warm meal, a hot bath and a sleeping pill. Before he went to bed, Woody called Stephanie and left her a message. By the time she called back, Woody was asleep.

"Hello?"

"Hello, this is Stephanie. I'm calling for Woody?"

"This is Jeff Pearlman, Woody's asleep. I've heard a lot about you. It's nice to finally speak with you."

"I've heard a lot about you too, about all the musicians you've helped. Thank you for helping Woody. How is he?"

"He's actually a mess. It's like he walked off a battlefield into my office. I'm taking him to see a doctor in the morning." Pearlman was sitting in his living room in a turn-of-the century armchair, sipping a glass of wine and reading a file for a court hearing the next day.

"Woody played a show in Marin a couple of months ago," she said. "He was assaulted afterward."

"He told me what he's been going through. In the meantime, his song 'Stephanie' is a huge commercial success and Ray Bell's blatantly trying to steal it. I heard Woody sing the song; there's no question in my mind that it's his. But he needs your help dealing with this. We both do." The pleasant tone of his voice put Stephanie at ease.

There was silence on the phone. "Stephanie?"

"I'm still here."

Pearlman chuckled. "Before Woody went to bed tonight, he told me you might be calling. He said, 'If she doesn't say anything, don't hang up, she doesn't talk during the pauses.'"

She didn't respond.

"I told Woody he can stay with me while we're developing our legal strategy. I've got an empty guesthouse. Will you come to the city? What Woody needs more than anything right now is you."

"I know it seems that way," she said, "but what he really needs is to get *himself* together. Since his hand was injured, he's been using alcohol and pills to deal with the physical and emotional pain. I know it's hard for him, but I'm taking care of my own life right now and, truthfully, he's a different person when he's on drugs."

"Sounds like you still care about him." Pearlman waited for her reaction, smiling to himself at the unusual pacing of the dialogue. This was his forte, talking on the phone, negotiating, and she was throwing him completely off balance with a few moments of silence. How long had he ever stayed in silence on a phone call?

After another long pause, she finally spoke up. "I'm afraid if we tried being together right now, it could make things worse. Being with him is like being on a roller coaster."

"He's definitely not the most socially adept person, but he's very talented. His music is extraordinary."

"I know it is," she said softly. "Believe me, I know."

Pearlman paused, realizing how much he was enjoying the relaxed cadence of their conversation. "I've had such an intimate relationship with the song "Stephanie,'" he said, "I feel like I know you. Everyone who hears the song feels a personal connection. That's what makes it so powerful."

"The music isn't mine, it's Woody's. It's an expression of *his* feelings. That's what you're hearing."

Pearlman considered what she'd said. "It's quite a paradox. He's in about as bad a shape as any artist I've ever seen. At the same time, he's got the greatest opportunity he's ever had to succeed as a songwriter. You might find him to be a completely different person once he gets the validation and credit he deserves."

Stephanie had come to the same conclusion watching Woody's gig at the Sweetwater. But then she'd seen the worst come out, the drugs and the selfishness. "Please tell Woody I called. Tell him good luck at the doctor tomorrow and I'll come to the city in a couple of days to say hi. Thank you for supporting his music."

From what she'd heard from Woody, Stephanie expected Jeff Pearlman to have a nice house. When she drove her Mustang through the gate of his Pacific Heights estate, her jaw dropped. She didn't know it was possible to have such a spacious, private setting in the middle of the city. Walking across lush grass to the guesthouse nestled in a stand of palm trees, she didn't see Woody until she was almost right next to him. He was sitting in a padded chaise lounge, wearing a Hawaiian shirt and, she noticed immediately, not playing the guitar.

He stood up slowly, they hugged, and he sat back in his chair. She sat down next to him. "This place is nice. How're you feeling?"

"Like a million bucks; all green and wrinkled." He gave her a weak smile, lifted up his new cast and made a motion with his left hand as if his cast was a guitar.

She rubbed his leg. "Jeff said you had surgery on your hand yesterday. I heard it went well."

"It was just an in-office procedure. The doctor was pretty cool; a friend of Jeff's. Seems like Jeff knows everybody. Bring your bathing suit?" Woody nodded toward the pool.

"You're pretty fortunate to have Jeff taking care of you like this."

"Yeah, he's been great. And the scene here is incredible. Actually, I think he's kind of lonely in this big place. It's probably why he works so much."

They sat quietly for a few minutes, a light breeze rustling the low-hanging palm fronds above their heads. With a view of the windy San Francisco Bay, they watched an enormous container ship making its deliberate way past Alcatraz through a maze of seemingly out-of-control little sailboats. From their Pacific Heights perspective, the container ship made everything look out of scale, like toys in a bathtub from different toy manufacturers.

Stephanie broke the silence. "You seem so much more peaceful than you were the last time I saw you.".

"I'm sorry about all that craziness with the drugs. I've been acting like a real jerk. I just kind of hit the wall." He took her hand. "There's no place like rock bottom to push off from."

Holding his hand in both of hers, she knew she'd made the right decision to give him the support he needed. This was a turning point in his life: he could realize his dreams, or go back to having nothing.

Pearlman had arranged for house calls by a therapeutic masseuse and a Chinese doctor who performed acupuncture on Woody. Within two weeks he was almost entirely off pain pills, his headaches had subsided and the surgeon was cautiously optimistic about the feeling returning to his hand.

Woody woke up every morning thankful for the positive turn of events. He was back with Stephanie, living in luxury, and had the best lawyer in California looking after his interests. The only thing missing was music. He spent his time writing poems, doing pencil drawings left-handed, and plunking on the grand piano in Pearlman's music room. It was a slow process.

Stephanie didn't say it, but she missed his music as much as he did. She knew that for him, not playing the guitar was like going cold turkey with any addiction. And he was doing it while he cut down on drinking, smoking and pain pills. She admired his tenacity. He had his bad days, sometimes being quiet for hours, often sitting at the piano with tears in his eyes. But for the most part, he was being positive. And she was amazed at how quickly he was learning to do things with his left hand. She especially noticed it when they made love.

Pearlman filed a copyright infringement complaint in Federal District Court against Ray Bell and met briefly with Woody and Stephanie every few days to discuss legal strategy. While he worked on Woody's case, he was putting in long days on complex contract negotiations between a bevy of upcoming San Francisco bands and the major-label record companies swarming around them. The musicians saw the explosion of new opportunities to play and record music, and the record companies saw the dollar signs. Pearlman's impossible job was to protect the musicians' interests, motivate the corporations to invest, and foresee the future.

It was late afternoon. Pearlman was at his office and had just hung up from a long conversation with a pleasantly stoned guitar player. The guitarist swore he'd heard a Warner Bros. A&R rep at a party say to him that if he signed with Warner's, he'd be entitled to "royalty." Pearlman decided to call it a day. He looked forward to seeing Woody and Stephanie. They'd been in his guesthouse for almost a month, but due to his busy schedule, he hadn't spent much time with them. When he did, he thoroughly enjoyed their company.

When Pearlman got home, they were outside on the lawn, Woody plunking out a rhythm on Pearlman's "beach" guitar, Stephanie dancing on the grass.

The doctor had removed Woody's cast and said it was time for him to slowly start using his right hand. Woody had rigged up a simple apparatus with a guitar pick super-glued between the thumb and index finger of a leather golfer's glove. It supplemented the strength required to hold a pick and he was just getting the hang of it.

Watching and listening to the catchy little melody, Pearlman was reminded that the quality of Woody's music was what this was all about. Through a musical instrument trader he knew, Pearlman had purchased another Martin guitar similar to the one he'd given

Woody at the recording session. He'd been waiting until Woody's hand healed to give it to him. This felt like the right time.

Woody's eyes lit up when he saw the distinctive gold wood finish. He put down the "beach" guitar, picked up the new one and kept strumming, tuning while he played. It was apparent to Pearlman that Woody was a completely different person than the half-starved drug addict that had burst into his office.

"Why don't you two come over in the morning and I'll make you breakfast," Pearlman suggested when Woody took a break from playing. "There's some business we need to discuss."

The next morning, Stephanie combed out Woody's hair, braided it halfway down his back, and they walked hand-in-hand across the beautifully landscaped grounds.

Stephanie helped Pearlman cook breakfast while Woody played his new guitar. "How long do these court things last?" he asked Pearlman. "I've heard lawyers can keep the process going forever."

Pearlman raised a sizzling stainless steel omelet pan off a gas burner and, with a flick of his wrist, expertly flipped the omelet in the air 180 degrees. "No business until after breakfast."

They enjoyed a simple meal, served on white Wedgwood china on a cobalt-blue glass table. The table reminded Woody of Orbit's plate-glass table. Orbit had created a living environment out of discards that, in some ways, was as comfortable as Pearlman's luxury home.

After breakfast they sat on Pearlman's deck in silk-covered rattan chairs, drinking coffee and enjoying the view. Woody carefully negotiated the cream and sugar left-handed without spilling a drop. "Jeff, your hospitality has been amazing. And whatever happens with my music, just having you work on it is –"

Pearlman held up his hand. "You better take a look at this." He put the new issue of Billboard Magazine on the table. Woody and Stephanie slid their chairs together and read the front-page story.

ONE-HIT WONDER RAY BELL SCORES ANOTHER, ITINERANT MUSICIAN CLAIMS AUTHORSHIP

Singer RAY BELL has his first song on the charts since his huge success, "BABY DON'T BE A BABY," almost five years ago. After speculation about BELL being a one-hit-wonder, his mega-hit "STEPHANIE" is charted at number one in twenty-five countries. The song will likely be nominated for a Grammy and is considered by some to be a shoo-in for Best Song of the Year.

In a move that's being talked about throughout the music industry, an unknown songwriter, CHESTER WOODS, who goes by the name "WOODY," has filed suit in Federal District Court claiming authorship of the song. Woody's attorney, JEFF PEARLMAN, was unavailable for comment.

According to Bell's attorney, MARIA ANGELISTA, Bell wrote the song and controls all publishing and copyrights. In a counter-claim for punitive damages and attorney's fees filed by Bell, he claims to be the victim of a frivolous lawsuit.

A supporting declaration by Bell asserts his proven track record as a recording artist and states that the alleged co-writer, Woody, is a mentally unstable street musician with no professional experience. According to music industry sources, the woman who is the subject of the now world-renowned love song is said to have been a topless dancer who was patronized by both Bell and Woody.

An anonymous source at the accounting department of A&M Records estimates that annual royalties for "Stephanie" will exceed $400,000. Because of the uniquely broad appeal of the song across genres, lifetime royalties generated from radio, TV, film, and recordings by other artists, are projected to exceed five million dollars.

Pearlman, the prominent entertainment lawyer who represents Woody, is Bell's former attorney and negotiated Bell's first record contract six years ago. Also of interest: Angelista was, until recently, an associate at Pearlman's law firm. Due to the potential conflicts, both counsel were required to get the court's permission to represent their respective clients.

Bell and Angelista have recently been seen together attending musical and social events.

All royalties being generated by "Stephanie" have been frozen in a court-ordered escrow account until a resolution is reached.

"Ray didn't write one note or word of that song!" Woody spilled his coffee.

"Easy does it there, cowboy." Pearlman cleaned the spill and poured Woody a fresh cup. "We'll turn this around when we present our side of the story to the press."

"That article is disgusting!" Stephanie's face was red. "What in God's name does my dancing have to do with Ray stealing this song? And they printed this!" Trying to calm herself, she took a sip of coffee and lowered her voice "You have the version of the song you recorded at the Palace. Doesn't that prove Woody wrote it?"

"It's good we have that version," Pearlman said, "but it doesn't show conclusively that he wrote it."

"Why not?"

"Because theoretically Woody could have first gotten the song from Ray, instead of the other way around."

"I showed him how to sing every note of that song." Woody was on his feet, pacing around the kitchen. "That guy couldn't write a decent song if his life depended on it! I can't believe this. It's like some kind of bad dream."

"I'm doing everything possible to protect your legal rights," Pearlman said. "We got a break with our motion for a temporary injunction. The judge is a Grateful Dead fan—I got him some backstage passes before he was a judge. Worldwide royalties from the song are frozen in escrow. But I put my reputation on the line with the court, saying I'll produce evidence that you wrote the song. Now we have to come up with it."

Pearlman tossed the Billboard Magazine aside. He didn't want the energy of that article on the table between them. "Maria is playing hardball. I can tell by how quickly she files responsive motions that she was prepared for this, ready with both barrels loaded. Before I got the injunction, she and Ray were probably accumulating five or ten thousand dollars a day since the song's been at number one. According to documents I subpoenaed from A&M, she's got fifty percent of everything: mechanical royalties, performance royalties, sync licenses, merchandising. She pretty much has the rights to fifty percent of Ray's soul, assuming he still has one. He must've needed this deal pretty bad."

"Maria Angelista worked for you?" Stephanie asked.

"I totally misread her. She's turned out to be one of the most ruthless people I've ever known. She saw the potential of Ray singing 'Stephanie' and got it released on A&M Records after she left my firm. They've been conspiring together to steal the song, and who knows what else. She and Ray make a perfect couple. Ray might be her only client. I had hopes of negotiating a deal, maybe give Ray something for singing the song and getting it out there. But they want everything. If they agree to a settlement, they'll be admitting they stole the song." Pearlman glanced over at Woody staring out the window with a steel-hard look on his face. "I know you wrote that song, Woody," Pearlman said quietly. "There's never been any question in my mind."

"I don't understand," Stephanie sighed. "How can they possibly prove Ray wrote it?"

"Angelista's ready to go to trial. She'll attack Woody's credibility and present Ray's professional recording history and references from the most influential people in the music business. Not only does she have, quote, 'music experts' who say they can prove Ray's other music is similar to "Stephanie," she's got musicians who Woody's played with that are prepared to testify that he's unstable and not credible. She's put together an airtight package of sworn affidavits, copyright registration, publishing agreements, the works."

Pearlman and Stephanie looked for Woody's reaction to all this. He just stared out the window. "But it can't be airtight," Stephanie pleaded, "it's all a lie."

Pearlman put his hands flat on the table. "Not only do we have to prove Ray didn't write it, we have to prove that Woody *did*." He turned to Woody. "So, what've you got?"

Woody looked over at Stephanie. "I wrote the song about *her*. She's living proof."

"I guess the fact that you two have been together is evidence of something. They're claiming that Ray could've written the song about her too." Pearlman gave Stephanie a penetrating look. "Do you and Ray know each other?"

Stephanie kept her eyes on Woody while she spoke. "I've met Ray a few times. I've never once been with him when Woody wasn't there."

The tension in the room was palpable. Pearlman was reluctant to stir things up any more, but he knew from too many bad experiences that if he didn't present his clients with the harsh reality of the other side's position, it could be a catastrophe in court. "Ray claims he had other women's names as working titles for the song," Pearlman said, "until he saw you dance."

Woody and Stephanie locked eyes across the room. "Like I said," she held Woody's stare. "I've never been with Ray except when Woody was there." She turned to Pearlman. "Is it possible that Ray was in the audience at The Chi Chi Club and saw me dance? Yes."

Pearlman intentionally changed the subject. "I don't suppose you've ever copyrighted any of your songs?"

"I've been a little busy writing songs," Woody said curtly. "I thought *you* were the lawyer."

Pearlman knew not to give the comment any energy. His office had immediately drafted the copyright forms after he agreed to represent Woody, but when Woody had disappeared, they'd put everything on hold. "The fact that Ray owns the copyright doesn't help matters. Still, it's not dispositive. The court will consider material evidence that tends to invalidate the copyright, if we can come up with the evidence."

Stephanie turned to Woody. "What about that cassette recording you made when you first taught Ray the song?"

"I gave it to Ray."

"You gave it to Ray? You didn't save a copy?"

"It was a funky work demo. I exchange tapes with guys all the time." Woody shook his head. "I have to admit, I had a funny feeling when I gave that tape to Ray."

"Do you have any other recordings?" Pearlman asked. "Earlier recordings of you singing the song where the date can be verified? Or recordings of other original songs with similar chordal or melodic patterns?"

"I've got every kind of recording known to man. I've got tapes of me farting through an Echoplex."

"Terrific." Pearlman was getting irritated. "It'll shift the burden of proof to the other side to prove you don't fart."

"What kinds of evidence would a court consider?" Stephanie asked.

"Anything that's relevant." Pearlman turned to Woody. "Are there musicians who could testify you wrote the song?"

"There's guys who know it's my song."

Stephanie raised her eyebrows. "Like who?"

"Like the guys I've jammed with."

"Who could testify in a court room? Crazy Carl, so spaced out he can't put two sentences together? Or Inky with those tattoos on his face."

"Roger, the keyboard player. I showed him the chords the day I wrote it."

"I thought you said Roger was doing time for his fourth DUI."

"Sounds like there might be a little credibility issue with your witnesses." Pearlman gestured to the Billboard Magazine on the chair next to him. "Ray will bring in a parade of rock stars and record company presidents who say he's the greatest guy and the greatest songwriter that ever lived."

"There's Murray," Stephanie said quietly.

Woody smiled. "There's always Murray." He snapped his fingers. "Remember those two women that were there when I taught Ray the song? They ended up leaving with him. They heard me show him how to sing it."

Pearlman cleared his throat. "Are you talking about the two women at the recording session in your apartment?"

"Yeah. How'd you know about them?"

"Those women are two of Ray's key witnesses. Maria claims they're intimately familiar with Ray's music and ready to testify they heard Ray teaching the song to *you*."

"That figures," he said bitterly. "Those air-head bitches."

"Ray's version of that night is that he was at The Chi Chi Club with Stephanie, then they went together to your apartment. Everyone that was there will testify that they saw Ray arrive with her. The two woman will testify that Woody played some of his own material, then, after everyone else left, Ray sang his song 'Stephanie' and you got upset."

"I got upset because that spaz couldn't get the melody right!"

Pearlman sighed. "Let's try to stay on point."

"Woody performed the song in front of a hundred people at The Sweetwater," Stephanie offered.

"Like everything else we're talking about, it happened after the fact, after they allege Ray had shown the song to Woody. When Woody played at the Sweetwater, it was already getting airplay." Pearlman punched his fist into his open hand. "We can't let those scumbags get away with this!"

Woody went back to pacing around the kitchen. "What about that shoe box of cassettes in your closet?" he asked Stephanie. "There might be a version I recorded when I was first working on it."

She looked at him evenly. "I threw them out."

"What?"

"Half of them were broken, you'd just smashed your guitar, and I was moving out. Don't blame me for this. You leave tapes everywhere you go. The tape you're looking for could be on the floor of your car."

Pearlman abruptly stood up. "I'm available to interview any

potential witnesses or audition recordings. It's time to get it together. We're only talking about millions of dollars and your entire music career." He turned to leave.

"Jeff," Woody said quietly, and Pearlman stopped. "How can you tell when a hippie's been in your house?"

Pearlman raised his eyebrows.

"He's still there."

Pearlman couldn't help but smile.

Two days later, after a long day at the office and a late dinner with some musician clients, Pearlman came home and saw all the lights on in the guesthouse. He found Woody and Stephanie surrounded by stacks of cassette tapes. Woody had on a pair of bulky headphones, trying to find any bit of a lyric or chord progression that showed the inception of his song. Stephanie was neatly labeling and cataloguing everything.

"Hi Jeff," Woody said too loudly with the headphones on.

"You guys having any luck?"

"Listen to this." Woody restarted a tape and handed the headphones to Pearlman.

He listened for a minute. "What am I listening to?"

""Stephanie." Those are the original chords. It's from a gig I did at a coffee house. It would've been on their calendar and they say the name of the place when they introduce me."

"Are there any lyrics?"

"No."

Pearlman picked up the headphones and signaled Woody to play it again. "This might be useful," he said after listening for a minute. "It could be helpful to our experts to show an example of your musical 'fingerprints.' They can use either earlier versions of "Stephanie," or other similar-sounding original songs. But I recognize the chorus because I'm listening for it. We need an example of the song that anyone could recognize." He set the headphones down, looking very tired. "Ray's experts will testify that the majority of rock songs all have similar chords. The beat and the melody are what make them unique. In songs like this, the vocals are what embodies the melody." Pearlman sighed and shook his head. "Sorry, I've had a long day. I know you guys are doing your best. We need something undeniable, and we need it soon." He took the latest issue of Rolling Stone from under his arm, set it open on the table and walked out.

The article had a half-page photo of Ray sitting at a white grand piano in a white tuxedo, with a woman with platinum blonde hair and a white evening gown lying seductively across the top of the piano. There were no black keys on the keyboard; they were all white. Underneath the picture it said RAY BELL'S "STEPHANIE" NOMINATED FOR GRAMMY, BEST SONG OF THE YEAR.

Woody threw the magazine in the trash and put the headphones back on. When he looked up and saw Stephanie reading the article, he tore the headphones off his head and slammed them on the table. "I can tell you what it says! It says Ray Bell writes songs about strippers! This is all bullshit!" He swept the back of his arm across the table, scattering tapes onto the floor, stood up and started toward the door.

Stephanie jumped to her feet. "You're not going to solve anything by throwing a tantrum! Our relationship stands on four legs, and two of them are yours. If you start flipping out, this whole thing's going to fall apart."

Woody looked at her blankly, picked up the keys to her car and walked out the door.

"Where are you going?" she yelled after him.

"To talk to Ray."

When Woody pulled Stephanie's Mustang up to Ray's apartment building, the door was wide open, a moving van parked in front. There were over fifty apartments in the tall building; someone was moving in or moving out. This was his chance to slip in, get upstairs and confront Ray.

On the drive over he'd obsessively gone over the possibilities of what he'd say. "Hey Ray, I'd like to get some gas money for driving over here, could I get that million bucks you owe me? Hey Ray, I'll make you a deal; sit down at your fancy-ass white piano and play the bridge to 'Stephanie' and you can keep all the money. Hey Ray, if you don't pick up that white phone and call A&M Records and tell them you didn't write the song, I'm gonna tear off your head and shit in your neck."

If Ray wasn't there, he'd just wait. Sooner or later Ray would show up. Unlike trying to deal with the ponderous legal system, Woody knew that in some parts of the world, if a man was owed money, he'd sit in front of the debtor's house, holding a solitary vigil for days or weeks, for everyone in the village to see until his presence couldn't be ignored.

Walking into the lobby of Ray's building, Woody saw the elevator stopped on the ground floor, full of white furniture. He took the stairs and ran up fifteen floors to Ray's penthouse apartment. The door was open, moving blankets on the furniture and white paper runners covered with footprints on the white carpets.

Breathing hard, Woody stopped a guy with a stack of boxes on a hand truck. "Where's Ray?"

"You're in my way, jack," the man grunted and pushed past him.

In the kitchen, Woody spotted a young man straining to tilt a refrigerator onto a dolly. Woody put his shoulder into it and helped him.

"Thanks."

"Is Ray around? I'm a friend of his."

"You a musician?"

"Yeah, me and Ray play together. I've got something important for him. I need to give it to him in person."

"Ray's not here. Maybe he's over at his new place, 6252 El Camino del Mar."

"Thanks, bro."

Woody drove across the city to Seacliff, an exclusive community of grand old estates perched on San Francisco's ocean cliffs. When he found the address and parked in front, it was the same scene, movers shuttling armloads of boxes and furniture. But this time it wasn't an apartment building, it was a ceramic-tiled circular driveway and ornate fountain in front of a sprawling luxury home.

Woody approached a woman with a clipboard, standing by a pair of open, hand-carved double doors. Without looking up, she asked "Main house or guest house?"

"Main house."

The woman pointed to the staircase behind her and looked past Woody to a mover with an upside-down armchair on his back. Like the previous place, there were paths of white paper runners on white carpeting.

Woody walked through a spacious entrance and up a wide staircase, into an empty living room with picture windows overlooking a swimming pool. Ray was in the middle of the room, talking to another woman with a clipboard. Woody got in a line of two men holding boxes, waiting their turn for instructions.

When he got to the front of the line, the woman saw that he wasn't carrying anything and hesitated. Just then, the mover with the chair on his back joined them. The woman said to Ray, "Dining room or living room?"

Ray looked up, saw Woody, and froze. The two men just stared at each other.

"Where do you want this thing lady?" the guy with the chair asked.

"Put it down right here," Woody said.

The mover complied. "Glad somebody around here can make a decision." He wiped the sweat off his forehead and walked away.

Woody sat in the chair, crossing his legs and smiling up at Ray. Two men holding the ends of a white couch walked up to them. The woman quickly consulted her clipboard. "This can be either living room picture window or music listening room with space for a coffee table."

"What's happening, Woody?" Ray's voice was tense.

"Me? I've been listening to 'Stephanie' on the radio. How about you? Been writing any songs?" A man carrying a framed gold record walked up and stood by the men holding the couch. "Bathroom," Woody told him.

The mover shrugged and walked away.

Ray started to say something when one of the movers holding the couch not so gently let his end down, leaving the man at the other end in an awkward bent-over position. "We're called *movers*, lady. Our job is to *move* stuff, not stand around holding it." The other mover dropped his end and the couch landed with a thud. They all heard a loud grunt and turned to see the body of a legless grand piano emerging ominously up the staircase like a big white ship being carried on its side by four straining men.

Watching the piano breach the top step, the small group in the middle of the room collectively pictured the bent-over men holding the thousand-pound piano while no one would tell them where to put it.

"I know where this goes." The woman with the clipboard went quickly toward the stairs. The other two movers left the couch where it was, leaving Ray and Woody alone.

"Have a seat Ray." Woody gestured to the couch.

"What're you doing here? What do you want?"

"I want my song back."

"Listen man, you don't come in here demanding anything! You chased me around trying to use *my* reputation and *my* voice. When I sing something I create a whole new piece of music. I made that song a song!" Ray's fists were clenched at his sides. "It was my voice and my name and my concerts that made that song into something while you were singing in the fucking shower!"

"Thanks for all your good work," Woody said. "Now can I please have my song back?"

"What the fuck are you talking about?"

The lady with the clipboard walked up. "Sorry to interrupt, but this can't wait. Do you want the keyboard of the piano facing north or south?"

"I don't give a shit!" Ray yelled at her.

She looked at him wide-eyed, dropping her clipboard to her side. Just then Maria Angelista came up the stairs, took in the scene and hurried across the room. Ray turned to Woody. "You can talk to my lawyer, asshole!"

"What's going on here Ray?"

"This is Woody," Ray snapped. "For starters, you can get him out of my house!"

Maria turned to Woody, still sitting in the chair with his legs crossed. "I'm Maria Angelista, Ray's attorney."

"Yeah, we met." Woody said.

She raised her brows. "I don't believe we have."

"We met at Pearlman's office. Remember?"

"I have no idea what you're talking about and you have no right to be here. If you have something to discuss with my client you can–"

"You remember," Woody interrupted her. "You showed me that black panther crawling up the inside of your leg."

"I'll discuss any legal issues you have with your attorney." She talked over him, but it was obvious that both she and Ray had heard what he'd said. "It's unethical for me to discuss legal matters directly with you when you're represented by –"

"Unethical!" Woody jumped to his feet. "You're both thieves! You outright stole *my* song because your dimwit client couldn't write one of his own!"

Ray took a step toward him. Maria put her hand on Ray's chest and spoke to Woody. "Since you're electing to talk without your attorney, what proof do you have that it's your song? Do you have any evidence to back up your accusations?"

"Evidence? What are you talking about? The three of us right here know Ray didn't write it!"

"You can't prove it." Her voice was steely hard, but under control. "We've got undeniable evidence and verified ownership rights."

271

"I don't have to prove shit!" Woody yelled, spitting at her. "I can sit down at that fucking white piano and play my song. Let's see your lamebrain client figure out where one fucking black note is!"

Realizing they were talking about him as if he wasn't there, Ray suddenly got his voice back. "You're jealous, that's what this whole thing's about! I wrote that song about your girlfriend's ass, and you can't handle it."

Woody moved toward Ray. Out of the corner of his eye he saw the smirk on Maria's face, and stopped himself.

"Go ahead, assault my client in his own home," she egged him on. "Let's see you do it."

Glaring at Ray, Woody felt a jolt of pain from just making a fist with his fragile right hand and wondered what would happen if he hit somebody with it.

"I want this asshole out of my house!" Ray snapped, and stalked away.

"You're trespassing," Maria said. "Leave right now or I'll call the police."

Woody sat back down in his chair. "This is *my* house. My song paid for it. I think I'll hang around and make sure it gets decorated the way I like it." Woody took out a cigarette, lit it, took a drag and flicked the ash on the white carpet.

Ray went out front to where a group of movers were standing. "Sorry boss," the biggest one of the group said. "We decided to take a break. It looked like you were having some kind of private meeting."

Ray took a wad of cash out of his pocket and peeled off a hundred dollar bill. "A crazed fan somehow got in my living room. Throw him out and keep him out."

The mountainous man walked up and stood in front of Woody's chair, his arms folded across his chest. "You got five seconds to get outta here on your own power."

"Five... four..." Woody counted out loud while he stood up and crushed his cigarette out on the carpet with his shoe. "three... two... I won." He turned and walked out.

Chapter 31

Balancing two bags of groceries, Stephanie let herself into the guesthouse that evening and found Woody at a clean table with a pad of paper, sketching a finely detailed pencil drawing of his right hand with his left hand. There wasn't a cassette tape in sight.

"What happened to this place?" She put down the groceries.

"I cleaned up."

"I see that. What happened with Ray?"

"I was wondering why the baseball was getting bigger, then it hit me."

She smiled. "So you saw Ray?"

"Yeah, then I came back here and imagined talking to a guy and getting some advice. The guy was me, in five years. We had a long talk." Woody looked down at his sketchpad for a few seconds, then back at Stephanie. "I decided I don't want to spend any part of my life dealing with someone like Ray. I don't even want to give him enough attention to take him to court." He paused again. "Let him have the song. It was my fault trying to get him to sing it in the first place. I knew he could sing it well, but it wasn't an artistic decision. I did it because he was Ray Bell. I was being disrespectful to my music and I lost a song. Karma. It's gone. I've got plenty more and I'll write new ones and I'll sing my songs myself." He looked down at his hand. "I'll get my guitar playing all the way back, or I'll compose on the piano. You and I know who wrote "Stephanie." That's what matters."

Without a word, Stephanie took her time putting away the groceries and settled into a chair, her legs folded under her. Just watching her calm expression made Woody feel better. After sitting quietly for several minutes, she finally spoke up.

"If that's your decision, I'll support it. There will be lots of challenges, but I think we'll be okay. We'll have to leave here. Jeff's been incredibly generous with us." She gestured to their surroundings. "But if you and I can use our energy together, as a team, instead of struggling with each other or with people like Ray, we can create any kind of life we want. It does feel like the universe is trying to tell us something."

"I love you."

When Pearlman went over to the guesthouse the next day, as usual, Woody was playing guitar and Stephanie was dancing. "We've got some business to discuss."

Woody played a minor chord.

"Maria sent me a fax this morning, a ridiculous one-time token settlement offer. In exchange, we have to drop the lawsuit and agree to release all future claims. The settlement would remain confidential, sealed with the court, and doesn't acknowledge any participation by Woody in the song composition. I told her to take the offer and shove it."

Pearlman waited for a response from either of them. There was none. He went on.

"I don't think we should back down, but there are some things you should be aware of. If we don't accept their offer and they prevail at trial, they're asking the court for costs and attorney's fees. They're also alleging defamation and asking for punitive damages.

Punitive damages are hard to get, but if we lose at trial, they could easily be awarded attorney's fees that could amount to hundreds of thousands of dollars. You'd have a judgment against you and any money you ever make would go to Ray until it's paid off. Backing up their offer, she included a half dozen signed affidavits from prominent industry people, all saying that based on their knowledge and experience, they believe Ray wrote "Stephanie."''"

Pearlman waited. Still no response. "They're also seeking a restraining order. Did you go over to Ray's house and threaten him?"

"How much?" Woody said.

"How much what?"

"How much did they offer?"

"Ten thousand dollars. It's ridiculous, the song's probably making ten thousand dollars a day right now. It'll continue generating income for the rest of your life, and your children's lives."

"Call her back, tell her she's got a deal." Woody said, "and you keep it. I know you've got more than ten grand into this mess."

"You want to take ten thousand dollars for a multi-million-dollar song?"

"It's like that Japanese haiku," Woody said. 'Barn's burned down, now I can see the moon.'"

"Woody's tired of fighting," Stephanie said gently. "We both are."

Pearlman took a moment to let her statement sink in. He was tired of fighting too, especially with no weapons. He felt like he was in a windowless courtroom trying to prove it was daylight outside. There wasn't the slightest doubt in his mind that Woody had written the song. And he knew with the same certainty that everyone that signed those affidavits knew Ray couldn't write a song like that. "Besides losing a fortune," he told Woody, "this will damage your reputation forever."

Woody shrugged. "I don't have a reputation. At least I'll get one. Bad breath is better than no breath."

"You'll be known as the guy who tried to steal Ray Bell's hit song. It'll make all your music suspect."

"They can't take away my ability to write more songs." Woody strummed a chord. "And when I do, they'll be as good as 'Stephanie' and then everyone will know who wrote it."

"There's really not much we can do anyway, is there?" Stephanie sounded resigned.

"It's hard to believe," Pearlman sighed, "but maybe not. There's definitely a good chance we would win at trial. But we could also lose. Bottom line, it's Woody's call on how we proceed." He felt the hopelessness Woody and Stephanie were feeling. "I've got one more thing I'm going to try. It's a long shot. If it doesn't work, maybe it is time to move on."

The week of the Grammys, Pearlman sat at his desk, flipping through a stack of urgent memos he'd mostly been ignoring. He had three clients nominated to receive awards and there were endless details to work out. But he could barely face up to the tasks knowing that the grand finale was going to be Ray Bell singing "Stephanie."

Pearlman hadn't formally responded to Maria's settlement offer. He'd been filing pre-trial motions, consulting music experts, doing whatever he could think of to strengthen their legal position. He'd interviewed a half-dozen of Woody's potential witnesses. Murray was the only credible one. Pearlman felt like the others could hurt the case more than help. He knew Stephanie would make a great witness if the case went to trial, but the subject of her being a stripper would definitely come up, and it was hard to know how a jury would react. And, of course, the closer Woody's relationship was shown to be with Stephanie and Murray, the less credibility their testimony would have. The other side would argue that Woody had two witnesses: his two best friends.

He imagined Woody and Ray both singing "Stephanie" to the jury. Would the judge allow them to actually perform? Woody would sound authentic, but Ray would have vocal coaches and piano teachers and by the time of trial he'd play a flashy, polished rendition that might seem more professional to the average person. And there was the problem of finding a jury that wasn't familiar with the song and had already associated it with Ray's voice.

Pearlman had often fantasized about Woody playing "Stephanie" to a jury of his peers and having them feel the same way he'd felt the first time he heard Woody play it in his office. But Pearlman also remembered how many times it took Woody in the studio before he actually sang it with passion. Woody would be a loose canon in a courtroom; it was impossible to predict how a jury would react to him. And Woody definitely wouldn't be singing to a jury of peers, he'd be singing to twelve people who weren't smart enough to get out of jury duty.

Opening a thick folder on his desk labeled "EVIDENCE," Pearlman went down the list of people who'd signed the affidavits saying they believed Ray had written the song. They were all in the music business and, the week of the Grammys, the music business was in chaos. But over the course of the last few days, he'd managed to speak with most of them and they'd all said the same thing: they hadn't really given the matter much consideration, they'd signed the statement because they believed it was true. They believed they were protecting an established recording artist from being harassed by a jealous street musician. It wasn't the first time any of them had heard of this kind of thing happening, and they felt it was incumbent on them to protect the entertainment industry from frivolous copyright allegations. In any event, none of them were about to retract their statements.

Pearlman knew he could deal with them all on the witness stand and bring out that what they were saying was based on hearsay and speculation. It was the kind of case he'd love to argue to a jury. But it always came down to what the client wanted, and Woody had lost his will to fight.

There was one phone call Pearlman had saved as a last resort, a call that someone with less experience in the music industry might think would be a no-brainer. But he knew it had little chance of accomplishing anything. And he knew the reason he felt that way was somehow related to the essence of the business of art; the ultimate oxymoron. Pearlman picked up the phone and called the president of A&M Records. He was immediately put through.

"Hello Jeff, how are you?"

"Fine, Marty, how about you?'

"Can't complain, but I do anyways. How're the kids? Have things lightened up at all between you and Amy?"

"Things are moving forward," Pearlman said, "at the pace of a glacier. Someone once told me that the time-span of a relationship is how long it takes to heal it after it's broken up. I never would've believed it."

"How long were you two together?"

"Fifteen years. How's your family, Marty? That's wonderful news about Heidi getting into Yale."

"I'm sure your letter of recommendation helped, Jeff, coming from such a distinguished alum. I can't thank you enough for that one."

"Everything in that letter is true. That daughter of yours is an incredible kid."

"What you did meant a lot to us. So I guess I'll be seeing you this weekend."

"Marty, I'm calling about the song "Stephanie." Are you familiar with the situation?"

"Of course I am. I've been following it very closely. I assumed I hadn't heard from you because you were trying to avoid the appearance of a conflict of interest while the case is pending. I certainly didn't expect to hear from you three days before the Grammys. So what have you got?"

"It's not Ray Bell's song. You and I both know he couldn't write a song like that."

"Do you have any proof?"

"The fact that we both know what I'm saying is true. Does that count for anything?"

"Jeff, as a friend, the word on the street is that you've lost your edge since your heart attack. People are saying you're representing some whacko that was stalking a stripper and became jealous when Bell wrote a song about her. From everything I've heard, your lawsuit is based on your client's jealousy, not on hard evidence."

"That's bullshit!"

"Sounds like you're personally involved in this case, Jeff. Is it true the guy's living in your guesthouse?"

Pearlman thought of the yoga class he'd attended that morning; a class given by Stephanie, on his front lawn, to him and Woody. "Yes Marty, I *am* personally involved. In fact, that's what this whole thing is about. It's not about legalities or the preponderance of the evidence… it's about art, the art that you and I have been talking about since high school. And now we both have all the money we'll ever need and it's about making some very meaningful choices. This guy Woody is an authentic hardscrabble artist, with no money, he's the real deal. There's something fundamentally wrong with the whole system, if you and I can talk like this, knowing what we know, and Ray Bell ends up getting credit for the song. Marty, gold is plentiful on this earth, old friends with silver hair are hard to come by."

"I certainly hope this doesn't end up affecting our relationship Jeff. But from what I can tell, your client's going to get thrown out of court. Don't let your own reputation be affected by this."

"He wrote the song, Marty."

"My legal department has reviewed all the filings, they tell me the evidence is heavily weighted in Ray's favor. Apparently your client has absolutely no credibility. Does he take any responsibility for that?"

Pearlman thought about the mindful way Stephanie paced her conversations. He waited.

"Jeff?"

Pearlman waited.

"Jeff, are you there?"

"I'm here."

"I thought I lost you."

"You did."

"Jeff, I'm not sure what you're asking me to do."

"One thing you can do for me Marty, right now, on a personal level. Just you and I on the phone today, no lawsuit, no courtroom… just acknowledge that you know it's impossible that Ray Bell could've written that song."

"Don't pull your lawyer cross examination stuff on me, Jeff. It's not A&M's case, it's Bell's. A&M has an airtight indemnity clause, we have no exposure. As far as A&M's concerned, all the press about your lawsuit has only helped record sales. That song has almost single-handedly saved A&M's bottom line this quarter. What do you expect me to do, pull the record out of thousands of stores and radio stations because you call up and tell me you believe some crazed hippie's story? Jeff, sometimes you're just too much of a soft touch, you always have been. This is very big business we're talking about. Take my advice, cut your losses and get out. Get a harassment-value settlement and move on. If your client's as broke as you say, ten thousand bucks would be a windfall."

Marty waited a long time for Pearlman to respond, but he didn't. "I really have to get going, Jeff. What do you say we get together for nine holes next week and talk about something besides business?"

"One last question Marty. How did you know about the settlement offer of ten grand?"

"Maria Angelista. She keeps me informed on everything."

Pearlman sat for a long time, his feet on his desk, staring out at the city. Forty-four floors up, he was in the clouds with only the orange tips of the Golden Gate Bridge jutting out of a thick blanket of fog covering the entire San Francisco bay.

The phone rang. Grammy week was always the busiest week of the year for him. He turned off the ringer and leaned back in his big chair, trying to make peace with his relationship with Marty Levine. Their friendship spanned almost their entire lives, yet there was some indefinable force that often came between them, obscuring what they both innately knew to be right from wrong.

Pearlman had considered the dilemma many times. For lack of a better explanation, he usually ended up placing the blame on capitalism, a system that endorses greed rather than compassion. He knew from experience that a scheme based on self-interest inevitably makes the more sensitive, creative people subservient to the hard-hitting, pedestrian thinkers; survival of the unfittest.

He was thinking of his own life compared to Woody's when the door to his office flew open and Brenda walked in, jarring him from his thoughts.

Pearlman's office was his private domain, a sanctuary over which he had complete control. Other than the one time Woody had done it, no one had ever come in unannounced. "Brenda! What are you doing here?" *She must have come up the back stairway,* he thought, *avoiding the new receptionist.* He made a mental note to have the locks changed.

She sat down in front of his desk. "I have something very important to talk to you about, Mr. Pearlman."

He could see she was dead serious. "If you have issues, Brenda, there are proper ways to resolve them. You don't work for me any more and right now I'm in the middle of some very –"

"Urgent matters." Brenda finished his sentence in her automaton receptionist voice. "I'm sorry, Mr. Pearlman is unavailable right now, he's extremely busy. No, tomorrow won't work. No, Thursday his schedule is full. Friday he's out of town. How about never? Does never work for you?"

He kept his voice even "What do you want, Brenda?"

She glared back with a look of determination unlike anything he'd ever seen from her. "I have something for you."

When she reached into her purse, Pearlman momentarily braced himself. She took out a cassette tape, leaned over his big desk and slid it toward him.

Pearlman picked up the tape. It was hand-labeled "Stephanie" with a copyright symbol and a date. He noticed that the date on it was less than a week before Ray had submitted his application to the federal copyright office. Pearlman knew the date well; he'd subpoenaed a copy of Ray's application.

Brenda gingerly took the tape out of his hand, walked behind his desk and flipped a hidden switch that opened a mahogany wall panel, exposing a multi-media entertainment center. Dropping the tape in the cassette player, she pressed *play* and sat back down.

There were twenty seconds of muffled background noises, then a female voice.

"Is anybody going to eat this last piece of pizza?"

"Ray." It was Woody's voice. *"Can we get a version recorded before my landlord comes back?"*

"Play the chorus again." Ray's voice was instantly recognizable.

When Woody played the chorus, Pearlman immediately recognized his distinctive guitar style. Ray sang along. Woody stopped. *"It goes up at the end, like this,"* Woody sang and played the part. *"It's close, but you're not getting the melody. I wrote the chorus so it sounds like it repeats itself without repeating. Try singing it with me."*

Pearlman leaned forward on his elbows, listening intently. The tape played on, Woody stopping to show Ray the phrasing to every line. They'd finally gotten one take of the song and Woody asked Ray to do it again.

"Woody!" Ray said in an unmistakable, clear voice. *"Stephanie's your girlfriend, Stephanie's your song, you've got every note and word figured out exactly like you want it. I'm just a singer. If you want me to learn your song, I need a budget."*

"I'll get some money together. Give me a couple of days. Can we just try it one more time?"

"Do you at least have the lyrics written out?" Ray asked.

"Did anybody see that napkin I had with the lyrics written on it?" Woody said. There were sounds of a cardboard box sliding across a table.

"Oh my God!" a female voice exclaimed. *"I had a slice of pizza and there was this napkin and I didn't even look at it and I'm like, this is such a bummer! I'm totally sorry!"*

There was muted laughter and the sound of high heels skittering across the room.

"You expect me to sing lyrics off a napkin covered with pizza sauce?" Ray's voice was loud and clear. *"Look man, this is completely unprofessional. I can't spend my time learning other people's songs without getting paid."*

The cassette wound to the end and clicked off. Pearlman looked across his desk at Brenda in disbelief. "Where did you get this?"

"I was at Ray's apartment one morning." She waited for Pearlman's reaction; he didn't have one. "Ray was sleeping and I was hanging around drinking coffee, looking for some music to play, and there was this cassette. Ray had told me it was his song and I heard about your lawsuit and..." Brenda shrugged.

"What do you want for this, Brenda?"

"Nothing."

"Nothing? You just decided to help Woody out of the kindness of your heart?"

"I don't care about Woody, I care about Ray. He taught me one of the biggest lessons of my life. I want to repay the favor. What he's doing is not right."

She bit her lower lip and looked down. "In my dreams I actually thought Ray was going to take me to the Grammys with him. I thought he cared about..." Her voice was breaking up. "I thought he was a caring human being. Then he wouldn't return my calls or even help me get a ticket for myself. Everyone knows he's going to get the best song award and I could see my plans shaping up for the evening, watching Ray on TV and drinking myself to sleep."

Pearlman saw the tears welling up in her eyes.

"I can't believe I was going to actually try to use this tape to make Ray take me with him, and they'd show me sitting in the audience, clapping for him, looking all proud."

She wiped her eyes. "I know it's pretty late, with the Grammys happening on Saturday. But I know you know a lot of people, and I thought if there's anybody that can stop this from happening...

283

what Ray's doing isn't right." She stood up. "I won't take any more of your time, Mr. Pearlman. Do what you think is best with that tape, but please don't tell anyone how you got it." She paused and Pearlman realized she was staring at the cassette player. "Woody's music is really beautiful. I hope someday I care about someone as much as he does in that song."

"Thank you, Brenda." Pearlman was on his feet. "If you decide you'd still like to attend the Grammys, I'll have a ticket under your name at the box office. Let me know if there's anything else I can do for you."

"Well, actually, there is one thing."

He raised his eyebrows.

"I wouldn't mind having my old job back."

Pearlman glanced at his watch; live broadcast of the Grammy's in 72 hours. He took out a fresh yellow legal pad, made a list of things to do and people to call, and divided the list into two columns: tasks that needed his personal attention, and things he could delegate to his staff. He had the phone numbers of virtually everyone that was performing or involved with production at the Grammys. But except for a few key people, he intended to try to keep the existence of the tape confidential, not bring it out until the moment of optimal impact.

It felt like a huge weight had been taken off his shoulders. What he was going to try to accomplish in the next three days was a daunting task for sure, but he was up to the challenge. This was the kind of action he thrived on, not groveling, being beaten down by greed. He took Brenda's tape out of the cassette player. *With this tape and Ray Bell's vanity,* he thought, *I can move the world. At least the Hollywood world.*

Pearlman's Rolodex started spinning. His first call was to his guesthouse, to Woody and Stephanie. He left a message: the three of them were going by chartered plane to Los Angeles in two days. Woody should go to Pearlman's downstairs closet and see if any of the tuxedos fit. If not, he should go out and rent one. And he might want to put a new set of strings on his guitar; there was a possibility he'd be performing at the Grammys.

Chapter 32

Wearing the first tuxedo of his life, Woody looked in the mirror. He looked ridiculous. It looked like it was buttoned up wrong, even though it wasn't. The tuxedo and bow tie were all he could handle. When Stephanie started messing with his hair, he shook it out and let it go au natural. In stark contrast, the sleek black evening gown Stephanie bought in Beverly Hills that day looked perfect on her.

Pearlman arranged to have a limo pick them up at their hotel, and he met them at the concert hall. A throng of onlookers had gathered out front, trying to get a look at the stars exiting their limos. When Pearlman opened the back door to Woody and Stephanie's car, the crowd ignored them.

Stephanie looked stunning. Woody's incongruous appearance in his ill-fitting tux brought a smile to Pearlman's face. *Wait until Hollywood gets a look at this,* he thought. Since the day he'd first met Woody, he'd wondered how he would react to sudden fame. The night was sure to be interesting.

Pearlman shuttled them inside, got them each a flute of champagne and they strolled among the clusters of beautiful people, handsome young men and women pirouetting around them with silver trays of hors d'oeuvres. Even the enormous chandeliers matched the style and color of the women's jewelry, everything working together to create one glamorous environment.

There were movie stars, musicians, politicians, sports stars, former presidents' children escorted by secret servicemen, and a colorful mixture of Hollywood *demimondes* making gaudy and revealing fashion statements. Proudly introducing Woody and Stephanie to people he knew, Pearlman seemed to know everyone. And almost everyone pretended to be absorbed in the conversation at hand while they furtively glanced around to see who else was in attendance. Constantly stepping away to a phone booth or a meeting in the hallway; in a relaxed, focused manner, Pearlman was subtly manipulating the evening's events.

He was standing with Woody and Stephanie and a small group of record company executives, everyone a little drunk, everyone talking at once, when he glanced up and saw Ray approaching from across the room with Maria Angelista on his arm. Gliding through the crowd, they were dazzling, catching everyone's attention. Ray looked like Adonis in a tuxedo, tall, dark and handsome with a gleaming white smile and sparkling blue eyes. Maria, with the poise and features of a professional model, wore a dress so low-cut in the front it looked like two separate pieces of fabric magically clinging to the two sides of her body.

As Ray and Maria got closer to their little group, Woody saw them, put his hand around Stephanie's waist and shuttled her out into the hallway. He pushed open a metal exit door and they stepped out onto a fire escape two stories above an alleyway. The steel, gray platform was wet and slippery from a light drizzle earlier in the evening. He kissed her gently and they both leaned against the railing, gazing at the alley below.

"I don't know how Jeff can be so confident he can pull this off at the last minute," Stephanie said. "He says he has something that absolutely proves you wrote the song. It sounds so mysterious."

They watched a white delivery van backing up below them.

"When I wrote "Stephanie,"" Woody said, "it was coming from a place of pain. An emotional replacement for what I really wanted. I was a total mess, freefalling. Writing that song was like building the airplane while I was flying it. But now that I'm not in constant fear of losing you, the song doesn't mean as much to me. It has a life of its own. If we get some money out of all this, that would be great. If not, I'll write more songs. I feel like as long as we have each other, we can do anything."

A young woman stepped out the delivery van below and began shuttling in food trays covered with aluminum foil. "Jeff says that if things go the way he's planned," Stephanie said, "you're going to sing 'Stephanie' tonight to an audience around the world of fifty million people. How do you feel?"

"Like I'm going to throw up."

She glanced up and was relieved to see he was joking.

"Will you come on stage with me?" He opened his hands to her. "Let me introduce you.

"Just go out there and sing your song. I'll be watching. Sing to me." Stephanie took Woody's hand and laid it lightly on her stomach. "Feel anything?"

"Indigestion?"

"I went to the doctor on Wednesday. I'm pregnant. I don't know for sure, but something tells me it's a girl. Sing to both of us."

Woody's eyes went down to her hand on his, then back to her face. He was trembling. Stephanie smiled, the most beautiful smile he'd ever seen.

Inside the auditorium, Pearlman was standing in a circle of entertainment executives and actors and actresses when Ray and Maria walked up. Everyone there was acutely aware of the dispute over the ownership of "Stephanie" and they all knew who the key players were. The electricity in the air was crackling with nervous small talk.

"If you believe the press, you're about to accept the award for best song of the year," one of the men said to Ray. "How do you feel?"

"A little nervous," Ray said. "But being nervous is a *good* thing. It keeps me on my toes."

"There's been a rumor that you're going to sing 'Stephanie' tonight as the grand finale," a woman said. "That's quite an honor. They rarely include a live performance of best song. The last time it happened, Frank Sinatra was singing." Everyone looked at Ray. He did his best to look modest.

"The chorus on that song sends chills up my spine," another woman said.

"Why don't you let Woody sing 'Stephanie' tonight?" Pearlman said to Ray.

Everyone in the circle froze. Maria's eyebrows went up. "Woody's here tonight?"

Pearlman glanced around. "He and Stephanie are here somewhere."

Ray gulped down his champagne. "It's my song, I'll sing it."

"The performance schedule for tonight has been set for months," Maria said officiously. "The programming, staging, lighting, everything is in place. Logistically, it would be impossible to include Woody in any way."

"Sorry for the short notice." Pearlman eyes were fixed on Ray. "Woody would like to sing his own song tonight. It would be quite gracious of you to let it happen."

"That's absurd," Maria snapped. "My client has all legal rights to the song and we've made our position clear. This is certainly not the time or place to discuss the matter."

"The arrangements have all been made." Pearlman kept talking to Ray. "I've worked it out with the program director, the orchestra leader, the camera crew, the —"

Ray turned to Maria. "It's *my* song. It's *my* song and I'm going to sing it!"

People within hearing distance were making their way over and a small crowd began to form. With Ray and Pearlman at six o'clock and twelve o'clock, on opposite sides of the circle, it had the makings of an old-west gunfight. Everyone there knew who Ray and Pearlman were. They could have been witnessing a songwriting dispute between Lennon and McCartney.

Pearlman slowly reached into the inside pocket of his tuxedo. The way he moved, the silver object he pulled out looked like a pistol, and everyone involuntarily took a half step back. He held it like a pistol, pointed it at Ray, and put his thumb to where the hammer would be. Instead of the hammer on a gun, it was the button on a battery-powered cassette player with a built-in speaker.

With an exaggerated motion, Pearlman pointed the player at Ray's chest, slowly brought his thumb down and pressed *play*.

Slightly tinny but still recognizable, Ray's voice came on singing the chorus of "Stephanie". Pearlman extended his arm further, holding the recorder in the center of the circle. As if it were choreographed, everyone simultaneously leaned in.

After one chorus, the singing stopped. Ray's voice was clear and damning.

"Woody, Stephanie's your girlfriend, Stephanie's your song, you've got every word and note figured out. I'm just a singer. If you want me to learn your song, I need a budget."

With a look of grim satisfaction, Pearlman hit the search/return feature and it played again. "Stephanie's your song, you've got every note and word figured out. I'm just a singer... Stephanie's your song, you've got every note and word figured out. I'm just a singer... Stephanie's your song, you've got every note..."

Ray reached over and violently tore the cassette player out of Pearlman's hand.

Ernie, the security guard from Pearlman's office building, suddenly materialized behind Ray. Pearlman had brought him along for just such an eventuality. Ernie clamped his over-sized hand on Ray's wrist. "You want to let go of that, Mr. Bell."

"Let him keep it, Ernie." Pearlman looked at Ray. "I've got plenty more copies. I've got a copy for every radio station in the country. In fact, my friend running the audio tonight has it cued up, ready to play on the air right before you accept your award. We'll play it for a jury of fifty million adoring fans and see if they recognize your distinctive voice. You can look like an asshole tonight Ray, in front of the world of music fans, or you can bow out gracefully and let Woody sing his song. Your call."

Pearlman turned to Maria. "I've also got a copy of the recording for the federal judge, to go with the motion for summary judgment I'll be filing Monday morning. I'm asking for fees, sanctions and to have you disbarred for suborning perjury. I've got a sworn affidavit from your former assistant Bruce saying you knew all along that Ray didn't write the song." He glared at her. "You're way out of your league, girl! After my civil suit bankrupts you, you're going to need your own attorney to try to keep you out of federal prison. You and Ray are about to finally get it; what you did is criminal."

"I'm hungry."

"That's because you're eating for two." Woody put his arm around Stephanie and they made their way toward the backstage area. The crowd and tight security became progressively more dense until they couldn't get any further. It was like an over-crowded subway, but everyone was dressed to the hilt and acting as if they were too important to be there. Woody saw someone nudge into Stephanie's stomach and felt a moment of panic.

"Woody? What's wrong?"

"It's too crowded in here." He'd had a flashback of the crushing crowds at Ray's concert and was leading her back the other way when a young woman put her hand on his shoulder.

"Woody?"

"Yeah?"

"I'm one of the production managers tonight. Come with me. I'll take you to where it's quieter and you can have your own space."

She opened a door, shuttled them into a utility hallway and

closed the door behind them. "My name is Gaia, I'll be your personal assistant for the evening."

She stuck out her hand and Woody shook it. Wearing a form-fitting tuxedo, pageboy haircut and diamond-post earrings, Gaia exuded an air of confidence that was contagious. "And you must be Stephanie. If you'll both come with me, I'll show you to your dressing room."

She guided them through the kitchen and down a hallway into a private room that was dramatically more quiet. "Please make yourselves comfortable. Your guitar's in the corner. I'll be back in a few minutes to check on you." She disappeared out the door.

The room was like a sealed catacomb in the center of the chaos. Along one wall a table was covered with a white tablecloth and silver trays of gourmet food. On the other wall was a large mirror framed with soft white light bulbs. Woody picked up his guitar and sat down on a luxurious silk-covered purple couch. Stephanie got herself a plate of food and sat next to him.

A young man in a tuxedo knocked lightly, came in, offered them each a glass of champagne and quickly left. When the server opened the door, they could see Ernie standing there, and a much larger dressing room packed with reporters and photographers.

Woody leaned back on the couch, strummed a few chords and hummed a melody that sounded like a lullaby. Stephanie recognized the song Woody'd been working on while he relearned to play the guitar. He'd regained enough strength in his hand to hold a pick for the duration of a song.

"How do you like the name Lillian?"

"It's perfect."

Woody was softly singing the chorus to his new song "Lillian" when Pearlman walked in with a briefcase and a bottle of champagne. "You guys doing okay?"

"Once again," Woody said, "you're Mr. Hospitality."

"Thank you for making us so comfortable," Stephanie added.

"The wine they're serving's not bad, but I brought something special for this special occasion." Pearlman expertly opened a bottle of 1959 Tattinger Champagne and poured them each a glass. Stephanie asked for just a small sip to make a toast. Pearlman lifted his glass. "To Stephanie." They clinked glasses.

"Well, it's all set," he said. "You go on in about an hour, last performance of the night. They'll announce 'Stephanie' as best song of the year, you'll walk out, accept the award and sing your song."

Woody strummed the first chord of the chorus and sang a sweet low "Stephanie."

Pearlman looked pleased. "I've always had a policy of not talking about business with a client at their own show, especially before they go on. With you I've broken every rule I've ever had. I've got a couple of surprises and I figured some good news might give you a little boost for your performance." Pearlman could see Woody was nervous and distracted but he just carried on in his relaxed, efficient manner.

Pearlman took an EP album out of his briefcase. The cover was a photograph taken by Stephanie of Woody sitting on a beach playing his guitar, his wild hair blowing in the wind, a sweet smile on his face. Above the picture it said "STEPHANIE," below the picture it said "WOODY."

"This is a rough workup of an idea for a cover," Pearlman said. "It's the solo-acoustic version I recorded at The Palace. I gave it to Warner Brothers right after we recorded it, but they put it on hold until the legal mess got sorted out. They're going to release it as a single, I confirmed it with them tonight. They've got this studio wiz, Brian Risner, who managed to take out the technical glitches. The Warner people think it's one of the greatest things they've ever heard. They think going back to the song's roots, following Ray's big production version with this acoustic version, will make it an even bigger hit than the first one. And with all the press there's been about the lawsuit... it's going to be incredible. Whenever you're ready, we'll get in the studio and record an album of your songs."

Just then a clean-cut young man with delicate features tapped gently on the door, came in and walked behind the couch. "Sorry to interrupt. You're Woody, aren't you? I need to give you the tiniest bit of shading so the lights don't bounce off your nose." He began purposefully dabbing at Woody's face with a cotton pad. When Woody flinched and turned away, the man adeptly reached to the other side. "This will just take a sec. At least you look like you get outdoors. Some musicians with their studio tans look like ghosts. Their skin is transparent. And I can tell you must have spent hours on your absolutely stunning hairdo."

The man disappeared as quickly as he'd appeared. Woody scratched his nose and Pearlman winked at Stephanie.

Picking up the Warner Brothers record, Stephanie looked at the picture of Woody and remembered that carefree, playful day on the beach. She wondered if, with everything that was happening in their lives, they'd ever be able to recapture the freedom they had back then. Then she wondered, as she had so many times, what kind of father Woody would be. Looking at the record, she tried picturing Woody with a baby in his lap instead of a guitar; it was a challenge for the imagination.

Woody got up off the couch and started pacing. "What's going to happen to Ray's version of the song? Are they going to keep selling it and playing it on the radio, or what?"

"What happens from now on, with any future licensing, is entirely up to us," Pearlman said. "In fact, in some ways it may be up to us whether or not Ray has a music career or if Maria Angelista ever practices law again, or maybe even whether or not they both spend some time in jail."

"Actually," Stephanie said thoughtfully, "I think Ray did a pretty good job singing the song."

Pearlman looked at her quizzically.

"I'm not saying he's a nice person," Stephanie said, "and I definitely don't think what he did was right. I'm just acknowledging that he has a nice voice. I guess I'm also saying that the world could use a dose of compassion and forgiveness any chance it gets."

"Ray does have a substantial range," Pearlman said. "Personally, I think Woody does a better job of delivering the song. So who's this Lillian you were singing about when I walked in?"

Stephanie blushed. "I've suspected that I was pregnant for a while. But with all the stress and uncertainty in the last month... I waited until Wednesday, the morning before we came down here, to see a doctor. I think it's a girl."

"That's wonderful news." Pearlman was grinning from ear to ear.

"We're not exactly sure what we're going to do now," Woody said. "Or even where we're going to live. You've done so much and, we've decided we don't want to keep living off you or take any money until I've actually earned it."

Pearlman held up his hand. "My second surprise." He reached into his tux and took out an envelope. There was a check inside made out to Woody for fifty thousand dollars. He and Stephanie looked at it in disbelief.

"It's an advance from my office, to keep you two going while we sort out the legal issues."

"That's incredibly generous," Stephanie said softly.

"Really man," Woody said. "You've already done so much."

"It's your money. You earned it. I prepared a letter of understanding that Ray and Maria both signed tonight. In exchange for me agreeing to not play that recording of you and Ray on the air, they relinquished all publishing rights to the song, past and future. And this is just the beginning. I think it's time to start looking for that house for your mother like you were talking about, and go ahead and find one for yourselves while you're at it. If it were up to me, I'd prefer you lived near San Francisco so we can continue working together in person. But you two, you three, can choose to live anywhere you want."

Woody leaned over and said something in Stephanie's ear. She kissed him on the cheek.

"Actually," Woody said to Pearlman, "there is someone else, besides Stephanie, that helped me write the song."

Pearlman raised his eyebrows.

"He didn't exactly contribute any notes or anything," Woody said, "but he helped create the environment, the context it came out of, you know what I mean?"

"Please, enlighten me," Pearlman said.

Woody lightly strummed his guitar. "Music is an expression of somebody's... everything... their world. In Victorian times people sat in the parlor in tight corsets, sipping tea with their pinkies sticking out. The music that came from that environment was highly structured chamber music; the first time people ever listened to music without dancing. Today people get stoned and write songs about going with the flow and letting it all hang out. My music –" he played a blues chord, "when I was hitting rock bottom, my friend Murray gave me and my guitar a place to be and some burnt pizza. For starters, I want to send him ten thousand dollars from this check."

Gaia came in the room and quickly walked over to them. "Everything's in place. Woody, your performance is scheduled to start in thirty minutes. In twenty minutes you and I will make our way to stage right. You'll wait there until they announce that 'Stephanie' has won best song of the year and you'll be escorted out by a young woman. Take your place, accept the award, and you'll have about ten seconds to thank anyone you want, or say nothing and just smile at the camera. Then follow the yellow tape on the floor and walk twelve feet to center stage to the vocal microphone. There will also be a mic in place for your acoustic guitar. As soon as you start playing and set the tempo, the orchestra will begin the piece according to the musical arrangement Jeff's provided."

Woody glanced at Pearlman.

"I had charts made of the version you and I recorded at The Palace," Pearlman said. "The band leader told me the arrangement is virtually identical to Ray's version."

Woody shook his head. "You think of everything."

"The orchestra is quite familiar with the song," Gaia went on in her pleasant but efficient manner. "After you start playing, go into the first verse at any time and the orchestra will follow. You'll perform the full song with the orchestra backing you up, then they'll continue to play the last chorus instrumentally while you walk off stage left and follow the yellow tape behind the curtain. All the musicians are extremely professional, they can turn on a dime. Whatever you do, they'll follow you." She gave him a moment to digest the information. "The production throughout the evening is designed to appear spontaneous and unrehearsed. There's not much you can do to mess it up. Everyone on the stage is a consummate professional, used to being on TV. They're ready to catch you if you fall. Is there anything I can do for you?"

Woody kissed Stephanie and stood up. "I'd like to talk to the band."

"Follow me." They walked through a maze of black curtains, Woody a few steps back, holding his guitar in front of him. A movement twenty feet away caught his eye.

Ray was standing in the wings, the collar of his shirt undone, his tuxedo bow tie at an angle, furtively glancing around. Their eyes met and Woody stopped in his tracks. In his mind, he saw the cocky smirk Ray had on his face earlier, thinking he'd gotten away with stealing Woody's song. Then he remembered how helpless he'd felt at Ray's new house and he heard Ray's voice in his head: *I wrote a song about your girlfriend's ass.*

Ernie was suddenly there, standing in front of Ray, blocking Woody's view of him. At the same time Gaia took Woody's arm. "Please come with me," she said softly, "we don't have much time before the orchestra has to be on stage."

"One second. I have some unfinished business." Woody walked right up to Ray until there wasn't much more than the width of his acoustic guitar between them. "Hi Ray."

"It was that bitch lawyer!" Ray said in an urgent low voice. "It was her idea to cut you out. The whole thing was her idea!"

"Get your new house decorated the way you like it?"

"There was nothing I could do! She had everything legally tied up so I couldn't even –"

"Maybe you could write a song about *her* ass."

297

"She put this binding contract together. If I didn't go along with it she was going to…"

Woody stopped listening. The difference in Ray's demeanor was dramatic. The smirk was gone, his blue eyes looked gray, sweaty locks of hair stuck to his forehead. He looked pathetic. Woody's anger evaporated. He only felt pity, and a sense of calm well-being.

"It was my idea to have you sing my song in the first place, Ray. Your voice worked great on it. You sang the melody and phrasing just like I asked you to. I want to thank you for that."

"I'm telling you, that fucking lawyer set the whole thing up. She –"

"I would've been fair with you, Ray. I know you know that. But you tried to take it all, and now you got nothing. It's called the blues." Woody brought his hand down across his strings and played a minor chord. "The blues, Ray. It's great for writing songs."

When Ray made a gesture with his hands, Ernie quickly stepped in front him and Gaia tugged at Woody. "We really need to get going."

Woody looked at Ray peering over Ernie's shoulder. He put his hands together, bent over the body of his guitar, gave Ray a formal little bow and followed Gaia behind a curtain.

She led him down a narrow hallway into a brightly lit room full of musicians. Stepping just inside the door, he immediately felt out of place, as if he'd walked into a stranger's party. When Gaia walked to the back of the room, he was about to turn around and walk out when a guy standing close by with a saxophone in his hands nodded to him. The man looked down at Woody's guitar. He checked out the mother-of-pearl inlay and his eyes traveled up the neck to the *Martin* headstock. "Nice axe." He went back to adjusting the reed on his horn.

Woody realized that everyone in the room was a musician. No one was hanging around partying; everyone was working. There were music stands, open instrument cases, practice amps and a Steinway grand piano. Everyone was focused, tuning up, adjusting bridges, valves, strings, every instrument gleaming and immaculate.

He was struck by the intensity of concentration being given to the minute adjustment of each instrument. He knew those adjustments made all the difference in these master musicians' ability to project the power of the music out into a large concert hall. Woody felt like he'd died and gone to musician heaven.

A guitar player, a young dark-skinned man, stood by the piano, adeptly strumming a Gibson semi-hollow-body electric guitar. Next to him, a tall attractive woman with gray-blonde hair, probably in her mid-fifties, was playing what looked like a mid-fifties Fender jazz bass. Woody noticed the fluidity of the line she was playing. He unconsciously strummed a chord that matched her notes. When the bass, guitar and piano went to the next chord, Woody recognized the chord change into the bridge of "Stephanie". He'd never heard the modulation from the chorus to the bridge played so smoothly. Fascinated by their interpretation of his music, he felt as if he were listening in on a conversation about himself.

"Woody, this is Jake Fraser. He's our musical director." Gaia was accompanied by a clean-cut, balding gentleman. The man could have been a librarian or an insurance salesman, but for the trumpet at his side. He was rapidly fingering the three valves while he held the horn with such a relaxed grip, it looked like he might drop it. Woody knew the man had probably held the instrument in his hands most days of his adult life.

"Thanks for the great song," Jake said. "I'm honored to play it with you."

Woody smiled.

"I like the way it drops to that E flat in the bridge."

It was the chord Woody already had his fingers in position to play. He strummed it lightly.

Jake and Gaia waited for Woody to say something. Woody just let the chord ring out.

Gaia looked at her watch. "Show time in thirteen minutes. Jake, will you and the other musicians please take your positions on stage."

"See you out there," Jake told Woody.

Woody cleared his throat. "How much playing time do we have?"

"Just under five minutes," Gaia said, "including the intro and outro. You're the closing performance. It's the longest slot of the night. You can continue playing to the live audience, but camera fade is at 4:50."

The other musicians were heading out past them. "Hey everybody," Woody called, "check this out."

They stopped, forming a semi-circle around him. Woody softly strummed a chorus of "Stephanie" while he spoke. "When we go into the last chorus...bring it down... way down... as quiet as you've ever played." He played softer. "Then come in like you're sneaking up on yourself, like the music is coming out of nowhere. Then keep playing, taking your time, taking prime time, slowly getting stronger, building it up and building it up, further than you think it can go, as if your life depends on it, as if all you can do is to keep playing."

Watching the band take the stage, Woody tried to clear his mind. He pictured a little mini-man, himself in a tuxedo, arms folded across his chest, standing guard on his forehead... *no thoughts allowed!* When Gaia put her hand on his shoulder, he jumped.

"Sorry," she said gently. "It's almost time. We have about one minute, then you'll be escorted out." Gaia nodded toward a woman in an evening gown a few feet away from them. Then they heard the Master of Ceremonies: *"Ladies and gentlemen! Moving on to our last award of the night."*

Stephanie appeared out of nowhere and gently put her hand on Woody's other shoulder. He jumped again.

The MC went on: *"Before we begin, I have a brief announcement; Ray Bell has withdrawn his name from the list of nominees for best song."* An audible gasp rippled through the crowd and people started talking. The MC nipped it in the bud. *"The remaining nominees are..."*

Woody held his breath and turned to Stephanie. "Will you come out there with me?"

She scanned his face; it was hard to read him. "Just swing by the podium, pick up your award, and go sing your song. You worked hard for this moment, it's yours."

"I never would've written the song if it wasn't for you." He raised his eyebrows. "Please?"

"We are pleased to announce that tonight's final award, for best song of the year, goes to… Woody… for composing the music and lyrics to the song… 'Stephanie'!"

"Woody," Gaia said urgently, "it's time to go."

He turned back to Stephanie. "Please?"

Gaia saw the blank expression on Woody's face. He'd stopped blinking. She turned to Stephanie. "Please?"

Stephanie wrapped her arm around Woody's arm, winked at the woman waiting to escort him to the podium, and walked him out there herself.

The audience response was slightly restrained, with an undercurrent of conversation and confusion about the unknown, unexpected recipient. Woody accepted the gold-plated gramophone award, cradled it in both hands and stood expressionless for a few moments until the audience quieted down. He cleared his throat. "I'd like to thank…" his voice started breaking up. He looked down at the award for a second, and started again. "I'd like to thank Jeff Pearlman for making all this possible… for his love of music… and for believing in me." He turned to Stephanie and took a long, deep breath. "And there's someone…" his voice quit working. His throat was so tight, air wouldn't come out. He reached for the glass of water on the podium, took a drink, and slowly set it back down. "I'm well aware…" his voice was a squeak. "I'm well aware," he said louder, "that everyone here tonight is wondering about my Grammy." He cleared his throat again. "Well… she couldn't make it. She's home in her pajamas."

There was an unnatural moment of silence as the audience took a second to get the joke; then an equally out-of-context burst of laughter in collective relief that Woody could get out a complete sentence.

"But there *is* someone here I'd like to introduce everyone to... Stephanie. I wouldn't be here without her." He handed her the award. "She deserves this as much as I do." When he kissed her, the audience exploded.

Stephanie walked off stage-right, holding the award in front of her. Woody walked ten feet stage-left to the orchestra. A young man handed him his guitar and slipped the strap over his shoulder. Woody stepped up to the microphone, put his head down, and froze. His heart was beating out of control. The deafening applause were creating oscillating waves of sound that pulsated in his temples, as though his head was expanding and contracting. Standing motionless, the noise in the room seemed to fade to a distant din as the pounding of his heart grew louder. The band waited, the audience waited, fifty million television viewers waited.

Woody turned his head slightly, peering out through the thick curly hair covering his face, and looked across the stage at Stephanie standing just behind a curtain. He was the only one in the concert hall who could see her. Their eyes met for a long moment when, almost imperceptibly, she started moving her hips side to side. He got the groove, the perfect groove, and started his song.

(image copyright ©2011, Susan J Weiand)

Greg Anton is a well-known drummer/composer on the San Francisco rock music scene. He has performed on over 40 albums and at concerts worldwide, most notably with his band Zero. He has published more than 50 original songs and has composed music for film, TV and theater. Greg is also a practicing attorney and a champion of medical marijuana rights. Greg has five children and lives with his wife Holly in Sonoma County, California. *Face the Music* is his first novel.

See more about Greg at gregantonmusic.com.

CPSIA information can be obtained
at www.ICGtesting.com
Printed in the USA
FSOW01n2306211214
4087FS

9 780986 008559